HUMILIATED ... HURT ... HEARTSICK

THE RESULT OF A

The French gold clock on the mantelpiece was striking nine. Sylvain paced the floor irritably. Randolph Baxter was to have come for dinner at precisely seven-thirty. Nana had poked her head in the empty dining room a dozen times. Delilah wore a displeased look. Even Edwin Fairmont, seated on Serena's favorite champagne brocade sofa, kept lifting his eyes to the gold clock.

When a carriage clattered to a stop outside, Sylvain yanked back the curtain in time to see Randolph step down, his golden head gleaming silver in the light of the early rising moon. He jerked open the gate, stepped inside the yard, and banged it shut with such force the whole fence shook. Then he stumbled and almost fell.

Sylvain knew something was wrong. She dropped the curtain and flew into the corridor. Heart pounding, she swung open the heavy front door and saw his disheveled hair, the glassy eyes, the unsteady stance.

"Randolph!" She stared at him. "What is it? What's wrong?" He stood looking down at her. He appeared angry and upset. Edwin Fairmont had stepped into the foyer. His question echoed his daughter's. "Son, what is it? What's happened?"

Randolph's green eyes blinked, and he swayed toward Sylvain. "I can't marry you," he muttered, his words slurring.

"But why, Randolph? I don't understand. What are you saying?"

"I'm saying" — he pointed a finger at her, and tears filled his bloodshot eyes — "I'm Randolph Baxter of the Mississippi Baxters. I'll not marry Jean Lafitte's bastard!"

MIDNIGHT AFFAIR

MIDNIGHT AFFAIR

Nan Ryan

PaperJacks LTD.

TORONTO   NEW YORK

AN ORIGINAL

PaperJacks

MIDNIGHT AFFAIR

PaperJacks LTD.

330 STEELCASE RD. E., MARKHAM, ONT. L3R 2M1
210 FIFTH AVE., NEW YORK, N.Y. 10010

First edition published July 1988

This is the work of fiction in its entirety. Any resemblance to actual people, places or events is purely coincidental.

ISBN 0-7701-0927-6

To

Glenda and Bill Howard,
My sister and brother-in-law,
For their unfailing support, encouragement, and love

Part I

Chapter One

**GALVEZ ISLAND
OFF THE SOUTHERN COAST OF TEXAS
LATE SUMMER, 1818**

Jean Lafitte was melancholy. Middle-aged and moody, the bored, lethargic Jean lay sprawled in his bright red canvas hammock, one long, well-muscled leg hooked over the edge, his foot resting on the smooth porch.

From the second-story veranda of his island fortress, Maison Rouge, Jean had an unobstructed view of the settlement he'd named Campeachy, of the bay on this eastern end of the island, and of the endless sea known as the Gulf of Mexico, which stretched for over a thousand miles.

A powerful telescope, close at hand, sat idle. Jean was not interested in viewing his domain on this sultry summer morning. He had not bothered to lift the powerful lens when two of his ships, heavy with booty from a Spanish vessel they'd sunk on the open seas, sailed into port shortly after breakfast. He'd waved away shouted invitations to hurry to the wharf and view for himself the chests filled with Spanish doubloons, the many bolts of fine silks and satins, the numerous crates of Madeira and brandy, the caches of spices and coffee and Cuban cigars.

Jean was tired, though he'd not overly exerted himself in weeks. He felt older than his thirty-seven years. His coal-black hair was graying at the temples, his once rock-hard belly was softening, the lines about his eyes and full mouth were deeper. His long, lean body no longer possessed the great strength he'd taken for granted in his youth. Even his quick wit and superior intelligence were seen less often by those around him.

The pirate chieftain yawned lazily, then sighed. He rubbed his weak left eye and draped an arm across his brow. Heavy lids shut out the daylight, and Jean Lafitte let the present fade away. It was no match for the past. It couldn't compare despite the comfort and grandeur of this newly constructed mansion. Within strong, high walls of rock and sand, where cannons were mounted on wooden platforms, the two-story, many-roomed Maison Rouge stood facing the bay. Topped with a towering observation deck, the spacious dwelling was elegantly furnished. Fine linens, fragile crystal, and a wealth of gold and silver graced his tables, while a well-trained staff of servants catered to his cultivated tastes and his adoring mistress lived only to do his bidding.

Still, he longed for the old days. He was not happy on Galvez Island. He missed his home, Grand Terre, his beloved bastion on Barataria Bay, south of old New Orleans. He missed the torrid days and nights there in his man-made paradise that rose from the Louisiana swamps — the days of glory when he was young and strong and commanded his army of privateers with such ease. An angry glance from him could make the most evil men come to heel.

Alone now on this sweltering morning, his white shirt damp with perspiration and clinging to his chest, he smiled wistfully, recalling those happier days — days when he'd sailed under a Carthaginian flag, his reputation for cunning and ruthlessness striking fear in the hearts of sailors from the Gulf Coast to Spain. The strolls with his brother through the Place d'Armes on warm Sunday afternoons, nodding and smiling boldly at the well-guarded Creole misses who sighed and flushed and stared with frank admiration at the Brothers Lafitte.

There were warm, flower-scented evenings spent at splendid quadroon balls where the loveliest of the young brown-skinned beauties were his for the asking, each watchful mother hopeful that the handsome, rich privateer might choose her precious offspring to be his mistress.

And sultry, sensual nights at Grand Terre when a prize ship was brought into harbor and gala celebrations lasted till dawn, torches flaring out over the water, and men, drunk on pillaged wines and brandies, singing and laughing and sating every appetite there on the beach: pagans in paradise.

Ah, but best of all was being publicly named a hero by Andrew Jackson for bravery and valor in the Battle of New Orleans, being invited by Jackson to a celebration ball for the elite of the city. Jean could still recall the undisguised looks of awe and adulation emanating from the eyes of men and women alike. Easily he'd charmed the aristocrats, and many respectable blue-blooded ladies had nervously stepped into his arms to be swept about the marble hall, their faces aglow with excitement, their full-lashed gazes unabashedly flirtatious.

It was immediately after that great triumph that General Jackson had personally persuaded the President of the United States to reinstate Jean's citizenship. It had been a glorious time. Rich and newly respected, Jean had seen his many warehouses filled to overflowing with valuable merchandise. Never had he been more prosperous, more daring, more alive.

Could he actually have expected such a sublime interlude to go on forever? Not really. It all came crashing down around his ears when Barataria was captured and destroyed by the United States, and his vast fortune confiscated. Escaping into the marshes, Jean watched in horror as his beloved sanctuary amid the swamps went under the torch. Grand Terre was no more.

In early 1817, Jean and a few of his men were forced to flee forever the setting of his greatest triumphs and defeats; they'd reached the bay of Galvez in April. He'd been here ever since.

Jean sighed once again and lifted his foot from the floor. Crossing his long legs at the ankles, he closed his eyes and let the still, oppressive air nudge him toward sleep.

While the morose man slept, the heavy summer air cooled slightly, pleasant sea breezes dried his damp white shirt and lifted locks of his coal-black hair. Jean slept on as those breezes turned into erratic gusts of wind and the sun disappeared behind dark, ominous clouds.

Serena held her long cotton skirts above her knees and smiled. Then she shouted happily and ran barefoot across the sand and into the surf. She lifted her skirts higher and waded out until the gentle waves swirled around her pale thighs.

She loved the feel of the warm salt water lapping at her bare skin. She turned around and around, clutching her skirts high, and laughed with a joy reserved for the very young.

How she loved it here! Since she'd been on Galvez Island, she'd been allowed to to things most sixteen-year-old young ladies could only dream about. If only her friends could see her now. They'd never believe that on this sweltering summer morning Miss Serena Donovan was out for a walk without gloves, bonnet, or shoes, unchaperoned, frolicking in the warm, salty waters of the Gulf of Mexico.

Serena laughed happily. How her life had changed! Was it possible that it had been only six months since her mother had died and she'd come to this strange new land to live with her father?

Wondering if the Almighty might strike her dead for her evil thoughts, Serena silently acknowledged that she'd never loved her mother as she loved her warm-hearted, affectionate father. And she was certain her mother had never loved her very much either. Too many times her elegant, proper mother had looked at her with barely disguised contempt. Serena knew the reason.

In Serena's blue eyes and light blond hair, Annabelle Donovan saw Serena's father, Taylor Donovan. Serena was a constant living reminder of the failed marriage her mother wished desperately to forget. Serena was never allowed to mention her father's name, and she was told nothing about him until her mother lay dying. Only then did Annabelle Donovan reveal the truth about her absent husband.

Less than a week later Serena went alone to the levee in New Orleans and boarded a ship bound for Galvez. She had no place else to go. Her mother had never remarried, and there were only distant relatives, none of whom offered a home to Serena. Her father had no idea she was coming. Would he want her? Would he let her stay?

Serena arrived at Galvez Island on a blustery gray day in February. No one was there to meet her. She hurried down the gangplank, her heart hammering. Men lounged around on the wooden wharf and boldly looked her up and down. It was evident they were not gentlemen. Serena averted her eyes as she passed them, ignoring the whistles and catcalls.

Not waiting for her heavy trunk to be unloaded, Serena set out to find her father. She would not ask these leering men on the waterfront. Surely there were decent, upstanding people living in this sprawling island community.

As Serena made her way along a wooden sidewalk that crossed the sand, she heard shouts and curses behind her. In seconds a throng of boisterous men surged forward, sweeping her along in their tide. Leading the procession was a wild-eyed, burly man who waved a pistol and bragged loudly that he was unafraid of Jean Lafitte. The man declared he'd not hold still for any punishment Lafitte might mete out. Boldly he shouted that he'd murdered the fat, rich matron on the open seas and taken her money and jewels. He was unrepentent and no man could make him so!

Shouts of approval from the crowd rang in Serena's ears. Desperately she tried to elbow her way free of the excited mass of men, but to no avail. She was pushed and jostled and carried with them, unable to separate herself.

All at once the mob halted. "I will not be flogged for my deeds!" shouted the man with the gun as he planted his feet apart before a large two-story house. "Hear this all of you: I'll kill Jean Lafitte if he tries — "

He never finished the sentence. A shot rang out and Serena bit back a scream. The sailor's gun fell from his hand. He swayed for a long moment, then fell forward on his face. Serena gasped. Above her, on the second-story veranda, a tall, dark man stood, imperturbable as a statue. From his pistol a blue spiral of smoke dissipated rapidly in the winter winds.

It was Serena's first glimpse of Jean Lafitte.

The impassive Jean turned without a word and strode back inside. Horrified, Serena stumbled away as the dead man was carried off. Eyes wide with fright, she burst into a saloon, not caring that it was filled with roisterous, drunken men and a few painted women. She pushed her way to the bar and demanded to know where she might find Mr. Taylor Donovan.

"You just did, missy," a voice boomed from just above her ear.

Serena looked up into a strong, broad face with a pair of eyes as blue as her own. Those eyes widened and blinked when she forcefully announced, "I'm your daughter, Mr. Donovan. I'm Serena."

Serena smiled, remembering. He'd not questioned her statement, but had swallowed hard, nodded, and immediately ushered her out of the saloon, pushing men aside with a swoop of his strong right arm, murmuring to her that this was no place for a young lady.

That was how it had been from the first morning. All the years he'd been absent from her life disappeared. The bonds of blood were strong. She was his daughter. He was her father. They'd found each other, and nothing else mattered.

With each passing day they grew closer, learned more about each other, and vowed they'd never lose touch again. Taylor Donovan told Serena that he would see to it she continued to be brought up properly. He insisted that come September, the two of them would leave the island and go back to New Orleans or some other fine city, where she could continue her studies.

September had seemed so far away when he'd told her of his plans. Now it was just around the corner. Serena kicked at the water and sighed. She didn't want to leave Galvez. She'd never been as happy as she was in this remote, strange community. She didn't care that the men who inhabited this city, including her dear father, were known to the world as privateers, or worse. Since they'd found out who she was, this odd assortment of humanity had been nothing short of polite in her presence.

She's seen the island ruler fewer than half a dozen times. From that first day, when she'd seen Jean Lafitte calmly gun down the sailor on the sand, Serena had regarded the tall, dark man with awe. Her father assured her that no finer man lived than Jean Lafitte, that it was unfortunate she'd witnessed the violent episode: Lafitte did only what was necessary.

Still, just thinking about the coldly handsome Lafitte made the wispy hair on her nape stand up. His men admired his indifference to danger, but Serena suspected the swarthy Frenchman was uncommonly brave because life meant so little to him. There was a brooding sadness in his dark eyes, a firm set to his full mouth. Never had she seen him smile. She wondered if he ever laughed.

An unmistakable laugh broke into her reverie and Serena promptly dismissed the privateer from her mind. She whirled about to see her good-natured father approaching.

"Serena Donovan," he gently scolded, "suppose some sea-weary sailor happened by and saw you with your skirts hiked up to your thighs?"

Serena saw the twinkling blue eyes and knew he was teasing her. But she didn't let go of the dress as she started toward him, splashing gaily. "He'd wish to high heaven he'd never looked because my papa would make him sorry he had eyes in his head."

"Aye, that I would, darlin'." Taylor shook his blond head. "That I would. No man on this island is fool enough to trifle with Taylor Donovan's daughter."

At the water's edge, he reached out and plucked his lovely, laughing daughter from the surf and set her down on the sand. He wrapped a long arm about her slender waist and kissed the top of her golden head as he drew her back toward the house.

"Child, I hate to spoil your enjoyment, but I'm afraid we're in for a bit of weather."

Serena had been much too preoccupied to notice that the morning sun had ducked behind billowing clouds or that the wind had picked up, changed direction, and was tossing the foamy waves a little higher than when first she ventured into the ocean.

Pushing an errant lock of long hair from her face, Serena looked up into her father's kind eyes. "Papa, are you worried? Will we be in danger?" She'd heard about the storms that occasionally slammed into the Gulf Coast ports.

Taylor Donovan smiled down at her and squeezed her waist. "No, Serena, we'll be safe, but I want you to stay close to the house until it blows over."

"As you wish, Papa." She patted his broad chest. "I'll race you back to the house." Before he could answer, she'd again lifted her long, full skirts and was flying barefoot across the warm sands toward the sturdy, well-scrubbed house they called home.

Taylor's laughter echoed after the nimble, sure-footed young girl. He didn't try to catch up. He stood enjoying the sight of the sweet, happy child who'd brought such joy to his life. Pride and love swelled in his powerful chest, and he was thankful for the unequaled blessing that was Serena.

He watched her until she disappeared inside the house. Then he lifted a big hand to shade his eyes. He looked again at the changing sky and didn't like what he saw there. Sea breezes that had only moments before been pleasant and calm were turning into powerful gusts, kicking up waves, blowing loose sand. By the time he neared his front door, big drops of rain were peppering his head and shoulders.

The Donovan house stood on the far western side of the island. Isolated from the rest of the community, it had once been the dwelling of a Mexican renegade who'd come to Galvez years before the arrival of Lafitte and his men. Away from the harbor, it was peaceful and private. The house itself was well built and sat on heavy four-foot-high pilings. The structure was tight and roomy, its high ceilings supported by a huge, heavy beam spanning the length of the house. If the home had any drawbacks, it was that at high tide, a small inland gully between it and the town could prove hard to traverse. On many nights, the Donovan home was completely cut off from the rest of the town.

Taylor Donovan didn't mind the isolation. It was a good, private home for his pretty daughter and should the weather take a turn for the worse, he could think of no safer place on the island.

A clap of thunder awakened Jean Lafitte. Lithely he rose from the swinging hammock on his second-story veranda and took up his telescope. Raising it to his good right eye, Jean trained the powerful lens on the port. His ships were bobbing up and down like corks on fishing lines. Waves tossed water high over their bows, and winds roared in off the ocean with mounting fury.

His lethargy evaporated, and Jean swung into action. In three long strides he was inside and crossing his bedroom. Down the stairs he hurried, issuing orders to his large staff. Stopping only to shove a pistol into the waistband of his trousers and shrug into a black oilskin slicker, he rushed out of the house and headed for the pier where one of his ships was moored while the others thrashed at anchor out in the harbor.

Sand blew into his eyes and stung his face. The sun had long since disappeared, and fingers of lightning now lit the dark summer sky, with claps of thunder close behind. Trees bent almost to the ground, and heavy squalls of cold rain quickly turned into blinding sheets that made Jean squint and raise his hand to rub the water from his burning eyes.

He leaped onto the gangplank of the *Orleans*, shouting to be heard above the roar of the wind and the waves. Seamen scurried about, making the necessary preparations, securing lines and battening hatches, while their leader, his dark hair plastered to his head, drew four of them aside; the others were to remain at their posts and ride out the storm.

The four men, all large and strong and intelligent, listened intently while Jean gave orders: They were to board the remaining eleven ships in the harbor and choose from each crew a half-dozen men. The group was then to mount up and meet Jean at the front wall of Maison Rouge. Not waiting for their reply, Jean whirled on one boot heel and dashed away.

The groom had Jean's milk-white stallion saddled when he reached the stables some time later. As he took the reins from the old man's hands, he saw that the stooped, graying servant was trembling.

"Clem," Jean shouted, patting the old man's shoulder, "it's just a little blow, nothing to worry about." He swung up into the saddle and rode out into the storm.

The seventy mounted men strained to hear Jean Lafitte's words above the screaming wind. Standing in the saddle, Jean cupped his hand to his mouth and shouted his instructions. In minutes the men separated into five groups and rode off in different directions, with Jean leading his bunch across the sands to the northeast.

They rode through the increasingly violent storm, pulling grateful women and children up onto the horses to be spirited back to the safety of Maison Rouge. Once their human cargo was unloaded, the men were off again to pluck more drenched and terrified inhabitants from flimsy structures that were already swaying and rocking on their foundations.

The cry of a child drew Jean's attention and he pulled up on the reins so abruptly that his horse reared, its front feet pawing the air. "You must move to higher ground," Jean shouted as he reached down to scoop the baby from its mother's arms. The young woman sobbed with gratitude when he extended his hand to swing her up into the saddle behind him.

His horse, dancing wildly, its big eyes wide with fear, neighed and blew as the house the mother and child just vacated lost its last roof to the terrible winds.

Jean dug his heels into the horse's flanks. As the big beast responded, Jean, the babe cradled in one arm, heard an earsplitting shout from the woman. His gaze followed her finger. A huge swell was surging up out of the gulf, joining with the incoming tide to form a dark wall of water. The gigantic wave was moving with remarkable speed. In seconds it washed over them. The woman screamed while her infant son squealed his outrage. Jean Lafitte said nothing but doggedly continued on his way and momentarily deposited the wet pair inside the high walls of Maison Rouge.

"Oh, thank you, thank you," the grateful woman cried, but Jean had already kicked his horse into a gallop.

It was midafternoon but as dark as night. The brutal winds continued to rip into the ocean, generating waves as high as a two-story building. The ships in the harbor bucked and pitched until hawsers snapped and the craft were blown out to sea. Men were tossed into the turbulent waters and drowned. Masts crashed into the decks, crushing sailors to death.

Jean and his men worked throughout the afternoon, transporting islanders to safety while the waters of the Gulf continued to rise at an alarming rate. Houses were swept away, debris floated on the tide, terrified people clung to uprooted trees and bits of lumber, their cries of fear and pain swept away on the relentless, roaring winds.

The walls of water rushing onto shore did not deter Jean and his men from making their treacherous way across the island. Though the raging tides rose belly-high on their horses and howling winds battered them, though salt water stung their eyes and burned their throats, and flying glass and splintered wood hurtled past their heads, the brave men went tirelessly about their tasks, combing the island for victims.

Hour after hour they rode and rescued, heedless of the danger of an increasingly angry sea, which threatened to swirl them away to a watery grave.

Long after darkness had fallen on the island, Jean Lafitte was still in the saddle and felt not the least bit weary. There was a glitter in his bloodshot eyes, and inside his chest his heart drummed. This rampaging storm was a challenge to him. He felt no fear, only stimulation and excitement.

For the first time in years Jean Lafitte felt vitally, totally, gloriously alive!

Serena Donovan had never been so frightened in her life. All through the long, dreadful afternoon she and her father had stayed inside their home. Serena had grown edgy from the too-near bolts of lightning and the booming thunder that shook the house.

At first her father had assured her that it would be a small island storm, potent but brief. She was not to worry; but even as he spoke, he set about nailing the shutters over the windows and Serena could see in his clear blue eyes undisguised concern.

Now as they waited for the storm to subside, Serena clung to his big hand and said a silent prayer for their safety. The walls seemed ready to shatter into a million pieces as the winds pounded relentlessly and the house groaned and shuddered. And all the while, the tide was rising around them.

"Serena," her father said in a calm voice that belied the fear gripping him, "I want you to do something for me."

She looked into his eyes. "What, Papa?"

"I'm going to lift you onto the roof. The water's lapping at the front door and the tide's not yet crested." His expression was grave.

Serena's head snapped around and she gasped. Water was seeping in under the door. Her hand flew to her throat, and she said quickly, "You'll come with me?"

"Yes, child." He pulled her to her feet. "Soon as you're safely up, I'll follow."

Bravely she nodded and tried to smile. They started across the room to the door. "Wait, darlin'." Taylor Donovan released his daughter's arm. "Stay right there; I'll get a slicker for you."

"All right," she cried above the howling winds, "but hurry."

The house rocked. Overhead a loud creaking grew steadily louder. Taylor Donovan was directly under the main supporting beam of the house. Suddenly Serena screamed. In one horrible instant a portion of the roof was torn from the house. The ceiling collapsed, bringing down the heavy beam and pinning her father beneath it.

Serena flew to his side and clawed wildly at the splintered timber. She pulled and pushed and shoved and cried, but the heavy beam would not budge.

Her father, though fully conscious, felt no pain. The joist had fallen across his legs, crushing them. Yet he thought not of himself, but of his daughter. "Listen to me, Serena!" He grabbed at her arm. "You must get out of here. Climb up on the roof. Now!"

"I'm not leaving you," she cried and snatched her arm free. Again she pushed and grunted and fought hysterically to lift the heavy beam from her father's shattered legs. So caught up was she with her impossible task that she was unaware of the water rising about her. Only when she glanced at her father's white face did this new horror register. Water was lapping at the back of his head.

"Oh, dear God, no," she sobbed. Futilely she tugged and jerked and pulled until she could no longer lift her arms. And still the water rose.

It was Serena's turn to be the brave, reassuring one. She crawled up behind her father and placed his head gently in her lap. "Don't you worry, Papa," she said calmly, "the storm's about to blow itself out. They'll come to help us then. They'll be here. You'll see."

Taylor Donovan smiled at his daughter, then took one of her small hands and brought it to his lips. He kissed it and said, "Serena, if you love me, you'll get up on the roof while there's still time. Please, darlin', do it for me."

"I'll do no such thing! I'll stay right here with you until they come for us."

Serena did stay, but the storm was not yet over. The winds continued to rage and the water continued to rise. Her heart thumping wildly, she managed to help her father sit up. Then she knelt beside him, her arm around his shoulders and her eyes on the swirling waters.

She could feel the cold, dark water at her hips, her waist, then her chest. "For God's sake, Serena," her father said through pain-thinned lips, "please go!"

"Never," she shouted and put her hands under his arms. Foolishly she tried to lift him higher. He groaned with pain, but Serena turned a deaf ear. She had to get him up. She had to pull him free of the beam. She had to! He would drown if he stayed where he was.

Tears streaming down her cheeks, she clung to him and yanked with all the strength she had left. The waters were rushing now, higher, faster, swirling up to his chin. Serena fell back to her knees and cupped his face in her hands.

"No," she moaned, "no, no, no."

"Save yourself, please," he begged, then added, "I love you, Serena."

It was the very last thing he said. The tide rose up to engulf him. His horrified daughter watched as he opened his mouth and gulped in the water so that he might get it over with as soon as possible and not struggle before her eyes. She fell upon him and kissed his wet head, clinging to him, reluctant to let him go.

The waters continued to rise.

Chapter Two

A strangely exhilarated Jean Lafitte led his exhausted minions across the storm-punished island, determined to save lives. Pushing his big white steed mercilessly, the lordly "Bos," his black eyes flashing, kicked his animal's sleek, wet flanks in an effort to win the all-important battle with the howling winds and raging seas.

It was dusk when Jean, standing in the saddle, water spiraling about his knees, looked toward the distant roof of the Donovan house. He quickly assessed the situation. Torrents of water cascaded swiftly down the wide, deep gully between him and the house; clearly it was too deep to cross. Jean looked again at the house, his eyes narrowing, a muscle twitching beside his full mouth.

"Don't try it, Jean!" Aumont Ledette called above the roar of the winds. "It's suicide, man!"

Jean turned to look at Ledette. "Donovan's little girl is in that house!"

"I know," his friend answered, "but the house is on high ground. They'll survive. Let's go!"

Jean cast one last look at the place, nodded, and reined his horse around as the angry waters continued their deadly rise.

When all the island dwellers who could be reached had been spirited to Maison Rouge, Jean finally went home.

It was past four in the morning when, as abruptly as it had begun, the storm was over. It had blown itself out, and in its place was an eerie calm. The waters dropped rapidly — a foot in less than ten minutes. By the time a half-hour had passed, they'd fallen four feet.

Jean Lafitte, freshly bathed and wearing clean, dry clothes, sat at the long carved table in his opulent dining room. He picked up a crystal goblet of fine wine and took a long pull. Ravenously he ate the cold duck and sliced bread a servant had placed before him. Alone in the big hall, with candles in heavy silver holders casting long shadows on the ornately molded walls, Jean felt his heart beating rapidly beneath his black shirt. There was a feverish gleam in his ebony eyes: he could hardly wait to finish his meal. He was anxious to be off once again. Jean motioned the servant forward to fill his empty wineglass. "Philippe, have Cook prepare foods that I can take with me. I'll leave in ten minutes."

"*Oui.*" The silver-haired servant nodded, stoppering the wine decanter and placing it on the sideboard. He asked no questions, but quietly exited the room to carry out Lafitte's order.

Restless energy still claiming his lean body despite the preceding arduous hours, Jean drained his wineglass, pushed back his chair, and rose. Into the corridor he strode, his boots clicking on the white marble, his tall, slim form made more so by the soft, blousy black shirt, snug black trousers, and black leather boots he wore. He turned to allow his valet to drape a long black cloak about his shoulders. Flashing the old man a rare smile, Jean took the black leather saddlebags from him, slung them over his left shoulder, and moved swiftly down the wide hall, a dark, mysterious figure disappearing into the night.

At the stables his men awaited him. Bleary-eyed and exhausted, they sat astride fresh horses and watched their leader. An alert groomsman tossed Jean the reins of a spirited black stallion. Nodding, Jean draped the saddlebags behind the saddle, put a toe into the high stirrup, and with a flourish, black cloak swirling around him, mounted the big beast and thundered away, his loyal lieutenants following close behind.

Sunrise revealed the staggering destruction left in the hurricane's wake. Across the storm-swept island Lafitte and his minions galloped, Jean's alert black eyes swiftly assessing the damage. Hardly a building was left standing; the powerful wind had leveled everything in its path. Livestock lay sprawled about, drowned in the watery wilderness, their carcasses already stiff.

To the harbor Jean rode, his face impassive save a strange, bright glow in his dark eyes. His armada had taken the brunt of the storm. From everywhere came the screams and groans of injured and dying seamen.

The expressions on the blood-streaked faces turned grateful as rescuers spilled onto the battered decks. Beams and debris were quickly lifted to free the injured while reassuring voices spoke words of comfort and promises of prompt deliverance from suffering.

No man worked harder than the island master. While the hot summer sun climbed steadily up into a blue, cloudless sky, Jean Lafitte, his cloak discarded, worked tirelessly alongside his men. Many pain-ridden sailors felt the firm, sure hand of their Bos on their feverish brows, heard his deep, calm voice speak their names with affection, watched his white, even teeth flashing in a bright grin, the likes of which they had not lately seen.

It was high noon, and the sun hovered directly overhead. The island was sweltering in the midday heat. Serena Donovan, her long blond hair a damp, tangled mass of curls about her stiff neck, sat on her heels, her arms around her father. She'd been like that for hours, since the eddying waters had closed over Taylor Donovan's head.

Staunchly refusing to leave him, she'd screamed and pulled and fought to save him while the briny waters lapped at her chin and washed into her mouth. Sputtering and shouting, she'd continued to tug and grunt and scream until her throat was raw, her voice was gone, and she was no longer able to lift her arms.

Still she remained with her father. There she sat when the waters began to recede and his dear face was once again visible above the tide. There she stayed when dawn broke and a soft pink light washed over her father's gray, still face.

She couldn't let him go; she couldn't. He was all she had in the world. She couldn't lose her father! So she stayed, her arms wrapped tightly around his broad chest, her chin resting on his gray head. Oblivious to the tattered dress that now exposed numerous bruises and cuts on her slender body, Serena clung to her father and hummed tunelessly.

He was tired. That was it. The storm had been wearying, and he needed rest. That's why his eyes were closed, why he wouldn't speak to her.

Serena smiled. Her father was merely dozing. Soon he'd awaken, rested and strong and vigorous as ever. Then the two of them would set about putting the house in order. He was a talented carpenter; why, in no time at all he'd have their home looking just as before, she was sure of it.

The smile still lighting her blue eyes, Serena put words to the tune she was humming. Her father loved to hear her sing. Often he'd told her she had the voice of an angel and that nothing was sweeter than to hear her going about her kitchen chores singing while he stretched out for his afternoon nap. Serena sang a lilting lullaby and gently swayed, her arms firmly about her father's girth.

There was nothing more to worry about. She'd sing to him and let him rest. Soon he'd awaken and everything would be as before.

It was nearing close of day when Lafitte and his band approached the remote island home of Taylor Donovan and his young daughter. Lafitte, his back regally straight, his eyes on the wreckage of the once sturdy house, pulled up on his horse. Calling for silence, he dismounted and moved forward. Jean had heard a faint sound coming from the half-collapsed dwelling.

He quickened his pace, his heart pounding. Onto the fallen gallery he leaped, ducking under a section of its roof that now hung precariously. Proceeding cautiously through splintered wood and tumbled bricks, Jean forced his way through the battered door, three of his men close behind. The sounds grew louder. Jean's flashing eyes swiftly surveyed what was left of the room. Then he saw her and held up his hand indicating that his men should come no farther.

For a time he stood looking at the young girl, her lovely face streaked with dirt, her dress in shreds, her tangled hair spilling down her back. His heart constricted. Motioning his men away, he shoved the smashed furniture and boards and broken pottery from his path and made his way to the girl whose slender white arms enclosed the dead man to whom she sang.

Jean slowly crouched down beside her.

"Child," Jean said softly. The humming continued. The girl didn't turn her head. She continued to stare dully into space.

Jean shook his dark head. Lifting a hand to her dirty, tear-streaked face, he gently cupped her cheek and murmured softly, "Sweetheart, it's Jean Lafitte. I've come to help you."

Slowly the fragile face turned toward him, and a pair of big blue eyes looked up into his. Calmly, she said, "I have to keep singing. You see, my father is sleeping, and I . . . I . . . he wants . . . " Her bottom lip began to tremble as though looking into Jean's dark eyes had brought her back to painful reality. "Please, won't you . . . won't you come back some other time? You see . . . Father's . . . he's . . . he's — " Her voice broke, and her eyes filled with tears.

"Sweet child." Lafitte's voice was low and warm. Looking steadily into her eyes, Jean gently pried her small hands loose and pulled her to him. While she leaned against his chest, Jean lowered the dead man's head to the floor. Then he picked up the trembling girl and rose.

The dam burst. Serena buried her face in Jean's throat and sobbed uncontrollably while he carried her out of the ruined house and into the fading sunlight. Inclining his dark head, he motioned his men to enter and prepare the body for burial. Jean went to his horse, got his black cloak, and wrapped it around Serena. Then he started walking, the girl clinging to him, crying her heart out. He strode away from the others whispering softly, "Oh, my child, my child . . . "

Down an incline he headed, leaving the others behind. He stopped a few feet from the water, still holding the weeping girl in his arms.

Serena lifted her flushed face and said tearfully, "My father is dead."

"Yes, child, he is, "Jean confirmed softly, and tenderly kissed a wet cheek when she again collapsed on him, burying her face in his shoulder. He stood there holding her for a long time. When finally her slim body no longer quaked with sobs, when she grew as silent as the man who held her, Jean Lafitte turned and retraced his steps.

At a peaceful, slightly elevated spot a hundred yards from what had been his last home, the body of Taylor Donovan had been lowered into a grave dug by Lafitte's men. When Lafitte carried Serena to the site, the earth had already been smoothed over and a crude marker had been driven into the sand to mark the spot.

Jean Lafitte gingerly stood Serena on her feet. Her eyes on the mound of earth, she slowly sank to her knees and clasped her hands before her. Jean stood behind her.

One of Jean's lieutenants stepped close and said near Jean's ear, "Bos, you know the tide'll rise with nightfall. We'd better leave. Otherwise, we'll be trapped here."

"Take the men and go," Jean said quietly. "We'll be right behind you." Nodding, the burly seaman took his leave, the others hastily mounting to follow. As the tired crewmen rode away into the rapidly falling twilight, they heard something they knew they would never tell anyone or discuss among themselves.

Jean Lafitte was singing a hymn.

He knelt beside her. Serena was singing, and Lafitte, as though he'd never missed one meeting of Sunday school, joined her, his rich baritone blending with her unwavering soprano. He knew every word of the sad refrain, and it was he, who, when the hymn was finished, began another.

At its completion, Serena turned to him and asked, "Will you please offer a prayer?"

Dark eyes kind, voice calm, Jean bowed his head. "Almighty God, accept into thy kingdom thy humble servant. Forgive him his transgressions and have mercy on his immortal soul. Comfort the daughter he leaves behind and watch over her all the days of her life in Jesus' name. Amen."

"Amen," Serena echoed softly.

Jean stood up. "Child, if we don't hurry, we'll be cut off. The tide is coming up."

"Yes."

His hand beneath her elbow, Jean drew her to her feet. Eyeing the rapidly rising tide, he guided her to his black horse. He swung up into the saddle, leaned over, and gave her his arm. Serena took it and he easily lifted her up behind him. She wrapped her arms around his trim waist, and Jean urged his horse into a gallop. The black cape flowed out behind Serena, whipping about the horse's shiny flanks.

The powerful black beast raced across the damp sand, his master urging him forward, anxious to cross the wide inland gully while there was still time. If there was still time.

But dark waters surged down the deep ravine, spilling over its banks. Jean pulled up on his horse, and the animal danced nervously in place. Jean's eyes scanned the foaming stream. Abruptly he turned the horse and sped in the opposite direction, searching for a safer place to cross. Again he pulled up on the reins and stood in the saddle.

"It's my fault." Serena's soft voice made him turn to look at her. "We stayed too long with father and now we —"

"It's not your fault and there's no harm done," Jean said kindly.

"But we can't get across, can we?"

"Not tonight," he answered calmly, "but that's no cause for alarm. I have food and water in my saddlebags. We'll go to Maison Rouge in the morning."

The fiery sun had slipped below the horizon, its afterglow still shedding light on the island when Jean and Serena returned to her devastated home. Her small hand clutching his, they entered the house by a back door. As they stood inside the dish-strewn kitchen, it was Serena who squeezed Jean's hand and said, "Come."

Through a half-obstructed doorway she crawled, Jean following, into an almost untouched bedchamber. Marveling that the violent storm had done little damage here, she looked at him and said, "This is my room."

"We'll stay here," he said with cool authority "Now, child, I have a canteen filled with water. You'll want to get out of those torn clothes and wash. Shall I help you?"

"I'll manage," she assured him, pulling the cloak tightly about her.

"Fine," Jean said and promptly pulled the long tails of his black shirt loose from his tight breeches. His nimble fingers swiftly unbuttoning the fine shirt, he explained,

"Your dress is ruined. You'll wear my shirt. It will cover you. I'll go into the other — "

"No," she said, stopping him. "I know the house better than you. I know where I can change." She took the shirt from his hand, turned her back, and slipped out of the cloak, releasing it to him. Hurriedly she fled.

In minutes she returned to him.

A candle flickered in the room. Jean had spread his heavy black cloak on the floor. He reclined there, his arms beneath his dark head, his eyes on the ceiling. Serena gripped the door frame and hesitated.

She'd removed her soiled and torn clothing and now wore only his black shirt. It hung almost to her knees, and its softness against her skin made her all too aware of her nakedness.

As if he sensed her presence, Jean agilely rolled to a sitting position. His eyes came to rest on her. She felt a momentary shiver of anxiety. In the candlelight the planes of his chiseled face were partially shadowed. His dark hair was disheveled and fell over his high forehead. His black eyes gleamed like an animal's.

"Come," he said and his voice was low, reassuring. Serena shyly joined him, dropping to her knees at the edge of the cloak. She sat back on her heels as Jean knelt and faced her. The silence was suddenly deafening; she could hear the sound of their breathing in the quiet room. Her eyes went to the bare, brown chest before her. It was muscular and covered with thick black hair. It looked strong and safe and warm.

"Will you hold me for a minute?" Serena said softly and found herself swept into his embrace before the last word was out of her mouth. Strong arms pressed her to the warm bare chest and Serena closed her eyes and put her grateful arms around him. Her head resting on his left shoulder, she could hear the steady, even beating of his heart and she silently gave thanks for his presence and let his strength flow into her cold, tired body.

Jean, his long arms around her, held her gently, meaning only to comfort, to protect. Silently he caressed her trembling shoulders through the soft fabric of his shirt. Unruly blond hair cascaded about her lovely face, its silky texture tickling his bare chest as she buried her face there. Small warm hands clutched at his bare back as though she might never let him go.

There in the candlelight they knelt, clinging to each other, saying nothing. It was Jean who moved first. His hands were on her shoulders, and gently, gradually he pulled back a little. Serena slowly lifted her head to look at him. His flashing eyes were on her face, and his mouth hovered just above her own.

It was Jean Lafitte who now trembled. He fought the emotions warring within his chest. A man who prided himself on his ability to remain firmly in control of any situation, he was shocked by the mounting desire this lovely young woman had stirred in him. She was looking up at him with trusting blue eyes, her soft lips parted and gleaming in the candlelight. Glorious blond hair spilled about her pale, beautiful face, and her small, warm hands remained tightly about his waist.

Jean, as he had for the past twenty-four hours, felt much, much younger than his thirty-seven years. The adventure of the storm had been like a mighty battle, his role that of a young warrior. And now, the battle over, the victor could claim the spoils. For this glorious moment in time, he was young and virile and full of hope. The delicate blonde looking into his eyes was not a helpless child depending on him for safety but his beautiful mate, at ease with her desirability and eager to know his arms. They were equals here. Zesty, youthful, passionate. Two anxious lovers alone in Paradise.

Jean's hand left Serena's shoulder and moved to her face. Long fingers raked through the spun-gold hair, and the cool reserve for which Jean Lafitte was famous evaporated into the sweet, humid air. He lowered his mouth to hers very, very slowly, giving her every opportunity to turn away, to stop him, to flee from his kiss.

She did not. Instead she lifted her lips to meet his and sighed softly into his mouth. Jean kissed her tenderly, and with the sweet joining of their lips a flame burst forth in both of them. He lifted his dark head to look at her. Her lovely face was aglow in the candlelight, cheeks flushed with color, supple body straining against him.

"Serena." For the first time he called her by her name and she felt her heart leap with joy. His mouth came back to hers in a deep, demanding kiss of passion. A deft brown hand found the buttons of her shirt and rapidly flicked them open. His lips never leaving hers, Jean pushed the shirt aside and pulled her closer.

Serena snuggled against him willingly, and when he eased her down on the floor, she closed her eyes and whispered, "Jean, Jean," and thought it was the most beautiful name she had ever heard.

Harsh reality arose with the morning sun. Jean's dark eyes slid open and the first thing he saw was silky blond hair fanned across his dark chest. He was no longer the young lover of the night before. He was, to his despair, a tired, middle-aged man who'd taken advantage of a sweet, innocent young girl. Experiencing a fiery pain in his stomach, Jean lay unmoving, feeling sick and saddened, knowing he'd never be free of his deep, depressing guilt. Nor should he be.

Serena stirred and Jean tensed. Lifting her head from his chest, she pushed back a curtain of hair from her face and looked at him. And she smiled, a sweet, charming smile that made Jean's heart hurt.

Unselfconsciously, she stretched happily and leaned over his face to kiss him. "Will I be your . . . your mistress now, Jean?" she asked sleepily. "Will I live with you?"

"My sweet Serena," Jean said quietly, "I have a mistress. I have a family . . . a son." He watched her bright blue eyes slowly fill with tears. "Oh, God," he groaned, cupping her sad face in both his hands. "Listen to me, child. I've done you a terrible injustice. It was unforgivable, wrong, inexcusable. I had no right, none."

Tears slid down Serena's cheeks and she blinked at him, his dark face a blur before her. "But I love you," she sobbed softly.

"No, dear," he murmured, "you don't. You feel you do now, but soon you'll forget this happened. You must." Jean sat up, bringing her with him. "Where did you live before you came to Galvez?"

"New Orleans, but — "

"You've family there?"

"No. I've no one."

"I'm sorry," he responded, then hurried on. "I'll take care of you, Serena. You'll need to finish your schooling. I'll send you back to New Orleans; you'll attend the Ursuline Academy. The sisters will teach you and watch over you. I'll send money and I'll . . . "

Serena remained silent. Her heart was breaking. She sat looking at the handsome face while Jean spoke, and she felt as though she were being sentenced to a term in some distant prison. Where was the warm, passionate man who'd taken all her love? What had happened to the tender lover who'd kissed her throughout the night and held her in his strong arms as though he'd never let her go? Who was this stranger who was calmly planning to send her away from him?

Jean Lafitte took from his little finger an extraordinary ring, a large glittering emerald set in gold filigree and surrounded by tiny pearls. "This is a very special ring, Serena," he said softly, lifting her hand. "I want you to have it." He slid it onto her middle finger and squeezed her cold hand. "Look at me," he commanded gently.

Serena lifted her eyes to his.

"You're a lovely, sweet child," he said, "and you have your entire life ahead of you. My dearest hope is that you will be happy. You will forget me, my dear, much sooner than you think." With that he leaned forward and kissed her wet cheek, and Serena knew very well, as his warm lips brushed her skin and his strong arms embraced her, that she would not forget this magnificent man. She loved him, and she would love him for as long as she lived.

She looked at the ring on her finger, and the pain in her heart expanded. He'd given her his beautiful emerald ring, a ring valuable and obviously precious to him. Still, it was not enough.

Was it all she was ever to have of Jean Lafitte?

Part II

Chapter Three

LATE APRIL 1829
THE U.S. MILITARY ACADEMY,
WEST POINT

Spring had come to New York State. The Highlands rose emerald green against clear blue skies. The Hudson River made its slow, steady way between the lofty Palisades, the sun's powerful rays transforming the peaceful water into gently rippling mirrors of light.

Red-breasted robins, perched in the budding limbs of the tall elms, chirped their happy welcome to the season. The morning air was warm and sweet, the pungent fragrance of mown grass and rich earth strengthened by a dawn thunderstorm.

On the Plain, where within the hour boy officers would pass in review, members of the Post band were setting up their instruments and music sheets on a wooden platform. The sound of a lone trumpet floated across the parade grounds to the dormitory known as Old South.

In a small Spartan room on the third floor, a massively built young man with unruly blond hair, a ruddy complexion, and pale blue eyes stood before the open window buttoning the eagle-stamped brass buttons on his single-breasted blue coat. The high, stiff collar of his uniform bit into his powerful neck, and the neatly pressed trousers strained across his powerful thighs. Cadet Lieutenant Cot Campbell was prepared for the ceremonies.

Across the sun-filled room, lolling on his bunk, his dark head resting on his rolled-up mattress, Hilton Courteen was not in uniform. Former Cadet Lieutenant Courteen's civilian trousers, slate gray and so fashionably long that they covered the tops of a black leather shoes, clung to his lean flanks while a soft, blousy shirt of purest white linen was open immodestly low, revealing his muscular dark chest. Feet crossed casually, Hilton blew perfectly formed smoke rings into the air and looked for all the world as though he had not a care.

A third occupant was mumbling to himself in the small, cluttered room. Jasper, his brown eyes flashing indignation and his shiny black face fixed in a permanent glower, meticulously packed Hilton Courteen's personal belongings. He muttered and worked, folded and grumbled, stopping regularly to shoot disgusted looks at his young master. Summoned to help the disgraced Hilton prepare for his leave-taking, Jasper was more ashamed of his charge than he'd been in all the days he'd been in attendance. Certain they'd never live down the shame, he was further incensed by Hilton's cavalier acceptance of the distressing situation. Didn't the young fool know he'd ruined his life and broken all their hearts?

Cot Campbell smoothed his cowlick and looked at his roommate."Dammit all, Hill, must you always be so stubborn? They had nothing concrete. All you had to do was plead innocence!"

Hilton Courteen, his full lips rounded into an O, forced the smoke out in carefully controlled bursts, so that a perfectly formed chain of rings drifted upward. Not until he had pushed all of the smoke from his lungs did he turn to look at his friend.

"Cot, old pal, while some might disagree" — Hilton looked pointedly at his unhappy manservant — "I consider myself a gentleman and a man of honor. Lying is beneath me. I refuse to do it."

A loud harrumph issued from the pursed lips of the displeased Jasper as Cot smiled incredulously. "My God, you have a strange set of values, Hill. You wouldn't dream of denying your guilt in order to save your military career, yet you have no qualms about dueling with intent to maim or kill. What kind of logic is that, pray tell me?"

Hilton placed his thin brown cheroot between even white teeth, agilely swung himself up off the cot, and ran a hand through his thick black hair.

"Southern," he drawled as he crossed the room and tossed his cigar out the window. Then he pivoted and shot his friend an impish grin.

Cot shook his blond head. The young Tennessean, a level-headed, slow-to-anger, ambitious young man, was exceedingly fond of the impulsive Alabamian with whom he'd shared quarters for the better part of four years. But, in truth, he had never really understood Hilton Courteen. While he admired his daring, wit, and intelligence, he despaired of the cool Courteen recklessness that had led his friend into this latest episode, which had resulted in expulsion from the Academy.

"Hilton, I'm every bit as much a southerner as you are, but the honor of being appointed to West Point is surely —"

"A southerner, Cot?" Courteen interrupted, grinning lazily "If they knew you weren't even a citizen of the United States, they'd kick you out, too."

Cot laughed. "I'm a native of the great state of Tennessee and you know it."

"Perhaps. But your daddy and your brother and any-one else who goes by the name of Campbell is down in Texas. Am I right?" His dark eyes sparkled. "Are they Mexican citizens yet?"

Cot Campbell's fair, broad face colored before he chuckled. "My little brother's been considering it. Says the Mexican government will give him some fine river land. All he has to do is become a Catholic."

"And perhaps marry a little —"

"We were discussing you, my friend." Cot waved his big hand dismissively. "Tell me, my unrepentant comrade, was it worth it? You took offense at meaningless words spoken in anger. What difference does it make what — "

"Cot," Hilton interrupted smoothly, "Samuel Dunlap flatly and without equivocation shook his blunt finger in my face and told me he considers me and all other southerners barbarians because we own slaves." Hilton shoved his hands into the pockets of his snug trousers while his lids slipped low over his black eyes. "Now, I'm not certain how you would have responded to such an insult, but no senator's soft son, who's spent the whole of his life in a Pittsburgh city residence without so much as a backyard, is going to tell me how we're to run our plantations. Sam's never been farther south than Phila-delphia, so I could hardly permit him to pass judgment on customs below the Mason-Dixon line."

"Granted. Still, I can't understand — "

"You're beginning to sound like a Yankee yourself, Cot. You've been up here too long. It's time you got back down South — or to Texas." He laughed then and added, "Tell you this much: Old Sam ought to be glad I had a go at him. That ugly devil's appearance will be vastly im-proved with a long scar down his jaw. He might have better luck with the ladies now that he's acquired a distinguishing mark of bravery."

Cot grinned and nodded his agreement as he took a pair of white gloves from a bureau drawer. Pulling them onto his ham-like hands, he said earnestly, "Still, you were a damned good soldier, Hill, and your grades were consistently high. Without your help I'd never have — "

Cot's sentence went unfinished. The door to the room burst open and a uniformed man marched in. Tall and slender, his carriage notably erect, the officer had light gold hair, a ruggedly handsome if too-lean face, and deep-set blue-gray eyes that flashed mischievously. Lieutenant Jefferson Davis, graduate of the Point the year before, was smiling broadly, his slim hand outstretched to Hilton Courteen.

"Didn't you learn a damned thing from me?" Davis teased, after nodding to Cot. "How the hell could you let yourself get kicked out?"

Hilton, fond of the rowdy Mississippian who'd been in constant trouble during his time at the Point, pumped Davis's hand. "Tell you, Jeff, without you around here, life's been rather wearisome, so I decided I'd had quite enough of West Point."

Jeff Davis roared with laughter, his eyes crinkling at the corners. Abruptly he pulled out of a straight-backed chair, took a seat, and said without preamble, "Hill, tell me what happened. I've only heard the rumors." All the laughter had left his lean face, and the light eyes darkened with interest.

Hilton shrugged. "Not much to tell, Jeff. I 'ran it' one evening, got safely past the sentry, hopped a sloop into New York, and was caught missing after taps. Nothing you haven't been guilty of dozens of times."

As Davis studied Hilton's dark face, disappointment clouded his blue-gray eyes. Without shifting his focus, he said, "That all there was to it, Cot? I heard — "

"You heard correctly, Jeff," Cot quickly affirmed. "He engaged in a duel with none other than Samuel Dunlap, Pennsylvania Senator Dwight Dunlap's only boy."

A wide, happy smile creased Jeff Davis's face, and he rubbed his hands together. "I knew it! I'm proud of you,

Hill. My God, if I'd only known, I'd gladly have been your second." He was bobbing his head for emphasis. "Tell me about it. What was the nature of the insult?"

"Slavery was the issue." Hilton's voice was flat.

Jeff Davis jumped up from his chair. "Why, that pompous, ignorant fool!" he thundered, his face reddening. "What in blazes does he know about — "

"Calm yourself, Jeff," Hilton admonished quietly, smiling fondly at his passionate friend. "Sit back down. What brings you to the Point this morning?"

Davis remained standing. Eyes still snapping, he said, "I was dining at a friend's home in New York, and Sam Houston was among the guests. He asked me to accompany him here today to review the troops. I agreed immediately. I'm on extended furlough, but I report to Fort Winnebago in the Michigan Territory on the last day in May." His face brightened. "Might do a little Indian fighting." Before Hilton could comment, Davis fished a gold watch from his pocket. "I'd better be on my way; it's almost time. You coming, Cot?"

"I'll be right along, Jeff."

Davis placed a firm hand on Hilton's shoulder. "Hill, won't your daddy intervene in this matter? You know, I was court-martialed and kicked out, but they took me back. I'm sure it could all be cleared up and — "

"No, Jeff," Hilton said, his lips compressed into a taut line in his dark face. "I will ask nothing of Reynolds Courteen."

"Independence is an admirable trait, Hill. Still . . ." Davis shook his head, then added, "We'll stay in touch, Courteen. Destiny has great plans for us both." He squeezed Hilton's shoulder, turned, and exited the room with the same brisk flourish with which he had entered.

After Jeff Davis's departure, a sad-eyed Cot Campbell, his face aflame with color, wordlessly embraced his best friend. Unabashedly he hugged the tall, slim man until

Hilton's deep voice said, "Campbell, get the hell out of this room."

Cot took a step back, raised a gloved hand, and snapped off a crisp military salute. Hilton returned the salute and watched the big man turn and stride from the room.

Jasper closed the last valise, his bottom lip trembling.

"That's it, Jas," Hilton told his manservant. "Let's go."

Hilton stepped into the hall. Old South was virtually deserted. All the cadets were outside preparing to assemble into marching units. Hilton descended the rickety stairs for the last time, an expensive gray frock coat slung over one shoulder, his handsome face expressionless.

No one, not even the faithful black servant following close behind, would have suspected that Hilton Courteen was sorry to be leaving the Academy. But it was true. Young though he was . . . still one month short of his twenty-first birthday . . . Hilton was wise enough to realize that the men he'd met at West Point were the cream of the country's crop: the smartest, the brightest, and the bravest young men in the nation.

As Hilton stepped out into the bright sunlight, a group of cadets called to him. One of them broke away from the group and came over to greet Hilton. Dark-haired and handsome, the tall cadet lieutenant moved with an air of assurance and grace. When he gripped Hilton's hand, his soft brown eyes were serious. Cadet Robert E. Lee said softly, "I shall never forget you, Hilton Courteen. I am saddened by this tragic turn of events. I feel the loss is West Point's as well as yours. Your brilliance in math and tactics has impressed me more than you know. You would have had a long and successful career in the army, sir. I wish you luck and pray we'll meet often."

Lee's warm brown eyes were filled with kindness. Hilton Courteen grasped Lee's hand and smiled at the soft-spoken classmate whose name had never had one single demerit placed beside it on the record of delinquencies. Hilton, like all the other young men who knew Robert Lee, was aware of the well-bred Virginian's leadership ability and unwavering integrity.

"Thanks, Robert," Hilton responded, then predicted sunnily, "I'm sure you'll be wearing the epaulets of a major by the time the first snow falls in Alexandria." Lee looked pleased. "Our paths will cross again," Hilton promised. "Good-bye, my friend."

As Robert Lee joined the other shiny-faced cadets, Hilton Courteen headed for the river. His long strides were purposeful. Quick though he was, however, he was unable escape the grounds before the band struck up a rousing march and the well-drilled troops passed in review before the banner-draped platform occupied by the distinguished guests.

Hilton slowed and paused, then watched, transfixed. Two hundred pairs of hands, gloved in snowy white, swung back and forth with crisp precision. Two hundred blue-clad chests, brass buttons gleaming in the sun, swelled with manly pride while two hundred pairs of eyes stared straight ahead.

And then Sam Houston was standing on the podium. The big frontiersman's voice boomed out. "When I look out this morning upon the gallant young men before me, my heart fills with unequaled joy. My fellow soldiers, I'm honored to be among you . . . "

Hilton turned and started walking. Soon he was picking his way down the steep, rocky path to the wharf. Behind him, Jasper hurried to keep up, all the while heaping criticism on Hilton's dark head. "Ain't nebber goin' to be able to hold my head up again. No, suh, I 'spect I spend the rest of my days feelin' shamed over this . . . "

Hilton smiled and, let the scolding go on. It obviously made Jasper feel better, and it bothered Hilton little, if at all. When the two reached the wooden levee, Jasper was puffing and out of breath, but still grumbling.

Hilton sat on an upturned trunk, looked up and down the calm river for a time, and finally swung around to look at Jasper. Smiling easily, he said, "Jas, you've made your point. I've disgraced you and you'll never live it down." He dropped his frock coat across one knee, laced his long fingers behind his head, and laughed.

"Well," Jasper sniffed, "you won't be laughin' once you is back home. Your pa ain't happy, neither. Not one bit!"

Chapter Four

RIVERBEND SUGAR PLANTATION
ON THE BANKS OF THE MISSISSIPPI
BELOW NEW ORLEANS
AUGUST 1831

Sylvain Fairmont stole silently down the great curving staircase, her gray eyes alert, her bottom lip sucked behind even white teeth. She paused when she neared the bottom, her small hands gripping the polished banister. Then Sylvain leaned over to peer into the library. Through the tall archway she saw Edwin Fairmont, hands folded across his stomach and gray head turned to one side, sleeping in his chair.

A surge of triumph raced through Sylvain. She crept down the remaining stairs, hurried across the wide entrance hall, and slipped out the heavy front door. Sighing with relief when she stepped out onto the sun-drenched gallery, Sylvain smiled and took flight. Like a spirited colt, she flew across the terraced lawns of Riverbend, her long, shining hair streaming behind her.

Delilah looked out of an upstairs window just in time to see the swirling yellow skirts rounding a purple azalea bush on the far edge of the vast yard. The slave shook her head. She knew Sylvain had managed to sneak past her father. Lord only knew where the child was headed.

Delilah turned from the window, eyes twinkling. The tall black woman had been Sylvain's personal maid for eight of the girl's twelve years. It was when Sylvain turned four that Delilah, only twelve herself, was informed she'd been given lofty position. Delilah, intuitive and bright, knew the reason: None of the other servants, including Sylvain's old nurse, could keep up with the active little girl.

Sylvain Fairmont possessed boundless energy, unending curiosity, and a patent disregard for convention. The child's precociousness and lack of inhibitions made Delilah's task a never-ending struggle. Still, though their battle of wills was ever constant, Delilah was often Sylvain's conspirator and protector.

Delilah went about Sylvain's big, airy bedchamber, picking up discarded clothing and books, wondering if the young mistress of Riverbend would ever learn to behave like a lady. Right now she hoped Sylvain would return to the house before noon. A guest would be calling at Riverbend, Delilah had been told, and Sylvain was to join her father, mother, and the gentleman caller for lunch. "And Sylvain is to be wearing a spotless dress," Mrs. Fairmont had informed Delilah. "Her hair is to be neatly brushed and ribboned, her hands and fingernails clean, her manners impeccable."

So Delilah, when she'd brushed the tangles from Sylvain's thick, dark hair, had cautioned the restless girl to stay indoors. She was to go directly to the music room, where she should practice her scales on the square piano for at least an hour, after which she would join her parents in the drawing room to wait for their guest.

The astute servant knew what had happened. Sylvain had found her father dozing in his chair, and to her that had meant freedom. She'd seized the opportunity to go outdoors and enjoy the sunny August day, and Delilah could hardly blame her. The child showed absolutely no talent for the piano, and she hated every moment she spent on the high stool practicing. Delilah's face broke into a broad grin.

Sylvain was a clever girl. She'd return before Edwin Fairmont awakened or her mother came downstairs. Delilah wouldn't tell on her, and no one would be wiser.

Sylvain scampered through the orchard, dodging low-hanging, leafy trees heavy with late-summer peaches, pears, and plums. Negro slaves, their voices raised in song as they harvested the ripe fruits, nodded and waved to Sylvain, and she shouted her greetings to them before disappearing into the dense forest.

Once she was in the lush, tropical woodland, Sylvain turned south. Picking her way cautiously through the verdant undergrowth, she glanced warily about for snakes and spiders. A well-worn path brought to her the stretch of bottomland bordering the cypress swamps, and within minutes she stood on a flat, grassy stretch surrounding an abandoned slave church.

Sylvain smiled as she looked up at the great carved cypress cross atop the steeple. Then she sat down upon the grass and removed her shoes and stockings. Though she'd been cautioned to stay away from the old church, Sylvain came here often. It was her special place at Riverbend.

Sylvain had no time to tarry today. No sooner had she taken off her white kid shoes and long white stockings, than she stood up and darted through the graveyard beside the chapel. Back into the forest she went, angling steadily toward the river. Through the underbrush she hurried, ducking and weaving, finally emerging onto the long, broad avenue that led to the levee.

Sylvain heard the sharp, loud blast of a whistle and felt her heart leap with joy. She flew headlong down the smooth, shady lane. A canopy of dark green leaves blotted out the sky, and Sylvain imagined that the huge, ancient oaks on either side of the river road were bending toward each other. Each time a spidery web of low-hanging Spanish moss brushed her hair or her face, she squealed.

Out of breath, she reached the wooden wharf in time to see the tall stern-wheeler round the bend. She took up her lookout on the splintered levee, lifting a small hand to shade her eyes against the blinding August sun. She stared, transfixed, at the approaching riverboat.

A beautiful sight she was! Gleaming white against the cloudless blue sky, she puffed thick, black smoke into the heavy morning air from two tall smokestacks. Sleek and long and proud and pretty, she made her way through the dark, murky waters, the giant paddle wheel turning slowly. Sylvain's gaze was drawn to the pilot house with its fancy gingerbread trim, and then to the texas deck, boiler deck, and hurricane deck where the railings looked like white lace.

Sylvain's wide gray eyes took in every inch of the imposing riverboat, from the flag proudly waving in the breeze to the red-hot boilers to the flint-faced pilot. But the bright smile soon changed to an expression of puzzlement. The boat appeared to be slowing, as if the captain intended to stop at the deserted Riverbend levee. That couldn't be.

Rooted to the spot, Sylvain watched as the captain raised his hand, a bell rang loudly, and the great wheel slowed and stopped. Sylvain, never noticing the tall, dark man lounging on the texas deck, spun about so rapidly that her bare left foot caught a needle-sharp splinter and she let out a yelp of pain, but she didn't slow down.

She had to get away. Someone was stopping at Riverbend. Eyes smarting from pain, Sylvain didn't stop to extract the painful splinter. Bent only on escape, she climbed the steps to the bluff and vanished into the cool, concealing forest.

Hilton Courteen, hands in the pockets of his tight buff-colored trousers, stood on the texas deck of the aging riverboat, *Jennifer J.*, the sun beating down on his dark head. He squinted, blinked, and raised a hand to shade his eyes. On the small levee not a hundred yards ahead, a young girl in a bright yellow dress was looking toward the steamboat. All at once she bolted like a frightened deer and disappeared into the trees. Hilton smiled.

He'd grown bored at the hotel in New Orleans and had hopped the steamer downriver, knowing full well he'd arrive before he was expected. He'd told the Fairmonts he would be on the noon boat. Edwin Fairmont had assured him a coach would be waiting to bring him to the house where he'd take lunch with the family. Afterward he'd be shown about the vast sugar plantation, which he was thinking of purchasing.

Hilton descended the gangway, nodding his adieus to pilot and crew. He stood motionless as the boat backed away from the landing and took up its slow, steady journey downriver.

Hilton shrugged out of his form-fitting jacket, folded it over his arm, and headed for the tree-shaded lane that would take him to Riverbend. He passed a large gatehouse, its windowpanes dusty from disuse, and noted the vines and weeds that threatened to take it over. Hilton frowned and moved on.

When he reached the broad avenue of huge oaks, Hilton sauntered along, whistling merrily. It wasn't long before he caught a glimpse of yellow on the left side of the lane. He stopped.

Again he saw it, daffodil yellow flashing brightly amid a sea of dark green. It disappeared. Hilton again began walking, eyes riveted to the dense thicket bordering the road. The yellow reappeared, streaked, and crashed. A loud shriek cut through the silence.

Hilton was into the woods with the speed of a jaguar. Dropping to his knees beside the prone form, his black eyes flashing with alarm, he lifted the child and saw immediately that she'd had the breath knocked out of her. He patted her back with a sure hand and said calmly, "You're okay, sweetheart. You'll be fine."

Sylvain clutched the dark stranger's forearm, her big eyes wild with fear. Finally her lungs filled with air, and she gulped and sputtered, her eyes stinging, her heart pounding, and her ears ringing.

Hilton said nothing, but smiled down at Sylvain and continued to gently pat her back. When she turned her frightened face to his, Hilton knew he'd never seen a more beautiful child. Huge smoke-colored eyes, shining now with unshed tears, were shaded by long thick lashes. Her pert nose, which was perfectly formed, was nothing short of adorable. Full, soft lips, rose-hued and dewy, opened to reveal small, white teeth. And a tousled mass of rich brown hair cascaded around her small oval face and over her slender shoulders. Even her smooth, flaw-less skin was remarkable — a strange golden color, like rich, light honey in the sunlight.

"Better?" he inquired softly, a smile playing about his generous mouth.

"Y-yes, thank you," Sylvain managed, then asked boldly, "Who on earth are you?" Shoving his arm away, she jumped up and bit her lip, cringing when she put her weight on her left foot.

"You're not all right." Hilton rose and put his hands on on her shoulders.

Sylvain shook her head. "I am. It's just . . . " She made a face. "My foot. There's a splinter in it."

Hilton hadn't realized until then that the lovely child wore no shoes. He spread his jacket on the ground. "Sit," he commanded and eased her down. "I'll see to it."

Crouching beside her, Hilton lifted the small dirty foot onto his knee.

"I asked who you are, sir," Sylvain reminded him.

He was intent on the nasty-looking splinter embedded in the tender sole of her foot, but he said, "I'm Hilton Courteen. I've come to call on the owner of Riverbend."

"I'm the owner of Riverbend," Sylvain informed him. "I'm Sylvain Fairmont. Ouch!"

"Stop squirming. You're a mighty small girl to own such a large plantation." He raised his eyes momentarily and gave her a teasing smile.

"Actually, Daddy owns Riverbend," she admitted, then added, "but I'm an only child, so that makes me the heiress, doesn't it?"

"I'd guess that it does."

"Why are you early, Mr. Courteen? You were supposed to arrive at noon on Cap'n Williams's *Helen Ann*, but you came down on the *Jennifer J.* instead, with Cap'n Walt Cochrane. Oooh, you're hurting me."

"Sorry," he said, "both for being early and for hurting you. You know the schedules well — you like the riverboats? Hold still for just one more . . . There!" he said triumphantly, and showed Sylvain the long, blood-smeared splinter.

"Thank you," Sylvain said, lowering her foot. "I love the river and the boats."

"I'm not finished," said Hilton, capturing her ankle and hauling the foot back onto his hard thigh. "You want the wound to get infected? You ride the paddle-wheelers often?"

"As often as possible. Mostly I just watch and wave to the captains. I know them all," she announced proudly.

"I see." He grinned and drew from his pocket a snowy white monogrammed handkerchief. Deftly he shook the folds from it and wound it around Sylvain's injured foot. Tying a neat knot over her high instep, Hilton smiled at her and said, "Now, Miss Fairmont, Dr. Courteen has finished. I prescribe limited walking, absolutely no running, and a bathing of the affected area just as soon as possible." He rose and held out his arms.

Sylvain looked up at him. She liked his face. It was strong and dark and handsome. There was about him, however, a devilish look. Could she trust him to keep a secret? She wasn't too sure. When she felt his strong hands beneath her arms, she pushed against his chest and demanded, "What are you doing, Mr. Courteen?"

"I'm picking you up," came the low, calm response. "I'll carry you." He swung her up against his chest and stooped to retrieve his coat.

Sylvain's gray eyes flashed. "You put me down this instant!" she ordered, looking squarely into his dark eyes. "I shall walk, thank you very much!"

No sooner had the words left her lips than she found herself deposited on her feet. "I was only trying to be of help," he said, slinging his jacket over his shoulder. He strode away.

Sylvain, her face screwed up in discomfort and surprise, limped behind him. "Will you wait a minute?" she said, exasperated.

Hilton turned, a grin spreading over his handsome face. "Change your mind? Want me to carry you?"

"No" She lifted her chin. "But you can slow down a little, if it's not asking too much." She smiled then, an endearing, lovely smile that enchanted Hilton Courteen.

He reached a hand out to her. Sylvain took it and together they made their way to the road. Sylvain was strangely impressed with this stranger's manner. He didn't defer to her as most people did. She had the distinct feeling she could put little over on this tall, dark man. She liked that. She promptly decided that she must win the favor of this Mr. Hilton Courteen.

Smiling sunnily up at him, she chattered gaily, telling him all she knew about Riverbend, answering his questions and admitting she hoped he would choose not to purchase the sprawling plantation. She did her best to look like an angelic urchin, fixing big sad eyes on his and explaining that this was her home, the only place she'd ever lived, the only place she wanted to live.

Hilton was touched and squeezed her hand. "I've only come to look at Riverbend. There's certainly nothing definite. In fact, I doubt very much that — "

"That's wonderful," Sylvain said quickly. "When Daddy told me you were coming to buy Riverbend, I sobbed for hours. I can't bear to leave here, Mr. Courteen. It's my home. I've lived here all my life!"

"That's an awfully long time," he said, smiling.

"Twelve years." She nodded. "I had a birthday in June. How old are you?"

"Twenty-three. I had a birthday in May."

Sylvain suddenly stopped. Courteen paused and turned to give her a questioning glance "Are you in pain?"

"No. I was wondering . . . " She chewed the inside of her cheek. "Can you keep secrets, Mr. Courteen?"

"I know secrets wild horses couldn't pull from me."

"You do?" Her eyes grew round. He nodded. "Come with me," she said and led him into the trees. Silently he followed, bending to push branches out of their path. He released her hand and moved her in front of him when the undergrowth became too dense for them to walk side by side.

They picked their way Indian file through the vines and bushes and soon stepped into a small green clearing. Before them a weathered building stood in the sunlight, a tall wooden cross rising from its steeple.

Hilton eyed the old chapel for a few seconds, then looked down at the big-eyed child gazing up at him. "It's a very private place, isn't it?" he said for want of a more suitable comment.

"Yes," she responded enthusiastically. "It's my secret spot at Riverbend. Want to go inside?"

"I can hardly wait." He knew what she wanted to hear.

Sylvain pointed out a loose plank at the back of the church. He easily pried it open, and the two of them slipped into the cool, musty room. Hilton looked about at the crumbling walls, the dusty altar, the dilapidated pews.

"Now I'll tell you the secret," Sylvain whispered to him. "There's gold buried in Seachurch."

"No!" he whispered back.

"There is. It was left here by pirates years ago. They never came back for it."

"Who told you?"

"I overheard two old slaves whispering about it one day a long time ago. And I know it's true. Turn your back a minute." Hilton turned away, hiding the smile that tugged at his full lips. Sylvain extracted a gold coin from inside her lacy camisole. "You may turn around."

Hilton lifted the hand she held out to him. "Why, that is gold, Miss Fairmont. A Spanish doubloon."

"I know. You may call me Sylvain if you like. I found it here at Seachurch. There's thousands of others just like it." She closed her fingers around the coin and, forgetting her modesty, pulled the yoke of her yellow dress out and deposited the doubloon back inside her camisole. "And they all belong to me."

"You're a lucky young lady," he offered. "Where are the rest of the gold coins?"

Sylvain made a face. "I don't know yet. I haven't found them, but I will. One day." She gave him a confident toss of her dark head. "Now we'd better be going, Mr. Courteen." Outside, Sylvain picked up her shoes and stockings, then turned to him and said, "Since you're so good at keeping secrets, perhaps you'd keep one more."

"Try me, Sylvain."

"Well, you see, I'm not supposed to be running about alone. I'm not supposed to come down to Seachurch. My parents are strict — unbearably so, I'm afraid." She looked pleadingly up into his eyes. "I shall surely be punished if I'm found out. It's unfair, don't you think?"

Hilton, his gaze dropping to the soiled bodice and skirts of her bright yellow dress, tried hard to keep a straight face. "Grossly," he solemnly assured her and was amused to see an expression of relief flooding her beautiful face. "What's the plan?" He folded long arms over his chest.

"If you would agree to go back to the landing, I'll have Delilah, my maid, delay our coachman's arrival. When he reaches the levee, you'll be there waiting, as though you'd just stepped off the *Helen Ann*." She was tilting her head thoughtfully, gentle breezes picking up strands of her long dark hair and blowing them into her face. "I, in turn, could hurry to the house, dash in the back door, and run up the servants' stairs to my room. Delilah will help me."

They were outside the old church now. Pounding the loose board back into place, Hilton said, "A brilliant scheme. I fully approve, my dear."

"Good!" She flashed him a dazzling smile. "Now we'd best go our separate ways."

"Indeed." He nodded his handsome head.

She turned away, paused and looked back at him. "Mr. Courteen," she said very softly, "you . . . you won't betray me, will you?"

Hilton Courteen smiled and lifted a hand to gently tug free a wisp of long sable-brown hair that had caught in Sylvain's parted lips. His voice soft and low, he said, "Sylvain Fairmont, I'd never betray you. Never."

Massive and magnificent, Riverbend was an impressive sight, even to a young man used to luxury. The big two-story cream-colored structure was at least seventy-five feet long and almost as deep. Eight enormous Doric columns supported the sloped roof. A broad gallery wrapped around the entire house, upstairs and down.

Two *garçonnières* — houses intended for heirs — flanked the great house; smaller versions of the original, they were themselves larger than most city residences. Sweeping terraced lawns and gardens in full bloom framed the palace on the hill. Riverbend was a lordly residence, a cool haven of grandeur nestled deep in the semitropical delta land.

The carriage rolled to a stop before Riverbend, and Hilton stepped out just as the tall front door of the mansion flew open. Edwin Fairmont, a welcoming smile creasing his fleshy face, came forward.

"Right on time, my boy," he said approvingly as he shook Hilton's hand. "Glad you could come, Mr. Courteen."

Hilton smiled down at the shorter man. "Thank you for sending a carriage along, Mr. Fairmont. I could have walked."

"I wouldn't hear of it," said Edwin Fairmont, patting Hilton's back and propelling him up the steps.

Edwin Fairmont led his guest into a spacious drawing room where the ceiling soared eighteen feet high and rosewood furniture gleamed in the afternoon sunlight streaming in the windows. The mistress of Riverbend sat on an elegant sofa of champagne brocade. Mrs. Fairmont nodded her delicate head and smiled when Hilton bent over her hand. The rotund and slightly rumpled Edwin Fairmont stood at Hilton's elbow, beaming down at his lovely wife. As Hilton released the lady's fragile hand, he hoped he'd hidden his astonishment.

Edwin Fairmont, whom he'd met before, he judged to be in his late forties or perhaps early fifties. Short, balding, with light eyes and ruddy complexion, the man was overweight, his belly straining against the buttons of his waistcoat.

But Mrs. Fairmont! She was extremely pretty and obviously much younger than her husband. Her pale blond hair shone in the sun, and her eyes, as azure as the

Louisiana skies, were big and beautiful, though their depths held an odd expression that hinted of a deep sadness. When she rose, Hilton saw that she was tall and regal. Smiling charmingly, she said, "Shall we go to the dining room where our lunch is waiting?"

When Hilton offered her his arm, she placed her hand on it and lifted her long, heavy skirts. Hilton was pulling out Mrs. Fairmont's high-backed chair when Sylvain Fairmont bounded through the arched doorway. Out of breath, her gray eyes sparkling and her dark curls dancing, the girl was a vision in a clean pink dress. She went straight to her father's chair. Throwing her arms around his neck, she gave him a peck on the cheek before her eyes went to the tall, dark man standing behind her mother's chair. "I'm not late, am I?" she asked sweetly, shifting her gaze to her father's face.

"Just in time," Edwin assured her, absently stroking her shiny dark hair. "Sylvain, dear, this is Mr. Hilton Courteen. He's the caller I told you about, come to look at Riverbend."

"Nice to meet you, Sylvain." Hilton smiled at her, and in his dark, expressive eyes she saw that her secret was safe. He had no intention of giving her away.

Sylvain said graciously, "We're happy you came, Mr. Courteen." She slipped from her father's arms and went to her place at the long, linen-draped table. When Hilton pulled out her heavy chair, she looked up at him and couldn't suppress a giggle.

Hilton pushed in the chair and glanced at Sylvain's mother. Now her dazzling blue eyes sparkled as she looked with love and pride at her lively daughter. Her voice was warm as she said, "Sylvain, you were favoring your left foot when you came into the room. Is your slipper too tight?"

Hilton, taking his seat across from Sylvain, dared not look at his co-conspirator. Wondering if the mischievous child would stammer, he could hardly keep from smiling when he heard her answer in a sure, sweet voice, "No, Mother, not at all. Nothing's wrong with the shoe or my foot." She flicked her snowy napkin open and spread it in her lap. "My, I'm starving. Aren't you, Mr. Courteen?"

"Yes, I am," he responded and watched Mrs. Fairmont lift a hand to jingle a silver bell. On her hand she wore a ring of such unique beauty, it caught Hilton's eye. A huge, flawless emerald set handsomely in gold filigree and surrounded with perfect, tiny pearls.

After lunch Hilton was given an extensive tour of the huge sugar plantation. Donning a broad-brimmed planter's hat, Edwin Fairmont mounted his favorite sorrel stallion. Hilton, who was bareheaded, selected a chestnut gelding, and the two of them cantered across the four-thousand-arpent spread, with Fairmont pointing out the slave quarters, the stables, the hospital, the plantation office, the smithy, the sugarhouse, and the fertile fields of sugarcane.

Pulling up on his horse, Edwin Fairmont pointed south. "That building you see over there is the old slave church. Hasn't been used in years. There was a great crevasse in the levee a long time ago, and Riverbend was flooded. The chapel almost collapsed, and it's unsafe now. No one ever goes into it. Beyond it are the swamps."

Hilton nodded and reined his horse around. It was evident that the chapel was not the only unused building at Riverbend. Many of the outbuildings stood vacant. Edwin Fairmont seemed to read the expression in Hilton's eyes. Sadly he confessed, "Riverbend has seen more prosperous times, I'm afraid. You see, Mr. Courteen, my health is not what it was, and I ... ah ... I've been considering selling for some time now. I'm an attorney and I plan to take up my practice again. Let someone younger be the gentleman planter." He laughed hollowly.

"I'm sure running a huge sugar plantation is a sizable undertaking," Hilton mused. "What's that building?"

"The sugar factory," Edwin said, his eyes clouding. "Or at least it was at one time."

Hilton eyed the vast wooden building with its peeling paint and boarded-up windows.

"Then you no longer . . . "

"No," Edwin admitted. "Truth is, Mr. Courteen, I've neither the slaves nor the money to operate Riverbend." He saw Hilton's look and said quickly, "Have you any idea how much it costs to run a plant this size?" Hilton shook his head. "A man needs scores of slaves and tens of thousands of dollars of credit." He fell silent, his eyes resting on the deserted sugar plant. "There was a time, Mr. Courteen, when . . . when . . . " He paused and sighed. His shoulders seemed to slump. Hilton felt a deep compassion for the man and felt almost guilty that he had already decided not to make an offer on Riverbend. And he wondered what had happened to bring Edwin Fairmont's downfall.

Back at the mansion Hilton took brandy with his host on the wide front gallery. Jasmine and camellia bushes, their branches heavy with blooms, filled the still afternoon air with a sweet fragrance. Droning wasps hovered over the blossoms, dizzy from the abundance of nectar. It was a peaceful, grand old place: impressive, enormous, remote.

"I'll be happy to show you through the rest of the house." Edwin took a long drink of brandy and stared straight ahead. "Ah . . . I'm afraid some of the rooms are — "

"Not necessary," Hilton interrupted. "Riverbend is all I'd heard that it was."

Edwin's round face broke into a big smile. "It is beautiful, isn't it?"

"Breathtaking, sir." Hilton drained his glass. "I don't know a damn thing about running a sugar plantation, Mr. Fairmont. As a matter of fact, I have very little knowledge of either cotton or sugar."

"But you were raised on a successful cotton plantation, son. Surely, you — "

"I was, but I paid little attention — none, my father said — to the running of the place. When I was seventeen, I went to West Point. I returned to Mobile just before my twenty-first birthday and found it was no longer my home." He smiled wryly.

"I'm afraid I don't understand."

"My father threw me out of the house. I've lived in hotels ever since."

"But ... but ... then, how do you propose ... that is, you led me to believe you — "

"I have money, Mr. Fairmont. Enough to purchase Riverbend, but I didn't come by it planting cotton."

Edwin's heavy eyebrows lifted. "You're a gambler?" he blurted out.

Hilton fixed him with a cool stare and gave no reply.

"Sorry, son, forget I said that. How old are you, Hilton?"

"Just turned twenty-three."

Edwin Fairmont shook his head. "No wife or children?"

"Happily, no."

Edwin sighed. "Riverbend would prove a bit lonely for a single man. We're a long way from New Orleans."

"Farther than I had expected, sir."

"You're not going to buy, are you, Mr. Courteen?"

"I'm sorry, sir." Hilton rose from his chair.

Edwin stood up. "Doesn't matter. Won't you stay for dinner?"

"I'd like to" — he extended his hand to the older man — "but I must be getting back to the city. You've been a kind and gracious host. I'm certain you'll find a purchaser for Riverbend. Where do you plan to go when you've sold the plantation?"

"Why, to your hometown, I believe. Mrs. Fairmont has expressed a desire to reside in Mobile, and I understand it's a quiet, genteel city."

"It's that, sir. A bit too quiet for me." Hilton laughed. "Look me up when you arrive."

"We will." Edwin walked the young man down the steps and out to the carriage that was pulling into the drive.

"Say good-bye to your family. You have a beautiful wife and daughter."

"Yes, I do," Edwin said proudly. "I'm a lucky man."

Edwin Fairmont, disappointed, sick-at-heart, turned and went back into the house.

Hilton, lounging lazily in the carriage, turned to look back at the mansion. His eyes were drawn to the upper gallery where a dark-haired girl in pink was waving furiously to him, her slim arm raised high over her head. Hilton's handsome face broke into a broad grin, and he blew her a kiss. The sound of her merry laughter floated down to him before she turned abruptly and disappeared.

At Riverbend landing, Hilton nodded to a cold-eyed stranger alighting from the steamer, but the sallow, ferret-faced man ignored the gesture. Pulling his dark hat lower over his eyes, the man, who was dressed entirely in black, brushed past Hilton. He was tall and thin and there was something menacing about him. In his right hand he carried an ebony walking stick topped with a gold gargoyle-head. He moved with a strange, gliding gait, as though he were slithering across the wooden jetty.

Hilton stepped onto the deck of the stern-wheeler and turned in time to see the dark man climb into the Fairmont carriage. His eyes narrowed and he wondered about the strange man's identity and the reason for his visit to Riverbend.

The boat slid out into the water, and Hilton yawned lazily. And he forgot all about the mysterious man. Ambling up the steps toward the pilothouse, he idly considered how he'd spend the evening in New Orleans.

A despondent Edwin Fairmont sat alone in his study after Hilton Courteen's departure. With his blunt fingers laced together on top of his desk, he shook his head and sadly faced the facts. Young Courteen had been his last chance, his only remaining hope of saving Riverbend from the grasping hands of the unprincipled Hyde Rankin. There was nothing he could do to stop Rankin now. Nothing.

Edwin looked about his favorite room, the place where he spent so much of his time. His beautiful wife and lovely daughter smiled down at him from a portrait above the mantel. Behind him tall French doors were open to the pleasant breezes from the side gallery. Across the room, priceless books lined the shelves, and a long worn couch under them had afforded him many an afternoon nap.

Edwin continued to reminisce until he was interrupted by his faithful servant, Delson, softly rapping on the door. The butler announced through the closed door that a gentleman had come to call. Edwin's stomach began to churn, and he closed his eyes briefly.

"Come in," he said finally, and slowly rose from his chair. Hyde Rankin came into the mahogany-paneled room and wasted little time. Propping his ebony cane with its grotesque gold gargoyle-head against Edwin's desk, he triumphantly presented Edwin Fairmont with a bank note and said coldly, "I'll take the deed to Riverbend." His thin lips widened into a wicked grin, and he added, "I'm sure you'll want me to leave promptly, lest I contaminate your charming wife and daughter with my presence."

Face crimson, teeth grinding, Edwin Fairmont pulled out the bottom drawer of his desk. Lifting a metal box, he took from it the yellowed deed to the vast plantation. With a breaking heart he relinquished the rich delta land to the malevolent man seated across from him. "The deed," he said tiredly.

Smiling coldly, the purchaser took it, slapped it against his palm, and said, "I shall enjoy living here. However, I'm a reasonable man: You may have until the first of the year to vacate." His eyes impaled Edwin Fairmont. "Don't think, however, that your moving to Mobile will free you of me. It will not."

"Haven't you taken enough?" Edwin Fairmont despaired. "You're buying this property with money you've extorted from me. You leave us with so little."

"Not true . . . not true at all." Hyde Rankin's evil smile disappeared and he added, "I just paid you a handsome sum for this run-down plantation." His eyes narrowed. "I don't care how you continue to get the money, but continue you will, or face the consequences." He smiled once again. "After all, now that I'll be residing in a mansion, I shall need money to lead the life of the country gentleman."

"Please," Edwin Fairmont entreated, "you own the land and most of the slaves now. Why don't you put the plantation into operation and earn some money?"

Laughter rumbled from the man. "Work? Why should I?" He crossed the room. Hand on the brass doorknob, he turned and said coldly, "Mobile is a charming city. I shall be more than delighted to visit you there on schedule, just as I've always done. I'm certain you'll rapidly build up a respectable practice. You once had a reputation as an able attorney." He opened the door and went out.

Edwin leaned back and gripped the wooden arms of his chair. He closed his eyes and grimaced. His stomach felt afire with despair and hopelessness. His chest ached with fear and dread.

The door opened, and Mrs. Fairmont swept gracefully into the room. Noiselessly she crossed to her husband. Without a word she put her hands to his face and pressed his head against her breasts.

"My dear, I'm sorry, so sorry," Edwin said into the sacheted silk of her frock.

Gently kissing the top of his head, she soothed, "Shhhh, Edwin, it doesn't matter. It doesn't matter at all."

Tears choking his voice, Edwin Fairmont pulled one of his wife's hands to his lips, kissed it, and murmured, "My sweet darling. Serena. Serena."

Chapter 5

Dense gray fog shrouded the riverfront, a thick, wet mist that dampened the skin as well as the spirits. Immense sycamores and cottonwoods, their branches bare, loomed black against the winter sky, and the moss-hung live oaks lining the river road took on eerie and forbidding shapes in the swirling mists. The heavy air was chill and biting.

Sylvain, a warm wool coat buttoned up to her chin, hurried down the avenue, her teeth chattering. Behind her the great house had been swallowed up by the murky veil. Leaving the road, Sylvain slipped through the wet undergrowth and low-hanging cypress branches and picked her slow, sure way toward a vague outline in the distance.

When she reached Seachurch, she hastily pulled the loosened plank away and ducked inside the chapel. From the pocket of her gray wool coat she produced a sulfur match, and within seconds a candle flickered in the gloom. Sylvain sat on the floor beside the candle, wrapping her arms around her knees and staring at the hypnotic little flame.

She sighed heavily as she looked around at the interior of the deserted old church where she'd spent so many hours. The candle's weak light cast shadows on the tall, crumbling walls, and she asked as she did every time she sat in this abandoned slave church: Where? Where was the treasure? It was here somewhere. She knew it. She'd never forget the night she'd overheard two old slaves whispering. They kept murmuring a name: Kashka. Kashka knew the secret, they said. But who was Kashka? There was no slave at Riverbend called Kashka.

Sylvain bit her lip. How *could* her father have sold Riverbend? How could she bear to leave this place that was her home? Why must they go away from here? Her mother had explained that her father was growing older and that running a vast plantation such as Riverbend was too trying for him. They'd decided it would be good for them all if they sold the sugar plantation and all of its headaches and took a smaller residence in a city where they could live a less complicated life. Besides, her mother had said, Riverbend was awfully secluded, and didn't Sylvain realize that very soon she'd become a young lady who would be attending parties and dances? Wouldn't it be exciting and advantageous to live in a city where she could meet lots of young people her age?

Sylvain screwed up her face. She didn't want to meet lots of young people her age. She wanted to stay right here at Riverbend and ride her horse and wander through the sugarcane and slip down to the river to watch the steamboats and sit here inside Seachurch until she finally figured out where the pirates' gold was hidden.

Unwrapping her cold hands from her knees, Sylvain rose agilely, wet her thumb and forefinger, and put out the candle. She squeezed back out through the narrow opening and carefully fitted the warped plank back into place, pounding it with her bare hand to make it more secure. Then she backed away and looked up at the imposing wooden cross. Water trickled down the weathered wood, as though this emblem of suffering and salvation were shedding tears.

Feeling a great tightness in her throat, Sylvain whirled away and scrambled back through the thick forest. Tears streaked her cheeks, and she dashed at them with the back of her hand as she ran away from the abandoned church with its great cypress cross. And its secret.

"Sylvain, you better get yourself in here right now." Delilah's voice cut through the fog. "We is ready to go. You hear me, miss?" Sylvain blinked back the last of her tears and saw the outline of the main house in the distance. The voice continued to call to her. "If I has to come lookin' for you, young lady, you is goin' to be in big trouble!"

"I'm right here, Delilah!" Sylvain bounded through the tall white gate and into the terraced yard. "I was telling the slaves good-bye."

Delilah, arms akimbo, glared down at the child hurrying toward her, dark brown hair flying wildly around her flushed face. Shaking her head, Delilah came to meet her, then took Sylvain's hand and jerked her up the steps onto the wide gallery and into the house. Inspecting her charge thoroughly, Delilah brushed the dust from Sylvain's coat, smoothed the dark hair, and ran a thumb beneath a wet eyelid. "Has you been cryin'?"

Brushing the servant's hand away, Sylvain shook her head. "No, I have not!" she said, but her voice quavered. "Oh, my baby," Delilah soothed, and pulled the child against her. Sylvain's slim arms went around Delilah and clung for dear life while she buried her face in the maid's ample bosom. Delilah crooned to her, cradling the dark head as she'd done so many times before. When the small body against her own ceased trembling, Delilah put a hand beneath Sylvain's small chin and tilted it up. Smiling down at the girl she often considered her own, Delilah said, "That's better. Your mama and daddy be comin' down soon. We gonna be smilin' when they does come, ain't we?"

"Yes, we are, Delilah." Sylvain took the offered handkerchief, blotted her eyes, and blew her nose. "We're going to pretend like we're happy to go, right?"

"Dat's right. We sure is."

The covered carriage was waiting at the edge of the yard. It would remain at Riverbend. This would be the last time the Fairmont family climbed into the gleaming black coach with its fine burgundy leather seats and the last time old Ned, the coachman, would drive the family to the levee. Ned was no longer a part of the Fairmont empire. Now he had a new owner.

Serena Fairmont, pale and lovely, took her husband's arm and regally swept down the steps of the great house, her head high, her expression serene yet unreadable. Edwin Fairmont, his hand supporting his wife's elbow and his eyes on her face, escorted her down the long walk to the carriage. Never had he loved his wife more than he did at that moment. As he had a million times since he'd married her, he felt he was the most fortunate of men. He was certain that this fragile woman's heart was breaking on this damp, gloomy morning, that to leave her beloved Riverbend was unbearably painful for her, though she had not complained or grieved. Not once had she hinted that his selling of the vast plantation was anything other than a wise decision. Here was truly a great lady.

Sylvain and Delilah followed closely behind. It was time to depart. The good-byes had been said, the trunks had been sent up the river, and the last-minute items had been packed.

Sylvain slowly turned around. A weak sun had managed to burn through the fog. The great mansion gleamed white in the filtered light. On both the upper and lower galleries of the magnificent eight-columned dwelling, the house servants — all twenty-two of them — stood, fear and despair in their sad eyes. They had been sold along with Riverbend.

Sylvain blew them kisses while Edwin and Serena waved. Delilah, sobbing loudly, got into the carriage.

Edwin handed his wife up inside, then his daughter. Old Ned, tears streaming down his withered black cheeks, clucked at the matched sorrels, and the carriage rolled away.

Down the levee road it rolled, under the canopy of live oaks, dappled sunlight now seeping through the branches. In silence they rode to the escarpment. Serena Fairmont's small hand rested in her husband's. Sylvain, seated beside the weeping Delilah, looked steadily out of the carriage window. Through the trees she got a fleeting glimpse of the tall steeple of Seachurch, its cypress cross rising to the sun.

While Serena and Edwin Fairmont resolutely accepted the fact that they would never again set foot on this delta-land haven, young Sylvain just as resolutely told herself that she would be back. She didn't know when or how, but she vowed she'd return.

This was Riverbend, *her* Riverbend. She'd find a way to get it back.

Chapter Six

The Fairmonts boarded a stern-wheeler at the landing and traveled upriver to New Orleans. At the bustling port they were met by a liveried coachman and transported to the luxurious Garden District home of Dr. Nicholas Delon. The prominent Creole physician and his attractive wife, Nadine, were old friends of the Fairmonts. Rosalie Delon, the couple's pretty daughter, was the same age as Sylvain, and the two were like sisters.

Rosalie, wrapless in the cold January air, came dashing out to meet her friend and threw her short arms wide to smother Sylvain in a tight embrace. They disappeared into the brightly lit house and up the carved staircase to Rosalie's enormous suite of pink rooms.

"I shall surely die of loneliness when you've gone," the short, plump Rosalie said despairingly, closing the door behind them and pulling Sylvain's wrap from her slender shoulders. "Have you grown some more?" She forgot the upcoming desertion momentarily to ponder an even more unpleasant possibility. Rosalie was destined to be a pretty, albeit petite, woman. Her father, though perfectly formed and dapper, was no more than five feet six. Her mother, Nadine, was barely five feet tall. How Rosalie envied the coltish Sylvain with her long slender legs and arms, her strange golden-hued skin that allowed her to play in the sun without benefit of bonnet and never so much as turn pink.

"Perhaps half an inch," Sylvain offered matter-of-factly. "I've not measured lately." She smiled at her friend. Then she pulled at a long dark curl and said, "Don't be such a goose, Rosalie. Ladies are supposed to be tiny."

Unconvinced, Rosalie tossed her friend's coat onto a chaise of tufted rose velvet and retorted, "Who wants to be a lady?"

Both girls cried, "Not me!" and burst into giggles. They crossed the carpeted room, kicked off their leather slippers, and climbed onto Rosalie's high, soft bed. While Sylvain stretched out on her stomach, face supported in her hands, Rosalie tugged at the bell pull. Within minutes a silver tray was set on the marble side table by the bed, and the two girls, wearing only their underwear in the cozy firelit room, drank hot cocoa, ate rich tea cakes dusted with sugar, and lamented the unkind fates that were about to tear them apart. Promising to write each other each week without fail, they recalled all their dear and wonderful times together as though they were elderly ladies looking back over long and adventurous lives.

A pensive Sylvain was still thinking of her friend Rosalie, and of the lost Riverbend, when Mobile came into view. Trying valiantly to cheer his family, a smiling Edwin Fairmont, arms around both wife and daughter, inclined his graying head. "There she is, the old port city." He looked from one pretty face to the other. "It's a handsome town, don't you think?"

"It's most attractive, Edwin." Serena smiled reassuringly at him. "I believe the Fairmont family is going to be quite happy here." She cast a hopeful glance at her daughter.

"Yes, Father." Sylvain tried to sound sincere as she looked up into his eyes. "Mobile appears to have great possibilities. We shall have grand times exploring the city."

The child was much too young to know how pleased her father was to see her glowing smile and hear her simple words. In fact, she was quite puzzled when he stooped, kissed her forehead, and squeezed her waist extra hard. She was just as puzzled by the mist of tears she saw shining in her mother's beautiful eyes.

It was necessary to stay in a hotel until a proper house could be located for the family. Sylvain did find residing in a hotel a new adventure — she'd never done so before — and she wasted little time in writing to Rosalie, excitedly relating how she was allowed to take all of her meals in the paneled dining hall with stylishly dressed travelers, prosperous Mobile businessmen, and elegant ladies and handsome gentlemen who came to the hotel to dine in the evenings.

Except when she took meals in the dining room and short strolls with her parents, however, Sylvain was told to keep to her room. It was small and stuffy and the sounds of passersby on the street below as they went in and out of the apothecary shop next door, the haberdashery across the street, and the crowded restaurants and coffee houses nearby seemed never to cease, even in the late evenings. The little room soon became a noisy prison to the young girl who'd grown up in the isolated tranquility of Riverbend, and she was relieved when, on their fifth evening in Mobile, Edwin Fairmont announced at dinner that he and Sylvain's mother had chosen a house.

He spoke of the new house and its choice location animatedly. Sylvain listened and felt her heart turn to stone. She'd hoped that her father would choose a place in the country, but he had not. They were to live in the city proper in a "town house."

The very next day Sylvain got her first look at their new home. The skies were leaden and heavy and the air frigid when she stepped down onto the Dauphin Street banquette. Before her stood a red-brick house of French Colonial design. Spanning the front was a porch with six very slender columns supporting the ornamental cast-iron balustrades that reminded Sylvain of homes she'd seen in the French Quarter in New Orleans.

Sylvain swallowed hard. Houses, almost identical to the one she was to live in, flanked the dwelling. They were so close! How could she breathe here? How could she survive among neighbors who could see her every move? How could she go barefoot? Turn somersaults? Talk to herself? Hide from Delilah?

"When the azaleas bloom in the spring, the balcony will be a perfect place to sit in the evenings." Serena Fairmont was indicating the bushes, their brittle, black twigs barren. "I can envision the pinks and purples, can almost smell their sweet scent." She was radiant, her cheeks flushed in the cold winter air, her big eyes sparkling.

"Yes, dear." Edwin Fairmont was nodding in agreement. Turning to his daughter, he said, "And you haven't seen the best part, Sylvain." He held out his hand, which she took immediately. "There's a walled courtyard in back of the house that offers complete privacy."

Sylvain brightened and walked around the house with him. A tall solid gate swung open and she stepped into the bricked courtyard. Appalled at the small size of the yard, Sylvain again hid her disappointment. Telling herself it wouldn't look so bleak and depressing in the spring, she noted the tall crepe myrtle trees and heard her father say, "Azaleas in the early spring, then the camellias and crepe myrtle. Roses will blanket the brick walls through July. Then in the late summer, Antigny vines will add to the color. What do you think, Sylvain? Is this fine enough for my little Louisiana princess?"

Sylvain looked up at the dear man whose thinning gray hair was blowing in the cold wind. Suddenly, her daddy looked very old to her. Never before had she noticed it. His face was heavily lined, his shoulders sagged notice-ably, and his hazel eyes held a tired, strange expression, though he wore a smile. Standing there in the windswept courtyard of this strange new house, Sylvain wondered if perhaps her daddy hadn't really wanted to come here either. Maybe there were things she did not know. Perhaps he hadn't wanted to sell Riverbend but had had no choice.

"Bend down a little, Daddy," she said, smiling at him. He complied. Taking his cold, lined face between her palms, she planted a big kiss on his thin mouth and said sunnily, "This new house is fine enough for royalty. It's very pretty. Now let's go inside so I can see my new room." Grinning broadly, he guided her into the house, excitedly telling her that there was a nice corner room with lots of windows that might suit her.

Sylvain was kept busy helping her mother and Delilah put the new house in order, lining the kitchen cupboards, filling the linen closets, unpacking the china and silver. The town house lost some of its starkness when Serena Fairmont's favorite pieces of fine, expensive furniture arrived from Riverbend. Sylvain watched her mother move gracefully about the drawing room, happily touching the numerous bookcases with their embossed volumes merged with the new, the elaborate gilt-framed mirror above the marble fireplace, the priceless gold chairs, the elegant long sofa of champagne brocade, with its intricately carved wooden arms and back. A smile of pleasure graced Serena's pale, lovely face as her delicate fingers lovingly plumped up the soft, shining cushions.

How many times Sylvain had heard her mother admire the beautiful couch. Of all the fine furnishings that had filled the large rooms at Riverbend, this shimmering sofa was undoubtedly her mother's favorite piece.

Taking one last admiring look at the couch, Serena Fairmont turned, smiled at her daughter, and said, "Now it's like home, isn't it?"

"Yes, Mother." Sylvain nodded her dark head.

But it wasn't really like home. Not like Riverbend. The house wasn't a fourth the size of the great house on the delta. So small was the dwelling that only five servants were necessary. Delilah, who'd come with the Fairmonts, watched after Sylvain and helped Serena dress. She was soon joined by Nana, the cook; Delson, Edwin's aging valet, who now served as both butler and coachman; Theo, Nana's husband, who served the meals, did the marketing, handled household repairs, and would serve as the gardener come spring; and Bodine, whose duty it was to keep the small, elegant house clean.

The house and walled garden stood on two acres of land, hardly a match for the four thousand arpents of Riverbend, with its twenty-two house servants and many field slaves. Here, there were no orchards, no row upon row of sugarcane, no sugarhouse, no stable of blooded horses, no slave cabins, no dense green forest, no private levee. And no Seachurch.

Sylvain, though she tried valiantly to pretend she was happy in Mobile, felt displaced and lonely. Bundling up against the chill, she slipped into the courtyard on a dreary day near January's end. She sat alone on the cold iron-lace settee beneath the bare branches of the crepe myrtle until her daydreaming was interrupted by her mother's approach.

Serena took a seat beside her daughter, cupped Sylvain's cold, smooth cheek in her hand, and said softly, "I know you're unhappy, darling, and I — "

"No, Mother." Sylvain shook her head. "I'm not, really I — "

"You needn't pretend with me. From the first moment you opened your eyes, I've felt everything that you feel." Serena's warm blue gaze lovingly caressed the young face turned up to hers. "You have no idea how special you are to me or how very much I love you, Sylvain."

"I love you, too Mother."

"I know you do, darling. And you love Daddy, and he's got some good news for you." She smiled and watched her daughter's luminous gray eyes widen with interest.

"He does?"

"He does and he'll be home very soon. Why don't we go indoors and wait for him?"

Sylvain bounded from the iron seat, nodding her agreement. "What is it, Mother? If you'll give me a little hint, I'll pretend — "

Soft, rich laughter issued from Serena's parted lips, and she shook her golden head. "Not a chance, but I'll race you to the house." She lifted her long heavy skirts, and Sylvain, squealing happily, flew across the yard ahead of her.

It was a good surprise. Sylvain was to attend Mobile's Mardi Gras Carnival with her parents. Her mood greatly improved, Sylvain counted the days.

Finally Shrove Tuesday arrived. Sylvain, dressed and impatient, waited with her father in the drawing room. She clapped her hands when her mother, stunning in a sweeping gown of apricot moiré taffeta, descended the stairs.

Upswept golden hair gleaming beneath the light of the high wall sconces, pale, full bosom exposed by the daring décolletage, waist as small as that of any single belle, Serena Fairmont smiled at her two admirers. Her emerald ring glittered when she lifted her slender fingers to caress her husband's shaking hands as he draped her wrap around her creamy shoulders. The ermine-trimmed brown velvet mantle swirled around her, its deep rich hue contrasting with her pale, delicate coloring.

"You're beautiful!" Sylvain touched the soft dark velvet, looking up at her elegant mother.

"And you are also," Serena assured her. "Shall we go?"

Walking between her parents, Sylvain was soon caught up in the gaiety and madness that was Mardi Gras. Throngs of happy Mobilians and visiting revelers swarmed the city streets to parade merrily behind the huge papier-mâché bull's head that had been brought over from France the year before. Fireworks lit the winter skies, and people danced in the streets and drank champagne and celebrated joyously. Masked revelers and costumed men and women sang and shouted and embraced.

Sylvain Fairmont loved every glorious moment of the exciting jubilee and when, much too soon, she was taken home and her parents proceeded alone to the fancy dress ball at the Condé Hotel, she chattered excitedly to Delilah. Talking rapidly, she hardly paused for a breath while Delilah, listening and nodding, undressed her, tucked her into bed, and blew out the lamp.

Sighing, Sylvain snuggled down under the covers, much too elated to sleep. And she decided on that cold February night in 1832 that she would never again miss a Mardi Gras celebration. For a long time she lay in the moonlight and saw again all the colorful costumes and masks, heard the laughter and singing. For the first time since leaving Riverbend, she drifted into sleep with a smile on her lips.

Sylvain made friends with the young ladies at Miss Ellerby's Academy on St. Michael, but none of the girls could take the place of her dearest friend, Rosalie Delon. How she missed her! They corresponded often, but it was not the same. Letters were a poor substitute for whispering together about the things that were happening in their lives. Besides, Delilah, Sylvain suspected, might on occasion read some of Rosalie's letters, so she'd warned Rosalie to be ever cautious and to disclose nothing that she didn't want "prying eyes" to see.

Of all the times to be away from her friend! Sylvain was growing up, and there were so many puzzling things she desperately needed to discuss with Rosalie and with no one else. Over a year had passed since she'd seen her friend. She'd been only a child when they parted. Now she was fourteen and very grown up. Was Rosalie all grown up too?

Sylvain didn't have to wonder about Rosalie's maturity for very long. The next letter she received spoke of an illness, a lingering weakness. Rosalie wrote that she felt as though she might never be well again, that she hadn't written sooner because she'd been much too ill. Since early May she'd been indisposed, and here it was late June and still she was sick. Could Sylvain please inquire of her parents if she might travel to New Orleans to comfort her sick friend?

Serena Fairmont received a missive from Mrs. Delon confirming her daughter's illness and asking that Sylvain be allowed to come for a visit. Sylvain started packing immediately.

Two days later she and Delilah were being warmly welcomed to the Delon home by Rosalie's worried parents. "Go right on up, my dear." Nadine Delon gave her a hug while Dr. Nicholas Delon nodded his agreement.

Pushing open the massive carved door to Rosalie's room, Sylvain peered inside. The heavy drapes were closed against the afternoon sun. Sylvain tiptoed across the thick carpet to the canopied bed. Rosalie's dark eyes opened, and she saw Sylvain standing over her. Neither girl said a word. Rosalie lifted weak, tired arms, and Sylvain fell on the bed with her. Laughing and crying, they embraced until the sick Rosalie, completely exhausted, fell back onto the pillow. "You're going to be all right now, Rosie," Sylvain said with great authority.

Dr. Nicholas Delon shook his head in amazement not two days later. There was a marked improvement in his daughter's condition that had nothing to do with medical treatment. Mrs. Delon tearfully gave thanks and told Sylvain how grateful they all were for her presence. Within a week Rosalie was out of bed and taking her meals in the dining room. And with the return of her good health came her usual good spirits. Spring afternoons found the two friends closeted in Rosalie's bedroom or sipping lemonade on the private back gallery. They had more than a year's worth of gossip to catch up on, and they were wasting no time. Far into the night, when the rest of the household was sleeping, the two friends, sharing Rosalie's big four-poster, chattered on as though they hadn't been together all day.

On one such night Rosalie, wearing a white batiste nightgown, sat cross-legged on the soft mattress chattering while Sylvain stood before the vanity brushing her long dark hair. "Good heavens," Rosalie interrupted herself, "you've been here all this time and I haven't yet told you about the most exciting man in New Orleans." She was smoothing the soft folds of her nightgown appraisingly over her newly formed curves. Drawing in her breath and thrusting her budding breasts out, she smiled. "Look, Syl, my bosom is growing."

Sylvain turned around. Then she glanced down at her own gently curving breasts and bit her lip. Sighing, she lifted her head and crossed the room. "I know. I'm so envious. Look at me. I look like a skinny boy."

"No, you don't," Rosalie consoled. "You're starting to grow there. Besides, I'm envious of you. You're tall as a tree and I'm still a midget." Her dark eyes traveled up her friend's slender frame enviously. Sylvain was studying her own small, rounded breasts, her fingers contouring their circumference, critically comparing them to the full, high breasts of her short Creole friend.

"Do you want to hear about the town's biggest rake or not?" Rosalie forgot about her full bosom and Sylvain's height.

"Yes!" Sylvain forgot, too. She climbed onto the bed and plucked a purple grape from a silver bow resting on the rose coverlet. "Who is he?"

Rosalie rubbed her small hands together. "There's so much gossip about him I hardly know where to start. Naturally he's so dark and handsome it takes your breath away, but his good looks are not the most appealing thing about him."

"No?" Sylvain picked more grapes. "Is he rich and charming, too?"

"Of course, of course, but there's much more. They say he has no heart, that he's gloriously wicked, and his exploits are the topic of conversations in the finest drawing rooms in New Orleans."

Gray eyes wide with interest, Sylvain asked, "Do you know him?"

"No," Rosalie admitted, "but I hope I'll meet him soon. When I'm allowed to go to the galas I'm sure we'll be introduced. But I'm not finished telling you about him. They say his wealth is a mystery. No one knows just where it came from, because his family practically disowned him when he was kicked out of West Point. They whisper that some of the most guarded of the Creole belles have risked scandal and disinheritance to be in his arms. I've overheard ladies murmur that he's male right down to his heels, and I've seen them flush with excitement just from talking about him."

Full lips parted over white even teeth, her gray eyes intent, Sylvain was rapt as her talkative friend continued her dreamy dissertation on the Crescent City's most notorious bachelor. "And they swear he wins or loses small fortunes on the turn of a single card and never bats an eyelash. He's reckless and daring and cares little for anyone. He's been in more than one duel and was expelled from West Point for dueling. Women fall hopelessly in love with him and never recover. Rumors persist that one of his rejected lovers threatened suicide, so brokenhearted was she when he tired of her. He's equally at home in the boudoirs of the most aristocratic of women or in the scarlet-sheeted beds of the Quarter's fancy ladies." Loving the shocked expression on the pretty face of her friend, Rosalie added eagerly, "They say he treats prostitutes like ladies and ladies like prostitutes."

"Rosalie Delon! That is terrible! I'm horrified at such a thought." But Sylvain was thrilled by the shocking revelations coming from her well-informed friend. A tiny chill of excitement lifted the wispy hair on the nape of her neck and she longed to know more about this fascinating mystery man. "What is this rake's name?"

"Courteen," Rosalie drawled out the name dreamily. "Hilton Courteen." Her dark eyes closed and she sighed.

Fully recovered, the bloom back in her cheeks, Rosalie could find no excuse to not accompany her parents on a long afternoon of making calls. Reminding their daughter that people had been very kind to her throughout her illness, they insisted she go along with them on their Sunday afternoon stops.

Reluctantly agreeing, she warned Sylvain of the dullness of the day's visits and told her there was no need for her to be subjected to the punishment. Grateful, Sylvain told the Delons she had a slight headache and said if they didn't mind, she'd stay behind and lie down. They were agreeable.

No sooner had their carriage rolled out of the drive than Sylvain began to hum to herself as she went through her many dresses to choose one of the prettiest. She'd not been out of the Delon house since arriving. It was a perfect early summer day, and she was going out for a walk.

Purposely waiting until Delilah had gone to her quarters to take a nap, Sylvain flew into action. Sneaking from the quiet house half an hour later, she headed toward the Place d'Armes.

Taking long, unladylike steps, she hurried along Chartres Street, turning the corner at St. Peters. A happy smile spread over her features as she passed the Cabildo and the busy arcades of the French Market. Through the busy square she strolled, pleased by the looks of admiration she drew from the young gallants gathered there, their fine tailored clothes bespeaking their affluence. It was a glorious warm day, and families had gathered to hear the band concert. Musicians in their snappy uniforms blended brass and reeds in a symphony of pleasing sounds.

Flower carts rolled by and richly dressed swains purchased clusters of cut lilacs for sweethearts and wives. Haughty Creole women carried bright silk parasols to shade pale, pretty faces and milky shoulders and bosoms. Lazy laughter and merriment were all about, and Sylvain was enjoying herself immensely.

In a lighthearted mood, she milled with the crowd, partaking of this life of indolent ease in the city she loved above all others. For a time she lounged on an iron-lace bench and listened to the music, watched the promenading couples, admired the uniforms of the *garde de ville*.

Soon she was up and moving again. Leaving the crowded square behind, she wandered down Toulouse Street past the Spanish governor's mansion, and found herself on Levee Street. It was not until then that she realized she was on her way to the river. Her pace quickened. Her pulse speeded.

Telling herself she would hasten to the jetty, watch the riverboats for only a few moments, then hurry away home, Sylvain, eyes snapping with anticipation, took purposely long steps, eager to reach the water. The smell of the river caused her to take a deep, long breath. Her gaze riveted to the wharf, she lifted a gloved hand to shade her eyes. There in the busy harbor was an infinite variety of boats: scows, canoes, covered skiffs, huge flatboats, and the impressive paddle-wheelers.

So enamored was she of this strange mix of vessels riding the calm, muddy water, Sylvain did not notice that she was the only unescorted female on this wooden pier full of men and cargo. She passed by rows of saloons on Tchoupitoulas, hardly conscious of the leering eyes that followed her.

She saw a praline seller twenty yards ahead, and her mouth began to water. How she loved the sweet confection. Calling to the squat black man, Sylvain removed her gloves and fished in her reticule for change. Choosing the largest praline she could find, she dropped the coin into the man's palm and walked away munching the sugary candy.

"Well, what have we here?" boomed a drunken voice very close to her ear. Chewing the sweet, Sylvain looked up into the dirty face of a tall, burly ruffian. "You look might near as good as that candy," he said.

Whirling away from him, Sylvain was horrified to see two more men, one short and heavy, the other tall and lanky, blocking her path. Both were dirty, drunk, and mean-looking. "Let's go," one said, and reached out to touch her hair.

"Get out of my way," she said, raising her chin defiantly.

"How much do you want?" It was the man who'd spoken first. "Let's go on into Contreras and get a cubicle." He took her arm. The half-eaten praline fell from Sylvain's hand.

Suddenly aware of their intention, Sylvain began to struggle and scream. The two men in front of her disappeared as she was whirled around with a force that made her come near to losing her breath. A viselike arm circled her small waist, bending her backward, his open mouth descending toward hers. The big, burly man said, "Sugar, you're prettier than anything I've seen down here. I'll buy you a whole cart of pralines when I'm finished with you. Now let's go."

Sylvain kicked and shouted. She was not that kind of woman! They were to let her go! She might have saved her breath. The three drunken carousers had found her alone on the waterfront, and that made her ripe for plucking. Sylvain felt the movement of the big man's body as he began to walk across the wooden levee toward a saloon. Her useless feet no longer touched the landing; he was carrying her under his arm as though she were a sack of flour. Sylvain screamed her outrage.

A gleaming black carriage rolled up, and a long-legged man in fine evening clothes swung down. In four long strides he reached the big man. A slam of his fist into a kidney caused the surprised man to drop his prisoner. Grunting with pain, the giant spun around and was caught under the chin with a quick, powerful uppercut.

"Run," said the tall, lean stranger as again his fist slammed into the man's bleeding face. "Run, girl," he repeated as the other two drunks lunged for him. Rooted to the spot, Sylvain watched as the two bullies pinned her savior's arms and the big man who'd dropped her stepped in to deliver a one-two punch to his flat, hard stomach. A groan escaped his lips, but he managed to free one long arm and wrap it around the neck of the short brute still holding on to him. He dug his thumb into the ruffian's Adam's apple until the attacker let him go.

Then everything was a blur. Sylvain waded in and beat on backs and kicked chins and screamed a warning when she saw one of the ruffians pull out a scaling knife. The long, gleaming blade caught the dark young man in the eyebrow, slicing a clean, white ravine through the dark brow. In seconds the white turned to crimson, and blood ran down into his ebony eyelashes.

Miraculously wresting the knife from the deathlike grip of his attacker, her defender heard it hit the ground and kicked it out of the way. Sylvain scrambled for it, beating the big man's accomplices. Teeth bared, she held them off, and when the dark man landed a crunching blow to his assailant, momentarily rendering him helpless, Sylvain shouted to him and deftly tossed him the knife.

Smiling now, the dark man flashed the knife at the trio and raised his other hand in an inviting gesture. "Come," he said coolly, taunting the three brawlers. "Who's first? Step up and I'll slit you wide open," he promised in a calm, deep voice. The three men looked from him to one another. Sylvain looked only at the man with the knife. He was smiling, relaxed, unafraid, self-assured. She never knew when the trio of accosters turned tail and ran.

She had eyes only for the tall, lean man who'd come to her rescue. She stared open-mouthed as he stood, feet apart, smiling lazily, his eyes black slits of fire in a darkly tanned face. His expensive evening jacket was open, white ruffled shirt torn, exposing a bare brown chest covered with black curly hair. His tight, dark trousers were dusty, and there was a rip in the fine fabric just below his left knee.

His jet black hair, shining in the Sunday sun, was disheveled and falling over his broad forehead. The knife cut in his thick eyebrow still oozed blood. A high cheekbone had already begun to discolor. His full bottom lip was split.

Effortlessly he sailed the nasty-looking knife into the river, pulled a snowy white handkerchief from his pocket, and lifted it to his eyebrow. His dark eyes came to rest on Sylvain, who finally found her tongue. Hurrying forward she said, "Thank you so much for helping me. I don't know what I would have done if you hadn't been here. You're Hilton Courteen."

He grinned and replied. "What's left of me." Holding the handkerchief to his eyebrow, he took her elbow, and guided her to the waiting carriage.

Inside, Sylvain took the handkerchief from his hand and dabbed at his cut. "Does it hurt awfully? Do you suppose it will leave a nasty scar? Shall we hasten to the doctor's?"

"A doctor is unnecessary. I'm sure I'll survive." He took the handkerchief back, pressed it to his split lip, and said, "You're Sylvain Fairmont."

She smiled. "Why, yes I am, but I'm surprised you know me."

"We met at Riverbend," he recalled. "You showed me your secret chapel. How could I forget?"

Her gray eyes fixed on the deep slash through his dark brow, she said, "I mean, I'm quite surprised you would recognize me." Her gaze slid down to meet his eyes. "After all, I was only a child then."

"Ah, that's true, and now you're a grown-up young lady." His mouth widened into a grin, pulling painfully at the newly split bottom lip.

"Why, yes, I am." Sylvain took a deep breath and lowered her lashes. She never saw the brief flicker of amusement in the black eyes fastened on her.

To Hilton Courteen she was still as much of a child as the little girl he'd met at Riverbend. True, she was much taller than when they'd met two years before, but she *was* a child, albeit a lovely one. He strongly considered lecturing her about walking alone through the city then decided against it. She was not his responsibility.

"Where can I take you, Miss Fairmont?" he inquired politely.

"I'm visiting the Delons. They live in the Garden District and — "

"Dr. Nicholas Delon?"

"Why, yes. You know them?"

"I've met the doctor and his wife." Hilton tapped the top of the carriage with long, lean fingers, spoke to the driver, and they were under way. He lounged back against the seat, making no effort to pull the tattered white shirt across his bare chest.

Sylvain settled back beside him and stole glances at him. He was undeniably good-looking. His heavily lidded eyes gave him a dreamy look while his full lips appeared fashioned solely for kissing beautiful women. There was an air of mystery and danger about him, and Sylvain caught herself recalling all that her friend Rosalie had told her about this man. He was even more handsome than she'd remembered and possessed a strong masculinity that was impossible to ignore.

Sylvain Fairmont was curious. Her face growing warm, she pressed her shoulders against the claret leather of the seat and turned to him. Favoring him with what she hoped was a highly seductive smile, she said softly, "It's still quite early, Mr. Courteen. Perhaps we could go to one of the cafés or coffee houses before you return me to the Delons." She let her long dark lashes flutter and inhaled deeply.

"That sounds enchanting. However, as you can see, I'm hardly presentable."

Sylvain laughed prettily. "How foolish of me. I'd completely forgotten about your torn shirt." She lifted a small hand to him, let her fingers tentatively skim down the torn white fabric and finally come to rest on the expanse of bare skin. His chest was warm and firm beneath her fingers, and she felt her heart speed alarmingly.

Hilton Courteen was faintly amused. Deciding that the best way to discourage her girlish flirtation would be to ignore it, he covered her hand with his own, squeezed it lightly, and unceremoniously placed it back on her lap. He pulled his dark jacket closed and said, "I understand you and the family now live in my old hometown. How do you like Mobile?" His dark eyes were friendly. It was not at all the expression she'd hoped to see there.

Precious time was passing. Sylvain couldn't let this unexpected opportunity go by with no results. Here she was, alone with the most infamous rogue in all New Orleans. Any Creole miss in the city would have known how to take advantage of the situation. She simply could not tell Rosalie that she'd been inside a closed carriage with the handsome, dashing Hilton Courteen and he hadn't even tried to steal a kiss.

"Dreadful." She sighed dramatically. "I find Mobile dreadful."

"I'm sorry to hear that. I had hoped — "

"There are no exciting gentlemen in Mobile, Mr. Courteen. That's why I'm visiting in New Orleans."

Hilton Courteen's dark gaze settled on her fresh, pretty face. "Oh? And you've found some to your liking here?"

"I have," she breathed and leaned a little closer to him. "You're here." She let her eyelashes brush her cheeks, then added, "You're still wearing your evening clothes. You've been out all night, haven't you? You like adventure, don't you, Mr. Courteen?"

For what seemed an interminable time, silence hung in the close quarters. Sylvain found she was holding her breath. She was looking directly into his eyes and her lower lip began to tremble ever so slightly. There was a heavy tension in the air, and she felt a strange kind of excitement she'd never known before.

Hilton Courteen's dark eyes slowly slid to her mouth, and she instinctively wet her dry lips with the tip of her tongue. He smiled at her — a slow, lazy smile that spoke of promised pleasures. His heated gaze never left her face as he reached up and languidly closed the wine velvet side-curtain. Then, reaching across her, he shut the curtains near her.

"In a hurry to grow up, Sylvain?" he drawled seductively.

She never had the opportunity to answer. With a quickness that rendered her speechless, he scooped her slippered feet from the floor and draped them across his long legs. Hands circling her waist, Hilton pushed her down onto the tufted seat. She was lying on her back, his torso pressing down on hers.

Eyes wide with surprise, Sylvain looked up into the dark, handsome face poised just above her own. He was speaking in a deep, calm voice. "Before you reach your destination, my dear, you can become a woman. Is that what you want?"

His lips hovered close to her own. His black eyes were glittering, a dangerous, heated light shining in them. The fresh wound in his dark brow still seeped crimson. A brown cheekbone, purpling into a nasty bruise, gave his handsome face a further look of menace. His broad chest was crushing her breasts; she could feel his heartbeat through her tight bodice. She was both terribly attracted and thoroughly frightened.

When his dark hand touched her face, Sylvain's heart stopped. All of a sudden the smile left his wide lips. A muscle flexed in his strong jaw and his mouth descended to hers. Her nerve gone, she turned her head at the last second. She felt his warm breath on her cheek, and the heart that had stopped began to pound once again. Pressing a kiss to the side of her throat, he spoke in a low, determined voice. "Tell me, sweet," he murmured, lips moving against her flushed skin, "Is this what you want? Shall I make you a woman? We have privacy enough, don't you think?" His brown hand left her face and slowly slid down until it rested on her hip. When he gave her skirt a quick tug, Sylvain found her tongue.

"No!" she cried, struggling wildly. "I want to get up! You let me up right now or I'll scream and — "

"You're sure you wouldn't like me to — "

"No," she screeched. "Don't say it, don't do it! Please."

Hilton slowly levered himself off her. Eyes round with fright, she lay panting, looking warily up at him. None too gently he lowered her feet to the floor and pulled her up beside him. He looked angry, and when she started to speak he silenced her with an uplifted hand. "Don't say a word; just listen."

"You can't tell me to — "

"Yes, I can. Now, be quiet." His dark eyes flashed and Sylvain, nervously smoothing the folds of her skirts, didn't interrupt him. "You've been very lucky two times this afternoon. I'd consider that quite enough testing of the fates, were I you. Do you have any idea what those three men back on the waterfront were going to do to you?"

She said nothing. "What in God's name were you doing down there alone? Tell me!"

Her chin quivering and her voice weak, she replied, "I wanted to see the riverboats, so I — "

"You've seen hundreds of riverboats." His face was suffused with color beneath its dark tan. "Little girls cannot walk around on the waterfront alone, do you hear me? What do you think those men had planned for you? A stroll on the decks of some paddle-wheeler? A companionable drink in one of the saloons?" A vein was throbbing in his smooth forehead. "Hardly, my dear. Do you know what they wanted?"

Sylvain, biting her bottom lip to keep it still, nodded.

"Fine. You know. Luckily I arrived in time. Then what did you do? You promptly forgot your danger, got into this carriage, and immediately started flirting with me."

"I most certainly did not," she defended. "I was just — "

"You were eager to know if all you've heard about me is true."

"No, I . . . that's not . . . I only wanted you to . . . to . . . "

"To what?" his dark, angry eyes held hers prisoner.

"I thought you might want to . . . to kiss me."

Hilton wrapped his long fingers around Sylvain's upper arm and pulled her close. "Kiss you? I ought to paddle you. While you may have heard unflattering things about me, Miss Fairmont, let me assure you I'm no spoiler of innocence."

Embarrassed, furious, and feeling terribly foolish and ashamed, Sylvain glared at him and said spitefully, jerking her arm away, "And let me assure you, Mr. Courteen, that I find you rude and arrogant. You would be the last man on earth I'd give my innocence to!"

She raised her chin, turned her head away, and seethed when she heard his low chuckling.

Refusing to look at him or to speak, Sylvain stared straight ahead and pretended she couldn't feel those dark, laughing eyes on her face. Hilton Courteen casually opened the side-curtains. When he leaned her way, she shot him her coldest look and jerked open the curtains on her side of the carriage.

When familiar landmarks and dwellings appeared to remind her they were nearing the Delon home, Sylvain swallowed her pride, reached out, and touched Hilton's forearm. As sweetly as possible, she said, "Please, Mr. Courteen, if you could have your driver stop here. You see, I . . . I'm . . ."

"You're not supposed to be absent, and don't wish to be found out," he finished for her, with such a knowing expression on his handsome face that she longed to slap him hard. Guiltily, she nodded.

Hilton tapped on the roof and the carriage rolled to a stop. Stepping outside, he held up his hand to her. Ignoring it, she stepped out of the carriage and, without so much as a good day, flounced away from him. She'd gone only a few yards when she sighed, paused, and turned around.

Hilton Courteen stood looking at her, a tall, slim figure leaning indolently against the carriage. Sylvain took a deep breath and went back to stand before him. "Ah, you . . . you mentioned that you know the Delons." He nodded. She looked up and said meekly, "You won't betray me, will you?"

He studied the lovely face with its lush little mouth, turned-up small nose, and big smoky eyes, and recalled vividly the twelve-year-old child who'd said those same words one warm summer day at Riverbend. She looked much the same. At fourteen, she'd grown taller, but she was in no way a woman. Gangling and awkward, she appeared all legs and arms to the man looking down at her. He never noticed the slight rounding of hips and breasts. He saw only a child.

Smiling down at her, Hilton raised slender fingers to pluck a tiny bit of sugary praline from her full bottom lip. He licked it from his finger, touched her cheek, and softly said, "Never, my dear."

Sylvain flashed him a smile of relief, whirled about, and hurried down the banquette, her full skirts swaying around her. The smile left her face the moment she turned from him. She did not like the cocksure Mr. Courteen. He wasn't all that handsome. He wasn't all that charming. Mr. Hilton Courteen could just go to blazes!

Hilton climbed back into the carriage. There on the seat lay a small beige glove. He picked it up and started to call to her. He didn't do it. He smiled, pressed the dainty, feminine glove to his lips, and inhaled deeply of the jasmine fragrance clinging to it.

Hilton tucked the glove into his pocket. Then he leaned back against the tall leather seat and promptly fell asleep. It was the first time he'd slept in thirty-six hours.

Chapter Seven

"Oh, Syl, I shall die of envy!" Rosalie exclaimed when Sylvain told her friend of the encounter with Hilton Courteen. "He actually tried to kiss you?"

Sylvain nodded, a pleased smile curving her full lips. "Of course, I didn't allow it." She felt only a small twinge of guilt. After all, Hilton Courteen had pushed her down onto the seat and bent over her. If she hadn't turned her head away, he would have ravaged her. "He was quite displeased that I rebuffed his advances."

Rosalie, her dark eyes round with interest and shock, said eagerly, "I imagine he was. Surely no other woman has ever turned him down." She shook her head and admitted, "I'd have gladly let him kiss me." Then her voice dropped and she added softly, "I can think of nothing more romantic than to receive my very first kiss from a man like Hilton Courteen. Perhaps I'll get the opportunity. Who knows?"

A quick flash of jealousy ran through Sylvain. The thought of Rosalie kissing the sleek, dark, sophisticated Hilton Courteen displeased her. "Rosalie, don't be a ninny. Mr. Courteen would find you much too young."

"What about you? You're my age and he wanted ... "

"Can't we change the subject, Rosie?" Sylvain lifted a hand to stifle a yawn. "I truly don't find this one all that interesting."

Sylvain remained in the Crescent City throughout the long, sultry summer. It was a lazy, glorious interlude; still, it was not long enough. Both girls were teary-eyed when they stood on the levee and embraced beneath a steamy September drizzle.

"It seems as if you just arrived," wept Rosalie.

"I know," Sylvain sniffled, clutching a parasol with one hand, Rosalie's trim waist with the other. "I had a wonderful time, Rosie."

"I did, too." Rosalie tried to smile.

"You'll come to Mobile for Christmas?"

"I promise, Syl. I'll be there if I have to . . . oh, no — " Her shaky voice was drowned out by a loud blast from the riverboat's whistle.

"It's time," said Nicholas Delon.

"Syl."

"Rosie."

They clung together, crying, until the doctor pulled his daughter away and said soothingly, "Rosalie, Sylvain must board, dear." He took Sylvain's elbow and escorted her up the gangplank while Rosalie sought solace on her mother's shoulder. Dr. Delon joined his wife and daughter and watched the *Majestic* back away from the wharf.

At the railing of the steamer's hurricane deck, a dark-haired girl waved wildly until she could no longer see the three Delons.

Then she turned to the comforting arms of Delilah. The tall black woman crooned softly, "Don't cry, honey. You'll see her again. Christmas'll come 'fore you knows it."

Sylvain never saw Rosalie Delon again.

By the time the *Majestic* anchored at Mobile, word had arrived of the yellow fever outbreak in New Orleans. The disease spread rapidly through the Crescent City, reaching epidemic proportions in a matter of weeks. One of the first victims was Rosalie Delon.

Dr. Nicholas Delon managed to get a short letter to the Fairmonts. In a clear, soft voice, Serena Fairmont read it to her husband and daughter:

> My dear friends,
> With breaking heart I write to inform you that our beautiful Rosalie has passed away. This terrible yellow fever epidemic claimed her overnight. The child was not yet strong from her prior illness; hence she had no chance.
> Rosalie's mother is naturally distraught, as am I. I'm sending Nadine at once to her native France. I shall remain here until the crisis has passed. If I survive, I will join my wife in Paris. Neither of us can bear to remain in New Orleans without our precious Rosalie.
> Sorrowfully,
> Nicholas Delon

Sylvain Fairmont was beside herself with grief. She flung herself into her daddy's arms and cried mournfully. And even as she cried for her dear, dead friend, she was filled with fear. Had the handsome, dashing Hilton Courteen also perished in the epidemic?

A full white moon shone through the open curtains. Bare branches of the tall elm tapped against the frosted windowpane. A chorus of happy carolers, their voices raised in Yuletide songs, floated up from the streets below. It was Christmas Eve. A time of joy and good cheer. Hot cider and roasted nuts. Mistletoe over the door and the scent of cedar filling the house. Roast turkey and plum pudding. Parties and church services. Visits from cold-nosed callers laden with gifts.

Sylvain lay wide awake in her chilly room. When her bedroom door opened quietly, she turned her head. The slim figure of her mother was silhouetted against the light. The door closed quietly and Serena Fairmont approached the bed. Wordlessly she held out her arms. Sylvain flew into them and said in a choked voice, "Mother, I was . . . I was . . . "

"Thinking about Rosalie," Serena soothed. "I know, darling."

"Mother, I don't think I shall ever love a friend again the way I loved Rosie."

Serena smoothed back the unruly brown hair framing her daughter's sad face. "No, my darling, you won't," she murmured. "And you will never forget her. But Rosalie is gone, darling; she'll never be back. You must go on without her."

I . . . I know," Sylvain sobbed, "I . . . I . . . Mother, how did you know I was thinking of Rosie?"

Serena kissed a tear-stained cheek. "She was to be here in Mobile this holiday season. I've not forgotten. Shall I stay here with you until you fall asleep?"

"Would you please?"

Serena turned back the covers and slid into the warm bed with her slender daughter. "Next Christmas, darling, will be better. Much better."

Hilton Courteen stretched his long legs to the blazing fireplace and picked up the bundle of unopened letters. It was nearing dawn on Christmas morning. He yawned sleepily and slid the silver-handled letter opener beneath the flap of the first white envelope. Robert E. Lee's neat, graceful hand was easily recognizable. Robert sent Christmas greetings from Fortress Monroe, Virginia, where he was a junior construction engineer with the U.S. Army. He and his wife, Mary, hoped Hilton would soon come for a visit and that the New Year would bring him much joy and peace.

Hilton smiled, dropped the letter on the rosewood side table, and picked up another. The big, bold strokes belonged to Jefferson Davis. Davis, who was still in the service, wrote from the wilderness of the Arkansas

Territory. He said little about his duties, but he spoke eloquently of a lovely young lady he'd met. She was Sarah Taylor, daughter of Colonel Zachary Taylor who had recently taken command of Fort Crawford.

The last was from Cot Campbell. Life in Texas was simple but satisfying, he had written. He'd never been happier, never planned to leave San Antonio de Bexar for the rest of his days. Couldn't Hilton come down for a long visit soon? There were no fancy gambling halls and elegant restaurants in the dusty Mexican city, but a man could always find a game of poker, a good meal, and perhaps a pretty *señorita* to cheer him.

Hilton folded the letter and dropped it on the table. The first pink tinges of a winter sun were slicing into the spacious New York hotel room. Hilton rose. Long, lean fingers went to the buttons of his white shirt. He undressed and slid naked between the chill silk sheets. Hands folded beneath his dark head, he mused sleepily.

It had been his best year ever. The investment he'd made in railroad and banking stocks were sound. Buying them had been a wise move. The city property he'd purchased in New Orleans would undoubtedly double in value within ten years. He'd managed to escape the dreaded yellow fever. He'd spent a busy autumn in New York conducting business and pleasure. And he'd met an extraordinarily beautiful French woman who'd insisted he come to Paris for a long visit.

Delphine de Carondelet seemed not to mind that he was considerably younger than she. He didn't, either. He found the sophisticated thirty-three-year-old woman a lively and enjoyable companion. A winter visit to Paris would be pleasurable. His business affairs were in good shape; no reason he shouldn't spend a few months abroad.

Hilton Courteen didn't envy any of the good friends who'd sent him holiday greetings. He was living the life he'd chosen, and the fact that it was Christmas and he was alone in a New York hotel room bothered him not at all. Families were nothing more than a nuisance. He was glad he was unhampered by one. He intended to keep it that way forever.

"Sorry, Grandmother," he murmured aloud, thinking of the twinkly-eyed, silver-haired little woman who had pleaded with him to come to Mobile for Christmas, explaining that since his mother and father had retired to South Carolina, he had no excuse not to come for a nice, long visit. Hilton loved the tiny, spirited Belle Courteen and admired her for not taking sides in his ongoing dispute with his father. She had never judged or censured him, nor had she lectured or preached to him. She had, in fact, hinted that she thought the elder Courteen, her son, was pigheaded and unyielding.

Hilton's eyelids grew heavy. He turned over onto his stomach and hugged the fat feather pillow in his long brown arms. Tomorrow he'd sail for Europe. Could anyone ask for a better Christmas?

A year had passed. It was Christmastime once more. Sylvain's pretty face was aglow with excitement. Dusk was creeping over the brightly lit Mobile town house. In moments she'd don her wrap and be off with the other cheerful carolers, and she could hardly wait.

Dressed and eager, she flew down the stairs and skidded to a stop in the doorway to the drawing room. Edwin Fairmont stood kissing his lovely wife beneath a giant sprig of mistletoe.

Face aflame, Sylvain stammered, "I'm sorry! I never thought . . . I mean I didn't know . . . "

Serena Fairmont, arms around her husband, smiled broadly. "Come in, darling, and let us look at you." She released Edwin and stepped away.

"You're the prettiest fifteen-year-old young lady in Mobile," said Edwin Fairmont proudly. "It frightens me."

"Why, Daddy?" Sylvain ran over to him.

He put an arm around her. "Too soon some young man is going to steal you away from us."

"Your father's right, Sylvain. You're so pretty. Now, you're sure you're dressed warmly enough?"

Sylvain spun away from them. "Yes, yes. My friends should be here. What time is it?"

Edwin Fairmont fished a gold watch from his pocket while Serena pressed, "Are you wearing your heavy underwear? The fur-lined boots? Where's your muff?"

Sylvain had no time to answer her mother's countless questions. By the time her father announced that it was six o'clock, a carriage rolled to a stop before the house, and loud, youthful voices announced that the happy carolers had arrived.

"They're here, they're here!" shouted Sylvain, rushing to snatch her hooded woolen cape from the coat tree in the corridor. "Don't worry. I'll be back by ten," she called over her shoulder and flew down the walk into the cold December night. The bells on the horses' harnesses jingled, and excited voices welcomed Sylvain into the packed carriage. The driver clicked to the four steeds, and Sylvain's sweet, clear voice joined the others in a joyful Christmas song.

"Should we have let her go, Edwin?" Serena said to her husband when he closed the door and drew her back into the warm room.

"Yes, Serena. She's young, but they're going to visit homes and sing carols, nothing more. She'll enjoy it." He held up to his wife the carved-crystal brandy decanter, eyebrows lifted in question.

She nodded and smiled. "That's true. She was so miserable last Christmas; it's rewarding to see her happy this season."

Edwin handed his wife a snifter of brandy, touched his glass to hers, and said, "May every Christmas find her as happy as she is tonight."

"And may they find us as happy, too." Serena sipped the warm, fiery liquid, set the glass aside, stepped into her husband's arms, and said teasingly, "Now, where were we when Sylvain interrupted us?"

Edwin downed his brandy in one swallow and bent to kiss his wife's parted lips.

The home of a distinguished Mobile merchant at the very end of Savannah Street was the last residence the carolers visited. The stately mansion was ablaze with lights; a holiday party was in progress. Sylvain and her friends stood in a neat row on the winter-browned lawn and began to sing. The heavy front door swung open, and several gentlemen ventured out into the cold while, within, ladies gathered at the tall French windows to peer at the young singers.

Nose cold, cheeks red, voice strong, Sylvain lifted her eyes to the smiling gentlemen standing on the broad gallery. She recognized the owner, wealthy, gray-haired Walt Bessamer. Flanking him were red-bearded, heavy-set Dr. Titus Nolan and the lanky Benjamin Thedford, professor at Mobile's Spring Hill College.

A young man, coatless despite the cold, stepped onto the gallery, and Sylvain's breath caught in her throat. He leaned a shoulder against a gleaming white column and casually crossed one foot over the other. His pale hair gleamed silver in the moonlight, but his classic, even features were partially hidden in the shadows. He was tall and slim, his tight-fitting fawn trousers encased long, lean legs and strapped over boots with square toes.

Sylvain realized she was staring and quickly lowered her eyes. Her voice was not as strong as it had been, and she had difficulty remembering the words. She fixed her gaze on a wreath of holly adorning the mansion's front door and clenched her cold hands together inside her fur muff.

When the song ended, applause came from the porch, and the carolers were invited to come in out of the cold. Sylvain let her eyes slide back to the light-haired young man. He was not applauding. He remained in the same casual stance, hadn't moved a muscle. And he was looking directly at her. Sylvain swallowed. The other carolers were hurrying toward the house. Her feet wouldn't work. She couldn't move. She stood there, feeling like a fool, rooted to the spot.

The young man pushed away from the white column and descended the steps, Sylvain knew he was coming to her. She drew a hasty breath and lifted her trembling chin. He stopped directly in front of her and stood looking down at her, as though carefully assessing every feature.

Smiling warmly, he lifted a slim hand and slowly pushed the heavy woolen hood from her head. "There," he said, pleased, "that"s much better." His eyes caressed the mass of shining brown hair framing her face as he took her cold hand and tucked it inside his arm while she stared up at him, dumbfounded. "Come," he urged and led her up the steps and into the house.

"I'm Randolph Baxter of the Mississippi Baxters," he announced as he slipped her cape from her shoulders. Tossing the wrap to a smiling black servant, Randolph Baxter escorted a very impressed Sylvain into the dining room where a buffet of fine foods was spread out on the sideboard and a huge silver bowl of rich, creamy eggnog graced the mahogany table. "And you?" He smiled warmly. "Besides being the loveliest girl in Alabama?"

Sylvain blushed, enthralled. In a voice none too strong, she said, "I'm Sylvain Fairmont, Mr. Baxter."

"You may call me Randolph, Sylvain. You and I are going to be very good friends." He favored her with an appealing smile, his sea-green eyes sparkling in a clean-shaven, tanned face. He picked up one of her hands and drew her with him to the table, nodding his golden head to the servant who was pouring the eggnog.

Sylvain found herself sitting on a velvet-padded dining chair sipping delicious eggnog and listening to Mr. Randolph Baxter explain that his family had only recently moved to Mobile. His father had purchased the old McConnell plantation, Oakgrove, west of the city. He, Randolph, was in his final year at University of Mississippi and was in Mobile for the holidays.

Sylvain was so caught up in Randolph Baxter's fascinating conversation that she never noticed they were being observed by a less than pleased young woman with flaming red hair.

Ginger Thompson — voluptuous, vain, and spoiled — stood in the arched doorway, seething. At seventeen, Ginger had a number of beaux panting after her, but she was bored with them all. She'd come with friends to this holiday party and met the handsome Randolph Baxter. Immediately she wanted him, and she intended to have him. She had no intention of letting that tall, gangling Fairmont girl stand in her way.

"There you are!" Ginger's petulant voice caused Sylvain to turn her head.

"Hello, Miss Thompson." Sylvain smiled at the redhead.

Ginger ignored her. She sashayed up to the couple, tapped Randolph's shoulder playfully, and reminded him, "I promised you a moonlight stroll around the gardens." She smiled seductively, and her lush, ripe bosom appeared ready to spill from the tight bodice of her dress.

Sylvain bit the inside of her cheek as Randolph Baxter's green gaze went to the white flesh so wantonly displayed. He was smiling, his lips stretched over even white teeth, and Sylvain had the impression he'd completely forgotten about her.

"It's a bit nippy out, isn't it, Miss Thompson?" Randolph let his eyes slowly move up to the redhead's pretty face.

"I'll keep you plenty warm," Ginger promised boldly, and Sylvain wanted to die.

"If you'll both excuse me . . . " Sylvain rose.

"Yes, we will," Ginger hurriedly assured her, not bothering to look at the younger girl.

"Wait," said Randolph Baxter, rising to take Sylvain's arm. To Ginger he said, "Find our wraps and I'll be with you in ten minutes." Satisfied and triumphant, Ginger tossed a smug glance at Sylvain and swept out of the room.

A commotion from the corridor saved Sylvain. The carolers were getting ready to depart. "I must be going, Mr. Baxter," she said weakly, wishing he were not standing so close, wishing he'd release her elbow, wishing he would not go for a moonlight walk with the experienced Ginger Thompson.

They stood in the wide hallway facing each other amid loud voices and laughter as the carolers thanked their host and hunted for their wraps. Sylvain heard nothing. She was looking up into a pair of deep green eyes whose owner was saying, "You must allow me to come 'round and call on you, Miss Fairmont." Her young heart pounded and her gray eyes grew huge when he slowly lifted a hand toward her throat. With one finger he idly circled the gold brooch pinned at the center of her high collar. "Say you want me to come." He smiled warmly and waited, his finger continuing to toy with the brooch.

"Yes, yes," she said excitedly, much too thrilled to be coy or coquettish. "When?"

Randolph Baxter grinned and dropped his hand. Eyes never leaving her face, he reached for the heavy woolen cape a servant held out. "Tomorrow afternoon at two," he said. "Turn around."

Obediently she whirled about, and closed her eyes in pleasure when his hands swept her cape around her shoulders and expertly hooked the braided frogs beneath her chin while she stood facing away from him. His hands went to her shoulders and gently squeezed them as he leaned close to her ear and murmured, "Until tomorrow, my dear Sylvain."

Sylvain didn't sing on the cold ride home. She sat quietly in the back of the crowded conveyance, reliving the glorious evening. Delicious little tingles kept skipping up her spine, and she lifted her shoulders and buried her chin in the heavy wool of her cloak. Stifling a happy giggle, she freed a hand from her fur muff and slipped it beneath the folds of her wrap. Fingers edged nervously up to the gold disk pinned to her dress. She traced the smooth edges of the brooch just as Randolph Baxter had done and felt again the strange sensations caused by the intimate gesture.

When the carriage rolled to a stop before her house, she was nudged back to reality by the girl seated next to her. Startled, Sylvain jumped slightly, then smiled and scrambled down from the carriage, calling good night to her friends.

She hurried inside and found her parents waiting up. Speaking rapidly, she related the events of the wonderful evening to them, ending with Mr. Randolph Baxter's intention to call on her.

"Isn't it all too exciting for words?" she cried happily, gave them both good-night kisses and flew from the room before the startled pair could respond.

"Delilah, Delilah!" She burst into her bedroom and grabbed the sleepy servant. Embracing her vigorously, she declared, "I've met the most charming man in the world!"

Delilah freed herself from the exuberant young woman and began unhooking Sylvain's dress. "You a might young to be meetin' young men." Her dark eyes snapped.

"He's tall and blond and has deep green eyes and a straight nose and — "

"Jes' calm yourself down. Ain't no sense gettin' worked up, 'cause you goin' to meet lots of boys, and you has to behave like a proper lady. Ladies don't get excited 'bout such things."

Unruffled, Sylvain stepped out of the balloon-sleeved woolen dress and sighed happily, "Who says they don't? Why, any girl in Mobile would be ecstatic over the attentions of Mr. Randolph Baxter. He's one of the Mississippi Baxters, you know. Ginger Thompson practically — "

"Ginger Thompson is a fast bit of baggage, you ask me! I seen how she made eyes at all the gentlemens las' year at the Mardi Gras parade. And right in the middle of the day, too!"

"You're a gossip, Delilah Fairmont! I don't want to talk about Ginger Thompson. I want to talk about Randolph Baxter." She sighed and lifted her long arms to slip into the batiste nightgown Delilah was holding out to her.

Delilah smiled at last and pulled the soft white gown down over Sylvain's dark head. "Honey, you talk to me all you like 'bout Mr. Baxter, but outside of this house, you jest act like a lady. And ladies don't go 'round ravin' like fools 'bout young men."

Sylvain turned and hugged her. "You're always right. I won't say a word to anyone, but, oh, Delilah," she whispered as she leaped into her high, soft bed, "he's sooooo handsome!"

Chapter Eight

Randolph Baxter arrived at the Fairmont home the next day at three minutes before the appointed hour. Delson, the aging butler, directed him into the drawing room where an excited Sylvain Fairmont waited expectantly with her parents.

Randolph stood for an instant, framed in the doorway, nattily dressed in tight-fitting trousers of dark brown wool, matching frock coat, snowy white shirt, and striped cravat. With his shiny blond hair carefully brushed and his tanned face glowing, he was the picture of health, vigor, and good breeding.

The young man strode forward toward Edwin Fairmont, who stretched out his hand and said, "Edwin Fairmont, Mr. Baxter. Welcome to our home."

"A pleasure," said the impeccably mannered Randolph Baxter, shaking the shorter man's hand firmly.

"My wife, Mrs. Fairmont." Edwin indicated the seated Serena. Randolph Baxter kissed her hand. "Mrs. Fairmont." She nodded, smiling.

"And I believe you've met my daughter, Sylvain." Only then did the green, sparkling eyes of Randolph Baxter turn to her.

"I met your beautiful daughter last evening at the Bessamers," he said graciously. "Miss Fairmont." He inclined his shiny golden head, but did not bend to kiss her hand. He stood, hands locked behind him, beaming down at her.

"Please sit down, Mr. Baxter," Edwin Fairmont said, indicating one of the matching gold chairs.

"Thank you, sir," responded Randolph Baxter. "If you don't mind . . . and if Sylvain doesn't . . . , I shall sit here on the sofa." With that he winked at Sylvain, plucked at the sharp creases in his elegant trousers, and sat down beside her. Spreading a long arm on the high carved back of the champagne brocade couch, Randolph Baxter made easy small talk with Sylvain and her parents.

He told them of his studies at the University of Mississippi, of his plans to make Mobile his home upon graduation, of his father's extensive renovation at Oakgrove, and of their plans to acquire even more of the rich, fertile land around Mobile. He was highly respectful of Edwin Fairmont, politely deferential to Serena Fairmont, and artfully flirtatious with Sylvain.

By the time Delson quietly entered, bearing a silver tray of hot coffee and pastries, the Fairmonts and their guest were thoroughly enjoying the afternoon. Especially Sylvain.

Her uncharacteristic attack of shyness had long since departed, and she was chattering gaily, waving her hands about to make a particular point, and easily charming the man seated beside her. At twenty, Randolph had courted a number of young girls in Mississippi, but had never cared more for one than another.

Drawn by the fresh good looks of the slender girl beside him, Randolph kept stealing glances at Sylvain and found himself wishing she were older. He had a feeling the very proper Fairmont family would give him no chance to be alone with their pretty daughter.

"So soon?" Sylvain frowned when he announced he really had to be going.

Randolph smiled at her, rose, and helped her to her feet. "Would that I could spend every hour of my visit here with you," he murmured provocatively, "but I've probably overstayed my welcome as it is." He glanced at the elder Fairmonts, smiling sunnily.

"Nonsense," Edwin Fairmont assured him. "We've enjoyed it."

"We certainly have, Mr. Baxter." Serena Fairmont had risen. "Do come again."

"You're kind, Mrs. Fairmont, Mr. Fairmont. I certainly shall call again." He looked once more at the beaming Sylvain, then took her hand in his and said, "Sylvain will see me to the door. Now good day to you both."

In the corridor he took the overcoat from old Delson's gloved hands and gave the servant a subtle but dismissive shake of his golden head. As soon as he and Sylvain were alone, he drew her hand up to his chest and said in a low voice, "Your parents have invited me to come again. What about you? Would you like that?"

"Very much," she said truthfully and felt her heart speed up when the warm fingers clutching her own squeezed gently and Randolph Baxter brushed her forehead with his lips.

Young Baxter came to the Fairmont house every afternoon during his long holiday leave. Edwin and Serena were approving. His reputation was without blemish. They'd heard that the Baxters were one of the wealthiest and most respected families in their home state of Mississippi. Every fashionable hostess in Mobile was clamoring for the pleasure of their company.

Randolph brought his parents to the Fairmonts' home one cold January afternoon, and the two couples took to each other immediately. Indeed they were so engrossed in their conversation that they paid little attention when Randolph announced casually, "Sylvain's promised to play the piano for me."

He swept her out of the room. There was not so much as a lag in the conversation.

"Randolph Baxter," Sylvain accused laughingly, "I never told you I played the piano."

"Do you?"

She lifted her slender shoulders. "A little."

"A little's all I care to hear." He grinned and propelled her to the music room.

She took a seat on the padded bench before the big square piano and blinked when he sat down beside her. Nervously she skimmed stiff fingers over the keys in a tortured tune while he leaned close and blew on a dark wispy curl beside her right ear. She stopped playing.

"Continue," he said. "If you don't, they'll wonder what we're doing." She struck a few chords. "Know what I want?" he whispered.

Eyes on the keyboard, she said, "I think so."

He laughed. "Then look at me, Sylvain."

Slowly she lifted her eyes, her fingers still stumbling over the keys. She turned her head and almost bumped noses with him, so close was he.

"I want to kiss you," he murmured, his green eyes on her mouth. She said nothing, but kept playing while his golden head bent and his hand went to the side of her throat. His mouth touched hers. It was warm and smooth and pleasant. Her fingers struck a sour chord, then paused.

Randolph's lips left hers. "Play, Sylvain," he gently reminded her. Then, "Will you write me when I return to school?"

"Oh, yes," she assured him. "Every day."

"You'll not let some other fellow steal your heart while I'm gone?"

The ear-punishing notes continued to engulf them. "No," she promised, but promptly added, "And you must agree to the same thing."

Randolph spread his bronzed left hand over the feminine ones atop the piano keys, ending the discord. "You may depend on that, Sylvain," he pledged gallantly and kissed her again.

The Baxters remained for dinner, which delighted Sylvain. But she was puzzled when, as they finished the dessert, Randolph said, "It's time we go."

She protested, as did Edwin Fairmont, who said, "Son, it's early yet. Why, we've not even had our cigars and brandy."

But Randolph was adamant. He spirited his parents to the waiting carriage and waved to a shivering Sylvain, who stood on the porch with her father, When the carriage turned the corner and disappeared from sight, Edwin hurried his daughter back inside the warm house.

It had been an eventful day in the life of Sylvain Fairmont. She'd been kissed by a handsome college man, who'd asked her to write to him. He'd even made her promise not to let another steal her heart while he was away.

Sylvain went to bed a very happy young lady.

At Oakgrove, Randolph Baxter shooed his parents from the carriage. Ignoring their questions, he directed the driver to take him to the home of one Miss Ginger Thompson. The wheels had hardly come to a halt before the modest dwelling when the front door opened and Ginder's flaming hair shone in the half-light.

Cape flowing behind her, she flew down the steps of her home and ran to the carriage. Randolph threw open the door.

"You're late, Randolph Baxter," she said peevishly.

"Am I?"

"Yes, you are, and I won't — "

"Yes, you will," he taunted and drew her into his arms. His mouth devoured hers in a heated kiss while his hands sought the lush curves beneath the cape.

"Randy," she sighed and molded herself to him.

Sylvain missed Randolph Baxter terribly when he returned to school. She wrote to him just as she'd promised and eagerly awaited an answer. When at last a short note from him came, she was overjoyed. She read and reread it until the paper was crumpled and worn.

He reminded her that she was to give her heart to no other, and he also spoke of the moment of shared intimacy in the music room. Did she know how much it had meant to him? Were ever a pair of lips sweeter than hers?

Sylvain hid the revealing letter under her mattress. She had no intention of letting Delilah snoop around and find it. She'd be sure to misunderstand and be shocked. She might even tell. Delilah did not like Randolph Baxter, Sylvain was certain of it. Why, she could not imagine.

After the first one, Randolph's letters came regularly, and Sylvain read them eagerly, then promptly and painstakingly answered. His last short note arrived only one day before Randolph himself.

Dated June 5, it predicted, "I assure you I'll be back in Mobile in time to help you celebrate your sixteenth birthday." She was descending the stairs the next morning when the knock came.

"I'll get it," Sylvain called to Delson and rushed to swing open the door.

Randolph Baxter stood smiling down at her.

"Why must you leave so soon?"

"Darling, I've been here in Paris for more than a year. I'd hardly call that leaving soon."

Delphine de Carondelet sighed and thrust a satin-cased pillow against the tall carved headboard. She sat up and snatched the downy comforter over her bare breasts. Her brown eyes were fixed on the dark, handsome man who was shoving his long, muscular arms into a clean white shirt. He turned to face her, as his lean fingers nimbly worked at the buttons.

"Delphine, it's been wonderful and I — "

"Then stay, Hilton," she pleaded, tossing the covers aside. Naked, she came to him, threw her arms around his neck, and whispered, "Stay, my love." She kissed his strong jaw.

Hilton's hands went to her waist. "No, Delphine. We've been over this a dozen times. Weeks ago I promised a good friend I'd be in Texas by mid-June. I intend to keep that promise."

Arms tightening around his neck, she said, "But what about me, *chèri*?"

His hands dropped from her. "Have I ever made a promise to you I have not kept?"

Delphine let her hands slide down his shirt front. Gently caressing, her fingers making small circles on the soft fabric and hard chest beneath, she slowly shook her head. "*Non, chèri*, you haven't . . . but I . . . I know if you go I'll never see you again."

Hilton covered the teasing fingers with his own. "Yes, you will. I'll come back to Paris, and you can come to New York." He pushed her gently from him. "Now, get dressed, love. This is our last night together and we're going to the theater." He gave her a flashing smile and reminded her of her words. "You're the one who said, 'It will be simply the most important performance of the year. All Paris will be there in their finest. We have to go!'"

"I did say that, didn't I?"

"Indeed you did, *mademoiselle*."

Delphine smiled saucily, took a step backward, and murmured, "Would you think me outrageous if I told you I don't wish to go."

Hilton crossed his arms over his chest and cocked his head. "Did I hear correctly? You'd miss the — "

"You did, *chèri*." She strolled toward the bed, bare hips swaying seductively. She stopped and slowly turned around, then tossed her hair back from her face, took a deep breath, and teased, "I'd like the performance of the year to take place in this bed." She gave him a naughty, challenging look.

Calmly Hilton Courteen flipped open the buttons and drew off the white shirt. Delphine climbed onto the rumpled, satin bed and waited breathlessly. Hilton, looking directly at her, stripped, tossing his fine evening trousers atop an open steamer trunk. Delphine felt her breath grow short when he started toward the bed. He was magnificent in his nakedness: tall, lithe, dark-skinned.

He rested one knee on the bed and reached for her. Pulling her up to him, he brushed warm lips to her cheek and said wickedly, "Let the curtain rise." His laughter filled her ears.

But not for long.

"Randolph!" exclaimed a delighted Sylvain Fairmont, and her hands went to her cheeks.

"I told you I'd be here in time to celebrate your birthday." He stepped into the corridor and cast a hurried glance around. "Where is everyone?"

Eyes only for him, she said, "Daddy's at his office; Mother's visiting."

"Good," murmured Randolph Baxter, and pulled the tall girl into his arms. With her hands trapped between their bodies, Sylvain had no choice but to spread them on his chest. She was opening her mouth to warn him about Delilah when his lips closed over hers in a warm, tender kiss.

The kiss continued until an indignant Delilah, hurriedly descending the stairs, cleared her throat loudly. Randolph lifted his head but continued to cling to Sylvain. Never one to keep an opinion to herself, Delilah, hands on her hips, said pointedly, "Gentlemens don't take 'vantage of a young lady's folks bein' out of the house, an' a young lady don't let no gentleman kiss her in broad daylight, 'specially when she ain't even sixteen yet."

Sylvain slowly turned. Chin high, she drew Randolph's arms about her waist and placed her hands atop his. "And respectable house servants do not go about snooping." She laughed then and added, "I shall be sixteen tomorrow, and I haven't seen Randolph since

Christmas." She leaned her head back against his shoulder. "Delilah, you simply must face the fact that I'm a woman."

Delilah's answer was a snort and a deadly flash of her dark eyes as she swept past the couple and into the drawing room. She took a seat on one of the gold chairs, folded her arms, and set her jaw, silently announcing that here she would stay for as long as the young male visitor remained in the house.

"She's impossible, I'm afraid," Sylvain murmured to Randolph.

He smiled and whispered, "I'll win her over, don't you worry."

Randolph came the next day to help Sylvain celebrate her sixteenth birthday. He brought her a lovely gold-backed looking glass with a long golden handle. Sylvain squealed with delight and held it up to her face. And when her father gave permission for Randolph to take her for an afternoon carriage ride, she was beside herself with happiness. Her parents stood on the sun-splashed lower gallery and watched the handsome pair drive away.

"He seems like a very nice boy." Serena Fairmont was smiling.

"Fine family, fine boy," Edwin agreed heartily.

Delilah, arms folded over her chest, stood on the upper gallery. She, too, watched the handsome young couple climb into the elegant carriage, but she was not smiling. A chill skipped down her spine despite the heat of the blinding June sun. Shrugging, she told herself she was being foolish. She went back into Sylvain's cluttered room and began hanging up the many discarded dresses her young charge had tried on before choosing just the right one.

"How about it, Jas?" Hilton Courteen sat sipping coffee in his New Orleans hotel room. "You coming to Texas or not?"

Jasper, taking a stack of clean shirts from a bureau drawer, turned and snapped, "I ain't never seen nothin' like you! We jes' get back from that awful place 'cross the ocean, and here you is leavin' again. What be wrong with you? You goin' to spen' your whole life driftin' like some homeless white trash?"

Hilton, his dark hands cupped around a slim cigar, puffed the smoke to life and eyed his manservant. He smiled lazily and drawled, "Isn't that what I am, Jas?" His dark eyes flashed merrily, and he rolled the cigar between straight white teeth.

"That's what 'ou act like, yessuh. But you is from one of the finest fa...ilies the South ever seen. I mean, your great-granddaddy was one of the first — "

"Spare me, Jas." Hilton poured himself another cup of black coffee. "Do you want to come to Texas with me or not? You needn't feel you must."

"What am I goin' to do if I don't go with you?" Jasper looked troubled.

"You have two choices: you may remain here at the hotel until I return or I'll take you down to Mobile and you can stay with my grandmother. It's up to you."

Jasper shook his graying head. "I sure don't wants to go to Texas. I hear they not civilized down there. Might lose my scalp to one of them savages." He dropped a stack of Hilton's shirts into an open valise and lifted his hands to his gray hair.

Hilton laughed. "That settles it. You'll stay here in the hotel."

"I don't like the idea of bein' here by myself." Jasper's lower lip jutted outward.

"Then Mobile it is." Hilton unfolded the morning newspaper.

"Mobile it is," repeated a relieved, smiling Jasper, turning back to his task. He took another stack of shirts from the drawer and stooped to pick up something that fell from their folds. On the wine carpet lay a small beige glove. Jasper picked it up. He frowned and crossed the room to the small trash basket, dropped the glove into it, and dusted his hands.

Hilton's dark eyes never left the newspaper, but he softly inquired, "What did you throw away, Jas?"

"Nothin' 'cept a lady's glove. Ain't no tellin' whose. Ladies always leavin' bits of their garments in your room. Ask me, they ain't ladies at all."

Hilton dropped the newspaper on the linen-draped table. Chomping down on his cigar, he rose easily. "Pick it up."

"What?" Jasper stared at his master.

"The glove. Take it out of the trash."

"What for? It ain't worth nothin'. Jes one glove and it — "

"Bring it to me." Hilton's calm, deep voice took on a determined edge.

His argumentative old servant promptly obeyed, snatching up the beige glove and handing it to the tall man.

Hilton gripped the small glove lightly in his left hand and said placidly, "You're never to throw this glove away. Is that understood?"

"Yessuh, it is, but why? I don't even know who it belong to."

"Never," said Hilton Courteen, ending the conversation.

Hilton Courteen was bone-weary when he pulled up sharply on the reins, bringing the well-lathered bay stallion to a halt. Squinting in the brilliant Texas sunlight, he saw in the distance the little Mexican town, the old provincial capital of San Antonio de Bexar.

It seemed like a lifetime ago that he'd put his man-servant on a riverboat to Mobile and boarded another for Galveston. The long journey across the gulf had been pleasant enough. Several well-heeled businessmen were on their way to the thriving Texas port, and after introductions were made, they'd passed the hours at a poker table.

In Galveston, Hilton had purchased the strong steed he now rode, packed a few items into his saddlebags, and set out, armed with a crude map. Now, days later, a full black beard hiding his lower face, his back aching from too many hours in the saddle, and his eyes burning from the relentless sun, he had arrived at his destination.

Awed by the immense size of this Mexican Texas, Hilton was likewise impressed with its wild beauty. An endless sea of waving grass and wildflowers blanketed the land. Geraniums, primroses, dahlias, and violets splashed vivid color over gently rolling hills. The deep, limpid pools where he'd stopped to bathe were covered with lilies. The streams were full of fish, and game was all about — deer, rabbits, wild turkeys. Herds of buffalo and mustangs roamed across the untamed expanse. Hilton was beginning to understand his friend Cot's love of Texas.

Hilton rode into San Antonio de Bexar and smiled at the brightly dressed Mexicans gossiping in the Main Plaza. Brown, big-eyed children scampered after him, calling to him in Spanish. Sleepy men wearing sombreros lolled against the flat-roofed adobe houses that lined the narrow streets. Guitar music drifted from a small cantina, and a huge, blond man strode from the dim, low doorway.

It was Cot Campbell.

"You son of a gun," Cot called cheerfully and hurried to drag the bearded Hilton off his horse. The two men stood in the middle of the dusty street embracing while the Mexicans stared and laughed and nodded happily. "Buy you a drink?" the big, ruddy-faced blond asked his old friend.

"I am a little thirsty." Hilton grinned and scratched at the bushy black beard flecked with trail dust.

"Good God, I hardly knew you, Hill. All that hair covering your face. Hell, you're near ugly as me." Cot guffawed loudly and slapped the leaner man on the back.

"True, but the way I smell makes up for it." Hilton laughed, indicating his sweat-stained shirt.

At sundown Hilton, freshly bathed and shaved, sat at a long dining table in the Campbell home. Built by Cot's father and his older brother, Jonas, the sturdy wood and stucco dwelling sat in the middle of a 4,428-acre parcel of land for which their father had paid the paltry sum of thirty dollars.

Cot's father had died the winter before. Cot, his brother, Jonas, Jonas's Mexican wife, and their two children lived in the house. Concepcion Campbell was a good cook. The platters of fried meat and fresh vegetables she served were delicious. After the heavy meal, she cleared away the dishes, poured the coffee, brought down the liquor bottle, and excused herself, admonishing her two small sons to wash up and get to their beds.

Cot slid the bottle of whiskey over to Hilton, then reached to the carved sideboard behind him and brought down three glasses. Hilton poured for them all while his black eyes went to Jonas Campbell.

"It seems," he said, lifting his glass in a toast, "that the brothers Campbell have found a peaceful and pleasant life on the frontier." They drank.

Jonas Campbell wiped his mouth on the back of a big hand and shook his corn-colored head. "We found it, Hilton. Trouble is, looks like we're losing it." He reached for the liquor bottle while Hilton's black eyes studied him.

Cot spoke, drawing Hilton's attention. "We'll be at war within a year, Hill, sure as we're sitting here." He refilled his glass, drank the whiskey down in one throat-burning swallow. "With the Mexicans."

Hilton looked from brother to brother. "I thought the Mexicans were your friends. After all, Concepcion and the boys . . . what . . . ?"

Jonas's ruddy face clouded. "Concepcion's family lives in Mexico City. That makes it doubly hard on us." The big man rocked back in his chair, balancing it on two legs. "Hilton, when Dad and I came down here eleven years ago, the Mexicans had the *empresario* program. They offered land at give-away prices. They were eager to get as many Americans down here as possible. Know why?"

"I've never thought much about it, Jonas." Hilton sipped at his second glass of bourbon.

"Indians, that's why. The Mexicans wanted us to handle the marauding Texas Indians so they'd be safe down South. Well, that was okay. I never minded an Indian scrape or two. Dad didn't either. We had the land, I met and married Concepcion, everything was fine for a time. Then Mexico ups and decides they'll allow no more immigration."

"Worse," Cot put in. "They abolished the sale and use of black slaves. Dad and Jonas with cotton and corn crops and no one to work 'em."

"Last year," Jonas picked up the conversation, "Stephen Austin, one of the original *empresarios*, went on down to Mexico City to press claims about the infringement of our liberties." He came down hard on all four chair legs and clasped his big hands on the table. "Know what happened to him? The bastards jailed him! He's still there."

"Is there no recourse?" said Hilton. "Have you no say in government?"

Jonas snorted loudly, and Cot poured yet another whiskey and said, "Hill, I'm sorry. Here it's your first night in Texas and we're loading you down with our territorial problems. Hell, tell us what's going on back in New Orleans."

"I hardly know myself." Hilton grinned lazily. "Been in Paris for quite a while."

Jonas, bleary-eyed and little drunk, soon shuffled off to bed, leaving the two old friends alone. They talked until far into the night, speaking of scattered comrades, recalling happy memories. sharing hopes and plans and the bottle of bourbon. Finally, when the bottle was empty, Cot said at last, "You're tired, Hill. We'll talk more to-morrow." He rose.

Hilton yawned, nodded, and scratched at the white scar in his left eyebrow. In the narrow hallway the two men shook hands. "It's good to see you, Cot," Hilton said again.

"Sleep well, my friend. We'll have the whole summer together."

Hilton enjoyed his long stay in Texas. It was a lazy, pleasant land, and it seemed no one was ever in much of a hurry. Americans took long siestas in the hot after-noon, just as the Mexicans did. Rousing after the sun had lost a little of its sting, Hilton and Cot would take Jonas's young sons down to the river to bathe in the sparkling clear waters, the little boys squealing and laughing, the men smiling and nodding to the pretty brown-skinned young women lounging on the shady banks beneath softly rustling cottonwoods.

In the evenings fires glowed in the yards and soft guitar music wafted from open doorways while overhead a million stars twinkled and sweethearts promenaded slowly around the plaza. Dances were held in a stone complex of buildings called the Alamo. The buildings, almost a century old, had been left by the Spaniards. A chapel stood at the corner of the stone and adobe build-ings. The Campbells attended Sunday services in the ancient church.

Days turned into weeks, and Hilton Courteen, wearing buckskins, his swarthy skin tanned deeper still by the bright Mexican sun, became well known around San Antonio de Bexar. And he began to hear more and more about the problems the Texans were having with Mexico. On a sultry evening in August, Cot told him a guest would be coming for supper.

"Jim Bowie's as wild as they come," Cot said to Hilton. "He grew up in your land, down in the sugarcane country of Louisiana. He swears he rode alligators, and I don't doubt it for a minute. He fought in frontier brawls, held off a swarm of Indians at San Saba, and made vast fortunes slave trading with that clever pirate, Jean Lafitte." Cot laughed.

Jonas had joined them on the porch. He crouched against the stucco wall and added solemnly, "Jim came out here in 1828. He turned Catholic, became a Mexican citizen, and married Maria Ursula de Veramendi, a blonde. Ursula was just nineteen then and the prettiest girl in San Antonio, not to mention the richest. Jim and Ursula had two children." He paused reflectively. "Jim was in Mississippi when the fever hit. Cholera. Ursula and the babies died. Now Jim lives all alone in the empty Veramendi house on Soledad Street."

Before Hilton could respond, Jim Bowie cantered up to the adobe. Hilton liked the man on sight. Tall, massive, and sandy-haired, Jim Bowie was smooth, polished, and spoke in a voice that was almost soft. Yet beneath his calm, pleasant exterior, Hilton sensed him to be hard and uncompromising. He listened intently as the big man's voice dropped when the subject turned to the Mexican dictator, Santa Anna.

"He's reopened the Customs House at Anáhuac." Bowie's eyes took on a dangerous glow. "He's slapped duties on the colonies and he's pouring troops into Texas as we speak, gentlemen."

"I hear he's ordered Bill Travis's arrest," said Cot heatedly. Bowie inclined his sandy head and looked at Hilton. "Mr. Courteen, we Texans were guaranteed self-government under the Mexican constitution of 1824. Our only goal is to build a secure future with no outside interference."

"Military occupation, martial law, the arrest of our friends — we won't put up with it much longer!" Jonas Campbell exclaimed.

A week later the Campbell brothers, Hilton, and Big Jim Bowie attended a banquet in Brazoria. Stephen F. Austin, who had just returned from his year's imprisonment in Mexico, got up to speak. The room fell silent. Austin told a hushed crowd that Santa Anna was revoking the people's rights. "A general consultation must be held."

"He's calling for a provisional government," whispered Cot Campbell. Jim Bowie nodded.

Stephen Austin made it clear how he felt about Mexican troops in Texas. "The people would not support any armed forces sent against this country. On the contrary, they would resist and repel it and ought to do so."

After the meeting, men gathered at the crowded, steamy saloon and talked into the dawn. A war with Mexico was inevitable, unavoidable. The Texans would stand against Santa Anna. Hilton Courteen listened quietly while the Texas rebels spoke passionately of the hated Mexican dictator. It was their fight, not his. Still, by the time he was ready to leave Texas a week later, he'd made up his mind. He'd help finance their rebellion. These Texans were brave and strong, but woefully underarmed for an all-out stand against their powerful enemy.

Cot Campbell was speechless when his old friend told him of his plan. Hilton explained that he was a wealthy man. His phenomenal success at the gaming tables had supplied him with huge amounts of cash. He'd invested that cash in holdings, which he would profitably liquidate to arm the Texans.

"You'd do that for the cause?" Cot stared at him.

Hilton laughed and clapped the bigger man's shoulder. "I'd do that for you, Cot."

"You'll get it back, Hill, I swear."

"I'm not worried about it."

"I know that. Just the same, I'll send you a singed note for every last bullet you supply."

"No need."

"I'll do it."

Chapter Nine

A marvelous Mobile summer gave way to a breathtaking autumn. And a tall, skinny girl gave way to a curvaceous, ripe young woman. Almost overnight Sylvain Fairmont matured. She reached her full height of five feet seven inches. Her breasts and hips took on the soft, seductive curves that caused men's heads to turn and their hearts to race. Masses of dark brown curls framed her golden-skinned oval face with its huge gray eyes, pert nose, and petulant mouth. Sylvain was a stunning beauty and rapidly growing aware of it.

Her native charm and friendly manner made her all the more appealing, and by the time the first leaves turned and fluttered down from the trees, Randolph Baxter was not the only young gentleman pursuing Sylvain.

William Greylord, hopelessly smitten, called often at the Fairmont town house. A wealthy merchant's son, the sandy-haired, massively built twenty-two-year-old Greylord flirted and flattered and hoped to steal Sylvain's heart.

Jake Robards was tall, pale, and shy. A quiet, poetic young man, he admired Sylvain's bubbling personality. Her opposite in every way, young Robards spent bitter-sweet hours penning love poems to a girl with "angel eyes and devil lips."

Tommy Mason was Edwin Fairmont's new law clerk. He'd been invited to have lunch with the Fairmonts.

Reluctantly he came. More reluctantly he left. From the moment he laid eyes on Sylvain, he was her slave. Sylvain found him funny and bright; he found her an irresistible mixture of sweetness and fire.

And there were other young gentlemen who came to call on one of the city's most desirable misses, but none was more determined — or more welcome — than the rich and handsome Randolph Baxter.

Randolph was a clever man who knew what he wanted. He wanted Sylvain Fairmont, and he intended to have her. Realizing that Sylvain was very young and was just experiencing the first rush of attention from men, he didn't press her but patiently stood by while the others called on her. He wasn't worried about the competition. He was certain he could win her, and besides, he had someone to keep him company while he waited for Sylvain to grow up.

Hilton Courteen sat in his attorney's upstairs offices on Chartres Street in New Orleans. The little lawyer took off his glasses, rubbed the bridge of his straight nose, and said authoritatively, "You, son, are a fool."

Hilton's generous lips curved into a grin. "Dave, my friend, I never pretended to be anything else."

David Garfield glared at the younger man. "Dammit, Hilton, this is hardly comical. You're telling me you intend to give your entire fortune to a bunch of frontiersmen out in Texas so — "

"Dave, I'm not here to be lectured like a naughty schoolboy. I want you to handle the liquidation of my holdings." He rose lithely from his chair and strode to the front window. "I have only a few close friends." He turned and slid his hands into his trousers pockets. "My best friend is in Texas. He needs help. It's that simple."

"It's not simple at all, Hilton. You're a very rich man and — "

"Turn it into cash. I'm going to buy arms for the Texas rebels."

"But — but, Hilton," the older man stammered, his face growing red, "don't you realize you could lose every cent you have?"

Hilton came back to the chair. Seated, he made a steeple with his long, lean fingers and said, "Cot will send a signed note."

"Note? Pshaw! What good will that do? What if your friend should loose his li — "

"He won't." Hilton interrupted. "Now, get my money for me. Those boys need arms, and they need them now."

David Garfield sighed wearily, replaced the glasses on his nose, and nodded. "Whatever you say. But, Hilton, are you fully aware you can come out of this no longer a rich man?"

Hilton grinned once more. "Should that happen I'll just have to earn another fortune."

"I suppose you mean by gambling."

"What else?"

"Hilton, a lot of men don't win at cards."

"That's their misfortune."

Two weeks later Hilton stood at the waterfront. Gangs of slaves sweated in the hot autumn sun while they loaded cannon and kegs of black powder onto a low, sleek schooner. By sundown the newly purchased armaments would be on their way to Galveston.

Hilton was pleased when he left the levee. Word of the revolution had reached New Orleans in the third week of October. Couriers told of a skirmish at Gonzales, the capture of Goliad. The small, ragged Texas army was rumored to be heading to Gonzales to escort Mexican General Cos right out of Texas.

New Orleanians were becoming interested in the plight of the Texans. Hilton stopped in at the Arcadian Coffee House and found a throng there. Within minutes they pledged $10,000 for the rebels. Back at his hotel, the Richardson, crowds swarmed through the lobby, everyone predicting great things for the Texans.

In Mobile, October 20 was a chilly, starry night. Crowds packed the courthouse, demanding independence for Texas. Sylvain held tightly to Randolph Baxter's hand and listened to the excited shouts and promises. The gentlemen set up a committee to organize help for the rebels, and they ordered that a copy of the proceedings be taken to Texas. They chose one of their respected leaders — dark, dashing James Butler Bonham, a South Carolina aristocrat — as the courier. Bonham spoke eloquently of the rebel cause and said he would not let the committee down.

"He's so brave," whispered an awed Sylvain when the tall South Carolinian stepped down from the rostrum.

Randolph looked at her. "You know, Sylvain," he whispered near her ear, "I've been considering going to Texas myself."

"Randloph!" Sylvain exploded, a flash of fear in her gray eyes. "You can't, you simply can't."

"I don't know," said Randolph Baxter. "We'll talk about it later." He turned back to look at the speaker.

After the rally, Randolph returned with Sylvain and her parents to the town house. Patiently he waited until Edwin Fairmont began to yawn and Serena finally said, "It's time for bed." She looked pointedly at Randolph. "It's quite late."

Randolph rose, nodding his blond head. "Yes, it is, Mrs. Fairmont. I must go, of course, but I wonder if I might have just a few minutes alone with Sylvain." He looked toward the big-eyed girl seated on the sofa. "There's something we must discuss."

Sylvain's heart froze. She knew what he was going to tell her: He was going away; he was going to Texas to fight with the brave rebels, and she'd never, ever see him again.

"Very well." Serena nudged her dozing husband. "Come, Edwin. Randolph wishes to speak with Sylvain."

Edwin Fairmont yawned and blinked. "Ten minutes, young man. Then she must come up to bed."

No sooner had the elder Fairmonts ascended the stairs than Randolph was beside Sylvain on the couch. He took her cold hands in his and said, "Sylvain, about Texas — "

"Oh, please, please," she said and jerked her hands free. She threw her trembling arms around his neck and begged, "Don't go to Texas. I couldn't bear it if you left. I couldn't." She buried her face in his throat.

Randolph's hands went to her slim waist. He pressed her close and soothed, "There, there, it wouldn't be forever. Besides, you have all your other beaux to keep you company."

Sylvain pulled back to look at him. "Randolph, I want only you. No one else." Again she flung herself into his arms.

"If that's true, Sylvain, will you stop seeing the others?"

"Oh, yes, yes."

Randolph kissed her temple. "Sylvain," he said in a low, soft voice, "I love you. I want to marry you one day."

Again she pulled back, eyes wide, lips parted. "You love me?"

"Yes, darling, I do." He smiled at her and kissed her turned-up nose. "Do you love me, Sylvain?"

For a long moment she stared at him, uncertain. He put his hand to her chin and drew her closer. His green eyes dropped to her mouth, and a thumb skimmed over the full bottom lip. He kissed her softly, withdrew, looked at her, and kissed her again.

She locked her arms around his neck and kissed him eagerly, passionately. His lips left hers and went to her hair. "Sylvain, do you love me?"

"I think I do, Randolph. Will you kiss me again so I'll be certain?" His mouth was back on hers and Sylvain sighed and responded fully, protesting when his lips left hers.

"Tell me now, Sylvain. Tell me."

"I love you, Randolph. I love you."

"And I love you," he murmured. "Very, very much."

"When will we be married?" She laughed happily and put her hands into his thick blond hair.

His fingers encircled her wrists and he drew her hands to his lips. Pressing kisses into the warm palms, he said, "It will be a while. We'll wait until you're eighteen. With your parents' permission we'll become engaged next spring."

"That's wonderful, but — "

"But what, darling?"

"You must promise you'll never go out with Ginger Thompson again."

He lowered her hands to her lap. "Whatever gave you — "

"My Delilah told me you've been seeing her, Randolph. You can't see her again. Not if you love me."

"I wouldn't dream of seeing anyone but my darling Sylvain."

"There's one more promise you must make. You must swear to me you'll think no more of going off to Texas and getting shot!"

He laughed happily and enclosed her in his arms. Against her flushed cheek he said, "If you don't want me to go to Texas, then I shan't go." Sylvain pulled his mouth down to hers and happily kissed him.

Sylvain's parents were overjoyed. Randolph Baxter would be an ideal son-in-law. He was rich, aristocratic, intelligent, respectful, a hard worker, and obviously in love with their beautiful daughter.

Edwin Fairmont had a talk with his prospective son-in-law. He coughed and hemmed and hawed and finally said what was on his mind: "Randolph, I know you're a fine, fine boy and that you respect Sylvain, but I . . . I . . ."

Randolph made it easy on him. "Mr. Fairmont, I know what you're concerned about, but you needn't be troubled. Sylvain is very young and innocent. I will not take advantage of her. You can depend on me. I'm a gentleman, Mr. Fairmont. I know how to treat a young lady."

Edwin Fairmont, blushing to the roots of his thinning gray hair, mumbled, "Thank you, son. I hope you don't think I've overstepped the mark here, but — "

"Not at all," responded Randolph. "I don't blame you one bit, sir. Sylvain's so temptingly beautiful it's hard not to . . . that is, she's a lovely girl as sweet as they come. I'll take good care of her."

A week after the Texas rally, Randolph escorted Sylvain and her proud parents to Mobile's Shakespeare theater. It was an exciting evening, and after the performance, a collection for the Texans was taken. Richly dressed theatergoers dropped bills into a silk hat, and $1,500 was raised within minutes. Sylvain sat holding tightly to her handsome sweetheart's hand, grateful he was not in far-off Texas.

Back at the town house, Randolph bade the Fairmonts a hasty good-night, pressing a kiss to Sylvain's glowing cheek. In a dream she ascended the stairs to her warm bedroom.

"Delilah," she called to her drowsy maid, "it was wonderful, a perfect evening. Randolph said I looked grown up and beautiful and that he never wanted to be out of my sight again."

Delilah took Sylvain's elbow and turned her, the began unhooking the tiny buttons going from collar to waist. "Uh-huh," she crooned. "Then where is he?"

"Why, he's home, or on his way." Sylvain looked back over her shoulder.

"Mighty early for an eager beau to be goin' home."

Sylvain frowned.

Randolph Baxter didn't go directly home. He hurried across town to Ginger Thompson's small house. Ginger came out to meet the carriage and climbed in. She snuggled close to Randolph under the plaid lap robe.

Soon the carriage was parked in the moonlight close to the Mobile River on a deserted bluff. The coachman, heavy overcoat pulled up about his chilly ears, sat patiently, awaiting instructions from his young master.

"Ginger, I'm not going to see you anymore." Randolph looked straight into her eyes.

"You can't mean that, Randy, you can't."

"I do. I've asked Sylvain Fairmont to marry me."

"When?" Ginger choked.

"Not for a couple of years, but — "

Relieved, Ginger said softly, "That's a long time. Two years. Wait until you marry her to stop seeing me."

"No, I can't do that."

"Can't you?" she whispered and pulled his head down to hers. Open-mouthed she kissed him, and as she kissed him, her hand slid underneath his warm brown cloak. She spread her fingers over his evening clothes, then let her hand slowly slide down over his chest to his belly and beyond. She found the placket of his trousers. Barely touching, she let her coaxing fingers slip up and down over the rapidly hardening male flesh. And still she kissed him, her tongue as bold as her hands.

When he reached for her, she abruptly pulled away. "Want me, darling?" she taunted.

Randolph gritted his teeth. "No. No, I don't," he ground out.

Her soft laughter filled the close cab. Ginger shrugged hurriedly out of her long woolen cape. Randolph Baxter swallowed hard. She wore only a thin satin chemise, one lacy strap slipping down a creamy shoulder, shapely legs naked to the night air.

"Good God, Ginger, what are you — "

She giggled and peeled the flimsy garment down to her waist. In a triumphant gesture, she tossed her head back,

124

plucked the pins from her unswept hair, and let the long, fiery locks cascade down her back.

She lowered her head, looked at Randolph who was breathing heavily, and said huskily, "Touch me, darling. Kiss me."

Randolph groaned and pulled her into his arms. His mouth, hot and searching, took hers in a searing kiss. His lips slid down to the full, swelling breasts he was fondling. Ginger arched her back and murmured, "Yes, darling, yes," and stroked the blond head bent over her.

His hand found hers and guided it again to the throbbing between his legs. Deftly she unbuttoned his trousers and released him. Enclosing him, she expertly caressed and stroked until finally he writhed and shuddered in release. He turned shamed eyes to hers. She smiled and whispered, "It's all right, my darling, all right."

Like a docile child he sat obediently, letting her undress him. By the time he was naked, he was fully aroused again. He pushed her down onto her back and mounted her, shoving his engorged hardness eagerly into her. They mated wildly, ramming and lunging and bucking, and rocking the carriage so violently that the poker-faced driver seated above them had to hold to his seat to keep from falling.

The sounds of their coupling carried in the chill night air. "Ah, Randy, darling. Will you do this to me again soon?"

A rasping male voice assured her, "God, yes, yes. Every night, every night. Oh, Ginger, Ginger . . . "

A dream awoke Sylvain in the middle of the night. In it she was wearing a wedding dress. Crowds of people thronged the church, everyone smiling and happy. She started down the long aisle on her father's arm. Randolph waited at the altar. His hand was out to her, beckoning her to him.

Suddenly her feet were heavy. So heavy she could hardly lift them. She struggled and fought her way down an aisle that grew longer and longer. She was tired, so tired. She could never make it, never. Randolph's hand remained outstretched. she had to reach him. *She had to*.

She kept going, slowly making progress, her heavy feet now sticking to the floor. On she went, determined to reach Randolph. She struggled, she plodded, she finally was within reach of Randolph's hand. She gave a shout of exultation and grabbed at his fingers.

Strong male fingers closed over her hand and pulled her forward. Sylvain looked up. The man wasn't Randolph. He was a stranger. Randolph was gone.

She screamed.

Her breath coming fast, perspiration dampening her chilled skin, Sylvain threw back the bedcovers and hurried to the window. Her eyes scanned the quiet street. She winced. There in the shadows half a block away, a tall, thin man stood lounging against a lamppost. His hat was pulled low over his eyes, his dark collar turned up against the chill. And in his right hand was an ebony walking cane, its gold head gleaming in the misty lamplight.

Chapter Ten

A scattering of scarlet clouds filled the late-afternoon sky. The cold, crisp air was biting. Winter refused to release its tenacious hold on the land. In mid-March, the city of Mobile continued to shiver. Sunset neared, and the temperature plummeted rapidly. It would be another long, cold night.

A dark young man stepped carefully from a leased carriage before a small, graceful dwelling on McGregor Avenue. A petite, white-haired lady drew back a corner of the heavy brocade drapes and peered out. A joyful smile lifted the corners of her thin, pale lips, and her dark eyes danced. She released the curtain, lifted her heavy skirts, and scampered into the marble foyer. Shooing the stern-faced butler away with a dismissive flutter of her fragile hand, Belle Courteen threw open the heavy front door.

"Hilton!" she shouted gleefully.

Black hair disheveled, his swarthy face covered with a stubble of dark beard, Hilton hurried in with a rush of cold air. Bending down to kiss a translucent, powdered cheek, he said warmly, "Could a wayward grandson find lodgings for the evening?"

Belle Courteen drank in the welcome sight of him, then said excitedly, "You came just in time. I'm to attend a most important affair, and you shall escort me."

Hilton took both her hands in one of his, and urged his grandmother into the warmth of the library. "Dear, that's not possible, you see I — "

"You have been in smoke-filled card parlors all night and all day?" She snatched her hands from his and pushed him toward the fire.

Shrugging out of his wrap, Hilton smiled. "How perceptive you are, love."

"Don't be insolent, young man. I will not tolerate it." She motioned the butler forward to take the discarded cloak. Hilton yawned, turned his back on his grandmother, and spread his fingers to the fire's warmth. "Are you listening to me, Hilton Daniel Courteen?"

Hilton grinned. His grandmother used his full name when she was irritated with him. Slowly he turned to face her, clasped his hands behind him, and rocked back on his heels. "Yes, dear, I'm listening. Just what may I do to get in your good graces? Name it and its yours." He gave her an exaggerated bow.

"That's better." Belle Courteen patted the knot of white hair at the back of her small head. "You will escort me to the ball this evening."

Hilton groaned but agreed. "I can hardly wait." He strode to round marble-topped table and lifted the stopper from a cut-glass decanter. He splashed cognac into a glass, raised it, and said, "I trust I'll have an hour or two to rest and freshen up." He downed the contents of the glass.

Belle glanced at the clock over the mantel. "There's less than three hours, and I want to fill you in on all the gossip." She was smiling sunnily, just as she always did when she had gotten her way.

"God forbid," said the sleepy Hilton Courteen. He started from the room. Belle Courteen fluttered after him.

"But, dear, you haven't heard about — "

"Belle Courteen, if I'm to be subjected to one of your infernal 'do's,' you can at least spare me your prattling about this city's gentry." He looked at her accusingly. She loved gossip; he did not. She was constantly annoyed that her handsome grandson seemed not the least bit interested in hearing what society was up to. More than once she'd had a choice bit of scandal to impart and he'd merely shaken his dark head and fixed her with a disapproving gaze.

"Hilton, dear, I just wanted to tell you about — "

He lifted a hand, silencing her. "I'll be your escort tonight. Now I'm going to bed." He grinned down at the tiny woman. "Think you can entertain yourself for a couple of hours?" His long fingers moved toward her snow-white hair.

The feisty little woman brushed his hand away. "I suppose I can. I've been doing just that for the last twenty years. After all, how often does anyone think of me? I'm alone here all the time."

Hilton climbed the stairs, impervious to the verbal attack meant to inflict guilt. He'd heard it dozens of times before. Now, as in the past, he turned a deaf ear. He was good to the scolding little woman reproaching him. He knew it; she knew it.

Downstairs, Belle Courteen began to smile. She returned to the library, delighted that her adored grandson would be at her side on this important evening.

At his second-story law offices on Royal Street, Edwin Fairmont waited. As he pulled from his waistcoat the gold pocket watch, he heard the distinctive step on the stairs. With a cold feeling in his belly, Edwin rose to stand behind his desk.

The door opened, and Hyde Rankin, dressed all in black, stepped in, the hideous, gargoyle-head cane in his right hand. The ferret-faced man smiled. "I hope I haven't kept you waiting," he said removing his black felt hat.

Edwin Fairmont ignored the pleasantry and pulled out the center drawer of his mahogany desk, from which he took a bank-note. "Take this and leave."

Hyde Rankin, an evil smile twisting his thin lips, said calmly, "I think not." Then he took a seat in one of the tall-backed chairs facing the desk. Crossing his legs, he dropped his hat on one knee and toyed with the vulgar cane, his fingers caressing the gold head with a kind of profane pleasure.

Feeling the icy fear closing around his heart, Edwin Fairmont said steadily, "What is it? What do you want?"

"Why, to visit a few moments," said Rankin.

"Take your money and get out!" Edwin thrust the bank-note across the desk, but Rankin made no move to take it.

"I understand your lovely daughter is seeing the Baxter lad." The color drained from Edwin Fairmont's round face. Hyde Rankin's evil smile broadened. "Friends tell me the handsome couple plan to wed. That must please you and the missus. The Baxters . . . why, they're real bluebloods, aren't they, Fairmont?"

"What in God's name do you want?"

"Why, the same thing you want. Your daughter's happiness."

Hating himself for begging, Edwin Fairmont, heart pounding now, pleaded, "Please . . . my God, please."

"God has nothing to do with it." Rankin rose and strolled about the well-furnished room. "I hold your daughter's happiness in my hands. Now, isn't that true?"

"Name your price," Edwin Fairmont said through clenched teeth.

"Twice that bank-note, Fairmont." Rankin walked back to the desk. "You see, you now have twice as much to lose. Your daughter has fallen in love with an aristocrat. How do you think the Baxters would react if I told them that — "

"Very well," Edwin Fairmont surrendered. Five minutes later Hyde Rankin, waving the valuable bank-note triumphantly, exited the office.

Pleased with the turn of events, Rankin stopped in at a small, out-of-the-way cabaret off Theater Street for a celebratory drink. Choosing a table against the wall, he placed his hat and gaudy cane on top of it and sipped a gin while his cold eyes took in the dimly lit room. It was hardly crowded. It was past the afternoon businessmen's rush and too early for the nightly patrons' arrival.

Two or three tables were filled, and a half-dozen gentlemen stood at the long polished bar. Rankin's attention was drawn to a table of laughing young men across the room. There were three of them. Two were rising, saying their good-byes. The third, a slim blond man, remained seated, shaking his head to their obvious invitations to leave with them.

After his companions had gone, the blond man's laughter quickly faded. He sighed and ran a hand through his thick, wavy hair. Then he turned his head and casually looked about. Momentarily his gaze came to rest on Hyde Rankin and his full lips stretched into a warm friendly smile.

Rankin's pulse quickened.

He downed the last of his gin and rose, moving directly toward the blond man's table, and said, "I'm Hyde Rankin. May I buy you a drink Mr . . . ah"

"Philip Neimyer." A pair of blue eyes lifted to Hyde Rankin's. "Sure. Sit down."

Hyde Rankin drew a deep breath, snapped his long fingers for fresh drinks, and took a seat across from the younger man.

An hour later a laughing Hyde Rankin stepped out into the cold March air as the carriage rolled to a stop before his Water Street lodgings on the riverfront.

Philip Neimyer, light hair blowing in the wind, was with him.

Edwin Fairmont shed his wrap and wearily climbed the carpeted stairs. Knocking lightly on the bedroom door, he put a smile on his face when his wife's sweet voice called for him to enter.

"Darling," he said and crossed to the bed where Serena lay. "How do you feel?"

"A bit better." She took her husband's hand, and he sat on the bed, facing her. "I'll be up and around in a couple of days."

"You do have more color." He lifted her hand and kissed it.

"You see, I told you it was only a cold. Nothing to worry about." She sighed. "I just hate it that we have to miss the Victory Ball. We promised the Baxters we'd — "

"The Baxters understand, Serena. Don't worry about that. I suppose Sylvain is already dressing for the affair."

Serena nodded. "She's been dressing for the past hour. She's so excited — " She paused, alarmed at his worried expression. "Edwin, what is it, dear? You look troubled."

"I wish I could keep my worries from you. I should spare you — "

"I don't want to be spared, you know that."

Edwin sighed heavily. He rose and paced around the four-poster, shaking his head wearily. "Rankin paid his call on me this afternoon." Serena sat up straighter, hand clutching her throat. "He doubled the amount he's been asking."

"Doubled! How could he? Surely you didn't — "

"Listen to me, Serena." Edwin came back to the bed. "The man knows of Sylvain's upcoming engagement. He as much as told me that unless . . . I had no choice. God! What are we going to do?" He looked so miserable his wife immediately started calming him.

"Oh, Edwin, my love, don't torture yourself this way." She reached for his hand and held it in both of hers. "Dear, it won't be too much longer. Randolph and Sylvain's engagement party is scheduled for next week.

A year from now they'll be married and then it will be easier."

Edwin looked at her quickly. "Darling, you don't really think that will end it, do you?"

She smiled at him and said, "Edwin, I'm aware that we're in financial trouble. We can't hold out forever. But don't you see that after Sylvain is safely married, we need not be social any longer. We can become happy hermits, you and I. Doesn't that sound enjoyable?"

"Dear, even after the children are married, the danger will not end. Surely you know — "

"Shhh." She put a finger to his lips, silencing him. "Edwin, I've had all the luxury a woman deserves in one lifetime. We'll live frugally, perhaps even move to another city and exist quietly away from our friends." He looked unconvinced. "And," she added breezily, "once Randolph and Sylvain are wed, there will be little the vile man can do to mar her happiness. Randolph *loves* her. He'll love her even more after a couple of years of marriage, after a child. Do you think for one moment it will make any difference if he finds out then? Let's have more faith in him than that. He's a fine boy, Edwin; you've said so many times."

"I have, I know." He tried to smile. "He is a good man, I'm sure of it. Perhaps you're right. All we need do is hold out a couple more years."

"That's all, Edwin. We can make it, can't we?"

"Yes, of course." Reluctant to tell even his trusted wife just how near financial ruin they were, Edwin Fairmont visibly brightened. "Now let's speak of something more pleasant. Shall I have dinner up here with you this evening?"

"I'd be honored if you would." She smiled and reached for the bed pull.

Dusk was falling when Randolph Baxter dashed into Oakgrove mansion. His startled father looked up when his son entered the high-ceilinged drawing room. Randolph swept off his heavy coat, revealing a burgundy dressing gown and silk pajamas.

"Son?" His father rose from his chair, his gaze assessing Randolph. "It's quite early yet. Still, don't you think it's time you were dressing?"

"Dad, I came to tell you I won't be dressing. I'm sick. I can't go with you to the Victory Ball."

Joan Baxter, Randolph's mother, descended the stairs at that moment. As she heard her only son announce he was ill, a worried expression clouded her face. She rushed forward, heart thumping in alarm.

"Randolph, darling," she sympathized, "what is it?" Tell Mother."

Randolph, hands thrust into the pockets of his fine robe, turned and smiled at her. "It's nothing serious. I'm coming down with a cold and I hardly think it would be fair to spread it about."

Already his mother's hand was clamped over his brow. "We'll all stay home. You can go upstairs and get right into your old bed. I'll have Winnie fix — "

Removing her hand from his forehead, Randolph kept the irritation from his voice. "Mother, you're terribly sweet, but that won't be necessary. I'm quite comfortable in the *garçonnière*. Besides, you must go. Sylvain is expecting us. We can't let her down."

"But, but — " Mrs. Baxter sputtered.

"The boy's right, Joan," Martin Baxter spoke up. "We're going."

Joan Baxter shot an angry glance at her husband, but did not contradict him.

Off the hook, Randolph said breezily, "Give my regrets and love to Sylvain. Tell her not to worry, I'll probably feel much better tomorrow."

As he turned to leave, his mother quickly caught his arm. "Darling, I'll stop by on our way out to see how you are."

"Don't you dare," he said, then caught himself. "What I mean, Mother, is that I plan to go right to sleep. I don't wish to be awakened."

"Very well," murmured Joan Baxter. Wistfully she watched her son go out into the chill night. She bit her lip and turned to her husband. "Do you think he'll be all right, Martin?"

"My God, Joan, he's a grown man. A little head cold never killed anyone."

Smiling broadly, a very robust Randolph Baxter crossed the huge terraced yard, slipped through the hedges and made his way along a stone footpath to his own *garçonnière*, nestled deep in the sheltering trees. He stepped inside, closed the door, and leaned back against it.

She came to him, eyes questioning.

"They believed me," he announced proudly.

"Then you'll stay here with me all night?" Ginger Thompson, flaming hair cascading down about her satin-clad shoulders, stepped up before him and pulled off his heavy overcoat.

"Yes, but this is the last time, Ginger. I mean it." He let the coat slide to the floor.

"You don't mean that, Randy," she said, stepping closer.

"I do. I've told you: I love Sylvain; I'm going to marry her."

Ginger pretended a nonchalance she didn't feel. Boldly untying the sash of his burgundy robe, she smiled up at him and murmured, "You love me, Randy. If you didn't, you wouldn't be here right now." Her fingers went to the flat pearl buttons of his pajama top. Deftly she flipped them open and Randolph's breath grew labored.

"You're wrong," he reminded her cruelly, just as he had dozens of times before. "I'm here because you feed a physical hunger. Sylvain is far too respectable to behave like you."

"Really?" she whispered and put the tip of her tongue out to lick her lips.

"Really," he echoed in a strained voice as she opened the top of his pajamas. She knew just what he enjoyed. She stroked his chest, arousing him with slow, sensuous touches. Her head was thrown back so that her hair fell down her back and her green eyes daringly locked with his.

When his blond head fell back against the door-frame and his chest began to heave, Ginger moved in for the kill. Her soft hands continued their caressing, and she whispered to him of all the forbidden things she was going to do to him on this cold March night. With each new, shocking promise, her voice dropped lower so that a highly excited Randolph strained to hear the crude words he'd never before heard from a woman. Hearing her utter such scandalous proposals was nearly as enjoyable as the carnal acts; more than once this uninhibited, wanton young woman had brought him to a rapid, wrenching climax with words alone.

Randolph was determined that would not happen now. He bit the inside of his lip and his head rolled to one side. "Ginger," he rasped, "please, please . . . "

Ever sensitive to his needs and desires, she murmured, "All right, my darling." She took a step backward. "Look at me, Randy."

He lifted his head and his eyes opened. Ginger slowly, very slowly, pushed the left side of her satin nightgown off her shoulder. The flowing sleeve hung loose, the gathered bodice rode low over her full, lush breasts. She repeated the action with the right side of the gown. Randolph waited. She made him wait, looking directly into his eyes.

When she saw the beads of perspiration forming on his upper lip, her hands went back to the satin. Languidly she lowered one side of the gown to reveal an alabaster, pink tipped breast. Randolph groaned, and Ginger released its twin, dropping the gown to her waist. She stepped into his arms and kissed him. His mouth was hungry, punishing, his hand cutting into the bare flesh of her back. Abruptly she pulled away.

Her eyes moved down over his body, and she smiled with satisfaction. The china silk of his pajama trousers stood out with his full arousal. She knew he couldn't hold out much longer. Hurriedly she stepped out of her gown and stood naked before him. Working quickly, she removed his pajamas, her hands following their descent to the carpeted floor. He dutifully lifted one foot at a time while she peeled the trousers from him. She rose.

"Lie down," she commanded.

Randolph stretched out on the floor. She knelt beside him. The stroking began once again. Knowledgeable, soft hands caressed the broad shoulders, muscled chest, flat belly, and long legs. She touched him everywhere but the one place he most longed to be touched. For that he would have to beg.

Shamelessly, he did so.

And when the experienced temptress had driven her lover almost over the edge, she quickly climbed astride him and leaned forward as he anxiously lifted his blond head from the floor. Greedily he kissed and sucked on her ripe, hard-tipped breasts while his hands kneaded the soft, rounded buttocks slapping against him.

While his elegantly dressed parents boarded a waiting carriage to go to the home of his betrothed, Randolph Baxter lay grunting on the floor, the flame-haired she-devil straddling him, taking him yet again to a sensual summit of carnal pleasure he could not get his fill of. And as the willful wanton guided him to ecstasy with her skillful body, she worked on his brain as well, murmuring, "You're mine, Randolph, only mine. You belong to me. You belong to me."

"Yes!" his voice as well as his body exploded with surrender. "Yours, I'm yours."

Chapter Eleven

Sylvain Fairmont, wearing only a lace-trimmed chemise, lay on her high feather bed planning the future on this cold March evening. And reminiscing. Her busy mind would speed ahead, then track back. Happiness was mixed with melancholy, expectation with regret.

Dreams of the happy years ahead as Randolph Baxter's wife brought a smile to her full, soft lips. Then memories of her glorious days as a child at her beloved Riverbend chased the smile away. She could see ahead: tranquil days at Oakgrove, the vast fifteen-thousand-acre cotton plantation at the western edge of the city.

A beautiful, gracious estate, Oakgrove reminded her of Riverbend. The huge white house was similar; Randolph's *garçonnière* was much like the two at Riverbend. Would she be as happy as she'd been at Riverbend?

Rosalie Delon's pretty face came unbidden to her mind's eye. A pain that was almost physical shot through her breast. How she missed her friend. How she needed her! She'd shared all of her secrets with Rosalie. She couldn't tell anyone else her most private thoughts.

Sylvain didn't dare tell anyone she missed Riverbend and New Orleans. She couldn't admit to anyone that Randolph's kisses were warm and pleasant but strangely brief and unemotional. Or that there were not as many of them as she wanted.

Sylvain closed her eyes and gritted her teeth as Randolph's stinging words echoed in her head. "Sylvain, darling, you are a high-born young lady. Please don't behave like a common . . . ah, like a girl with no breeding."

How hurt she'd been! And confused. All she'd done was kiss him the way she wanted him to kiss her. He'd acted as though she'd done something outrageous. She didn't understand. Baffled, she asked him, "Don't you want my kisses? Don't you find me appealing?"

"Darling, of course I do. I'm going to marry you, aren't I?"

"Yes, so I don't see why — "

"Sylvain, you're a lady. You must behave like one. After we're married, it'll be different. You'll see."

"Oh, Randolph, I can't wait, can you? Then you will hold me and kiss me and make love to — "

"Sylvain!"

"If you don't quit daydreamin', you is goin' to be late." Delilah came into the room and drew Sylvain back to the present.

Sylvain sat up and scooted off the bed. "I know." She smiled at her maid. "I was just thinking about how lovely this winter has been. The holidays with Randolph, and Mardi Gras, and how . . . well, next week — just seven more days until the engagement party!"

"Ummm, yes, child. I sure hope Miz Serena be feelin' better by then."

"Me, too. Now, help me dress. You're right, I must hurry. Randolph and his parents should be here shortly."

"Where you say ya'll goin' tonight?"

"To the Condé Hotel Victory Ball for the Texas rebels." Sylvain lifted her arms while Delilah eased the lilac velvet dress down over her head. "Daddy says those poor Texans need all the help they can get. A bunch of them are under siege right now in an old mission. Thousands of Mexicans are swarming in on them."

"My, my, you is pretty." Delilah smiled as she hooked Sylvain's new dress. The latest in fashion, its sleeves were smaller and tighter than the balloon sleeves that had been popular for the past several years. The bodice, too, was tightly fitted. Lined and boned, it hooked up the back, its neckline skimming Sylvain's smooth shoulders and dipping to deep V between her high, rounded breasts. The skirt was very full and just short enough to give an occasional glimpse of her square-toed slippers.

Sylvain's heavy sable-brown hair was parted in the middle and pulled flat over her well-shaped head. Long, shiny ringlets covered her ears and fell down her back. She had never looked more beautiful in her young life.

She checked herself in the gilt-trimmed mirror and said, "Know what I need to make everything perfect, Delilah?"

"Honey, you is about as perfect as you ever goin' to be in this world." She stood staring at her grown-up charge, wondering where the mischievous little girl had gone.

"Mother's emerald ring." Sylvain snapped her fingers in an unladylike manner. "I must wear that ring tonight!"

Sylvain was disappointed when the Baxters arrived with the news that Randolph was ill and would not be going to the ball, but her spirits rose rapidly as she neared the stately old hotel on Broad Street. A cortege of carriages had pulled up before the imposing four-story building.

Amazed by the size of the crowd, Sylvain found herself swept up a wide center staircase to the giant ballroom on the hotel's second floor. There in the banner-draped hall, lavish gowns and opulent jewels abounded. Elegantly turned-out gentlemen in fine evening wear waltzed with alluring ladies who displayed bare backs and shoulders.

Mobile's elite had gathered on this gala evening to raise money for the Texas rebellion. As Sylvain passed a wealthy silver-haired gentleman, she heard him say to his companions, "Why, only yesterday the *Mobile*

Examiner's headline declared, 'Texans under Siege at San Antonio de Bexar's Alamo.' "

There was champagne and music and gaiety. Happy faces were awash from the light of hundreds of candles burning brightly in the multitiered chandeliers.

The excitement was almost palpable. Sylvain was completely caught up in the merriment. Drifting away from the Baxters, she took her glass of punch and went to join a group of young ladies she had met at Miss Ellerby's Academy. They were disappointed that her handsome fiancé was not with her. She explained that he, too, was terribly disappointed but asked that she extend his warm greetings and remind them of the engagement party next week.

"Randolph says he . . . he . . . " Sylvain stopped talking as she became aware of a commotion. Abruptly the laughter and conversations subsided and a low, strange stir rippled through the crowd. Her classmates were no longer listening. Their eyes had strayed from her. Slowly she turned around.

Sylvain drew a sharp breath.

Framed in the open archway, a tall, cloaked gentleman removed his black top hat. He leaned down to help a tiny white-haired woman out of her fur-trimmed cape. With a graceful flourish he swept his silk-lined cloak from his shoulders and handed both wraps to a servant.

Sylvain recognized him immediately.

He stood there across the room, relaxed, elegant, and very handsome. His black swallow-tail coat was superbly tailored, straining across broad shoulders and draping perfectly to a trim waist. Matching dark trousers clung to his slim hips and long, well-shaped legs. The white dress shirt, with its small stiff collar, and his carefully tied white cravat, accentuated the dark handsomeness of his smoothly shaven face. His curly jet-black hair gleamed in the candlelight.

"Hilton Courteen!" Sylvain said under her breath and felt faint. He was even more handsome than she had remembered. She didn't doubt for a second the tales of his conquests.

There was not a single female present, young or old, plain or pretty, single or married, who was not achingly aware of his virile presence. Ladies a dozen times more worldly and sophisticated than Sylvain Fairmont could not keep their appreciative gazes off the notorious man whose escapades multiplied almost daily, who was reputed to be the consummate lover.

Hilton escorted his grandmother into the room, nodding and shaking hands with old acquaintances. His dark eyes languidly surveyed the crowd. His gaze reached Sylvain — and lingered. Hilton saw a breathtakingly beautiful young woman. She was much taller than her companions . . . and much lovelier. He continued to look at her and his heavy-lidded eyes widened. He recognized Sylvain.

She smiled prettily at him, and Hilton felt his stomach muscles tighten involuntarily. He slowly lowered his eyes and began to talk with his grandmother, but his thoughts were on the dark-haired, golden-skinned beauty across the room.

Sylvain caught his look of interest. Pleased and flattered, she hardly heard the fluttering young girls surrounding her. "That dreamy man looked at you, Sylvain! Do you know him? Is he a friend of Randolph's? Will you introduce us?"

"Hmmm?" she said, and began to plot. She was terribly attracted by Courteen's dark good looks and his air of easy command. But she vividly recalled how foolish he'd made her feel that summer day in New Orleans. He'd told her she was a child and that he should paddle her. Sylvain began to smile. And to plan.

I'm no child now, Mr. Hilton Courteen, she told him silently. *I'm a woman and you will have a difficult time denying it. Before this evening ends, my arrogant friend, you'll try to kiss me just as I wanted you to that day in New Orleans. You'll be dying to kiss me, Courteen, and I'll let you think you can. But when the time comes, I'll laugh in your face!*

"Sylvain, answer us." A short blonde tugged at her elbow.

"What? I'm sorry I — "

"Do you know that man?"

"Which man, Vivian?" Sylvain asked breezily.

Vivian sighed.

"Oh, dear Lord," whispered a chubby brunette, "he's coming our way."

Sylvain gulped and told her pounding heart to slow its pace. She tossed her curls and looked directly at the man striding purposefully toward her. Her fingers tightened on a half-filled glass of fruit punch.

As Hilton approached, he hoped no one, including the object of his attention, knew what he was thinking. He was bowled over by the young enchantress. That gold-hued skin, the shining dark hair! And she was tall! A tempting goddess rising above the encircling entourage of short, fresh-faced females. His eyes slid from her oval face to the fitted gown of lilac velvet. Its lines revealed a waist long and narrow and breasts high and full. His heated gaze rested on the swell of sweet bare bosom above the snug bodice, and his breath grew short. He yearned to press hot kisses to the smooth slope of her long, elegant neck.

His eyes met hers.

"Miss Fairmont."

"Mr. Courteen."

"I hardly recognized you, Sylvain," he said softly, and Sylvain felt a shiver run through her when she heard the smooth baritone voice that suited him so well.

"It's been a long time since New Orleans, Mr. Courteen," she managed, smiling at him.

"Much too long," he responded as he took the glass from her stiff fingers and set it on a passing waiter's tray. "May I?" He inclined his dark head toward the dance floor and offered her his arm.

"I'd enjoy a dance," she said and laid her hand on his sleeve.

She cast a triumphant glance at the gaping girls around them and walked regally to the floor, hoping her knees would not buckle.

Hilton Courteen took her in his arms and masterfully led her around the polished floor, displaying an ease and grace rarely seen in a man so tall.

Sylvain was woman enough now to recognize the light in Hilton's dark eyes. There was no mistaking his interest. He no longer thought of her as a child. This was going to be easy. In half an hour she'd have him trying to kiss her.

She smiled fetchingly up at him and let her eyes go to the white scar slicing through his dark left eyebrow. Saucily she said, "Oh, dear, Mr. Courteen."

"Call me Hilton, sweetheart. What is it?"

"Your eyebrow. You've a scar from that day you saved me on the waterfront in New Orleans." She wet her lips and waited for him to make some flattering reply like: *You've left your mark on me, Miss Fairmont*, or perhaps *I cherish the scar; it reminds me of you*. That's what Randolph would surely say. Or Billy Greylord or Jake Robards. Or even Tommy Mason or any one of a dozen young gentlemen who'd paid her court.

Hilton shrugged lightly. "I've got lots of scars." He smiled lazily and idly toyed with her emerald ring.

Fighting to hide her irritation, Sylvain asked, "Is this affair important to you because you are concerned with the Texans, Mr. Cour . . . Hilton?"

The smile left his full, sensuous lips. "Yes." His thoughts flashed to his friend, Cot Campbell, who was fighting for his life at the Alamo.

Puzzled, she said, "I, too, came because I wish to help the Texans."

The smile crept back to his lips. "Your parents are here with you?"

"No, my mother is ill and . . . "

Hilton took a deep breath. He was gloriously engulfed in lilac velvet and frilly petticoats and jasmine perfume and sweet, girlish conversation.

The handsome couple danced as one and looked only at each other. Sylvain chattered incessantly while a tolerant, enchanted Hilton nodded and smiled and let her abundant, uninhibited charm take a firm, stubborn hold on his heart.

"The weather shouldn't be this cold in March, do you think? . . . We moved to a town house on Dauphin Street . . . Daddy's law practice is most profitable, naturally . . . still miss Riverbend so much I could cry . . . What? . . . No, no, I never found the treasure, but I will one day . . . " On and on she rambled gaily, bent on charming this tall, exciting man. And for that reason, the one subject she failed to mention was Randolph Baxter and the fact that she was soon to be engaged.

Hilton spoke little, but his dark, smoldering eyes were communicating with her in a way that made her feel hot and dizzy and wonderful all at once. She felt gloriously giddy and was certain that when the song ended, he'd demand that she remain in his arms.

But all he said was "Thank you, Sylvain," and led her back to her circle of friends. "It was pleasant seeing you again."

Before she could protest, the dark, mysterious man was drifting back through the crowd, away from her. She watched, furious, when he took a gorgeous, willowy blonde in his arms. His dark face was pressed close to the creamy cheek of the smiling, deliriously happy woman, and Sylvain Fairmont wanted to die.

The party progressed. Hilton Courteen did not come back for a second dance. He did, however, seem to be watching her. More than once Sylvain looked up and caught his intense gaze on her.

Excusing herself from her friends, she made her way around the floor. She passed directly in front of Hilton Courteen and a small knot of gentlemen engaged in conversation beside a drink trolley. She looked pointedly at him, then hurried on. She ducked behind a row of potted palms, glanced nervously behind her, and rushed to the tall French doors. She opened one and stepped out onto the cold, deserted balcony.

Sylvain inhaled the frigid air, rubbed her cold arms, and walked to the railing. She clasped the smooth, cold iron and looked out over the brightly lit city. And she wished she'd had enough gumption to wear a coat. It was freezing outside!

What if he hadn't seen her go out? What if he'd seen her and decided not to follow her? What if she stood out here in the cold all night alone and . . . Sylvain heard the door directly behind her open, sounds of the orchestra growing louder for a second, then subsiding as the door closed. Not daring to breathe, she clutched the railing more tightly and prayed it was he.

"A little chilly to be out without a wrap, isn't it, sweetheart?" His deep, sure voice sent a thrill through her. Brown hands wrapped themselves around the railing on either side of hers. Sylvain could feel the heat emanating from his body and knew he was standing behind her, very, very close.

To her horror she found she was speechless. She tried to speak but her throat was tight and aching. She couldn't even get out his name.

"Sweetheart, turn around." His warm breath ruffled her hair.

Slowly Sylvain turned. Hilton Courteen didn't move back. He continued to stand where he was, hands on the railing, his long arms enclosing her. He smiled down at her and said, "You're far too lovely to freeze." With that he unbuttoned his dark tailcoat and drew her hands inside. "Put your arms around me, Sylvain." Wordlessly, she obeyed. She put her palms on his trim waist and smiled when he drew his coat over her bare shoulders and locked his hands behind her.

"Still cold?" he inquired softly, his dark eyes holding hers prisoner.

Her feet were icy, but her cheeks felt feverish. "A little," she murmured and winced when he pulled her even closer.

For what seemed an endless time he stood holding her against his hard, tall body. There was a promise of security in his strength — and a threat of danger in his dark eyes. Sylvain suddenly realized her hands were eagerly exploring his smooth, warm back and that his were moving insistently over her waist and hips, pressing her to him.

Their eyes were locked, and she knew the moment had arrived: He was going to kiss her, she was sure of it. Hilton leaned toward her, and his hand came to the crown of her head. She caught her breath. She feared his kiss, yet didn't move. She stared at him, fascinated by his dark, brooding gaze.

"Sylvain," he said, "why do you fear me?"

"I . . . I don't," she murmured and feared him more than she'd ever feared a man. Feared his masculinity. His devil-may-care attitude. His wildness. His fire. His passion. Was afraid if she surrendered to him, she'd be consumed by the blazing flames of temptation.

"You need never fear me, sweetheart," he murmured in that soft-tongued southern voice, and covered her parted lips with his own.

All Sylvain's well-laid plans were forgotten. The thought of turning her head at the last moment never occurred to her. A tiny gurgle of fear and wonder came from her but was swallowed into the hot commanding mouth of Hilton Courteen.

Sylvain was dazed by some unfamiliar desires, a hot yearning so alien to her she wasn't sure what she yearned for. She knew only that she was drugged by this man's deep kiss. His lips were masterful and persuasive. His tongue was doing strange and wonderful things to the inside of her soft, fleshy lower lip. In a possession so complete he left not one sensitive area of her mouth unclaimed, he kissed her long and ardently.

Hilton felt her surrender, total and girlishly sweet. She held on to him and opened her mouth to his kiss, eagerly letting him explore the sweetness behind her teeth. Her small hands clung to his back, and he thrilled to the almost painful raking of his flesh as she became completely uninhibited in her passion.

Sylvain gradually realized their burning mouths were not the only parts of their bodies involved in the fiery kiss. Hilton's lean, masterful hands were sweeping over her back and waist and hips, pressing her close to his tall, trembling body. She could feel her swelling, aching breasts being crushed against the flat, hard muscles of his chest. And through the folds of her full lilac skirts, his hard, sinewy thighs were pressing hers.

Swept away on a tide of emotion she'd never felt before, Sylvain experienced startling, strange sensations she couldn't put words to. But she didn't want to; she wanted only to feel, to live, to melt, to remain in this magnificent man's arms for eternity.

Hilton was just as intoxicated. They kissed through several breaths before he finally dragged his mouth from hers. They both gasped for air, shifted their bodies to new positions, murmured unintelligible words of endearment, and kissed once more. Their eager lips finally parted. Hilton buried his face in the mass of dark glossy curls, chuckled happily, and said, "Sweetheart, let's leave this party. I want to take you someplace where we can be alone."

Sylvain, her cheek pressed to his chest, his thundering heartbeat filling her ear, squeezed her eyes shut and felt

like weeping. Reality came marching back, and she became painfully cognizant of where she was, and with whom.

Hilton slowly lifted his head. She couldn't look at him. He put a warm hand to her chin and tilted her face up to his. She blinked at him in the silvery moonlight and felt the full measure of her guilt weigh down on her sagging shoulders, turning her passion to punishment.

"Sweetheart," he said softly, "what is it?"

Sylvain bit her trembling lip and looked up into those beautiful black eyes. "Mr. Courteen, I can't, I . . . "

"Why, darling? What is it?"

Looking straight into his eyes, she said falteringly, "I am to be engaged next week. I'm in love with another." She dared not breathe.

Coolly, Hilton nodded. He released her, freeing her arms from inside his coat. He took a step backward. "I see. And who is the lucky man?"

Sylvain's eyes drifted down to his dark throat. "Randolph Baxter. Of the Mississippi Baxters."

"My congratulations to Mr. Baxter and my best wishes for happiness to you."

"Thank you." She hugged herself and asked nervously, "Do you know Randolph?"

"I've not had the pleasure." Silence fell between them and Sylvain felt she would surely scream if he didn't stop being so kind. She found herself wishing he'd scold her as though she were a naughty child, as he'd done that day in New Orleans. She could take that better than this cool, dignified acceptance.

"You must think me terrible." She was ready for her lecture.

"Not at all," he corrected and his lips turned up into a smile. "After all, you came out here to be alone. I followed and took advantage of you." His mocking grin told her he was on to her.

"That's not exactly the way it was."

"No, Sylvain, it wasn't. You drew me out in the moonlight. But tell me, sweet, why? To prove you could do it? You proved it. I came, I kissed you. Is the test completed now?"

Sylvain hung her head. "It wasn't a test. It was . . ." She sighed wearily and lifted her head. "You made me feel like a fool that day in New Orleans and I . . . I — "

"You wanted to pay me back?"

"Yes."

Hilton laughed, teeth flashing starkly white against his swarthy face. "It might have started out that way, but it became more, didn't it?" His piercing gaze dared her to deny it.

"Yes, it . . . Do you think my behavior shocking?"

"Sweetheart, I think you're a lot like me. You see something you want and you reach out for it. I don't think that's so bad."

"But I'm engaged . . . I love Randolph."

"I know you do."

"Then how could I . . . that is . . . "

"I'm afraid, my dear Sylvain, that what just happened between us had little to do with love and marriage."

"I feel so guilty. I led you on. I let you think I . . . I'm terribly ashamed."

Hilton smiled at her, that dreamy, endearing smile that tore at her already aching heart. "Sylvain, you're so much woman, so warm and giving. And such a dazzling charmer. It's most appealing. Don't ever change."

"How can you say that? I was shameful, you should hate me."

"I could never do that, darlin'," he drawled and touched her cheek. "But I'll tell you something. Unless you want the gentry of Mobile gossiping about you, you'd better get back indoors."

"What about you? They'll talk about you, too."

Hilton threw back his dark head and laughed. "Sweetheart, I'd be dead if they didn't. Now, go."

"Yes, sir." She nodded and backed away. She'd almost reached the tall French doors, when she stopped. "Hilton?"

"No, Sylvain, I won't tell anyone about this."

"Thanks," she said sheepishly,

Hilton smiled warmly and said, "But I'll tell you something, sweetheart." His voice was warm, gentle.

"What, Hilton?"

"Always kiss Randolph Baxter of the Mississippi Baxters the way you kissed me and he'll be a happy man."

Chapter Twelve

"Oh!" Sylvain whirled and hurried back inside.

Hilton chuckled and watched her flounce away. And when she'd disappeared, he groaned with relief.

He was glad she was engaged, glad she was to marry another. Girls like Sylvain Fairmont spelled trouble. A beautiful young virgin eager for love was hardly the kind of companion to make a man's life pleasant. He wanted no part of her.

Hilton lit a cigar and stood at the railing. He looked out over the twinkling lights of Mobile, but he saw only a dazzling oval face framed with shimmering dark curls. He heard a sweet, childlike voice whispering his name in abandon, and tasted honeyed lips eagerly seeking his. He felt soft, female curves pressing insistently against his body.

Hilton shook his dark head and tossed away the half-smoked cigar. Yes, he was damned glad the charmingly bold Sylvain Fairmont was engaged. His advice to her young man would be to marry the girl as quickly as possible. There was a lot of fire and passion just waiting to be tapped, and if she went about kissing men the way she'd just kissed him, some unsuspecting fellow was going to take her to bed. Hilton shivered, and his long legs felt weak. He had the distinct feeling that one night in bed with Sylvain would be the most disastrous thing that ever happened to a man.

Sylvain, cheeks flushed with anger and remorse, sidled back into the crowded ballroom, looking warily about for the Baxters. Had they missed her? Had anyone seen her leave? Did the entire room know she'd been out in the cold moonlight behaving like a low woman of the streets?

Hands nervously smoothing her tousled curls, she made her way back to her prospective in-laws feeling miserable and guilty. Their warm reception added to her shame.

"There you are, Sylvain." Martin Baxter turned and drew her into his outstretched arm. "Are you having a good time?"

"Why, yes, lovely." She smiled at him.

"Where have you been, dear?" Joan Baxter asked pleasantly.

"I've been with my friends from Miss Ellerby's," she said evenly and hoped lightning wouldn't strike her dead.

"Oh." Joan smiled and tucked a wayward curl behind Sylvain's ear. "Who was that handsome gentleman you danced with earlier?"

Sylvain's throat tightened. "That was Hilton Courteen. I've known him since I was a little girl."

"I see. Well, we'd best not tell Randy. He'd be very jealous."

Sylvain reddened. "That's flattering, but Randolph has no reason to be jealous."

"I was teasing you, Sylvain." Joan Baxter laughed gaily. "Darling, why don't you dance with Sylvain?" She looked at her husband.

"I'd love to," said Martin Baxter and led Sylvain onto the floor.

Martin Baxter talked the entire time he spun Sylvain about, but she heard little of what he said. She nodded and murmured yes or no at the appropriate times, but her thoughts remained on the cold hotel balcony where moments before she'd stood warmly in Hilton Courteen's embrace.

Hating herself for her disgraceful behavior, Sylvain relived the passionate encounter on the porch. She saw again a pair of black, brooding eyes, heard a deep, warm voice speaking her name, felt incredibly hot lips moving forcefully on hers while male hands roamed provocatively over her body.

" . . . and then in a year or so you'll present me with my first grandchild. Won't that be wonderful?" Martin Baxter was waiting for an answer.

"Yes," Sylvain managed. "Wonderful."

Sylvain tried very hard to keep her eyes off Hilton Courteen for the rest of the evening, but she had little success. She was all too aware of the moment he reappeared in the room. And when, a half-hour later, a bewhiskered gentleman stepped up on the dais and gave a short speech calling for money to arm the Texas rebels, Sylvain couldn't help noticing that Hilton dropped only a few bills into the top hat, no more than any of the other well-heeled gentlemen had given.

She was glad. She told herself he was not very generous. He'd admitted his very best friend was under siege in Texas, yet he apparently cared so little he gave only a minimum amount of money to the cause. Already she admired him less. He was a selfish, hedonistic man, caring only for his own comfort. That's why he'd kissed her as he did. He was not a gentleman like her Randolph. Randolph never kissed her that way; he had far too much respect for her. Mr. Hilton Courteen had no principles, and all the gossip about him was undoubtedly true. Thank the good Lord above she loved a decent man like Randolph Baxter. Pity any woman who cared for the heartless, disrespectful Hilton Courteen.

No sooner had the collection been taken than Hilton Courteen escorted the small white-haired lady to the door. They donned their wraps and departed. Sylvain

154

sighed with relief — and wondered why she soon felt restless and bored.

More than an hour passed before Martin Baxter said, "Ladies, it's getting late. Shall we go?"

Sylvain was quick to agree.

"Night, darling'," Hilton said when he escorted his aging grandmother inside her home.

"Good night?" She shot him a furious look. "Where do you think you're going, young man? It's past midnight."

"I'm over twenty-one, Belle."

"Hilton, you only slept a couple of hours. Surely you need to go to bed."

"I'm not tired, I'm restless."

Belle clicked her tongue. "You are always restless. When are you going to find a nice girl and settle down?"

"I'll see you tomorrow." He tipped his hat and went back to the carriage. "Thomas, take me to the Paradise Club on Water Street."

"Oh, Mr. Hilton, that be mighty rowdy place, they tell me."

Hilton chuckled and settled back on the seat. "I'll watch my step, Thomas. I'm just going to play a few hands of poker."

"Yessuh." The driver nodded and spoke to the horses.

At four o'clock the next morning, Hilton sat in a smoke-filled room at a card table covered with green baize. His evening coat had long since been discarded, the white cravat untied, shirt unbuttoned, sleeves rolled up over dark, muscular forearms. Hilton's white teeth clamped down on his cigar. Blue smoke curled up into his narrowed black eyes. Dark stubble covered his jaw.

Hilton slowly fanned out the five cards he'd been dealt. A quick look and he pressed them back together, his face expressionless. He drew no cards. The man on his left, a

Mobile cotton planter, drew two. The three other players drew three cards each.

On the next round of betting, the Mobile planter raised $500. Hilton saw him and raised $1,000. The remaining players dropped out, and the planter called Hilton's raise. He then fanned out his cards. A full house, aces high.

Hilton smiled and shoved his cards to the center, face down.

"Take it down," he said and watched as the smiling planter drew the large pot to him. It had been that way all night. Hilton couldn't win a pot. He'd had second-best hands all evening, like the king high full house he'd just shoved to the stack.

He rubbed the back of his neck, snuffed out his cigar, and waited for his next hand. The door of the small gambling house burst open, and an excited river man hurried in. A sleek schooner had just pulled into port with the word.

The Alamo had fallen! All the valiant defenders had perished.

Hilton felt the harsh blow in the pit of his stomach. He said nothing. He shoved a fresh cigar between his tight lips. Then he reached into his wallet and drew out the neatly folded note Cot Campbell had sent him months before. Holding it between two fingers, Hilton put it into the candle's flame. When the paper blazed, Hilton lit his cigar with it. He dropped the burning paper into a crystal ashtray at his elbow and watched through heavy eyelids while it curled into blackened ash.

He coolly picked up his cards and opened the betting.

He was no longer a wealthy man. Cot Campbell had not been a part of the provisional government of Texas. Hilton's fortune had died at the Alamo with his friend.

Sylvain tossed and turned in her bed. Plagued by guilt and shame, she found that sleep eluded her. She tried to shake off her melancholy by promising herself she'd be

156

extra kind and attentive to Randolph the next time they
were together.

It helped little. Certain she was bad, she feared the
Almighty would punish her for her sins. Face flaming in
the darkness, she agonized, feeling she'd let her parents
down as well as Randolph. Tears slipped down her hot
cheeks. Her beautiful, refined mother would never, ever
have behaved so wantonly.

Sylvain prayed an extra time that cold night. She
asked for forgiveness and understanding and promised
she'd never again behave so badly. "Please, God," she
entreated, "if you'll just overlook this one terrible trans-
gression, I vow I'll be a good girl for the rest of my life.
I'll be a true and faithful mate to my kind, beloved
Randolph, and I'll never again even look at a rogue like
Hilton Courteen."

She sighed and felt a bit better. Cleansed. More relaxed. Sleepy. But as she drifted off toward the peaceful
release of much-needed slumber, Sylvain squirmed and
stretched and trembled with the wicked awakening of
her burning body.

"Courteen! Let me go!" she murmured and drew her
knees up to her chest.

A week had passed since the gala at the Condé Hotel.
Hilton Courteen was back in New Orleans. He entered
his Richardson Hotel suite just at sundown. He'd spent
the last twenty-four hours at the card tables.

Once again he'd lost.

Hilton picked up a stack of letters from the marble-
topped table in the sitting room. Bored, he rifled through
them until bold, familiar handwriting caught his eye. He
dropped the remaining mail back to the table. The long
white envelope in his hand, Hilton sat down in the brown
velvet wing chair by the window.

The last red rays of the dying sun streamed in through
the parted drapes as Hilton tore open the envelope and

lifted the letter dated March 5, 1836, in hands that had begun to tremble:

> Hill old friend,
>
> There's a lull in the Mexican bombardment at the moment. Everyone's writing to loved ones. Isn't it a damned shame I don't have anyone but you to write?
>
> God, I'm sorry about your money, Hill. I've left you a poor man and I'll not live to make it up to you. Can you ever forgive me?
>
> Our messenger is ready to depart. Just as well... my hand is shaking so badly I can hardly write. I'm scared, Hill. I'm going to die and I'm terrified.
>
> I love you, my friend, and if you care for me, please never tell our West Point classmates that old Cot Campbell died a coward.
>
> Good-bye
> Cot

Hilton slowly lowered the letter. The sun had slipped below the horizon, and the spacious room had become shadowy and dim. No fire burned in the grate and it had grown uncomfortably chilly.

Hilton made no move to light the lamps or start a fire. He sat alone in the gathering dusk while memories of the laughing, good-natured Cot Campbell filled his thoughts. Now Cot was dead. A hero's death at the Alamo. His body had been lifted onto the flashing sabers of the victorious Mexicans, tossed onto kindling wood in the town square, and burned along with those of his comrades.

Hilton slowly leaned forward. Elbows resting on his knees, he put his face in his hands. And for the first time since he was a little boy, Hilton Courteen cried.

On that same evening a radiant Sylvain Fairmont officially became engaged to Randolph Baxter. Sylvain and

Randolph lifted champagne glasses in a toast at precisely midnight and kissed happily while everyone applauded. The pretty pair stood in the drawing room of the Fairmont town house and accepted hugs and kisses from over one hundred well-wishers.

The long dining table groaned under a buffet of smoked meats and salmon, shrimp and chicken salad, roast tenderloin, lobster medallions, boiled crab, fruit salads, and cheeses. Fine wines and imported champagne flowed freely. People milled through the rooms talking, laughing, and commenting on what a perfect couple the young pair made.

Serena Fairmont, though still quite weak from her recent illness, managed a couple of hours' celebrating with their guests. Sylvain saw in her mother's lovely blue eyes just how happy Serena was that her daughter was going to be the wife of Randolph Baxter.

Sylvain clung tightly to Randolph's arm. This was good. This was right. Their families were delighted and she was, too. She and Randolph would have a long happy life together and lots of blond children to love. And as the years went by, they'd be closer than ever.

Hilton Courteen's dark visage flitted through her mind, but Sylvain quickly dismissed him. What she'd felt in his arms was low and vulgar. A physical hunger that, as he had pointed out, had little to do with love and marriage. She didn't need or want that kind of relationship. She wanted only her handsome Randolph, a man who was upright and kind, who loved her and her alone and was going to make her his bride. It was in his arms she wished to lie each night, his lovemaking she craved.

Sylvain was a happy young woman.

But Sylvain frowned when, after all the guests had finally said their good-nights and departed, Randolph announced it was time he, too, left.

Lifting her eyes from her sparkling diamond engagement ring, she protested hotly, "Randolph, no!"

"But, Sylvain, it's after two o'clock in the morning! My parents left an hour ago."

"Yes," she nodded, "and mine are in bed. We're alone at last, darling. Can't you stay for a while?" She smiled prettily and brought her hand up to his jaw.

"Sylvain, soon we'll be married and . . . "

"I know. Won't it be wonderful?"

"Yes, it will. But until then, dearest, I must go."

Sylvain sighed. "I suppose you're right. I love you, Randolph." She leaned toward him and pressed her lips to his.

Randolph kissed her, murmured "I love you too," and pulled her to her feet. "Walk me to the door."

Arm in arm they strolled to the corridor, and when Randolph had donned his coat, Sylvain threw her arms around his neck and whispered, "Darling, kiss me the way you'll kiss me when we're married."

Randolph laughed. But he pulled her to him and kissed her hungrily. When finally their lips parted he was breathing heavily and his green eyes were glazed. "Good night," he breathed and hurried out the door.

Sylvain stood where he'd left her. She smiled, pressed her hands to her cheeks, and flew up the stairs, happy, hopeful, in love.

Randolph stepped into his darkened *garçonnière* at Oakgrove. He tossed his coat to the rack and walked into the parlor. Bright moonlight streamed into the room.

Something moved.

"Who's there?" he said, alarmed.

She stepped into the silvery light.

"Ginger!"

"Yes, love," she said and came to him. She was naked in the moonlight, her pale body gleaming, her long red

160

hair spilling about her shoulders, a shiny lock curling seductively over her right breast.

"Dammit, Ginger you can't stay here. You've got to leave."

Undaunted, she swayed to him. His eyes went to the bouncing breasts, the flat stomach, the shapely thighs with that thick triangle of auburn hair between them. "Oh, God," he moaned.

She laughed, a deep, husky laugh. Draping her arms around his neck, she nuzzled his throat and murmured, "Let me stay for an hour, Randy."

"No, absolutely not."

"Five minutes?" she breathed and bit him playfully.

"Ginger, I'm telling you for the last time, I'm in love with Sylvain Fairmont."

"Ummm." She smiled and her hands went to the waistband of his trousers. He stood rigid and unmoving while the brazen girl unbuttoned his breeches and pushed them to the floor. Her hands playing over his trembling thighs and her eyes looking into his, she slowly slid to her knees before him. "Tell me, Randy," she breathed, leaning to him, "does your sweet little Sylvain do this for you?"

"Yes, it would. Besides, where have you got to go?"
She was beginning to pout prettily.

Hilton scratched his jaw and looked at her. She'd
innocently asked a question that pricked him. Where *did*
he have to go? Where was he needed? What did he do
that made any difference?

"I think," he said thoughtfully, "I'll do the only thing
I'm trained to do."

"And what's that?"

"I'm going to join the United States Army. Perhaps
they need me."

"I doubt it," she said petulantly.

"Me, too." Hilton grinned. "But I intend to find out."

Sylvain recognized Dr. Talbot's carriage parked in front
of the town house. She felt an icy chill of fear, despite the
warmness of the humid August day.

"Delilah," she said, turning to the black woman,
"Mother is worse."

Delilah, almost lost in a sea of boxes and packages,
reached over and took Sylvain's cold hand. "Don't go
jumpin' to conclusions. He come by to check on her all
the time. Don't mean she's feelin' bad."

Sylvain gripped the strong black hand. "I know, but
she wasn't feeling well this morning. That's why she
couldn't go shopping with us. She looked pale, and I'm
afraid ... "

Her words trailed away and Sylvain bit the inside of
her cheek. Delson had barely stopped the coach before
Sylvain was out and running toward the house. Delson
and Delilah gathered up the many packages and followed the worried girl inside.

Nana, the cook, stood in the foyer, wringing her hands
and crying. "I done sent Theo to fetch Mr. Fairmont. He
be here 'fore we knows it."

Sylvain gave no reply. She bounded up the stairs, her
heart hammering in her breast. She stood outside her

mother's closed door. Commanding her body to stop its trembling, Sylvain balled her cold hands into tight fists at her sides and listened through the door.

She heard the kindly doctor's gravelly voice. "Now, Mrs. Fairmont, I warned you about overexerting. You're not strong. You must spend more time in your bed."

"Doctor, I have one child. Sylvain is the most precious thing on earth to me. She's to be married in less than a year, and I'm going to see to it she's married in grand style. There's so much that must be done."

"Uh-huh," Dr. Talbot mumbled. "Well, you'd better let someone else do it for you if you want to around to see your only daughter walk down the aisle."

Sylvain squeezed her eyes shut and felt she might faint. Quickly she collected herself and softly knocked on the door.

"Come in," Dr. Talbot called.

Sylvain put a bright smile on her face and walked into the room. "Mother," she said, rushing to the bed and taking her mother's frail hand, "I'm sorry you're not feeling well. I'll bet Doc Talbot can fix you right up, though." She smiled and glanced at the stooped, white-haired physician.

"No, I can't," the stubborn old man snapped. "You can, though, young lady. You and your daddy."

"Just tell me what do to, Dr. Talbot."

"Pay him no mind, darling," Serena said calmly and brought Sylvain's hand up to her lips.

"Missy, you are causing too much of a stir around here," the doctor said gruffly. "Oh, sure, I know, you're engaged to be married, but you're not the first young lady in Mobile ever to walk down the aisle."

Fighting desperately to keep her voice even, Sylvain pleaded, "Tell me what I must do, Dr. Talbot!"

"Let your mother rest and relax. She can't go rushing about town shopping for fancy gowns for all your foolish parties and soirees. She tells me the two of you are supposed to take a packet to New Orleans this autumn so you can buy your trousseau."

Sylvain nodded guiltily.

"Well, you mother can't go!" Dr. Talbot shook his white head. "She's not able, and if you ask me, it's tomfoolery anyhow. Don't we have shops here in Mobile good enough for you, young lady?"

"No, we do not," Serena answered for her distraught daughter. "For over a year we've had our hearts set on buying her clothes in New Orleans, and we intend to do just that." She winked at Sylvain.

The doctor snorted. "Fine. Fine. Buy everything in New Orleans, but you, my dear Mrs. Fairmont, will not be there to do the picking. Sylvain will have to find someone else to go with her."

"Mother, I don't need to go to New Orleans. We can . . . "

"Shhh, darling." Serena smiled. "Your trousseau is coming from New Orleans."

Serena Fairmont remained unwell through the remainder of the hot, humid summer. She tried valiantly to hide her condition, but Sylvain and Edwin Fairmont both saw in her clear blue eyes a look of weariness that never seemed to leave.

Nonetheless, in October, Serena announced to her worried husband that she would escort their lovely daughter to New Orleans to buy her wedding dress and all the clothes she would need for an extended honeymoon. Edwin begged her not to go, promising that as soon as he was not quite so busy at the law office, he'd take Sylvain to New Orleans.

Serena touched her husband's cheek. "Darling Edwin," she said in her soft voice, "don't you understand this is not something that occurs every year? We have but one daughter. She'll be married but one time. Please, my love, say I may go. You'll never know how much this means to me."

Edwin brought her hand to his lips and kissed it. "My dear, I can refuse you nothing, but you know how worried I am . . ."

"After she's married, Edwin, I promise I'll spend my days resting." She laughed then, a warm, tinkling sound that filled Edwin Fairmont with pleasure, just as it always had. "Any time you look for me, they'll tell you, 'The lazy scamp is in her bed.'"

"Go, then, darling, but take Delilah along, and promise me you'll not overdo."

Serena kissed her husband soundly. "I promise."

The October weather had been crisp and clear and the visit to New Orleans was nearly perfect. Sylvain ordered her wedding dress; the modiste promised it would be completed and sent to Mobile well in advance of the June wedding date.

Sylvain, Serena, and Delilah spent wonderful hours picking traveling dresses, afternoon frocks, ball gowns, frilly, frothy underwear and nightgowns, bonnets and parasols and shoes. They visited the most exclusive shops in the Quarter and chose the finest, most costly apparel, Serena happily telling her daughter she was not to worry about money. "After all — "

"I know," laughed Sylvain, "a girl marries only once!"

"Exactly."

It was not until the day before they were to leave New Orleans that it happened. It was early afternoon. Sylvain and her mother had enjoyed a splendid lunch at the Café des Améliorations on the corner of Rampart and Toulouse. Sylvain's eyes widened when the dark-skinned waiter brought her the delicious-looking aperitif. Serena Fairmont laughed softly.

"Mother," Sylvain trilled excitedly, "my very first cordial! Thank you so much."

Serena Fairmont's gentle laughter rose above the din of male voices surrounding them, and her blue eyes shone with that inner light that often appeared when she gazed fondly at her spirited child.

"Enjoy, darling.' Serena sipped black coffee. "I shall never forget the first aperitif I tasted. I was just about your age."

"Really, Mother?" Sylvain drank, licked her lips, and nodded her approval. "Tell me about it? Where were you?"

Serena's voice was soft. "I was right here in the Vieux Carré, darling. Edwin had taken me to the Theatre d'Orleans to see a musical comedy. Afterward, we stopped at a little café for a midnight supper." She paused, reflecting. "It was my eighteenth birthday."

"Mother! That's so romantic. I'll bet you looked beautiful. Did you have a wonderful time?"

Serena again laughed and reached for her daughter's hand. Lacing her frail white fingers through Sylvain's long, golden ones, she confessed, "I did, darling, but to tell you the truth, I was torn. Your father wanted me to stay in the city for the night at a hotel."

"Surely you said yes."

"I told you, I was torn." She squeezed the strong young fingers. "You see, it was the first time I'd ever been away from you."

"Oh, Mother, don't tell me you . . . "

Serena was nodding. "I made him take me home to Riverbend. I couldn't abide the thought of being away from my infant daughter even for one night."

Sylvain made a face. "I'm not like you, Mother. When Randolph wants me to spend the night in a hotel, I'll do it. I don't care if we have six babies at home." She quickly blushed, realizing what she'd just said.

To her relief, Serena laughed heartily. "Darling, you're absolutely right. I should have stayed in the city with your daddy." She smiled and added, "When we got to Riverbend that night, you were fast asleep in your crib and never knew I was there." Serena paused, smiling wistfully, "I sat and watched you sleep. You were beautiful, so beautiful." Her blue eyes took on a distant, serene expression.

"Mother, speaking of Riverbend, why don't we go out there this afternoon?"

Her mother's gaze swiftly locked on Sylvain's, and a tightness appeared about her soft mouth. "Sylvain, what a foolish — "

"But it isn't! I miss Riverbend so much, and I know very well you do too. We could call on Mr. Rankin and . . . "

Serena's breath grew short. "Certainly not!"

"Don't say no, Mother. I understand Mr. Rankin is married now and that . . . "

Serena interrupted sharply. "Just where did you hear that? Why would you be talking about Mr. Hyde Rankin? I can't believe he would get married."

"Why not? Mother, why are you getting excited?" Sylvain shook her dark head. "One of my friends at Miss Ellerby's has an aunt who lives in New Orleans. She told Virginia that Mr. Rankin married a plain-looking woman who moved to New Orleans from North Carolina."

"It makes no difference. We certainly will not visit Mr. Rankin." Serena's blue eyes flashed.

Sylvain stared at her mother. "Mother, for as long as I can remember, you've become angry when I mention Mr. Rankin's name. Why? What is it you don't like about him?"

"That's ridiculous, Sylvain, it's simply — "

"It is not. I was always shunted away to my room when Mr. Rankin was coming to see Daddy. Why? I was allowed to meet all our other guests. I used to wonder if the man had two heads or something, so I sneaked out onto the balcony to get a look at him. I saw nothing all that threatening about him."

"It's time we got back to the hotel." Serena's voice sounded weak.

"Mother, why won't you tell me about Mr. Rankin? Who is he? What is the mystery about him? And what about Kashka?" She saw her mother's displeased look, but hurried on, "I know, I know — Kashka's dead. I know that, but surely you know something about him. Please tell me."

Serena sighed heavily. "Dear, I've told you before: The man called Kashka died before I came to Riverbend."

"Yes, but surely some of the others knew about . . . about — "

"Sylvain, darling, I wish you would forget that story about any treasure hidden at Riverbend. It's a myth, nothing more. You heard the slaves whispering, and you took every word they said for gospel." She sighed once more. "Forget about hidden gold. Forget about Hyde Rankin. Forget about Riverbend."

"But I can't, Mother," Sylvain replied. "It's been so long, and I . . . It's not yet two o'clock. We could take a paddle-wheeler downriver. If you don't want to call on the Rankins, we could just stroll up the river road and . . . "

"No!" Serena's usually warm, modulated voice grew shrill. She rose abruptly from the table, almost over-turning her coffee cup. "We are not going to Riverbend! And you must promise me you'll never go there alone or with one of your friends. Not even with Randolph, do you hear me?"

Sylvain's mouth gaped open. Never had she seen her mother behave so strangely. Serena started for the door and she was trembling. Sylvain left the cordial forgotten on the table. She rushed to her mother's side, at a loss to understand the sudden change in her mother's gay mood.

"What is it, Mother? What have I done?"

Serena shook her blond head. "Get us a carriage, I don't feel well."

"Of course, I . . . oh, Mother, you look so pale."

Back at the hotel, Serena put up no argument when Delilah took one look at her and bossily announced,

172

"You is goin' to let me undress you and put you to bed."

Sylvain waited alone in the sitting room, pacing back and forth, wondering again, as she had dozens of times in the past, why her mother refused to speak of Hyde Rankin, why she hated the strange man so much.

Sylvain whirled anxiously when Delilah closed the door to her mother's bedchamber. "Is she all right?"

Delilah wore the same tight expression she'd seen on her mother's lovely face. "Your mama be real tired. She goin' to nap till dinner time."

Sylvain caught Delilah's sleeve and clung. "It's more than that. I mentioned Hyde Rankin's name at lunch, and that seemed to distress her."

Delilah's nostrils flared and her black eyes grew hard. "I tol' you not ever to speak 'bout that man!"

"Good grief," Sylvain exploded, "you'd think Hyde Rankin was the devil himself."

"Maybe he is." Delilah pulled away from Sylvain's grip and shuddered.

There was no sun the next day when Sylvain, Serena, and Delilah boarded the paddle-wheeler *Savannah* for the trip home to Mobile. The weather had taken a turn. It was uncomfortably chilly. The skies were low and leaden, the threat of rain increasing hourly. The wind kicked up, buffeting the wooden-hulled steamboat. Waves in the Gulf of Mexico were higher than usual.

An hour out of New Orleans, Delilah pressed a hand to Serena's forehead. It was hot and clammy. She turned to Sylvain. "See can you find a doctor. Miz Serena be feverish."

Sylvain flew from the cabin, fear causing the blood to roar in her ears. Luckily she soon found a physician in the main saloon, and she and the dapper doctor hurried below. By nightfall Serena Fairmont was a very sick woman. Her fever was dangerously high, and her chest rattled when she breathed. Her lovely face was as pale as the sheets on which she rested.

The doctor was extremely attentive. He gave her medicine from his black bag and stayed at her bedside, refusing to leave her even to have his dinner. He was calm and reassuring and capable. At one point he turned to Sylvain and smiled. "Don't look so worried, child. I'll take good care of your mother. Why don't you to to the dining room and eat?"

"I'm not hungry," Sylvain responded.

"Please, darling." Serena's eyes slid open. "You must eat. You too, Delilah."

Delilah stubbornly shook her head and folded her arms across her chest. She wasn't budging. Sylvain, feeling if she sat helpless for one more minute she would surely scream, said, "Perhaps you're right. I'll have a quick dinner and hurry right back."

Sylvain didn't go to the dining room. Instead she stood at the bow of the deserted hurricane deck, gripping the wooden rail and looking out over the murky water. She inhaled deeply and paid no attention to the fine mist of rain falling on her face and hair. She fought the urge to weep, telling herself it would do little good.

She stood there in the cold rain blaming herself for her mother's illness and wondering what it was about Hyde Rankin that could make her mother so upset. Serena had felt fine throughout the busy week. They'd had a wonderful time shopping and dining and laughing together late at night in their hotel room. Her mother had looked rested and relaxed and happy. Until yesterday at lunch.

Whatever it was, Delilah knew about it too, but she refused to tell Sylvain. Oh, she pretended innocence and staunchly stuck to her guns, but Sylvain knew better. She'd question Delilah again once they were back in Mobile.

Sylvain stood alone in the gloomy twilight and gave a silent prayer for her mother's recovery. And she vowed she'd never again plague the dear, delicate woman with her upsetting questions.

Chapter Fourteen

Ginger Thompson's pretty face was almost as red as her flaming hair. Angrily she whirled about and shook her finger in her mother's astonished face. "Listen to me, old woman," she said venomously. "I am not like you! You have no backbone, no will."

The small, pinch-faced woman's pale eyes filled with tears as she valiantly tried to defend herself. "Ginger, please don't be cruel. Your father is a very strong man and he — "

"My father is a failure! And you? You've spent the whole of your married life pretending this miserable house is a palace and that you're content."

"But I am, Ginger. I'm married to a respectable merchant, and I have a beautiful daughter." Mrs. Thompson managed a weak smile.

"You may be happy, but I am not. And I'll not waste my life the way — "

"Ginger, I know you're upset because that young man you fancied is going to marry Miss Fairmont, but Stephen Roper is so fond of you and — "

"I am not going to marry Stephen Roper! He's stupid and dull and poor! A clerk in Father's dry goods store? Never! I'm going to marry Randolph Baxter, do you hear me? I'm going to be rich and reside at Oakgrove and lead the life of a fine, respected lady."

Her mother wrung her bony hands, frightened by the furious gleam in her determined daughter's eyes. But, uncharacteristically, she spoke up once again, "Ginger, I'm sorry you can't have the things you want. But you must face the truth: Young Baxter chose Miss Fairmont, not you. You've not seen him now for weeks, have you?"

Ginger's small hands smoothed at the soft green velvet of her afternoon suit. She appraised herself in the mirror and smiled at what she saw. Then she turned and said cruelly, "No, I've not seen Randy lately, and it's all your fault."

"My fault?" Mrs. Thompson clutched at her throat. "Darling, what have I done? How could I — "

Ginger turned and fixed her mother with an icy stare. "You heard me, it's your fault, yours and Daddy's. He's nothing but a common storekeeper, and you've convinced him that's good enough. Well, it isn't. Not for Randy, not for me." Ginger turned back to the mirror. "Sylvain Fairmont's family and position lured my love away from me, and I have no intention of sitting quietly by while he marries her."

"But what can you do, Ginger?"

Ginger turned and brushed past her mother as if she were not there. She stepped into the narrow hallway and took a parasol from the worn mahogany rack and yanked open the front door. Hand on the brass doorknob, she glanced back at her mother. "I told you, Mother, I'm not like you. I don't lie down and let life roll over me. I've got a plan." Her lips curved into a pleased smile.

Mrs. Thompson reached a tentative hand out to touch her daughter's shoulder. "What is it, dear?"

Ginger pulled away, her lovely face registering disgust. "None of your concern, old woman," she snapped and rushed out the door.

Ginger hurried to her destination, which wasn't far. She'd noticed the sign when it had first gone up more than a year before. She'd walked past it dozens of times and had, on more than one occasion, nodded to the large chestnut-haired man who went in and out of the building several times each day. She assumed he was the MacCarren of the sign over the door, but wasn't certain.

She neared the Broad Street address and found to her dismay that she was nervous. She'd never spoken to an investigator before. What if he questioned her motives? What if he made her explain everything and then refused to be a party to her spiteful snooping? Suppose he charged outrageous prices? What if he refused to help her?

Ginger stood before the closed door. Two windows with frosted panes made it impossible for her to see inside. Perhaps the investigator was out. Maybe he was away from the city working on some important case and wouldn't be back for weeks.

She took a deep breath and tried the door. It swung open, and she stepped inside the room. A large man looked up from a stack of papers. When he saw her, he smiled and stood up. Stretching his hand across the cluttered desk, he said cordially, "Come in, miss. I'm Spence MacCarren. How can I be of service?"

Ginger didn't miss the appraising look he gave her, or the heat that leaped into his clear blue eyes when she smiled prettily at him. "Mr. MacCarren," she said as she shook his large hand, "I'm Miss Ginger Thompson, and I have a problem you must help me solve."

"I'll do my best, Miss Thompson." He released her hand. "Have a seat, please, and tell me what's on your mind."

Ginger took the high-backed chair, settling her full skirts about her small feet and hooking the handle of her dainty silk parasol over the edge of MacCarren's scarred desk. "I'll come right to the point. I'm in love with a man who is planning to marry someone else. I won't allow it to happen. You must investigate the girl and her family. There has to be some sort of scandal in her background . . . bank robbers or smugglers, perhaps, or Negro blood. Something! You must find it for me."

"You sound like a very determined young lady, Miss Thompson."

"I just told you, I will not let him marry her. Will you help me?"

"Miss Thompson, my services are not cheap." He lifted his heavy eyebrows and fixed her with a hard stare.

"I have some money, not much, but ... what do you charge, sir?"

"Twenty dollars a day, plus traveling expenses."

Ginger bit her lip, then nodded her agreement. "You'll have to travel to New Orleans, I'm sure. Her family came from there. I have three hundred dollars. Can you begin today?"

"Three hundred will see me through only a couple of weeks, Miss Thompson."

"Perhaps you'll find something in that length of time."

"And if I don't?"

"We'll discuss it when the time comes."

Spence MacCarren nodded. "Tell me everything you know about the girl and her family."

A sun-filled, warm October drew to a close. The blaze of color that had tinged the towering trees had long since disappeared. Golds and rusts and oranges faded to lifeless browns. The dead, crisp leaves rustled plaintively and quivered to the earth.

The November sky was low. Bare black branches of oaks and elms seemed to punctuate the covering blanket of gray. Chill air, heavy with humidity, stung eyes and reddened noses. Night winds howled and sought entrance into warm, lighted houses. The temperature fell almost to freezing and hovered there for a fortnight.

It was nearing midnight. Rain had begun at midafternoon and rapidly turned to sleet. Tiny pellets of ice, blown by a strong north wind, lashed at the tall French doors. Candles flickered in a silver holder atop the square piano. A chill clung to the shadowy corners of the spacious room, but the pair seated on the floor near the crackling fire were far from cold.

Sylvain sighed with pleasure and relaxed in Randolph's strong arms. He looked down into her large gray eyes and marveled at their clearness, at the length and thickness of her dark eyelashes. His gaze slid to her mouth and stayed there. Her lovely lips were parted, the bottom one trembling slightly. He bent his blond head and playfully nipped at the quivering sweetness and whispered huskily, "Are you cold, my darling?"

Her face and throat flushed, her breath rapid and warm, Sylvain murmured happily, "No, Randolph. If anything, I'm too . . . I'm warm."

Randolph chuckled, then pressed his lips to her cheek and whispered, "I want you always to be warm here in my arms."

He cradled her close against his chest, one arm tight around her. They sat on the carpet before the fireplace, she with her legs curled to the side, skirts spread about her, he with one leg stretched out, the other bent at the knee, foot flat on the floor.

His mouth sought hers once again, closing over the sweet parted lips in a hungry kiss. Sylvain responded eagerly, her mouth opening to him, her hands anxiously touching his chest, his blond hair, his face. And when the long kiss came to an end, she pressed her head to his shoulder and sighed.

Randolph's fingers went to the row of tiny covered buttons at her throat. Deftly flipping two or three open, he murmured softly, "Sylvain, I love you very much. You believe that, don't you, darling?"

"Yes, of course," she breathed, her eyelashes fluttering open, their silkiness pleasantly tickling his cheek.

As his fingers busily continued their task, he whispered hoarsely, "I'm glad, my love. I would never do anything to hurt you, I want you to know that. I've been sure of few things in my life, but my love for you is as certain as the rising of the sun, as lasting as eternity."

"I feel the same way," she assured him. "I love you and I . . . What are you doing?"

He smiled and kissed her pert nose. "You said you were too warm." He undid yet another button, one that rested on the gentle rise of breasts.

"But, I . . . that's not — "

"Shhh," he scolded gently and kissed her again.

Sylvain resistance fled with the persuasion of his lips. She grew pliant in his arms, her eyes closing once again, her slender body melting against his.

"Oh, God, Sylvain," he murmured hoarsely, and his lips slid away from hers, down over her chin. His hand gently brushed aside the opened bodice, and he pressed fevered kisses along the slender, golden column of her throat and down onto the swell of her breasts.

"Randolph," she gasped as he urged her back over his supporting arm. His mouth moved lower, sending glorious shivers throughout her body.

Against the rapid rise and fall of her breast, Randolph's lips played, pressing, teasing, pushing the lace-trimmed satin of her chemise lower, then lower still, yearning to plunge deeper until the sweet rosy nipple was his to draw upon.

He lifted his blond head and looked at her. Her head was thrown back, so that the long brown hair spilled over his arm. Her eyes were closed, and the firelight played on the planes of her perfect face and throat and bosom. She was so tempting it took all Randolph's willpower to keep from taking her there on the floor of her home with her parents sleeping upstairs.

As blood rushed through his veins and his heart hammered a powerful cadence, his chest constricted and his groin ached. His clothes felt tight and binding. Perspiration beaded his upper lip and hairline. He sat there holding the warm, plaint girl in his arms and battled valiantly with propriety. He loved her deeply. He desired her with a raging passion that threatened to be his undoing.

Sylvain opened her eyes and she smiled sweetly. "Randolph," she softly whispered, "we mustn't."

Trapped by the trust in her big gray eyes, he said softly, "I know, Sylvain, I know." His hand again went to the tiny buttons of her dress. Before he attempted to rebutton them, his fingers gently brushed the bare flesh he'd exposed. Instinctively her back arched to him and she bit her lip with the joy of his touch.

Shakily, she murmured, "No, please, Randolph," while every bone and muscle in her body cried out for him to continue, to spread his warm fingers on her waiting flesh, to cup her swelling breasts in his hands, to let the tips of his fingers search out the taut crests.

"I won't, my darling," he said and pulled her head against his chest.

Her eyes fell on the evidence of his desire. Face flushing, she would never have admitted, even to Randolph, that she was tempted to place her hand on him. But she was terribly curious and wanted to know how he felt. She longed to let her fingers travel over the strange, hard contours straining beneath his trousers.

Randolph set her away from him and began buttoning her dress. As he worked, he spoke in a soft, loving voice, "You're so sweet, so beautiful, I must keep you safe." His hands went to her narrow waist, and he eased her with him up from the floor.

He pulled her close and inhaled deeply of her clean, shiny hair. "It's late, and I must go. Think of me when you're in your bed."

Her arms held him tightly. "I shall, Randolph. And you? Will you be thinking of me?"

For the first time he could answer truthfully. He had stopped seeing Ginger Thompson. Now when he left Sylvain, he went directly to the Oakgrove *garçonnière* and tossed and turned in his bed thinking only of the sable-haired, gray-eyed charmer whose trust he no longer betrayed.

"Yes, darling, I'll think of you. And I'll pray for the days and nights to speed by." He pulled back so he could look down at her. A muscle jumped in his jaw. "I can't wait until we're married. Why must we wait until June? I want to be with you now. I want you with me in bed on these cold winter nights. Let's elope. Let's go tonight and — "

"Randolph, darling." Sylvain shook her head and laughed softly. "We can't do that. Everything's planned. I've ordered my wedding gown." She skimmed a slender forefinger over his bottom lip. "I want to be married in the church, darling. Say you understand."

Randolph sighed, then smiled at her. "I do. I'm being selfish. We'll marry in the church. Anything you want. I love you. Oh, God, how I love you."

She nuzzled his neck happily. "And I love you, too," she sighed.

Serena Fairmont was determined to hide her illness from her daughter. She wanted nothing to dim the happiness of her only child.

The girl's joy was like brilliant warming sunshine in the deep of winter. Serena spent many a cozy afternoon ensconced in Sylvain's bedchamber, an appreciative audience of one, applauding gaily while her daughter whirled about the room, modeling one of the many new, gorgeous gowns sent from New Orleans. Never had mother and daughter been closer than they were during that long, cold winter.

Sylvain did not mention it, but she was alarmed by her mother's constant pallor, the tired look that had crept into the clear blue eyes, the loss of weight.

Sylvain was wise enough to know that the upcoming wedding meant almost as much to her mother as to her.

She suspected it was because her parents had had no church wedding. Serena had told her they married quietly. Only Edwin's sister had been present to witness the short ceremony.

But for the twinges of worry over her mother's health, Sylvain was happy. She loved Randolph Baxter with all her young and trusting heart and was certain the years ahead stretched full and rewarding before them.

She had no idea why Randolph had become so much more loving, but she was delighted that he had. From the beginning of their courtship, she'd yearned for the closeness they now shared. At times the depth of his passion, and her own, frightened her. His kisses had changed; now they were the kisses of a man. They'd become very much like the heated, breath-stealing kisses of that dark man who'd swept her off her feet on a cold stone balcony so long ago. They'd become the kind of kisses she'd always imagined a man shared with his wife.

Sylvain no longer had any doubts about Randolph's love for her or hers for him. All was right between them, and if there were nights when she had difficulty falling asleep after he'd left her, she knew that was as it should be. She was inflamed by his caresses, and only the marriage bed would quench the raging fire. She could hardly wait.

"I'm sorry, Miss Thompson," Spence MacCarren said, looking up from his desk, "but I've not found a thing in the Fairmonts' past. I'm afraid you've sent me on a wild-goose chase."

"Don't tell me you've given up." Ginger glared at him.

Spence MacCarren leaned back in his chair. "I spent over a month on the case, Miss Thompson. I found nothing." He paused, cleared his throat, and continued. "I gave you more time and effort than most of my clients receive."

Ginger sighed. "You mean you'll not go further without more money."

"Exactly. I'm sorry, truly I am."

Ginger's lovely face clouded. "But I know you'll find something if you keep at it a while longer. Please, can't you — "

"I don't work for nothing, Miss Thompson."

"No, I . . . I'm sure you don't." Ginger rose slowly from her chair. She had no more money to give him, but an idea was taking hold in her busy brain. She put her gloved hands on the edge of his desk and smiled at him. "Mr. MacCarren, are you married?"

"I'm a bachelor, Miss Thompson. Why?"

Ginger began to smile. Slowly she circled his desk until she was standing beside him. "Do you find me attractive, Mr. MacCarren?"

Spence MacCarren let his eyes travel slowly over her ripe body, closely scrutinizing every lush curve. "I find you very beautiful, Miss Thompson." His eyes returned to hers.

She gave him a seductive smile, then turned and walked away from him while he watched the provocative sway of her full hips. She moved gracefully to the door and the heavy bolt, locking it. She pulled the heavy shades down over the windows and turned. The room was cast into dimness, a small lamp on MacCarren's desk the only light.

Ginger slowly walked toward him, peeling off her dark gloves as she came. She dropped them on the desk, took the pin from her velvet hat, shoved it into the crown of the feather-trimmed bonnet, and let the bonnet fall on top of the gloves.

Spence MacCarren's interested gaze never left her. Anticipation was building pleasantly inside him. He gripped the arms of his high-backed chair when she reached up under her heavy skirts and petticoats and released her linen pantalettes, letting them slide to the floor, and kicking them away with the toe of her kid slipper.

MacCarren's face was scarlet and his heart thumped against his ribs. Ginger laughed and stepped around the desk. Smiling down at him, she edged between him and the heavy desk to stand before him, very close, her eyes holding his. Slowly she sank down to the floor, her skirts mushrooming around her.

His bent knees were wide apart. Ginger sat on her heels between his parted legs. "I have no more money, Mac, but perhaps I can please you all the same." Her hand boldly went to his groin. He groaned and squirmed when her fingers enclosed the hardness beneath his trousers. "Do you want me?" she asked huskily, her hand sliding up and down his throbbing erection.

"God, yes," he breathed.

"You'll help me?"

His big hands reached for her as he moaned, "I'll help. Come here."

With passersby but a few feet away beyond the locked door, Ginger Thompson, skirts shoved up to her waist, straddled an excited Spence MacCarren, her hands brazenly guiding his shaft into her waiting softness. Carriages creaked, horses snorted, and men shouted on busy Broad Street, but Spence MacCarren, confidential investigator, never heard any of it. Naked from the waist down, he sat in his chair and thrust himself into the shameless young woman who sat astride him, his big hands cupping her round buttocks, his eyes on the bare breasts spilling from her opened bodice.

Expertly she ground her bottom against him and whispered, "You like that, Mac? Anything you want me to do, I'll do it. Just promise you'll keep looking. I can't let him marry her. I love him, I really love him."

"Sure you do," said Spence MacCarren. "I'll keep working as long as you do."

Ginger ground her pelvis against him with renewed vigor.

Spring came early to Mobile. The crepe myrtle in the courtyard behind the Fairmont town house exploded into vivid purplish pink, its blossom-heavy limbs bending almost to the ground. Roses climbed the high brick walls, and the camellias looked as though they'd open at any moment.

Sylvain and Randolph spent love-sweetened hours seated on the white settee, the scent of roses filling their nostrils while they kissed and clung and counted the days until their wedding. Their evenings together were becoming a pleasant torture. Their kisses grew hotter, longer, more desperate. Their hands roamed and touched and teased. Their bodies strained and pressed and rubbed.

They were so much in love they felt they couldn't wait one more week, one more day, one more hour. Randolph was not the only one who couldn't sleep. Sylvain tossed in her bed each night, her flesh sensitive to her nightclothes, her lips soft and swollen from Randolph's kisses, her blood afire.

And finally, there was but one week until the wedding. Sylvain awoke with the sun and smiled. "One week. Just one more week and we'll never be apart." She slid from the bed and pulled her nightgown up over her head. She started when her door flew open. She held the gown in front of her and stared at Delilah.

"You might have knocked, you know, I . . . " She stopped suddenly as fear closed over her heart. "What is it, Delilah? What's wrong?"

"Child, your mama . . . Miz Serena, she . . . " She choked and the words trailed away.

Sylvain's gown fell forgotten to the floor. "What about Mother? Tell me, Delilah!"

"Oh, dear God, she dying! Miz Serena's dying!"

Chapter Fifteen

Sylvain stood staring at Delilah, who was nearly hysterical. She waved her long arms and babbled excitedly, tears coursing down her frightened face.

"Stop. Stop it, Delilah! You must get hold of yourself. You'll be no good to Mother in this state. Has the doctor been summoned?" The sobbing woman bobbed her head, sputtering as she tried to speak.

"Is Daddy with her?"

"Yes, Mr. Edwin be in there."

"Listen to me, Delilah: Please go back to my mother. I'll come as soon as I've dressed."

"Yes'm." Delilah turned and hurried from the room.

Sylvain moved with sure, determined steps toward her large dressing room. The morning was already hot, and a sheen of perspiration covered her slender body. But her heart was cloaked in icy fear. She shivered and gazed at the gooseflesh covering her sweat-dampened body.

She did not weep.

Sylvain was strangely aware it was she who would have to be the strong one. She was certain of it when, dressed and composed, she entered her parents' bedchamber and saw her distressed father, shoulders slumped, eyes red-rimmed.

Softly Sylvain crossed the room and put a hand on her father's shoulder, but he did not look up. Dr. Talbot stood on the other side of the big four-poster. His eyes lifted from the ashen-faced woman in the bed and looked directly at Sylvain. Her question was answered.

She bit the inside of her cheek and commanded her shaking knees to support her. Then she leaned down and gently kissed her father's balding head, squeezed his shoulder, and murmured softly, "Daddy, don't. Mother could wake up any second, and we wouldn't want her to see us weeping."

He turned tear-filled eyes to her. "You're right, I . . . I'm sorry. I'll . . . " He drew a handkerchief from his pocket, wiped at his eyes, and blew his nose.

"That's better." Sylvain smiled at him, leaned over the bed, and picked up her mother's small, cold hand. Holding it in both of her own, she spoke to the woman whose brilliant blue eyes were closed: "Mother, darling, we're here. Daddy and I are here. We won't leave you. We'll never leave you."

And they didn't.

Through the long, unseasonably hot June day, Edwin Fairmont and his daughter sat by Serena's bedside. Hourly Serena Fairmont's condition worsened. Unconscious, she lay unmoving, her long golden hair spilling onto the pillow like a gleaming silken fan, her black lashes rested in spiky crescents on milk-white, sunken cheeks, dark shadows beneath her closed eyes. Serena's lips appeared more blue than pink.

The afternoon dragged on endlessly. The room grew steadily warmer. The double doors were thrown open to the balcony, but not a breath was stirring.

The sun finally slipped toward the horizon. A soft light bathed the quiet chamber and its three silent inhabitants. The lilac glow, the unbroken silence, and the uncommon heat combined to cast an eerie pall over the room. Sylvain sat rigidly on a chair by the bed. She felt as though she were outside her body, observing these mute people in this too-warm room, their sad faces suffused with a strange pastel illumination.

When Serena's blue eyes fluttered restlessly, then opened, Sylvain was out of chair and at the bed. Edwin's face lifted from his chest and he, too, rushed to his wife. Serena smiled weakly up at him and said softly, "My darling, you look so tired. You must rest."

He tried to speak, but choked. He grabbed his wife's hand and shook his head.

Sylvain smiled at her mother and said, "Is there anything we can get you? Are you comfortable?"

"The two people I love most in the world are with me. What more could I want?" Serena's smile was weak, her usually brilliant eyes dim.

Sylvain nodded. "We don't want to tire you. I'll step outside and let you visit with Daddy."

"No, darling, wait," Serena's eyes went to her husband. "Edwin, my love, let me speak to Sylvain for a moment. Then you'll come back to me?"

Swallowing hard, Edwin managed to whisper, "Yes, dear. I'll be right outside." He blinked back his tears, released her frail hand, and left.

"Shall I light the lamps?" Sylvain asked when her father had gone.

"No, it's so peaceful like this; let's wait. Sylvain, I keep the emerald in the top drawer of the chest. There's a silk-covered box. Get it for me, please."

"Yes, Mother." Sylvain was glad her mother had given her the small task to perform, something to do. She took the ring from the box and came back to the bed. "Shall I put it on your finger?"

"No, darling, Put it on yours."

Sylvain felt fear tightening its grip on her aching heart. "But it's your ring, Mother. It's special and you — "

"You have no idea how special that ring is, Sylvain." Serena's voice was so low Sylvain had to strain to hear. "Promise me you'll keep it always, darling." Serena paused, drew a troubled breath, and softly added, "He would have wanted you to have it." Tears gathered in the corners of her eyes.

"Who, Mother? Daddy?"

"Yes, your father," said Serena Fairmont, the tears spilling over and sliding down her cheeks. "Promise me something else, darling."

"Anything, Mother." She gripped the emerald ring in her fist so tightly it cut into the soft flesh of her palm.

"Watch after Edwin. He's such a sweet, dear man; he'll need you."

Sylvain didn't tell her mother that she was speaking nonsense, that nothing was going to happen to her, that she would get well and look after her husband. Sylvain knew, just as Serena did, that she would not live through the night. "I shall. You can depend on me."

"I know I can, Sylvain. You're so strong, so much like ... so like ... " Serena's golden head turned away for a moment. She blinked and turned back to Sylvain. "There's something else, dear."

"Yes, Mother?"

"Tell me ... say you forgive me for ... I ... we ... "

"Shhh." Sylvain took a soft linen handkerchief from her pocket and dabbed at her mother's eyes. "Forgive you? What for? You must forgive me. I always wished I could be more like you."

Serena Fairmont looked up into the beautiful face of her daughter and saw, as she had every day of the girl's life, the hauntingly handsome face of the man who'd fathered her. His swarthy skin had softened to a pale honey in Sylvain. His black eyes had lightened to a smoky gray. Her long, lean body was so like his, the set of her strong jaw, the high cheekbones, the graceful way she moved, her quick mind, her air of command.

"I have always been grateful you're so much like ... like ... "

"Like my father?" Sylvain supplied the word, though in truth she felt she was not at all like Edwin, either in looks or in temperament.

"Yes," Serena choked. "Sylvain, I love you, and I'm so proud of you. You'll make Randolph a good wife, and I know you'll both be happy. Darling, don't postpone the wedding. Please don't. Kiss me good-bye."

Without a word, Sylvain leaned forward and kissed her mother's cool lips. Then for a long, peace-filled moment, she laid her dark head on her mother's breast and pretended she was a little girl once again. Serena stroked her child's hair.

The long moment passed. Sylvain lifted her head and smiled at her mother. "I'll send Daddy in," she said, and left the room. And she knew, as she walked away, that she would never again be held in her mother's arms. Nor would she ever again feel like a little girl.

Her childhood was gone forever.

Sylvain stood in the hallway with the grim-faced servants. Theo had been sent to summon Dr. Talbot. Nana had deserted her kitchen to stand watch with the others. Old Delson, his gray head bent, gnarled hands clasped in front of him, had kept watch all afternoon. Bodine, the housekeeper, slumped against the wall, head bowed. Delilah was quietly watching her young mistress.

Sylvain opened her hand. The flawless Colombian emerald glittered in the light from a wall sconce. Sylvain lifted the ring, turned it about, and read the inscription inside.

La croix.

She slipped the beautiful ring on her finger and silently vowed never to let the ring out of her sight. Then she heard the muffled cry from within and she knew.

Serena Fairmont was dead.

"Randolph, we'll have to postpone the wedding." Sylvain sat with him on the iron settee in the courtyard. The young couple had stolen a few minutes away from the crowd of mourners who'd called at the town house.

Randolph gently caressed her slender shoulder and soothed, "Whatever you want, Sylvain. I'll do anything to make this easier for you."

She leaned against him and sighed. "I know. I need you now, darling, and I wish we were already married. But Daddy is so distraught. And people would talk if we went ahead with our plans."

"That's true. We'll wait a few more months. Perhaps come fall, we can still have the church wedding."

"Thank you, Randolph, for understanding. I love you."

"I love you, Sylvain."

"I'm in luck, Mac!" Ginger Thompson breathlessly swept into the Broad Street office of Spence MacCarren. "Sylvain Fairmont's mother died. Isn't that wonderful?"

Spence MacCarren's thick eyebrows arched, and he clicked his tongue. "You are a cold little piece, aren't you, Ginger, my dear?"

"Oh, I'm not glad the poor woman died. But don't you see that this gives me more time? The wedding will surely be put off, and you can continue your snooping." She whirled about the room happily, skirts and frilly petticoats swaying around her. "It's fate, I tell you. Randolph Baxter was not meant to marry Sylvain Fairmont. He was meant to marry me!"

Spence MacCarren watched the excited young woman spin about the floor and knew he was every bit as heartless as she. And just as immoral. Eyeing the well-turned legs exposed with her giddy reeling, he realized she'd done as he'd asked: She'd come to him wearing no stays or corsets, no chemise or pantalettes. Ginger was naked beneath her petticoats, and that knowledge was enough to spur his lust.

He rose and went about clearing off his large desk while Ginger continued to dance and spin. When the

polished surface was bare, Spence circled the desk and
lounged back against it. He clapped his hands and urged
her to spin faster and faster. She did and her full skirts
billowed out about her, rising higher and higher until the
big man's eyes were locked hungrily on her bare thighs.

In two long strides he reached her. He lifted her off her
feet and sat her on top of the desk, then pushed her
yellow muslin skirt and lacy petticoats up to her waist.
With one hand he opened his trousers and released his
pulsing flesh. His other hand sought the damp warmth
between her legs. Ginger giggled, unhooked her tight
bodice and opened it. Her breasts bobbing with each
movement, she lay back on the desk, arms flung over her
head.

"You'd better hurry, Mac," she warned and laughed
deep in her throat.

"Why?" he asked, moving into position.

"Because you forgot to lock the door."

The wedding was set for the first Sunday in September.
There was less than a week left before Sylvain Fairmont
would become Mrs. Randolph Baxter. The long, sad
summer was drawing to a close. Sylvain had shared her
father's grief; she'd been strong and patient and understanding. She'd suffered with him, she'd clung to him
while he sobbed, she'd made him eat when neither of
them was hungry, invited friends to the house to cheer
him, and longed for the day when she'd become Mrs.
Baxter, when she could lie in her husband's arms and
lose herself in his loving.

Sylvain and Randolph faced the fading September sun
seated beneath a white gazebo on a tiny island in a pond
behind Oakgrove. Huge oaks, dripping Spanish moss,
hid the embracing couple from the white plantation
house.

"Think of it, darling," Randolph said, his voice
warm. "In a few days you and I can walk from this

summerhouse over to my *garçonnière* and hide from the world for as long as we please."

"Pray God nothing happens to — "

His lips silenced her. Randolph kissed her soundly and murmured, "Nothing will happen. You'll be my wife this time next week."

"I will," she breathed, and clung to him.

It was less than twelve hours later that Miss Ginger Thompson hurried to the Broad Street office of Spence MacCarren. He'd sent a message that he had news for her.

"What is it, Mac?" Ginger's eyes flashed with excitement.

Spence MacCarren grinned, leaned on his desk, and indicated a chair. "I think I've just solved your little problem."

He told her calmly that the young lady known to Randolph Baxter and the rest of the world as the aristocratic Sylvain Fairmont was in reality the illegitimate offspring of the ruthless pirate Jean Lafitte. Enjoying the look of astonishment in Ginger's wide eyes, he went on: "I met a young man in a New Orleans saloon who was once the lover of a priest named Hyde Rankin. The boy, Steve Crowell, was very, very drunk. He told me everything. Rankin was a priest at Ursuline, but even then his desire for young boys was an obsession. It seems a Sister Sylvain, one of the nuns, caught Father Rankin with a young boy student. She saw to it the man was defrocked and cast out of the church. He went, but with him he took a very important document."

"What?" Ginger's eyes were as round as saucers.

"Sylvain Fairmont's birth certificate. Her mother had named Jean Lafitte as the child's father."

"The stupid fool," Ginger breathed.

"Rankin needed money, so he paid a visit to poor Edwin Fairmont and told him about the birth certificate.

Fairmont loved his wife and her daughter so much that he paid Rankin to keep their secret. But Rankin is a greedy man. He continued to blackmail Fairmont until he could no longer afford to keep his big sugar plantation on the delta."

"But this is wonderful!" Ginger exclaimed. "The high and mighty Miss Sylvain Fairmont is a common bastard. The offspring of a murderous pirate. Too good to be true!"

Spence MacCarren smiled. "It's true, Ginger. You think it's enough to keep the Baxter boy from marrying the girl?"

Ginger burst out laughing. "I can see you know little about the Baxters of Mississippi. Their ancestors were English and French royalty. They're so intent on keeping the lineage spotless, they wouldn't dream of allowing their only son to marry a pirate's bastard child!"

MacCarren leaned back in his chair. "That's good, but will they let him marry you?"

Ginger gave him a smug look. "They won't be all that pleased, but they'll agree. You see, Randy is a weak man. He'll need someone strong like me when the blow falls. The elder Baxters will be relieved I'm there to keep him from going to pieces." Ginger rose. "I assure you, I'll be Mrs. Randolph Baxter within six months."

Spence MacCarren smiled. "Does this mean our relationship is over?"

Ginger blanched. "Mac, you . . . you wouldn't spoil things for me. You'll not — "

"Blackmail you?" he finished the sentence. "No, Ginger, I'm no blackmailer." He stood up. "After you've paid me today, we'll wipe the slate clean."

"But, Mac, I . . . Oh, very well, let's get on with it. I want to go shopping." She grinned and stepped into his arms. "I must have a new frock for my visit to Oakgrove this evening, don't you agree?"

"I don't believe it!" Randolph Baxter's handsome face was dark red. "You're lying, Ginger."

"I wish I were, Randy," Ginger said softly, her eyes skipping from him to his shocked parents.

She'd arrived, uninvited, at Oakgrove half an hour before Randolph was to go to the Fairmont home for a quiet dinner. Ginger had sat in a wing chair of fine soft velvet quickly relating all she'd found out about the Fairmonts. Now, however, she was growing very nervous. Randolph's deep love for Sylvain was evident; he was extremely distraught and defensive. For the first time, Ginger wondered whether her revelation would make the difference. He was ranting and raving and declaring he'd marry Sylvain no matter what. It was something Ginger had not anticipated.

Randolph stalked across the room, removed the stopper from a decanter of Kentucky bourbon, and splashed a healthy portion of the dark liquid into a glass. He downed it in one swallow and poured another. His green eyes narrowed as he looked at Ginger with barely disguised hatred.

"If you've shared all your good tidings, Ginger, why don't you leave?" His voice was menacing.

"If that's what you want, Randy." Her voice was tremulous.

"No, wait," said Martin Baxter. "Let's go over this one more time. Are you positive, young woman, that what you've told us is true? Can you prove it?" He fixed Ginger with a hard, piercing look.

"Yes, Mr. Baxter, I can. It's all true, I swear it." And Ginger told them again facts of Sylvain's parentage, while Randolph paced the floor and continued to drink bourbon.

"Now will you get out of here?" Randolph growled when she finished.

"Yes, Ginger," Joan Baxter put in. "Perhaps it would be best if you leave. Randolph's naturally upset and — "

"Of course, Mrs. Baxter." Ginger nodded and rose. She cast one last anxious glance at Randolph and murmured, "Randy, I'm so sorry . . . I know you feel terrible about this whole thing, but I couldn't let you go on not knowing."

He didn't reply. He seemed to look right through her, and Ginger's unease grew.

After her departure, Randolph, whose speech was beginning to slur, said, "I don't give a damn. I love Sylvain and this changes nothing."

Martin Baxter poured himself a whiskey, took a drink, and spoke. "You're wrong, son, this makes all the difference. There will be no wedding, at least not to Miss Fairmont. Or should I say Miss Lafitte?"

"Damn you, Father." Randolph glared at him. "She's a sweet, lovely girl and I'll marry her. With or without your blessing."

"But, darling." His mother rose and went to him. "You can't do that to us, or to yourself. Why, the whole city will be reeling with the sandal. A pirate's daughter! You must forget her at once." She put a hand on her son's chest and patted him.

Randolph brushed her hand away roughly. "I can't forget her! I'm in love with Sylvain. Can't either of you understand that!"

"Oh, we understand," Martin Baxter assured him. "She's a pretty child and you care for her. Well, that doesn't pose a monumental problem, son. People do fall in love, as the saying goes, but love isn't enough to build a marriage on." He shook his head. "No, Randolph, you'll marry a respectable young lady to bear my grandchildren."

"Damn you, Father! You think only of your grandchildren. I'm talking about the woman I love, the woman I want to spend the rest of my life with."

His father turned to his wife. "Joan dear, perhaps you could leave us for a minute. I'd like to speak to Randolph man to man."

"Of course, darling." She turned and left the room.

Martin Baxter swirled the whiskey in his glass. "Randolph, I know you care a great deal about Sylvain. But don't you see that you can still have her? The solution to your little problem is so simple: You marry a quiet, understanding, respectable woman to supply you with heirs to the Baxter fortune, and you make Sylvain your mistress. Set her up in a place of her own, if you like, make her comfortable, visit her whenever you please. Everyone will look the other way. It's done all the time, and it works rather well." He gave his son a pleased look.

Randolph tossed back another whiskey and jammed a finger into his father's chest. "I am going to marry Sylvain Fairmont, Father, whether you like it or not."

"No," his father said evenly, "you are not." He set his glass on the table and strode to the fireplace. He shoved his hands into his pockets and turned to face his son. "Randolph, as you well know, I'm one of the richest men in Alabama . . . one of the richest in the entire South."

"Father, please — " Randolph began.

"If you marry Sylvain Fairmont, you won't see one nickel of my fortune. I'll disinherit you so rapidly you won't know what happened. Do I make myself clear, young man?"

Randolph tried to focus his eyes. "You can't mean that."

"Ah, but I do. You're my only child, Randolph. My only hope for grandchildren. My only dream of immortality. Do you suppose I'm going to allow you to breed with some swinish, swarthy pirate's issue?"

"My God, how can you be so cruel?" Randolph shook his blond head unbelievingly.

"Cruel? I don't see it that way, not at all. I love you, Randolph, and I've built up vast wealth for you and the generations to come after me." Martin Baxter turned and gripped the marble mantelpiece. His back to his son, he said quietly "With love comes knowledge, familiarity, understanding. I know you, Randolph. You could no more bear being poor than I. You'll find it much easier to give up a girl than money. Women are easy to collect, money is not." He turned and left the room.

The French gold clock on the mantel was striking nine. Sylvain paced the floor irritably. Randolph Baxter was to have come for dinner at precisely seven-thirty. Nana had poked her head in the empty dining room a dozen times. Delilah wore a displeased look. Even Edwin Fairmont, seated on Serena's favorite champagne brocade sofa, kept lifting his eyes to the gold clock.

When a carriage clattered to a stop outside, Sylvain yanked back the curtain in time to see Randolph step down, his golden head gleaming silver in the light of the early rising moon. He jerked open the gate, stepped inside, and banged it shut with such force the whole fence shook. Then he stumbled and almost fell.

Sylvain knew something was wrong. She dropped the curtain and flew into the corridor. Heart pounding, she swung open the heavy front door and saw his disheveled hair, the glassy eyes, the unsteady stance.

"Randolph!" She stared at him. "What is it? What's wrong?"

He stood looking down at her. He appeared angry and upset. Edwin Fairmont had stepped into the foyer. His question echoed his daughter's. "Son, what is it? What's happened?"

Randolph's green eyes blinked, and he swayed toward Sylvain. "I can't marry you," he muttered, his words slurring.

"But why, Randolph? I don't understand. What are you saying?"

"I'm saying" — he pointed a finger at her, and tears filled his bloodshot eyes — "I'm Randolph Baxter of the Mississippi Baxters. I'll not marry Jean Lafitte's bastard!"

Chapter Sixteen

"Lafitte's bastard?" Sylvain said slowly, thoroughly baffled by Randolph's wild declaration. Behind her, all the color had drained from Edwin Fairmont's face.

"Don't pretend to be shocked, Sylvain. It's I who have suffered a great shock this night!" Randolph's bleary eyes took on a fierce glow, and he grabbed Sylvain's arm.

"Please, Randolph." She looked at him incredulously. "You don't know what you're saying, darling!"

"Don't I?" His hand tightened on her arm, his face hardening with pain and rage.

"Release my daughter at once, Baxter." Edwin Fairmont stepped closer, putting a protective arm around Sylvain's waist.

Randolph laughed hollowly and dropped his hand. "*Your* daughter, Mr. Fairmont? Hardly. Why she's not even — "

"That's enough. Leave this house at once, young man!"

Sylvain's bewildered gaze never left Randolph. His words made no sense to her, but she was aware that he was terribly upset and that she had to make things right. Shrugging away from Edwin Fairmont, she seized Randolph's lapels. "What are you saying, Randolph? What has happened to make you behave this way? Tell me what is wrong."

"Wrong?" he thundered. "Everything is wrong!" His hands covered hers. "You've ruined my life."

"But how? You're speaking foolishly, Randolph. What does a dead New Orleans pirate have to do with us?"

"Not us, Sylvain. You. The man was your — "

"Damn you, Baxter," Edwin Fairmont erupted, his face purple with rage. "Get out of my house this minute!"

"No, Daddy, he . . . I . . . " Sylvain tightened her grip on Randolph's lapels. Suddenly she discovered she was trembling. Her world was spinning out of control. "Randolph, you've made a horrible mistake." She tried to laugh, failed, went on. "Why, it's preposterous, don't you see that?" She cast a worried glace at Edwin Fairmont. "Tell him he's wrong, Daddy. Tell him we know nothing of Jean Lafitte. Tell him you're the only father I have ever had."

The look of misery in Edwin Fairmont's pale eyes frightened her far more than anything Randolph had said. And there she read the staggering truth.

"Yes, Mr. Fairmont, tell her." Randolph's eyes remained on her face. "What an actress you are, Sylvain," he said through clenched teeth. "You know very well this man is not your father. You betrayed my trust. You let me believe you had an impeccable background when all along you . . . Oh, damn you, damn you," he muttered. He pulled her roughly to him and kissed her fiercely, then pushed her away from him.

Sylvain stood, stunned and heartsick, as Randolph Baxter stormed out of the house, down the steps, into the carriage. And out of her life.

She slowly turned sad eyes on Edwin Fairmont. "Is it true?"

"Oh, darling . . . " Edwin Fairmont felt his chest constrict with pain. "Sylvain, Sylvain."

"Please." Her voice was soft. "Tell me."

Edwin put an arm about her, led her into the drawing room, eased her down onto the brocade sofa. Then he poured some brandy into a snifter and sat beside her, urging her to drink, holding the glass to her lips, murmuring encouragement.

When the glass was emptied, he set it aside and said, "Sylvain, I'll tell you everything, but first I want to say that I love you more than you will ever know." She nodded and took his hand. He drew a deep breath. "To me you are my beloved daughter just as surely as if I had fathered you." He saw her expressive gray eyes flicker. "It's true that another man is responsible for you being on this earth, but I'm so grateful to him." He squeezed her hand and cleared his tight throat.

"I'm really Jean Lafitte's daughter?"

"Yes, Sylvain, you are, but — "

"And who was my mother?"

"Serena was your mother."

The pupils of her gray eyes dilated and she murmured, "Then my mother and Lafitte . . . they were . . . " Her words trailed off, and she closed her eyes and shook her head.

"It wasn't what you think, Sylvain. Shall I tell you all I know?"

She opened her eyes and turned to him. "Please. Everything."

"Very well." He coughed, patted her hand, and began. "In the early summer of 1819 I returned home to New Orleans from an extended trip abroad. When I arrived, I went immediately to Ursuline Academy to see my sister." He smiled sadly, and explained, "Sister Sylvain, the woman for whom you were named. While I was there I met the most beautiful young woman I have ever seen. Serena Donovan had long golden hair, alabaster skin, and sad blue eyes." He fell silent.

"Please go on," she prompted him.

"I saw at once that the girl was pregnant. I asked my sister if I might speak to Serena. She agreed and I spent the long, warm afternoon seated beside Serena in the courtyard. She told me the child she was carrying had been fathered by Jean Lafitte, whom she had loved very much. She explained that she'd met Lafitte when she lived on Galvez Isle with her father. A disastrous hurricane had hit the island and her father was killed. Lafitte saved her life and he ... that is — "

"I see." Sylvain took her hand from his and massaged her throbbing temples. "But of course Lafitte didn't love her."

"I didn't say that, Sylvain. I'm sure he cared a great deal for her, but you see, he had a family of sorts, a common law wife. So Lafitte sent Serena back to New Orleans. He never knew she was carrying his child."

"So my father ... Lafitte ... never knew about me?"

"No, no, he didn't." Edwin swallowed hard and continued. "I loved your mother before that long, warm afternoon had ended. I asked her to marry me and she agreed. Sister Sylvain revealed that Lafitte had legally deeded Riverbend to Serena. The deed was to be presented to her when she reached twenty-one years of age or when she married, whichever came first."

"Riverbend belonged to Jean Lafitte?" The old stories of hidden booty leaped into Sylvain's mind.

"Yes, it did, and Lafitte gave Riverbend to Serena. So you see, he must have loved her." Edwin smiled weakly. "My arrangement with Serena was quickly settled. No one knew I had returned from abroad. We would quietly wed and I'd tell the world I'd met and married an American girl in Europe. We'd married abroad, she'd conceived, and we had come back and purchased Riverbend for our home. By the time you were born, we'd be safely ensconced at Riverbend, Mr. and Mrs. Edwin Fairmont."

"And did you carry out the plan?"

Edwin Fairmont sighed wearily. "Two nights later Serena went into premature labor. Sister Sylvain called me to the convent and when I arrived, your mother was in terrible pain. The doctor was with her, as was a priest. We should have married the day we met, but still I thought it would make little difference, no one would know."

"How *did* they know?" Sylvain bit the inside of her cheek.

"Your mother was so slim, so small. She went through a terrible ordeal delivering you, and when finally at five in the morning you arrived, she was groggy and pain-drunk. When the physician asked for name of the father, she answered truthfully." He looked at the floor.

"She told him that Jean Lafitte was my father."

"Yes." Edwin lifted his head and hurried on. "We were married the next day, and less than a week later the three of us quietly moved to Riverbend. Soon I called on old friends, told them I'd just arrived from Europe, that I was married, and that my child had been born upon our return. We threw parties at Riverbend. Everyone came and marveled at the beauty of my wife and my daughter. I was a proud and happy man, Sylvain. I loved you both so very much."

She smiled and touched his cheek. "I know you did, Daddy."

His sad heart speeded at the word that had taken on new meaning in the last terrible hour. "Our life was wonderful. Your mother was kind and affectionate, you were a joy, all was splendid . . . Then, ah, Sister Sylvain caught a priest in a compromising situation. She saw that he was banished from the school and the church. He left, and with him he took your birth certificate."

Sylvain's mouth rounded into an O. "Hyde Rankin," she breathed.

"Yes, Hyde Rankin. Soon he showed up at Riverbend threatening to expose our secret to the world. I couldn't let that happen, I couldn't. So I paid him." Edwin shook his head and wrapped a hand around the back of his neck. "I thought that one payment would be enough to silence him. I gave him a handsome sum and told him I never wanted to see him again. But he returned a year later and demanded more money."

"He's been blackmailing you all these years, hasn't he?"

Edwin nodded sadly.

"And now the vile man has told others even as he took your money." Sylvain began to shake once again. "Now Randolph knows, and he . . . he no longer wants me."

"Dear God, child, I'm sorry, so terrible sorry." He pulled her into his arms as big tears filled her eyes. She clung to him and tried very hard to keep from crying, but the tears rolled down her cheeks unbidden.

Unable to fully comprehend all that this kind man had told her, Sylvain knew only that Randolph Baxter no longer wanted her, now that he knew she was a pirate's illegitimate daughter. Her life was over. All over.

"Oh, Daddy," she sobbed, burrowing her face into his shoulder, "what shall I do? I love Randolph so much."

Edwin Fairmont tightened his arms around her. The anger and outrage he felt were increasing by the second. To see this dear girl so deeply hurt was too much for the man who had always and would always consider her his daughter. He kissed her flushed temples and vowed to himself grimly, "Randolph Baxter will pay. He's going to pay for this."

He remained seated patiently on the brocade couch holding Sylvain until she was all cried out. He patted and soothed and promised. He kissed her, comforted her. And when at last she slumped against him, her red-rimmed eyes finally dry, her slender body no longer shaking, he picked her up in his sturdy arms and carried her to her room.

Delilah, her black eyes somber, waited there. She'd heard the exchange, the accusations, the sobs. She'd been standing silently by, waiting her turn to minister to her brokenhearted young mistress. She stepped forward immediately and said to Edwin Fairmont, "I stay with her. Jes' put her on the bed."

"Thank you, Delilah." He carried Sylvain to the four-poster and gently placed her on the silk counterpane. Then he kissed her and whispered, "Rest, child. You will feel a little better in the morning."

He went quietly down the stairs and summoned his faithful servant. "Delson," he said evenly, "you're to go at once to the home of my young law clerk, Tom Mason. Bid him come here immediately."

"Delilah," Sylvain said, her voice tired and weak, "did you know I am a pirate's daughter?" She turned to look at the grim-faced black woman who was unhooking her tight green dress.

"I always knowed, child."

"Why didn't you tell me? Why didn't anybody tell me?"

" 'Cause it didn't make no difference. You're Mr. Edwin's daughter just as sure as if he begat you. Stand up now, honey."

Sylvain stood, her arms hanging limply at her sides while her servant peeled the frilly dress off. "Randolph doesn't love me anymore. He's not going to marry me, Delilah."

"Step out now, lamb." Delilah pulled the dress and petticoats away from Sylvain's feet. "That man ain't good enough for my angel nohow."

"I love him, Delilah. I want to be his wife, but now he doesn't . . . Dear God, what have I done to deserve this?" She was beginning to tremble again.

Delilah swept the slim girl into her strong arms. "You ain't done nothin', not a thing, and neither has your sweet mama. That poor woman suffered all those years — so 'fraid you was goin' to be hurt. I jes' thank the Lord that gentle soul be up in heaven and not have to know 'bout this."

"Delilah, how did you learn the truth?" She gently pulled away from the servant's embrace and slumped back onto her bed.

Delilah handed her a white nightgown. "Honey, ain't a lot goes on that us darkies don't know 'bout. I heard all 'bout it when I was a child back at Riverbend."

"I see." Sylvain wearily slipped on her gown. "Did you know about Hyde Rankin?"

"Yes, child, I did." Delilah frowned. "That man be the devil hisself, for sure. He has the sin of Sodom, that one does."

"What does that mean, Delilah?"

"Nothin'. I be speakin' out of turn."

"Tell me, I want to know."

Delilah sat down on the bed beside Sylvain. "Did your daddy tell you 'bout your aunt, Sister Sylvain, catchin' that devil-man doing somethin' bad."

"Yes, but what?"

Delilah's big eyes rolled. "She come upon him in the smokehouse with a young boy."

"And?"

"He was doing things with that boy. You know, like men and women does when they be married."

"My God!" Sylvain murmured. "You mean he was — "

Delilah nodded. "Sister Sylvain, she throwed him right out of de convent, she did."

"Delilah." Sylvain clutched the woman's arm. "How long after Hyde Rankin left the school did my Aunt Sylvain die?"

"Not even six months, best I recalls. And you know what I always suspected?"

"That maybe Hyde Rankin could have — "

"They foun' her dead in the convent courtyard one morning at dawn. She had a powerful nasty bruise on her head." Delilah frowned. "The doctor say she fell, but I

208

don't believe it. I think that devil-man came back and kilt Sister Sylvain. That's jes' what I think!"

"Is there nothing the man won't do?" Sylvain rubbed her temples.

"I 'spect not, honey. He be evil through and through."

"Delilah, did you know a slave named Kashka at Riverbend?"

"I hear of him, but I don't remember him. He died when I was little. I know why you're askin'. I hear those whispers 'bout hidden treasure at Riverbend."

"Do you believe it?"

"Naw, I don't. They say ole Kashka was the only one who knew where the gold be buried. They say your mama ask after him first thing when she moved to Riverbend, but he was already dead before she got there."

"You mean my mother . . . Who told her to ask for him?"

Delilah lifted her shoulders. "They say Lafitte told Sister Sylvain to tell your mama to ask for old Kashka. I don't know why, though."

Tom Mason shook hands with Edwin Fairmont. "What can I do for you, Mr. Fairmont?"

"I wish you to carry a message to Randolph Baxter at Oakgrove plantation."

Tom Mason looked puzzled. "To Miss Sylvain's betrothed?"

Edwin gritted his teeth. "I'm challenging Baxter to a duel. Will you deliver the invitation and be my second?"

Young Mason's jaw dropped. He leaped from the chair he'd just taken. "Sir, you can't be serious. You're going to duel with the man your daughter plans to marry?"

"She's not going to marry him, Tom. Will you deliver the message?"

"I . . . yes, sir. If that's what you wish."

"Go at once, I'll be waiting here for you."

Tom Mason rode out to Oakgrove and returned within an hour. "At dawn," he said. "He's chosen pistols, sir."

"Fine," said Edwin Fairmont and poured himself a stiff drink.

Sylvain and Delilah continued to talk through the long night. Sylvain wept again as she spoke of Randolph Baxter, her mother, and of the buccaneer Jean Lafitte.

Exhaustion finally became a balm for her pain, and she slipped into a deep sleep just as the first pale light of the summer sun drove away the darkness.

Delilah gently pulled the coverlet up over her slender frame and murmured softly, "Sleep, my baby, you jes' sleep. Delilah be right here with you. Goin' to be a better day today." She tiptoed to a chair and sank into it wearily, her eyelids heavy. "Randolph Baxter!" she spat. "I knowed he be weak. Ain't no man at all." Her head fell to one side, "She better off without him." Delilah dozed.

A loud pounding on the bedroom door jarred both women fully awake. Sylvain sat up in bed as Delilah hurried to the door.

Delson stood there, big tears rolling down his cheeks. "Come quick," he cried, "Mr. Edwin done been shot!"

Sylvain, clad only in her nightgown, flew down the stairs. Edwin Fairmont lay upon the champagne brocade sofa, his eyes closed, a bright blossom of blood on his chest. Tom Mason knelt beside him.

Sylvain fell to her knees and grabbed one of Edwin's hands. "Daddy," she whispered, swallowing the lump in her throat. "Speak to me, please speak to me." Without taking her eyes from his white face, she cried, "Tom, what happened?"

"Miss Sylvain, your father met Randolph Baxter in a duel for your honor."

"And Randolph?" she whispered, loving him in spite of all that had happened. "He's unhurt. Baxter got the draw. Your father never got off a shot." Tom cleared his throat. "I believe Baxter drew prematurely."

"Is the doctor coming?" She smoothed a thin lock of gray hair from her father's forehead.

"He's on the way. I sent Theo for him."

"Daddy," she murmured again, "you'll be fine. The doctor will be here soon."

Edwin Fairmont's eyes opened. He looked at Sylvain, tried to speak, and stopped breathing.

Chapter Seventeen

Ladies of the gentry soon stopped calling at the Fairmont home. By autumn society was in a tumult over Sylvain's right to admittance. Come winter it had been unequivocally decided: Sylvain Fairmont had no place among them. She did not belong.

"A sweet child," one would say. "Still . . . "

"A *buccaneer's* offspring," another would put in. "And her mother, rest her soul — why, that woman was no better than the harlots down on the waterfront," sniffed Laura Lancaster, the banker's wife, a plump, pretty brunette with small, bejeweled hands, enormous breasts, and a distinct sense of superiority. "I almost have an attack of the vapors when I recall all the times they dined in our home."

Sylvain had seen so much tragedy in such a short time that she hardly realized — or cared — what the city's elite were saying about her. The long, sweltering fall had passed in a fog of pain and confusion. The deaths of Edwin and Serena Fairmont, the cruel jilting by Randolph Baxter, had left her so hurt and lost she'd hardly considered the chilly behavior of her former friends.

She was grateful for the privacy, preferring to sit for hours alone in the bricked courtyard, her thoughts tumbling in all directions like the brittle runners of dying rosebushes spilling over the high brick walls of her sanctuary. She needed the solitude and the quiet. She was barely aware that day after long autumn day passed with no callers.

Night after moonlit night Sylvain sat alone and relived happier times spent in the now-dormant courtyard: the chilly days when Edwin Fairmont would rake leaves from the brown, dying grass, his face ruddy and glowing, his pale eyes shining with happiness; the warm spring days when her mother would read poetry aloud, her soft voice like an angel's whisper in the quiet afternoon; and the balmy starlit nights when Randolph sat with her, his arms around her, as he murmured passionately that he loved her.

Sylvain said good-bye to them all in that sad eighteenth autumn of her life, and by the time the first frost came, she had put her grief behind her and stepped into her role as head of the Fairmont household. She visited the empty law offices on Franklin Street. Tom Mason had taken a position with another law firm. He'd sent the office keys to the town house but had not bothered to call. Sylvain looked, for the first time, at the many leather-bound ledgers Edwin Fairmont kept. She packed up all the files. And finally she went through all the bank drafts he'd written.

Her rage mounted with each one she saw. Vast sums of money had gone to Hyde Rankin. The vile man had bled Edwin Fairmont of his entire fortune. Sylvain could only shake her head in despair. There was nothing left. Nothing. Even the town house was so heavily mortgaged that she would have to sell it.

Stacks of unpaid bills swam before her shocked eyes. There were duns from the modiste for the expensive wedding gown that she would never wear and countless bills for frocks, hats, underwear. None of the trousseau had been paid for. There were repair bills for work done on the house, duns for the expensive new Aubusson carpets laid in the town house for the wedding reception, bills from Dr. Talbot, from grocers, from stables and carriage owners.

Sylvain's head throbbed. Frightened, with nowhere to turn, she sat alone in an office where the lease had not been paid and wondered what would become of her. And what of Delilah and Delson, Nana and Theo and Bodine? How would they survive? How could she feed them? Where would they live?

Fighting the panic threatening to overcome her, Sylvain rose, took her velvet bonnet from the rack, tied the taffeta bow beneath her proud chin, and went directly to the Mobile National Bank. The bank's president and owner, Newton Lancaster, rose when she entered his office.

Without preamble, Sylvain told him she was aware her father had borrowed a large sum of money on the town house. She intended to sell the property and repay the debt without delay. Lancaster eyed the brave young woman and said, "That's wise, my dear. It so happens I know a charming couple who might be interested in purchasing it. Shall I tell them they can come around someday soon?"

"The sooner the better," said Sylvain evenly. "Good day, sir, and give my best to Mrs. Lancaster." She saw embarrassment flicker in his eyes, but thought nothing of it. She had no idea that the banker's sharp-tongued wife was going about Mobile ridiculing her.

"Ah, yes, yes, I will. Laura, I'm sure, will come to call soon." His face went pink with his lie.

It was on her walk home that Sylvain was snubbed for the first time. Two handsomely dressed ladies, who'd taken coffee in the Fairmont parlor many times, passed Sylvain on the street. She smiled at them and automatically stopped to exchange pleasantries. They nodded briskly and hurried on, leaving her standing there, gaping after them. She looked around, puzzled, and saw a group of gentlemen talking low and laughing, their eyes upon her.

She recognized the dry, metallic taste of fear in her mouth. She was standing on the busy sidewalk, alone and terrified. Her heart thumped against her ribs, and her knees were rubbery. As she stood rooted to the spot, she could hear snatches of conversations drifting from across the street: "A pirate's daughter . . . Serena Fairmont bedded the blackguard . . . old Edwin probably never knew . . . "

Suddenly her fear was replaced with rage. Gone was the metallic taste, supplanted by the bile of hatred. Sylvain spun around and stepped off the wooden sidewalk. Heedless of the carriages and carts clogging the bustling streets, she stormed across the avenue, fists clenched, jaw set.

She walked right up to the large gathering of elegant, idle men and said courageously, "You call yourselves gentlemen but you don't know the meaning of the word! Hear me, all of you: Say what you will about me, speak ill of Jean Lafitte if you must, but say one more defamatory word about my mother or Edwin Fairmont and you'll answer to your Maker!"

They all stared at the tall, wild-eyed young woman. Passersby on both sides of the busy street paused to look and listen. No one made a sound.

Her gray eyes wintry, Sylvain glared at them a moment longer, then turned and walked away. Only then did a ripple of nervous laughter escape their lips. She never heard it; the blood was pounding too loudly in her ears. Never had she been so angry, so consumed by wrath. She was nearing the town house before her heart slowed its furious beat and she had ceased grinding her teeth.

In a small yard before a house one block from her own, three pretty children were playing tag. Sylvain recognized them. She stopped, as she had always done, to call to them. But the Walden trio, Susie and Louise and Timmy, did not fly to the fence to greet her. They bobbed their heads almost shyly, and from the house a woman's harsh summons made them skitter away immediately.

"Good afternoon, Eliza," Sylvain said to their stern-faced mother. But Eliza Walden, whom Sylvain had known since she moved to Mobile, closed the door after her children and never acknowledged the greeting.

Inside her own home, Sylvain sighed wearily and sank onto the brocade sofa. Handing her bonnet to Delilah, she asked pleasantly, as if nothing had happened, "Will you bring me some coffee, Delilah? I'm chilled. And the *Mobile Examiner*, too."

Delilah's broad face looked troubled.

"What is it, Delilah?"

"Honey, you don't need to read that paper. Ain't nothin' in it worth seein'." She blinked nervously.

Sylvain eyed her servant suspiciously, then rose and went to fetch the newspaper. Unfolding it, she sauntered back into the parlor and sat down. A sick feeling wrenched at the pit of her stomach. The headline on page three made her eyes widen and her hands tremble. "Miss Ginger Thompson Becomes the Bride of Mr. Randolph J. Baxter."

Sylvain didn't read the rest. She couldn't. Tears blurred her vision. Delilah took the paper from her cold hands and sat down beside her. "I'm so sorry, honey. I jes wish there was somethin' I could do."

"You're here," Sylvain said and gripped Delilah's strong hand. "That's enough. Don't ever leave me."

"Never," said Delilah fiercely and meant it.

Lieutenant Hilton Courteen was not the only young officer at the St. Louis, Missouri, home of Robert Lee on the cold Thanksgiving of 1837, but he was by far the favorite of the Lee children. And of Mrs. Lee as well.

While a cozy fire snapped and crackled in the grate and mouth-watering aromas wafted in from the big kitchen, Hilton sat on a horsehide sofa in the parlor of the roomy two-story home and listened distractedly to the conversation of the half-dozen young officers who'd been invited to share a turkey dinner with First Lieutenant Robert Lee and his family.

While the officers talked about devising some means by which the channel of the Mississippi River at St. Louis could be cleared of the sand banks that were making navigation impossible on the stream's western side, Hilton made silly faces at the baby in the crook of his long arm. Six-month-old William Lee gurgled and blew bubbles and tried to reach Hilton's newly grown mustache. William's five-year-old brother, Custis, and his three-year-old sister, Mary, were perched on Hilton's knees, giggling and poking their infant brother.

The two older children were delighted that their "Uncle" Hilton had come for dinner. They knew he would stay long after the other soldiers had gone. And they knew he would tickle them, wrestle with them, and play with them for as long as their mother would allow.

The Lee children considered Hilton Courteen their personal playmate, and they loved him almost as much as they loved their indulgent father.

"Him have no teef." Mary stuck her pudgy finger into her infant brother's tiny mouth.

Hilton gingerly removed the probing finger and smiled down at her. "Darlin', he's too little to have teeth."

"I've got lots," she proudly announced and showed them to Hilton.

"And pretty ones they are," he assured her, patting her back.

"Uncle Hilton," Custis asked, "will you spend the night?"

"No, Custis, I can't do that."

"You can sleep with me. I've got my own bed." The dark-eyed little boy put his hand on Hilton's face.

"That's grand, Custis, but I — "

"Children, you are smothering Lieutenant Courteen." Mary Lee bent to take her infant son from Hilton's arms. "Now jump down and go bother your daddy." She took Custis's elbow and helped him to his feet.

"No!" shouted the willful three-year-old Mary, lunging at Hilton and throwing her arms around his neck.

"Robert," Mrs. Lee said, turning to her husband, "can you do something with your daughter? She's been misbehaving all morning."

Robert Lee smiled placidly and left his spot before the fire. He picked up his daughter, touched his wife's plump cheek, and said, "She's only expressing her desires, dear." He winked at Hilton. "Reminds me a bit of the lady for whom she's named."

Mary pretended to hit her husband while all the young officers laughed. Tweaking her husband's bushy mustache, she warned, "If you don't wish to be served the turkey gizzard, Robert, you'd best watch your tongue."

Hilton took his seat at the long dining table and bowed his dark head while Robert gave the blessing. The conversation once again turned to the army activities at the fort while the ravenous soldiers ate the bounty before them.

After the heavy meal, the children were put down for their naps while the gentlemen enjoyed coffee and cigars in the parlor. One by one the young men departed, but Hilton remained. He and his old West Point classmate visited privately while Mary busied herself in the kitchen.

A cloud of smoke drifted up about his classic features as Robert said, "You were wrong, Hilton, my friend."

"I've been wrong many times," Hilton agreed, smiling. "What are you referring to this time, Robert?"

Robert tapped ashes into a crystal ashtray. His brown eyes were wistful, almost sad. "When you left the Point you told me I'd a major by winter. It took me seven years to make first lieutenant." He sighed. "Do you suppose it will take another seven before I reach captain?"

"Robert, I can't understand why — "

Uncharacteristically, Robert interrupted. "You know I think I shall tell my sons not to make a career of the army. Become a rich planter or a politician first and then come into the army as a commissioned officer. It's the only way to get ahead, it seems to me."

Hilton leaned forward and said diplomatically, "Robert, perhaps the timing of my prediction was off. Still I know you'll rise to the top before your career is over. You're not yet thirty. You'll make your mark."

"You truly believe that, Hilton?"

"I do, my impatient friend. Yes, indeed."

"And I do also." Mary Lee joined them. She sat on the arm of her husband's chair. "He'll succeed yet, I just know it."

Robert smiled up at her. "It will require a feat greater than the one I'm assigned to now, my dear." He took her hand. "Clearing the Des Moines Rapids of rocks is hardly an occupation for heroes."

Mary sighed. "Lieutenant Courteen, do you feel you're wasting your time being assigned to this important engineering project?"

Hilton felt himself flushing. Before he could reply, Robert told his wife, "Mary, Lieutenant Courteen is leaving within the week. He's been ordered to Florida."

Mary's eyes grew large. "The Seminole War?"

"Yes, Mrs. Lee," Hilton replied almost sheepishly.

The woman who loved Robert Lee tried very hard to be gracious. "We shall miss you, Lieutenant," she managed, but Hilton could read the displeasure in her eyes. Mary Lee was ambitious for Robert. Too ambitious, some said. She was bitter that it had taken her brilliant husband so long to be promoted. Much as she loved him, she would happily have seen him off to Florida to fight the Indians. She knew that only in battle would he attain the captain's bars he so richly deserved. "You'll write us."

"Count on it," said Hilton Courteen.

Sylvain looked at the five faithful servants and saw that their eyes were wide with fear. She poked at the fire, brushed her hands off, and turned back to them.

"You all know I've sold this house to a couple recently moved to Mobile from Kentucky," she said. "We . . . I will be moving before the Christmas holidays." She drew a deep breath, hugged her arms to herself, and continued. "Mr. and Mrs. Paul King have graciously informed me that all of you will have a home here with them. You'll like the Kings, I'm sure."

Nana and Theo looked relieved, as did Bodine. They loved Sylvain, but knew she could not take care of them, and they were grateful they would have a home. Such was not the case with old Delson. Tears filled his eyes and he began to tremble. Sylvain saw his despair and quickly told him, "Delson, Delilah is coming with me. You may come also, but I want you to realize that you will have a much better life if you stay with the Kings."

"I don't want no fine life, Miz Sylvain. I jes wants to watch over Mr. Fairmont's only child." He rubbed his eyes on the back of his hand.

"Then you shall come along to take care of me, Delson." Sylvain smiled at the old man and knew full well it would be the other way around. Still, her heart lifted at the look of joy and relief that leaped into his eyes.

"I be lots of help to you, Miz Sylvain." He bobbed his head gratefully.

"I know you will," she said softly. "Now you all may go back to your packing chores." She dismissed them and went into the foyer for her wrap. "I won't be home until the dinner hour. I'm sure I'll find employment very soon." She donned her wrap and was gone.

The cold winds stung her cheeks and made her eyes water. Her full skirts and petticoats billowed about her, slowing her progress. She was freezing by the time she had walked the ten blocks to the city's finest shopping district.

She hurried into Meredith's Millinery on Conti Street, setting the bell above the door to tinkling. Mrs. Meredith

220

Thornburg, the plush shop's proprietor, glanced up from the plumed hat she was carefully placing on the head of a customer.

"I'm quite busy," she said sharply and turned her attention back to the lady looking into a gilt-framed mirror, turning this way and that, admiring herself.

"That's fine, Mrs. Thornburg," Sylvain said pleasantly, "I shall wait."

The customer heard her voice, turned to look directly at Sylvain, and lifted her nose in the air. Under her breath, she murmured something to Meredith Thornburg, and Sylvain had a very good idea what it was. Steeling herself, she remained at her post, intent on speaking to the shop owner.

It was two hours before Meredith Thornburg turned her attention to Sylvain.

"Mrs. Thornburg, I understand you're looking for someone to help you out here in the shop, what with the holidays coming on. I'd very much like the position." Sylvain smiled despite the coldness she saw in the milliner's eyes. "Mother and I always had such lovely times shopping here, you were so — "

"I'm sorry, Miss Fairmont," the older woman cut her off. "I have no position open for you."

"But you . . . There's even a sign in your window. I'd work very hard and be a great deal of help to you."

"Only ladies of quality come into this shop. I can't . . . " Meredith Thornburg lowered her eyes. "I'm sorry."

"Are you?" Sylvain gray eyes narrowed. "Don't be. Don't ever be sorry for me!" She whirled and left the shop, slamming the door behind her. Up the street she marched to an exclusive boutique where Serena Fairmont had spent thousands of dollars in the past five years. The result was the same. She tried a dry goods store three blocks away. Even there, she was turned away.

Cold, disappointed, and weary, Sylvain started home as the weak winter sun began to slip below the horizon.

Lost in thought, she didn't notice the two young boys following her as she brushed past holiday shoppers and businessmen. The pair trailing her were soon joined by others, schoolboys passing time in town. Gradually their number swelled to half a dozen and their loud talk and laughter finally drew Sylvain's attention as she neared the edge of the business district.

She turned and saw the boys mimicking her walk, mocking her. And one, the tallest of them all, obviously the self-appointed leader of the gang, cupped his hands to his mouth and hollered, "There goes the bastard!" He laughed uproariously and looked around for approval from his friends. He got it. They all began to call in unison, "Bastard! Bastard! Bastard!"

Sylvain, the blood rushing to her face, her stomach feeling as though someone had viciously slammed his fist into it, started to reprimand her youthful traducers, but stopped herself in time. They were only children. And they were only repeating what they'd heard from their elders — what the entire city of Mobile was saying.

Hand at her throat, Sylvain hurried on, heart pounding furiously in her chest. Hot tears stung her eyes and she bit the inside of her cheek, willing herself not to cry. If only she could get home. *Please God, let me make it home!*

Sylvain hurried down the street, her lungs burning, her slim body trembling. Head spinning, thoughts tumbling, she asked herself what her mother would have done at this minute. *No!* she thought. *Better still, what would Jean Lafitte have done?*

It helped. It helped a great deal. Her strong chin rose slightly. The tears stopped threatening to spill. Her legs felt stronger.

She'd heard enough about Lafitte to know that little, if anything, had ever frightened him. He'd apparently been capable of striking fear in the hearts of the most hardened men. She could almost feel his blood surging through her veins, could almost hear his calm, cool voice whispering to her to stand up to her tormentors.

Abruptly, Sylvain halted, turned around, and fixed the boys with a look so cold and menacing that she heard several of them gasp. Two boys turned and ran. Even the leader stopped short, his last insult dying on his lips.

Sylvain said nothing, but turned away and strolled down the street. it was a minor battle, but victory was sweet. She savored it as she walked through the gathering darkness, and it was not until she was safely inside the warm town house that she allowed herself to consider the luxury of weeping.

Even then she waited. She greeted the servants cheerfully and told them she hadn't found employment but something was sure to turn up soon. She ate her dinner, read the newspaper, and soaked in the hot bath Delilah had drawn for her.

Alone at last in her bed, she heard again the cruel word, "Bastard!" She wept and shook with fear and despair. And she wondered: Was it that Jean Lafitte had never been afraid or was it that he just never let anyone see his fear?

Wise beyond her years, Sylvain felt certain it was the latter. All at once she almost loved the dark man who was her father. Of course he'd been afraid, she told herself, many, many times. But he'd been strong enough to hide his fear from the world.

She'd be like him. She'd be like her father. The cold, uncaring world would never again know she was afraid. If she was Jean Lafitte's daughter, then by the Almighty, she'd behave like it.

Sylvain slept better that night than she had in months.

Lieutenant Hilton Courteen, granted a two-week furlough before he was to report for duty in Florida, alighted from the leased carriage at the remote Mississippi cotton plantation, Briarfield. His eyes went to the front portico where a tall, spare man stood looking down at him.

"Jeff!" Hilton called and Jefferson Davis lethargically lifted a slim hand to wave.

"Welcome to Briarfield," the unsmiling Davis said tiredly and disappeared inside.

It was a very changed Jefferson Davis whom Hilton had come to visit. The stoic Davis's once alert, blue-gray eyes were now dulled with sadness, and the mischievous grin was no longer in evidence.

At a small dinner party that evening in Hilton's honor, Davis ate sparingly, spoke little, and seemed bored and distracted. After the meal, he wandered alone into the newly planted yard, saying only, "Brandy's on the sideboard, Hilton. Will you pour?"

Hilton's dark eyes followed his slim, melancholy friend. "Cognac?" He rose at once, looking at his table companions. He cheerfully acted as host, leading the conversation, bidding good night to departing guests.

When only one couple remained, Hilton took a seat across from them and saw his concern for Jeff Davis mirrored in their eyes, though none mentioned it. Brian Le Noble, a large man with iron-gray hair, strong features, and a quick, biting wit, told Hilton he was a transplanted easterner.

The big man smiled broadly. "Know why I came on down south?"

Hilton returned his smile, looked at Le Noble's serenely beautiful blond wife, and said, "That is no mystery to me." He addressed Mrs. Le Noble. "My dear, you're a southerner, are you not?"

Alexa Le Noble, regal, self-assured, and charming, favored Hilton with an engaging smile. "From my accent, you know very well that I am, Lieutenant. Natchez is my home, the only place I've ever lived."

"Aha." Courteen grinned and his gaze swung back to Brian Le Noble. "Can't say that I blame you, sir." He looked again at the lovely Alexa. She had lifted a slim hand to her husband's shoulder, and her sparkling green eyes were on his strong face.

"Lieutenant Courteen," Le Noble said proudly, "I met this sweet woman in New York. She'd come with her parents for the winter social season. I was fortunate enough be at the theater on a cold January night. Alexa and her parents were in the box next to mine." He turned and smiled at his wife. "Before the curtain went down I'd decided to make her mine."

"Lieutenant Courteen," Alexa spoke in a soft, pleasing voice that enchanted Hilton, "are you married? Is there a wife down in New Orleans?"

"No, Mrs. Le Noble," he replied smoothly.

"Did you know Sara, Jeff's wife?"

"I met her once," said Hilton, the smile leaving his face. The three then spoke of their deep concern for Jeff, the Le Nobles telling Hilton that they'd tried everything they could think of to draw him out of his despair. Nothing worked.

Later that night, after the Le Nobles departed, insisting Hilton and Jeff come for dinner at their home on Friday night, the two former West Point classmates drank in the parlor. Jeff Davis, his tongue loosened by liquor, stared into the fire and said flatly, "I'm tired of living, Hill. I wish I'd died with Sarah."

"You don't mean that, Jeff. You're young and — "

"I'm old, my friend, in spirit. My dreams are dead, my purpose gone, my existence pointless." He drained his glass, his brooding eyes staring fixedly, his slim shoulders slumped, his chin on his chest.

Hilton had hoped Jeff's grief would have eased by now, that the wound would be healed. Looking at the lined face of his gloomy friend, Hilton said softly, "Jeff, you loved your wife very much, I know, and she — "

"Loved Sarah?" Jeff interrupted. "I worshiped her!" He turned to look at Hilton. "Three months, Hill. Three short months together, that's all we had. She was twenty-one, just a girl. She died in my arms, and I could do nothing to help her, nothing."

"I'm sorry."

"I had the fever, too. Why in hell didn't I die? Will you tell me that?"

"I can't, Jeff. But I'll tell you this. Since you didn't, you'll to have get on with your life."

It was as though Hilton hadn't spoken. Jeff Davis mused, "My precious Sarah died two years and three months ago, and never a day goes by . . . never an hour passes, that I do not wish I'd died when she did."

"It will not always be so, Jeff. You told me once that destiny had great things in store for you. Perhaps that's why you were spared."

Jeff Davis didn't reply.

The weather matched Sylvain's mood on moving day. The sky was bleak, the cold air heavy with moisture.

She watched her mother's fine brocade sofa being carried into the tiny parlor of the small house she'd leased on Water Street. The poorly built clapboard structure had little appeal. It was identical to the houses around it. On the lower floor were four rooms with scarred wooden plank floors: a modest parlor, a kitchen large enough for serving meals, a tiny bedchamber opening into the parlor, and a screened-in sleeping porch. Upstairs were two decent-sized bedchambers. Behind the house, a small smokehouse stood inside a fenced yard that had never been planted with any kind of greenery. Dormant weeds spread below the one bare-branched willow tree.

She'd chosen the house because it was inexpensive and because there were three bedchambers, but one of them would stand empty. Old Delson had died quietly in his sleep a week before in his quarters at the Dauphin Street town house.

Sylvain ran her hands over the fine brocade of the sofa, so out of place in this modest dwelling. And she smiled. As long as she could touch her mother's favorite pieces of furniture — the sofa, the gold chairs, the square piano, the elaborate gilt-framed mirror — this shabby Water Street house would hold a bit of home.

Part III

Chapter Eighteen

The day was unusually warm for February. The sky was a cloudless blue, and a hint of an early spring was in the air. Sylvain thought absently that the weather in Mobile was near perfect for Mardi Gras. Then she laughed at herself for her foolishness. What difference did it make to her? She would not be celebrating this year. She wouldn't be among the gay crowd parading down Theater Street behind the huge bull's head.

Last year's celebration came back vividly to Sylvain as she trudged wearily toward her waterfront house. Randolph Baxter's handsome face rose before her as though he were standing there, so close she could reach out and touch him. Sylvain shook her head to clear it and continued on her way.

She didn't discover she'd taken a wrong turn until she saw the slave block looming before her. Sylvain halted and debated. She could turn around and walk back up Bellview or she could continue along Bellview past the slave block to Water Street.

Her tired, swollen feet decided for her. She'd endured another fruitless day hunting employment, and now she was weary and wanted a bath. So she went on her way and soon was near the strange, crowded place where

Negro men, women, and children were sold to shouting, laughing gentlemen attired in their finery.

A sobbing young black girl stood alone on the platform. The auctioneer was calling for bids, a broad smile on his face. "A fine body!" He grabbed the frightened girl's elbow roughly and turned her around for the crowd's inspection. "She can work twelve, fourteen hours pulling your cotton and still have the energy to take on your strongest bucks. Meant for breedin', she is!"

Appalled yet fascinated, Sylvain unobtrusively edged closer. The weeping girl was sold for $750 and hurriedly shunted from the platform into the hands of her new master.

A Negro man was led onto the scaffold. A buzz went through the gathering. All eyes went to the huge black towering over the barking auctioneer.

The black stood with his feet apart. He wore only a pair of white plantation breeches. A Goliath in stature, his deep chest was broad, his shoulders wide and powerful. Muscles bulged in his big arms and in the enormous thighs straining the worn fabric covering his long legs. His color was a light tan, and the smooth bare flesh shimmered with perspiration. His head was noble, his face intelligent, his dark eyes sullen.

The bidding began at once and excitement mounted. More than one gentleman clamored for the chance to own this magnificent specimen. One in particular seemed so determined to purchase the black man that he topped every bid. Sylvain moved to a better vantage point so that she could see the persistent bidder.

Hyde Rankin.

Sylvain expelled a breath and stared at the ferret-faced man who'd stolen Riverbend and ruined her life. Rankin was smiling as he raised a hand excitedly to shout another increase. A young man with blond hair put a slim hand on Rankin's arm and leaned close to whisper something to him. Rankin nodded and continued bidding.

Sylvain held her breath, praying some decent, honest planter would top Rankin's bid and take the noble black away from the clutches of one so thoroughly wicked. It didn't happen. When the bidding ended at $2,000, Hyde Rankin was the owner of the huge man.

Heartsick, Sylvain turned and hurried away. Swollen feet forgotten, she rushed toward the waterfront. What was the despicable Hyde Rankin doing in Mobile? She thought about what Delilah had told her — and she remembered the young man she'd seen whispering into Rankin's ear. Her stomach did a turn.

Whatever did the strange pair want with the enormous light-skinned black man? She was afraid of the answer.

The winter weather had returned by the next morning. Sylvain drew on her warmest woolen cape and pulled the hood up over her head. Delilah took her arm and said, "Honey, it be too cold to go out today. Jes' wait till next week. Then you can go lookin' again."

"It's all right, Delilah. I'm not going far." Sylvain smiled and explained, "I've finally begun to understand that the shopkeepers in Mobile are never going to allow me to work in their stores. You see, my presence offends the genteel ladies and — "

"Don't talk like that, Sylvain. You is — "

"A bastard, Delilah. That's what I am and what I will always be. So I will go where such a stigma is not important."

Delilah's eyes widened. "You not goin' . . . you not intendin' to . . . ? Her hands went to her heart. "Lord, no. I lock you up before I let — "

"No, dear, dear Delilah, I didn't mean that." Sylvain laughed heartily. "There's an abundance of prostitutes in this port. I have no intention of joining their ranks."

"Well, don't be scarin' me like that," Delilah sniffed, relieved.

"Sorry, I only meant I've decided to look for a position down here on the waterfront."

"Doin' what?"

Sylvain lifted her slender shoulders. "I'm not quite sure." Twenty minutes later she stopped outside a ship chandlery half a block from the levee. She went in, nodded pleasantly to two older ladies who were fussing over a cloth-covered tray resting on a long wooden counter.

"I wish to see John Spencer," she said.

"I'm John Spencer," came a low, raspy voice from behind her. Sylvain turned to see a short middle-aged man with light brown hair, muttonchop sideburns, thin pink lips, a bulbous nose, and a warm green eyes.

Sylvain thrust out her hand. "Mr. Spencer, I'm Jean Lafitte's daughter and I need employment. I want to work for you!" She heard the horrified gasps from the pair at the counter, but looked steadily into John Spencer's eyes.

"And what do you know of this kind of business, my dear?" He was smiling, whether at her or with her, Sylvain was not certain.

"Nothing, sir, but I'm very quick. I'll learn rapidly and work very hard."

"I'm sure that's true, but I hardly think a ship chandlery is the place for a refined young lady." Sylvain heard snorts of disgust from the ladies.

"Perhaps you didn't hear me. I told you, I'm Lafitte's daughter, and I . . . What is it?" John Spencer was studying her intently.

"Child, your father was one of my very first customers at this store."

"My . . . Lafitte was here?" she asked incredulously. "He came in this shop?"

John Spencer was nodding vigorously. He took Sylvain's elbow. "Come, meet my sisters. You're lucky they are here. They've brought me my breakfast. Hester, Marie, say hello to Miss Lafitte."

The one called Hester, the plumper and older of the pair, sniffed and said rudely, "I thought your name was Miss Fairmont." Her thin eyebrows lifted accusingly and Marie nodded approval at her sister's barb.

Sylvain looked from one plain face to the other. She laughed softly and replied, "You know what? I, too, thought my name was Miss Fairmont." With that she burst into laughter. She laughed at them. At herself. At life.

While the women stared at her, John Spencer laughed and when finally he and Sylvain calmed themselves, he told her, "Dear, you will be an asset to this establishment. You've got your father's wit and charm. I'll wager you have his ambition and intelligence as well. Start work tomorrow morning. Nine sharp."

"You're a kind man, John Spencer," said Sylvain. She rushed happily to the door, then paused to turn and look at the sisters. "Is it a family trait?" The sound of his laughter followed her out the door.

"How dare you, John!" stormed Hester Spencer when Sylvain had left. "We know about that woman! Why, her mother lay with a pirate. Can you imagine such a ghastly thing!"

"Yes, I can," said the wise, understanding John Spencer. "I liked Jean Lafitte. But even if I had not, I'd still have hired his daughter. She's alone and needs help. You claim to be Christians. Where's your compassion, your understanding, your love?" He looked at the pair of spinsters and wondered, as he had so many times, if they had any conceivable notion of what it was to be young and in love, to make a mistake born of passion. He thought not.

Marie spoke up. "Why, John Spencer, surely you don't expect us to condone what you're doing. How can you ask us to . . . to associate with a . . . a — " Her face went crimson and she couldn't say the word.

"Bastard?" he supplied and watched his sisters exchange glances. "That won't be necessary, my dears, but
if you don't wish to be around her, then you'd best stay
upstairs in your quarters, because that child is going to
work in this store."

"But, John, we can't — "

"I have nothing more to say on the matter," warned
John Spencer, lifting the napkin from the tray. He picked
up a piece of bread, took a bite, and turned his attention
to the morning newspaper.

Lieutenant Hilton Courteen, sweat staining the blouse
of his blue army uniform, body aching from fatigue,
rested against a cypress stump deep in the Florida
Everglades. He smoked his last cigar and questioned
what he was doing here in this tropical terrain pursuing the elusive Seminoles with whom he secretly
sympathized.

This was their land, their home, their world, and they'd
been told to leave it. Could he blame them for not
obeying? Hilton leaned his head back and let his heavy
lids slide low over his burning eyes.

He'd heard how Andrew Jackson had issued the edict
to the Seminoles. "I tell you that you must go and that
you will go," he had warned them. The Seminole chiefs
in the meeting at Fort King had been ordered to sign
away their Florida lands. The young brave Osceola had
plunged his knife into the document and cried, "The
only treaty I will ever make is this!"

Hilton drew on his cigar and cringed. That same young
brave had become the chief of the Seminoles. He'd ridden into St. Augustine under a white flag of truce sent to
him by General Jessup. Jessup then violated his own flag,
arrested Osceola, and imprisoned him. The proud Osceola
had died of malaria in prison. Rumor had it that the
attending doctor had cut off the Indian's head for a
souvenir.

Chief Coacoochee, or Wild Cat, was the main thorn in the side of the United States Army now. Captured with Osceola, he'd escaped and fled back into the swamps to tell his people the white man could not be trusted. Hilton thought Wild Cat had a point.

"Mount up, men," General Zachary Taylor's voice shook Hilton from his reverie. "I know damned well that bastard Wild Cat is near here. We'll flush him out if it's the last thing we do."

Hilton pulled his forage cap low on his forehead, rose, tossed away his cigar, and mounted a big bay stallion. He and a thousand other soldiers headed deeper into the swamps. Not an hour later the general ordered his men to dismount.

"Horses are useless in these damnable swamps. We shall proceed on foot."

To the left of the soldiers stretched an endless savanna, to their right an impenetrable marsh. And dead ahead, across a sea of razor-sharp sawgrass, lay a thickly foliaged hammock. There were no Indians in sight.

Taylor asked for volunteers and, to Hilton's chagrin, the tall, imposing general pointed a blunt finger in his direction and said, "You, there, Lieutenant, you say you'll go in?" His steely eyes were fixed on Hilton.

"Yes, sir," said a reluctant Hilton Courteen and divested himself of all equipment save his weapon. He and the other volunteers formed two lines, then crept into the eerie silence of the swamp where they heard only their own footfalls and the occasional call of a bird. They crossed the waving sawgrass and neared the hammock.

Hilton felt the hair stand up on the back of his neck. He was sure hostile eyes were upon them as they moved deeper and deeper into the jungle. A low-hanging wisp of Spanish moss touched his face and startled him so badly he almost called out.

In the woods of the savanna, hundreds of Seminole warriors were waiting. From the edge of the marshes,

Wild Cat's steady gaze observed the unsuspecting soldiers. The calm young chief waited until they were at point-blank range to give the order.

Shots erupted from the dense growth all around the trapped soldiers. Hilton's fear evaporated. Before the echo of the first report died, he had raised his breech-loading Springfield rifle and begun to fire at the swarming warriors.

He recognized the handsome Wild Cat as if he'd known the man all his life. He aimed at the young chief's naked chest, but never pulled the trigger. A bullet caught Lieutenant Hilton Courteen in the upper right quadrant of his back. His dark eyes flickered in surprise as he slumped to the marshy ground.

The dour sisters were nowhere in sight when Sylvain Fairmont arrived at the chandlery the next morning at the appointed time. John Spencer looked up from a ledger book, smiled broadly, nervously tugged at a sideburn, and said cheerfully, "Morning, Miss Fairmont. Right on time. Good, good."

Sylvain shrugged out of her cape. "Mr. Spencer, I'm Miss Lafitte, not Miss Fairmont."

The middle-aged man came around the counter. "Tell you what. So there'll be no confusion, I'll call you Sylvain, you call me John. How would that be?" His friendly eyes twinkled as he relieved her of her wrap.

She smiled at him. "John," she said softly, "I like you."

He chuckled. "I'm delighted that you do, Sylvain. Come, I'll show you around while we have no customers."

John Spencer was warm and likable, but a poor businessman. He led Sylvain through a maze of merchandise and provisions, much of the inventory hidden so completely she doubted he knew where or what it was.

Pails of tar, coils of rope, barrels of rye, nails, whale oil, tallow, candles, decking, and ducking were carelessly strewn about the store. Above them, the sail loft held more discarded refuse than sailcolth.

But Spencer seemed unaware that anything was amiss. Sylvain suspected he'd been looking at the disorganized shelves and rows for so long that he'd grown accustomed to the clutter.

"This isn't the most profitable business on the levee, but it feeds us," he mused, laying a broad hand on a pile of warped lumber. "Why don't you sit there on the rye barrel, Sylvain, and let's visit a moment?"

She blew dust from the barrel, sat down, and folded her hands in her lap, her quick mind already planning how she would clean, rearrange, discard, and better display merchandise.

John Spencer crossed his short arms across his sturdy chest and said apologetically, "Sylvain, my sisters were rude to you yesterday and — "

"John, don't apologize. I understand."

The chandler lowered his head, sighed, then lifted it. "May I tell you a bit about my family?" Sylvain nodded. "Hester, Marie, and I were born and raised on a farm outside Cleveland, Ohio, near the shores of Lake Erie. Papa was a preacher and a strict disciplinarian." John uncrossed his arms, lifted a hand, and absently tugged at a sideburn. "He thought sin was hiding around every corner, lurking behind every door, concealed in any place where there was love and laughter. He believed the devil was always poised to pounce on the unsuspecting."

Remembering, he laughed, then hurried on. "I'm afraid my sisters learned the lesson too well. They thought anything Papa said was gospel. When he lost Mama, he preferred that his daughters never marry, that they stay at home to care for him."

Sylvain raised her well-shaped eyebrows. "Could it be the holy man was guilty of the sin of selfishness?" She grinned at John Spencer.

He laughed aloud. "You're a smart young woman. It's tragic that Marie and Hester were not as clever." John shook his head. "I met and married the cutest little girl in Ohio, said good-bye to friends and family, and brought my bride to Alabama with very little money in my pocket. We bought this chandlery from an old man who was eager to retire, moved into the quarters upstairs, and were the happiest two people on earth." He fell silent, sighed, and squatted down on his heels.

"My sweet Lily was soon carrying our child. She was a tiny girl, hardly five feet, and . . . and fragile." John cleared his throat. "She died in labor along with my son."

"Oh, John." Sylvain's voice was soft. "I'm sorry."

John stood up and shoved his hands into his pockets. "I was alone then, but not for long. When Papa died, I sent for Hester and Marie. The three of us have lived here together ever since. Neither has ever had a beau. They've been sheltered all their lives, even here in this bustling port. They go nowhere but to church services and the market, and I escort them whenever they set foot outside that front door."

"You're a good man, John Spencer," said Sylvain gently. "I'm glad you've told me all this. I"ll be most respectful of the sisters, and perhaps in time, they'll see that I have no horns or tail." She laughed, jumped down from the barrel, and said, "Put me to work, John. Where do you keep the broom?"

John Spencer grinned at the lively young woman whose sunny smile warmed his heart.

It was a very tired Sylvain who said good night to John Spencer at six that evening. He had teased her through-out the day about "going like a whirlwind," and now she was feeling the effects. Never in her young life had she worked so hard; still, she'd hardly made a dent.

She had hummed as she went about the monumental tasks. She'd tied her dark glossy hair up in a snood, then swept and dusted and waxed. She moved boxes, unpacked crates, discarded trash. And she'd met each patron who came through the creaking front door.

Burly seamen, fresh from months in the Atlantic Gulf, looked at her with keen interest. Lonely sailors, ambling into the chandlery to purchase provisions, pick up mail and messages, or pass some time with John Spencer, were very surprised to see pretty Sylvain. And unkempt ruffians, drunk on cheap whiskey, stumbled into the establishment, blinked at the sight of the beautiful and obviously refined young woman.

"Sylvain," John Spencer quietly told her when she was ready to leave, "I keep a loaded revolver on the low shelf under the cash drawer. Should danger ever befall you . . . "

As she told Delilah of her busy day and of the plans she had for the chandlery, the black woman listened and smiled. Much as she'd hated the thought of her charge taking a position at the chandlery, Delilah was delighted to see a spark of Sylvain's old liveliness returning. The girl's expressive eyes gleamed with excitement, and roses had returned to her golden cheeks.

When Sylvain yawned, Delilah said at once, "Bes' be gittin' in bed, honey." She turned back the covers and Sylvain, nodding, dropped her hairbrush, and slid between the sheets.

" 'Night, Delilah," she said drowsily, closed her eyes and immediately fell asleep.

" 'Night, honey," Delilah whispered, blew out the lamp, and raised the window a few inches to allow fresh air into the tiny bedchamber.

Sylvain didn't know how long she'd been asleep when she was awakened by an unfamiliar sound. Opening her eyes groggily, she raised herself up on her elbows. From the open window came thudding sounds. Sylvain pushed her long dark hair from her face, threw back the covers, and crossed the room. Pulling back the lacy curtains, she looked out the window.

She gasped in horror.

In the tiny barren yard next door, a naked black man was tied to a big oak tree. Hands and ankles cuffed in irons, the poor soul was being beaten by a tall, slender man wielding an ebony cane.

Sylvain didn't hesitate. Heart racing, she flew to the bureau, jerked open the top drawer, and took out a large oxblood leather box. Snapping it open, she drew from its bed of red velvet a long, pearl-handled dueling pistol, leaving its twin in place. Biting her trembling lip, she shoved a lead bullet into the chamber of the heavy silver pistol, grabbed a woolen shawl from the armoire, and threw open her bedroom door.

Delilah, eyes round with fear, stood in the narrow hallway. "You ain't goin' over there!"

"Yes, I am," Sylvain called over her shoulder as she ran down the stairs. She rushed out the back door and across the yard, long dark hair whipping about her shoulders, her white nightgown swirling about her slender body, her feet bare upon the cold ground.

She shoved on the tall gate between the yards. It swung open and she swept through it just as another punishing blow fell across the bloodied back of the chained black.

Aiming her heavy gun at the skull of the man with the cane, Sylvain said levelly, "Hit him once more and I'll blow your head off."

The stunned man turned and Sylvain exhaled loudly. Hyde Rankin, eyes alive with excitement, lips curled evilly, stood staring at her, the ebony cane with its bloodied gargoyle head raised in his hand.

Rage drove away any fear she'd had. "Drop the cane this minute and cut him down," she ordered, fighting a strong compulsion to pull the trigger and watch the despicable man's head explode into a million pieces.

Hyde Rankin rapidly recovered from his surprise. He lowered the cane, but did not drop it. "Your noble

display of courage and concern is touching, but mis-
placed. This slave is my property and I'll punish him as I
see fit."

"You die if you touch him." Sylvain's voice was firm,
her hand steady. She cast a hurried glance at a slim,
blond man clad only in a dark satin robe who stood in
the rectangle of light streaming from the back door. To
Rankin, she said again, "Release him immediately, I'm
out of patience."

"Damn you, you little bitch," snarled Hyde Rankin.
"This nigger is mine. I paid two thousand dollars for
him."

"I'm buying him," said Sylvain. "Cut him down. Now!"

Hyde Rankin furiously strode to the trussed man.
"You'll pay me or wish you had," he barked angrily,
reaching up to untie the man who hadn't made a sound
throughout the merciless beating or the exchange following it.

"You'll get your money tomorrow," Sylvain said icily,
her gun still trained on Rankin.

Once the ropes were removed, Rankin grabbed the
man's arm and spun him around. Sylvain saw the shamed,
pained dark eyes for only a second before the gigantic
black lowered his head. It was the magnificent light-
skinned slave from the auction!

With her free hand she pulled the shawl from her
shoulders and stepped forward. Still pointing the pistol
at Rankin, she managed to wrap the shawl around the
slave. Then she slipped her arm about his waist, and
immediately felt blood saturate the long sleeve of her
nightgown.

"Can you walk?" she asked softly.

"Yes" was all he said.

Ironed hand and foot, the massive man hobbled across
the yard, Sylvain straining to support part of his weight.
The strange pair made slow, steady progress while behind them the blond youth said petulantly to Hyde

Rankin, "We're just as well rid of him. He was no enjoyment at all," and Sylvain realized why they were beating the proud black.

They'd purchased him not for work but for pleasure, and the regal slave had refused to do as they commanded. Sylvain's heart expanded with admiration and regard for him.

"The smokehouse will be fine," said the huge man.

Sylvain tilted her head to look up at him. "You'll come inside," she told him firmly. "Delilah, Delilah!" she shouted when they neared her back door.

"You can't bring no naked nigger in this house," Delilah said loftily, her eyes fixed on the tall, manacled man.

"Help me get him inside or I'll turn this gun on you!" Sylvain spoke sharply.

Delilah snorted, but stepped forward. "Where you aimin' to put him?" She seemed reluctant to touch the injured man.

"In the bedroom off the parlor." The two women managed to get the enormous man to the bed. "Lift your arms over your head," Sylvain said gently. He promptly obeyed, raising his cuffed hands high in the air. "Now we'll lay you down on your stomach." With his help, the two women got him on the clean white bed. Delilah, seeing for the first time the badly lacerated back, cried out. She began to tremble and her hand flew to her mouth.

Sylvain sat on the bed by the the prone man. "Delilah, go for the doctor and then for the blacksmith." She took the linen case from a feather pillow and began to stanch his wounds.

"But . . . but it be the middle of the night. I can't go after no doc — "

"Go!" commanded Sylvain, and Delilah flew upstairs to dress. When she was gone, Sylvain heated water, bathed the deep gashes, and marveled that the man still had made not one sound.

Calmly, in a voice rich and almost melodious, he said, "My name is Napoleon."

Sylvain's eyes were on the ribbons of raw flesh slicing across his back. "Napoleon," she said, "I'm sorry you're in pain. Is there anything I can do?"

"You're doing it," replied Napoleon, his cheek pressed to the mattress, his dark eyes closed. "Thank you for saving me."

"You're ... you're ... " Sylvain couldn't get out the "welcome." Crisis past, the rush of adrenaline long since used up, she choked, and tears rolled down her cheeks.

But when she continued to gently bathe his back, he said soothingly, in precise, perfect English, "Don't cry. I'm fine. Just fine."

The next day Sylvain went to the Mobile National Bank. With her she took Edwin Fairmont's matched pearl-handled dueling pistols and her mother's beautiful emerald ring, the ring she'd promised never to let out of her sight.

She placed pistols and ring on Newton Lancaster's mahogany desk. "I need to borrow two thousand dollars, Mr. Lancaster. I've brought these items to use as collateral."

The president of the Mobile National leaned forward, picked up the ring, and twisted it about on a blunt forefinger. He studied it silently, laid it back on the desk, and flipped open the leather box containing the expensive dueling pistols. He touched a gleaming silver barrel and leaned back in his chair.

"Miss Fairmont, I'm sorry. I can't loan you money on these items."

"But why not?" Sylvain said incredulously. "The ring alone is worth that much and the pistols were specially made in — "

"I'm sure that's true, still ... I have stockholders to satisfy. I have to be very careful about making loans." He leaned forward, touched the emerald, and said, "Tell you what. You seem to need money badly, so I'll help you out. I'll buy the items outright for two thousand."

Sylvain thought for only a moment. She had no choice. She had to have two thousand dollars today. "Done," she said, rising. "Please give me the cash at once, I must hurry."

Sylvain went directly to Hyde Rankin's house. She knocked forcefully on the front door, stood on the small porch in the cold late afternoon air, and heard a commotion within. Muffled voices, quick footsteps, laughter, and finally the young man with blond hair threw open the door.

"I've come to pay for my slave," she said without preamble.

The young man smiled, his soft lips curling into an amused grin. "I'm Philip Lawson. Welcome to my house. Won't you come inside?"

"No." Sylvain shook her dark head impatiently. "Here." She thrust the money at him.

"Bring the lady in," said a low voice. Philip Lawson smiled broadly. "You heard Hyde. He wishes you to come inside."

"I don't care what he wishes," Sylvain said coldly. "I have no intention of — "

Hyde Rankin, wearing only a pair of black trousers, appeared in the doorway, and Sylvain winced. He was even more frightening in the daylight. His long, thin face was sallow and pockmarked, his light eyes beady and cold. His narrow chest and long, skinny arms were covered with hair so thick he looked more like an animal than a man. His thin lips were stretched into an evil smile.

"You've brought the two thousand in cash?" His voice seemed to come from low down in his chest. Sylvain shuddered when he draped a long, hairy arm around the slender blond Philip and drew the youth close to him.

"Take your money," she said coolly, "But should that Negro die, I'll see to it that you are tried for murder!"

Hyde Rankin laughed. Giving Philip's shoulder a squeeze, he released him, then reached out and took the money. Sylvain turned to leave, but he caught hold of her wrist.

"Don't threaten me, I don't like it," he said menacingly.

Struggling to free herself of the long fingers wrapped around her wrist, Sylvain looked into his eyes and said, "I'm telling you that before my life is over, you'll pay for everything you've done. Everything!"

"I doubt that," he said softly, his face close to hers. Then he laughed and added, "You hate me? Well, girl, I'm as displeased as you about this unhappy turn of events. Now that everyone knows you're a pirate's bastard, you're worth nothing to me. It's I who should kill *you*." His eyes narrowed.

Sylvain gritted her teeth. "I don't frighten easily, Rankin. As you just pointed out, I have nothing left to lose." With that she sank her teeth into the back of his bony hand.

"Damn you!" he shrieked and immediately released her. Sylvain hurried off the porch as he shouted after her, "You miserable bitch! You'll be sorry you did that, do you hear me?"

Sylvain flew across the yard to her house. Delilah threw open the front door. Saying nothing of the incident next door, Sylvain related the other events of the day.

"You sold your mama's emerald!" Delilah was outraged. "How could you do sech a thing!"

Sylvain inclined her head toward the small sleeping chamber off the parlor. "Human life has more value than a piece of stone."

Chapter Nineteen

"She's a bastard and we're going to tell her so right to her face," Hester Spencer said righteously.

John Spencer's back stiffened. "You'll do no such thing!"

"And," Marie chimed in, "that tall black who follows her around is nothing more than an uppity nigger slave with that Oxford English accent. We're tired of them both."

John Spencer whirled on the pair. "Two and a half years they've worked here, and look what this chandlery has become!" He pointed out the row upon row of provisions, casks of good wines, great wheels of cheese, tins of coffee and tea and ship's biscuits, sacks of flour and sugar.

"Look around you!" he demanded, directing their attention to the shelves neatly stacked with new rope, nets, navigational instruments, lanterns, and carpentry tools. There were blankets, tailored bunk sheets, pillows, duck seamen's breeches, cotton shirts, woolen jackets, and knitted caps.

The sisters, cowed by their brother's unusual display of anger, watched him stalking between the rows of merchandise, yanking at his sideburn.

"Perhaps she has been of help to you, John," Hester ventured. "Still, we don't — "

"Help?" John interrupted furiously. "Our income has quadrupled since Sylvain came here to work for me." He

marched up to Hester and pointed an accusing finger
in her face. "You're worried about her coming to
your Fourth of July party?" He laughed sharply. "Set
your mind at ease, Hester. Even as you stand here be-
littling her, Sylvain is lugging sacks of flour aboard
the *Susan A.* and the *Black Widow* to show Captain
Andrews and Captain Jonathan Peck the fine quality of
our staples."

A wharf rat ran down the middle of the wooden dock.
Sylvain kicked at the fat rodent with a toe of her worn
slipper and continued on her way. She smiled and nodded to the roustabouts lounging against crates and bales
of hay. She recognized old Amos Dexter, whose full
white beard and mustache made him look like Santa. She
called to the old steamboatman, and he beamed and
lifted a bottle that had been passed from hand to hand.

"Not today, Amos," Sylvain said cheerfully and laughed.
She'd known old Amos from the first week she'd worked
at the chandlery. He drank too much, but he was good-
hearted, a loner who'd spent his life at sea.

"Can we carry that, Syl?" It was one of the fresh-faced
Cole twins. Sylvain smiled and released her burden to
the big hands of Keith Cole. Keith and Ken fell into step
next to her, and talked excitedly of their upcoming voyage. Just nineteen years old, the identical twins were tall,
slender boys with thick brown hair, ruddy complexions,
and infectious grins. The happy-go-lucky pair were fa-
vorites of Sylvain. They, like most of the river people,
knew her real father was Jean Lafitte and envied her
such an illustrious parent. The twins brought her gifts
from exotic places and visited the chandlery any time
they were in port.

"Got time to walk over to Land's End for some seafood
gumbo?" asked Ken Cole.

"Afraid not, Ken. Maybe we can get together later this
evening."

"Nope," Keith shook his head. "We sail at sundown." He broke into a wide grin, "The West Indies, Syl. Can you beat that?"

"Could I stow away?" she teased gaily, suddenly feeling carefree and happy on this oppressively hot July day. "This is it. Keith give me the flour."

They stood before a tall side-wheeler, its engines building steam. Roustabouts gleamed with sweat as they carried huge crates and barrels up the narrow loading planks to the deck of the *Susan A.* Captain Steve Andrews, cap pushed back on a full head of bright red curls, shouted orders from the main deck.

"We got time. We'll take the flour aboard for you." Keith looked down at her.

"You'll do nothing of the kind," she said pertly. She lifted the heavy flour sack, settled it on a slender shoulder, and said, "Have a good journey, you two. Come by the chandlery as soon as you return." Sylvain started up the gangplank of the *Susan A.*, then turned to look at the two boyish faces. "Bring me a seashell from Barbados, all right?"

"Yes, ma'am," they said in unison and watched the flash of snowy white petticoats sway beneath her faded green summer dress.

The late-afternoon sun had grown even hotter when Sylvain wearily stepped down from the *Susan A.* and once again made her way along the levee, the sack of flour balanced on her left shoulder. Dozens of steamers crowded next to sailing ships with their high, proud masts and furled canvas sails. There must have been thirty or more, all shapes and sizes, but Sylvain, feeling perspiration dampen the back of her dress, didn't see the *Black Widow.*

She passed the tall stern-wheelers tied up to the landing posts and wharf-boats and told herself the *Black Widow* must surely be nearby. When she finally caught sight of the side-wheeler, she let out a sigh of relief and hurried toward the big boat.

Captain Jonathan Peck stood on the busy boiler deck. Sylvain waved to him, and the tall, slender man nodded and took a long pull on his pipe. In a voice as threatening as storm at sea, he shouted to the deckhands, "Get that cargo up that ramp! We sail at sundown and I'm not aiming to go out empty!"

Sylvain laughed and darted past two big black men groaning under the weight of an ornately carved piano.

"Well done," Sylvain complimented when the pair deposited the piano on the main deck. "Cap'n Peck," she shouted happily and descended the stairs to the boiler deck.

The sound of a woman's laughter caused her to pause and turn. Hand shading her eyes, Sylvain looked up to the high texas deck.

And her heart stopped.

There in the brilliant July sunshine, leaning over the varnished railing, stood Mr. and Mrs. Randolph Baxter. For a frozen moment she stared at them, and they at her.

Blond hair gleaming in the sun, green eyes fastened on her, Randolph stood tall, handsome, and elegantly turned out. His voluptuous, red-haired wife, Ginger, was clinging to his arm. She wore a beautiful traveling suit of the palest yellow linen, the bodice dipping low to display her generous bosom. Upon her flaming hair, a small, fashionable bonnet sat at a jaunty angle.

Sylvain turned her head away and hurried down the long gangplank, her heart pounding furiously. She'd escaped the unpleasantness of seeing Randolph since that horrible night so long ago when he'd killed Edwin Fairmont. Until today. Now he stood above her, silently appraising, unabashedly assessing, and in all likelihood, thanking the gods he was married to Ginger and not to her.

Commanding her hands to stop shaking, telling herself she hated Randolph Baxter with all her heart, Sylvain lifted her chin, stiffened her back, and gracefully descended the wooden planking. From the railing above, a woman's laugh mocked her.

Captain Peck met her at the foot of the stairs, smiled warmly, and said, "We'll go up to my cabin." He took the sack of flour from her, turned her around, and followed her up the steep stairs. Sylvain, eyes carefully trained on the steps, climbed to the hurricane deck.

Inside Captain Peck's gracious cabin, she took a seat at the long, polished table and nodded when he offered coffee. She sipped at the scalding black brew while the captain relit his pipe and poured himself a jigger of Kentucky bourbon.

He downed the whiskey, grimaced, wiped his mouth on the back of his hand and said, "So you have flour that's free of weevils, girl?"

"I guarantee it, Cap'n." Sylvain shoved the sack of flour toward him. "Cut it open, go ahead. No charge. We want your business at the Spencer Chandlery."

Captain Peck drew on his pipe, raised his eyebrows, and said teasingly, "Why should I buy all my provisions at Spencer's? There are other — "

"Cap'n," Sylvain cut in, "Spencer's now has the best selection in port. Anything you need for a voyage, we can get it for you. I want to set up some kind of agreement between us. You give me your sailing schedules and a list of supplies you'll need; we'll fill the orders and deliver the provisions right to the deck of the *Black Widow*."

"Hard to refuse an offer like that." He grinned and sucked on his pipe.

"Impossible," Sylvain assured him. "I'm telling you, Cap'n Peck, you let me know what you need, and Big Napoleon will have it loaded in plenty of time, no extra charge to you."

"You're quite the little businesswoman, aren't you, my dear?"

"Yes, I am," she said with confidence. "If you're a businessman, and I know you are, you'll accept my offer."

Captain Peck shoved the whiskey glass aside, took a scaling knife from its small scabbard beneath his left arm, and slashed into the sack of flour. With the knife's gleaming tip, he drew furrows in the powdery white stuff, hunting for unwelcome bugs. He saw none.

Sylvain gave him a triumphant look. "Well?"

"Pure as snow, miss. Pure as snow." He reached across the table. "Shake my hand, partner."

Sylvain smiled and grasped the big, callused hand. "You'll not regret it," she promised. She rose. "And now I must go. It's almost sundown."

Captain Peck stood up, his head almost touching the stained ceiling. "And it's almost time I was off. Going to the Bahamas, I am. Loaded down with valuables and only two passengers."

"Two passengers? That's all?"

The tall man winked and said, "A wealthy young couple wants their privacy. I'm to take 'em on down to the Bahamas and lie at anchor until they get bored." He took Sylvain's elbow and escorted her to the cabin door. "Best lookin' youngsters you ever saw, and so much in love it's downright embarrassing to watch 'em. The pretty gal can't keep her hands off her husband." He chuckled. "Yes, sir, they're just crazy about each other, I reckon."

Sylvain stepped out onto the deck, anxious to be off this vessel that was transporting the Baxters to an island paradise. She started down the companionway, surprised to see the sun was slipping rapidly westward, turning the water to a vast brick-hued mirror. Lights were blinking on some of the vessels, and the sounds of fireworks began to fill the evening air.

"Wait, Sylvain." Captain Peck caught her arm, stopping her progress. "Look there, child. It's the *Gulf Princess* steamin' in from Florida. Have you ever seen a grander sight?"

Sylvain reluctantly turned her attention to the huge side-wheeler heading into the berth next to the *Black Widow*. She slid through the water, high and proud, dwarfing all the other boats around her. Her snowy white railing gleamed pink in the setting sun's rays. Her chimneys, twin pillars that stood forward of the texas deck, rose high into the air, black and straight and impressive. Her hull was slender and long. Amidship, the enormous wheelhouses loomed against the sky, the paddle wheels concealed within.

Sylvain looked up at the pilothouse atop the texas roof. The glass temple glittered brilliantly, its cupola decorated with intricate woodwork that looked for all the world like fine lace.

What a grand and beautiful boat she was! Sylvain felt her heart lift a little at the sight of such a glorious craft sliding gracefully into port. "She's a beauty, Cap'n. What's she transporting?"

The captain had to shout to be heard above the sudden snapping and cracking of fireworks from the port and the loud blast of the whistle from the imposing vessel sliding in beside them. "I have no idea." She nodded, said good night, and walked purposefully down the gangplank, the lovely summer's evening already spoiled for her.

On the high texas deck of the *Gulf Princess*, a tall, dark man stood alone. He was attired in full dress uniform, the light blue jacket with its gold braid and captain's bars straining across wide, powerful shoulders, the immaculate white trousers clinging to long, well-shaped legs, and his tall black boots freshly polished and gleaming. Captain Hilton Courteen propped a foot on the white railing, braced an arm on his knee, and let his dark eyes move casually to the smaller vessel to the right of the *Princess*.

He saw her.

His foot came down from the railing. He gripped the smooth wood for support and blinked, straining for a better look. At that moment she paused, turned, and looked up.

"Sylvain!" he shouted.

She never saw him. Soon she was down the long companionway. Again and again he shouted, but she never heard him. The fireworks were cannonading with regularity now, and docked steamers were blowing their ear-shattering whistles in celebration of their country's birthday.

Hitlon stood watching the beautiful young woman descend to the crowded dock and wondered what on earth she was doing on the Mobile waterfront.

His legs felt unsteady. He inhaled deeply of the humid heavy air, his heart thudding in his chest. What was it about her that so fascinated him? Why did he feel this sudden rush of longing at the sight of her?

"My God, what a woman," Hilton mused aloud, his words drowned out by the fireworks and whistles and shouting and laughter filling Mobile Bay on this sweltering July 4, 1840.

Chapter Twenty

"Hilton Courteen!"

Hilton, standing on the levee, turned, smiled, and shook the outstretched hand of Newton Lancaster. "Newton," Hilton said graciously, "good to see you."

"And you, Hilton." Newton Lancaster released his hand and clapped him on the shoudler. "A captain? My, my you must be personally responsible for wiping out scores of those savages."

Neither proud or ashamed of his accomplishments in Florida, Hilton smoothly changed the subject, leaning close so that the banker could hear him above the din of fireworks, "Newt, what brings you to the pier tonight?"

"I'm celebrating, Hilton." Newton Lancaster pointed to a sleek schooner lit by Japanese lanterns. "She's mine, and I'm having the biggest Fourth of July party this city's ever seen. How fortunate for us you've arrived to join in the merriment."

Hilton smiled and shoved his hands into his trouser pockets. The image of Sylvain quickly flashed through his mind. Was Lancaster's party her reason for being on the levee? Was she at this moment aboard the schooner sipping champagne and chattering gaily in that sweet, unforgettable voice. Would he be allowed to spin her about the polished deck for one breathless dance despite the fact she was a married woman.

"Lead the way, Newt," said Hilton and felt his blood race when he climbed the gangplank of the party boat and heard the sweet sounds of a violin wafting from the afterdeck. Lifting a fluted glass of champagne from a waiter's silver tray, Hilton let his dark eyes casually survey the glittering crowd. Shaking hands with old friends, bending to ladies to accept their welcoming busses and hugs, he circulated from stern to bow, disappointment rapidly replacing expectation.

She wasn't there. He'd checked below decks, wandering in and out of open staterooms and gaudy saloons, intent on finding her, but to no avail.

"You're not having a good time." A soft voice made Hilton turn.

"I'm sure that will all change, now you've come to my rescue," he said gallantly and smiled warmly at a short, voluptuous young woman with shiny chestnut curls, wide green eyes, and a pouty mouth.

Delighted with his response, she stepped closer. "I'm Grace St. Claire, and I've never danced with a captain." She lifted a small hand and let her fingers skim over the silver bars on his shoulder.

Hilton set his champagne glass down on the smooth railing. "I'm afraid, my dear Miss St. Claire" he drawled as he took her in his long arms, "you'll find that captains dance just like other men."

Grace St. Claire stood on tiptoe and happily wrapped her arm around his neck and placed her small hand in his. Enthralled, the young woman melted against him, pressing her cheek to his broad, hard chest. Hilton danced her about the slick deck, telling himself that here was a beautiful woman, a lovely lady with full, feminine curves, a kissable mouth, and an adorable smile.

It was, after all, a party, an occasion for celebration and merriment. Wishing the willing woman in his arms were not so short, Hilton told himself he was being foolish. Most women were short. And most men were glad that they were. He'd heard many gentlemen boast about how tiny their wives and sweethearts were, what a feeling of power it gave them to escort their doll-like ladies about, how pleasing it was to look down upon a fair face that barely reached to their shoulders.

Hilton didn't feel that way. He preferred tall women, women who fit comfortably into his embrace, women who didn't make dancing an uncomfortable exercise in bending and stooping, as he was doing now. Women like . . . like . . .

"You were wrong, Captain." The chestnut-haired girl shook him from his reverie.

"I was?"

She smiled up at him, wet her full lips, and said, "Yes. Dancing with a captain is the most exciting thing that's ever happened to me."

"My dear, the pleasure is all mine."

"Call me Gracie. And what's your name, Captain?"

"Forgive me," Hilton said. "I'm Hilton Courteen and I — "

"*The* Hilton Courteen?" Gracie St. Claire gasped.

"There's only one, far as I know."

"Oh, Captain Courteen, I've heard so much about you."

Hilton stopped dancing. "There's still time to flee," he teased.

She gripped his neck more tightly. Voice quavering, she said, "That's the last thing I want to do."

Hilton gave no reply. He picked up the steps of the dance, spreading his brown hand over the generous expanse of bare, soft flesh above the low back of her white organdy gown. When a waiter came by, he reached out, took another glass of champagne, and graciously shared it with his partner.

"What's this medal for?" Gracie said several dances later, fingering the stiff blue and white ribbon with its small gold medallion.

Hilton shrugged, didn't reply, then delighted Gracie St. Claire by removing the gleaming medal from his uniform and deftly pinning it to the V of her daringly low-cut bodice. As he did so, his fingers brushed her sensitive flesh, and he announced dramatically, "Miss Gracie St. Claire, you're awarded this medal for courageous shipboard dancing above and beyond the call of duty."

Breathless, happy, and speechless, the young woman looked down at the shiny gold medal nestled between her breasts and felt she might faint. Hilton held firmly to her small waist, took yet another glass of champagne, and lifted it to her dry lips. She gulped the fine wine down as if it were water.

Hilton Courteen laughed, took the empty glass from her hands, lowered his face to hers, and kissed her.

"Hilton Courteen!" A woman's voice pulled him from the deep caress. He lifted his head and looked down into the smiling eyes of Laura Lancaster. "Is Gracie going to claim you all evening?" She tapped his shoulder with her fan and looked at Gracie's glowing face.

"I most certainly am," Gracie declared, pulling Hilton's arms more tightly around her.

"You heard the lady," Hilton told his hostess.

"I did, but I shall not allow it," Laura Lancaster announced. To Gracie she said sweetly, "My dear, I'm delighted for you. However, you can hardly expect to monopolize all the time of our glamorous guest." She smiled and added, "I am, after all, your hostess, the one who invited you. Now, be a good girl and let me have a dance with our handsome captain."

Gracie St. Claire remembered her manners. "Of course," she said, releasing the tall man. She looked up into his black eyes and said gently, "I'll not lose you, will I? You'll come back?"

Hilton touched her cheek. "Count on it."

He took the big-bosomed Laura Lancaster in his arms and led her around the floor. While she questioned him about his adventures in the Florida Everglades, Hilton answered, noncommittally. His hand holding hers felt the smoothness of a fine stone, and his gaze went to the ring she was wearing.

His feet missed a beat.

"Sorry, Laura," he said and picked up the dance. His eyes went again to the glittering emerald set in filigreed gold and surrounded by tiny pearls.

Vividly Hilton recalled having seen that ring on the hand of Sylvain Fairmont one long-ago night at the Hotel Condé Victory Ball. He'd commented on its beauty, and Sylvain had told him that the ring was very special, that it was her mother's, that it was priceless and precious.

Although he longed to ask Laura what she was doing with Sylvain's ring, Hilton held his tongue. But when the song ended and Gracie St. Claire came hurrying back to him, he found that he'd lost what little interest he'd had in her.

He was delighted when Newton Lancaster moved through the crowd at midnight announcing that tables of poker were being set up in the main deck saloon. Stopping beside the couple, Lancaster said, "Cap'n Courteen, surely we can count on you to fill a seat?"

"Will you excuse me?" Hilton said to a disappointed Gracie St. Claire. He kissed her cheek and added, "We'll meet again."

"I hope so," she said dispiritedly and sadly watched the tall, broad-shouldered captain walk away. She touched the gleaming medal between her breasts and smiled again. It had already been the most exciting night of Gracie St. Claire's life.

"And I raise you five hundred, Newt," said Hilton, his jacket cast aside, shirt unbuttoned halfway down his dark chest.

Newton Lancaster stole a glace at Hilton's stony face, but he read nothing there. He looked again at the pair of kings and threes in his hand, then scratched his chin and pondered. Courteen must have three of a kind, Newton thought. No use throwing good money after bad. He tossed his cards on the table face down.

Hilton threw in his own hand and pulled the stack of chips to him. His luck had been good this evening for the first time in years. The other players at their table had fallen out after a couple of hours and only Hilton and Newton Lancaster remained, playing head-to-head poker.

Hilton was delighted with the turn of events. A plan had quickly taken hold in his brain and as the hours passed and his luck held, he grew more hopeful of its success. It was not money that Hilton Courteen desperately desired. It was Sylvain's ring.

At a few minutes before five o'clock in the morning, Newton Lancaster finally pushed back his chair and lifted his hands in defeat. "I can't beat you tonight, my friend. If my count is correct, I owe you five thousand. I don't have that kind of cash on board, but if you'll step around to the bank in the morning..."

Hilton toyed with the deck of cards, yawned sleepily, and leaned back in his chair. "Tell you what, Newt," he said easily," I was planning to leave Mobile rather early." He dropped the deck on the table and ran a lean hand through his unruly black hair. "That's a nice ring Laura is wearing. Must be worth...ummm...a couple of thousand?"

"Yes, I'd say the emerald would cost a couple of thousand."

"You owe me five, the ring's worth two..." Hilton slowly rose, plucking at the creases in his tight white trousers. "Let me have the ring and we'll call it even."

Newton Lancaster stood up. "God, Hilton, I don't know. Laura is fond of that ring."

Hilton lifted wide shoulders. "Laura has lots of rings."

"True, true." Newton stroked his chin. "You have a deal. I suppose you want the emerald now."

Hilton yawned dramatically. "I'm dead tired, Newt."
He picked up his uniform jacket and slung it over a
shoulder. "Get the ring from Laura and I'll be on my
way." He started for the stairs.

"Very well." Newton Lancaster stepped past him.

Five minutes later Hilton was descending the gang
plank to the deserted wharf, the emerald resting on
his little finger. A waiting Lancaster carriage took him
to Belle Courteen's darkened dwelling on McGregor
Avenue.

Hilton lifted the heavy door knocker and waited. The
carved door was opened a crack, and his grandmother's
butler peered at him warily.

"My Lord, Cap'n Hilton," the old servant said, a happy
grin creasing his face.

" 'Morning, James." Hilton stepped into the corridor
and shook the old man's hand. "You doing all right?"

Beaming at the tall soldier, James said spiritedly, "I be
jes' real fine, Cap'n Hilton, never feel better. How 'bout
yourself?"

"A little tired, James. Jas been behaving himself?"

"That Jasper be hard to git along with sometimes,"
James said carefully.

Hilton laughed. "I've noticed that." He started up the
stairs, saying, "Go back to bed, James."

"Yassuh, Cap'n Hilton."

At the top of the stairs, Hilton didn't pause before the
guest room where he always slept but continued down
the dim corridor to his grandmother's room. Knocking
briskly, he entered before the sleeping woman had time
to awaken.

"Wake up, Belle," he said cheerfully. He lifted the
globe from an oil lamp and lit it.

"What . . . why . . . ? The tiny silver-haired woman
sat straight up, her black eyes alert in an instant.
"Hilton Daniel Courteen, how dare you come barging
into my boudoir in the middle of the night! You have no

better manners than those red savages you've been fighting."

"I'm glad to see you, too, darlin'," Hilton leaned down, gave her a quick kiss, and tugged playfully at the long silver plait draped across her right shoulder.

"You get out of here and let me dress! What time is it? Why didn't you arrive last night like you promised?"

Hilton lifted a satin and lace bed jacket from the foot of Belle's bed and offered it to her. "You needn't dress, I'll stay only a moment. Sit up and I'll help you."

Glaring up at her tall grandson, Belle slid her arms into the sleeves of the bed jacket and brushed his big hands away when he attempted to tie the satin ribbons beneath her chin.

"If you're going to remain in my bedchamber, for heaven's sake draw up a chair and behave like a gentleman."

Hilton grinned, hauled a straight-back chair close to the bed, took a seat, and said, "Tell me about Sylvain Baxter."

Belle's silver eyebrows shot up. "Sylvain Baxter? Boy, you stayed out in the sun too long. You're talking nonsense."

"Dammit, Belle, you know exactly whom I'm referring to. She was born Sylvain Fairmont, a tall, lovely dark-haired girl with big smoky eyes and gold skin. She married that . . ."

"She married no one." Belle folded her arms across her chest and leaned back against the cushioned headboard.

"Married no one?" Hilton's black eyes widened. He left his chair and slid onto the bed to face her. "I don't understand."

Belle Courteen gave him a disgusted look. "How many times have I tried to tell you the news and what did I get for my efforts? A scolding. A dismissive shake of your head. A bored look."

"My God, will you get on with it?"

"Don't you swear in my house, young man. I don't care if you are some big brave hero, I'll not permit it and I . . ."

"Please." He felt he'd shake her if she didn't tell him what she knew. "Sylvain? I promise not to swear, but tell me."

"It happened quite some time ago, Hilton. You'd just left for Florida. Sylvain and that young Baxter boy were to be married, but her mother died and the wedding was postponed. Then somehow . . . I don't really know the details . . . it came out that Sylvain was not really the daughter of Edwin Fairmont. She's the daughter of the pirate Jean Lafitte."

"Jean Lafitte?" he echoed dumbly.

"Yes. When the Baxter boy heard the news, he refused to marry her. Edwin Fairmont called him out, and the boy shot and killed him."

Stunned, Hilton stared at his grandmother as she went on. "It seems a defrocked priest knew of the child's parentage and had been blackmailing the Fairmonts for years. Because of him, Edwin Fairmont died penniless and in debt. The poor child was jilted by her sweetheart, lost both her parents, and was deserted by her friends.

"My God," Hilton said finally, his heart aching for the fiery beauty. "How is she managing? Who takes care of her?"

"No one. They tell me she took a job at an unprofitable chandlery on the waterfront and turned it into a success. I understand she's got a keen business sense and drives a hard bargain." She chuckled lightly. "Guess she takes after that scamp Lafitte. He was quite a man, I'll tell you that. More than once when I was in New Orleans with your grandfather, I saw the handsome corsair in the company of the town's most influential men. Why, I even recall one time he was . . . "

"Belle," Hilton interrupted, "the chandlery. What's the name of it? Where is it?"

"Spencer's. John Spencer's. It's down on the pier someplace. Why?"

"I'm going to see her, Belle." He was smiling, his dark eyes flashing in the dimly lit room.

"Hilton, I have nothing against Sylvain Fairmont, but I think it would be foolish for you to see her. They say she's not the same proper young lady she once was." Her voice turned conspiratorial. "She goes about with the river people, the roughest in the harbor. She's been known to enter the grog shops, and some of the harlots on Water Street call her by her first name, so friendly is she to them. She lives in a little house down there. They tell me she's got a big black man living right in the house with her."

Hilton smiled again. "Her new friends are a more human lot, I'll wager, than the bluebloods who turned their backs on her." He rose. "Belle, wake me no later than nine o'clock. I'm going to see Sylvain."

"Don't go yet. Now that you've wakened me, tell me about the Seminoles. Tell me why you were breveted to captain. I want to hear all about these last two and a half years."

"Nothing to tell, dear," said Hilton Courteen and left.

At precisely nine o'clock there was a knock at Hilton's door. It didn't wake him; he'd been awake since before eight, shaking uncontrollably beneath the white muslin sheet.

Jasper, grinning happily, hurried into the room. "Land sakes, it be good to see you." As he neared the big bed, his smile left his wrinkled face. "My boy be sick," he said, his eyes troubled. Hurriedly placing the breakfast tray on the mahogany night table, the stooped servant put his bony hand on Hilton's face.

"Hello, Jas," Hilton managed, his teeth chattering. "I'm a little cold."

"You is burnin' up with fever," said the servant, swiftly pulling the heavy counterpane over Hilton. "I'll git Miz Belle."

Hilton's grandmother bustled into the sun-filled room a few minutes later and leaned over her grandson. "Darling," she soothed, pushing the damp hair off his hot face, "what is it?"

"Nothing to be alarmed about, Belle. I contracted malaria down in the Florida swamps, and it flares up on me now and again." He was still shaking violently.

"Bring coverlets and quilts from the hall closet, Jasper." To Hilton she said, "We'll make you comfortable, Hilton. We'll get you warm."

Hilton shook throughout the hot summer day, freezing beneath three downy covers, his dark face fiery to the touch. Finally around four that afternoon, the fever broke. Hilton began perspiring and was soon kicking off his covers.

He turned his head and saw his grandmother seated beside his bed. Jasper stood by the window. "Belle, if you'll have the cook fix me a bowl of rice." She rose immediately.

"Anything you want, angel." She mopped at his wet brow with her handkerchief.

"Rice is all I can manage." She nodded and was gone. "Jas, if you'll be good enough to draw me a bath."

"Yassuh, I do dat' rat away. Help bathe my boy too if he be needin' it." The old man scurried from the room.

Sylvain was in the storeroom and didn't hear the bell tinkle. She came back into the chandlery's main room and stepped behind the wide counter. Thinking herself alone, she sat on a high stool and thumbed through a wholesale catalog, unaware that someone was studying her.

The man stood quietly across the room from her, arms folded across his chest. He was grateful for this time to look at her while she was ignorant of his presence.

How beautiful she was! Her long, thick hair was pinned on top of her head, and shiny curls looped haphazardly about her crown. Wisps of fine, glossy hair had escaped their restraints and curled appealingly around her neck and face. She'd sucked her bottom lip behind her even white teeth and was chewing on it. There was a small smudge of ink on her left cheek just below the long, feathery lashes.

She wore a simple calico dress in a pink and white floral print. The tight bodice buttoned to her chin, but she'd opened a few of the buttons, obviously fighting the heat of the July day. A sheen of perspiration covered her throat, and her damp golden flesh fairly shimmered.

She was absolutely breathtaking, more so than any woman he'd ever seen in his life, and he desired her with a passion he'd thought was dead. He crossed the room and spoke her name.

"Sylvain."

She looked up, blinked, and let the catalog drop to the floor.

"Randolph!"

"Yes, it's me," he said with difficulty, his speech slurred from too much wine.

"What are you doing here?" She jumped down from the high stool and came around the counter. "You were on your way to Nassau."

He smiled and shook his head. "I saw you and I couldn't go. Ginger went without me." He stepped closer.

She took a step back. "You're drunk."

"No, no, I'm not," he stammered. "I . . . want you, I've come to tell you that."

Sylvain glared at him. "Don't talk such foolishness. Get out of here right now, Randolph Baxter. I don't want you here."

"Don't say that, Sylvain, please don't say that." He advanced on her. She again retreated. "I've come to tell you I was wrong. I made a mistake, darling. I shouldn't

264

have listened to them, I should have married you." His green eyes were red-rimmed, his blond hair disheveled.

"Please leave, Randolph. I won't listen to any more ..."

"You've got to, Sylvain. I love you, I want you. I'm a very rich man, darling. I'll get you a nice house, I'll fill it with fine furniture, and I'll dress you in fashionable clothes."

Sylvain's surprise turned rapidly to rage. "You miserable drunk! Weak rich man's boy! You're suggesting I become your mistress. Is that it, Randolph?"

He bobbed his head happily. "You can come with me right now. I'll put you in a hotel until we can find the proper house." He was grinning triumphantly. "Yes, that's it. We'll go to the Hotel Condé ... we'll make love and ..."

"Get out of here, you disgusting, filthy, stupid — "

"Darling, don't. I love you. I must have you. I never loved Ginger, you know that. It was you from the beginning. No one but you."

"Randolph, I want you to go. You have a wife and child, but even if you didn't, I'd still have nothing to do with you." Her hands went to her slender hips. "You killed my father! Shot and killed him, and for that reason alone I shall hate you until the day I die!"

"Sylvain, he wasn't your father. You know that. Your father was — "

"Damn you, Baxter," she shouted. "You're a weak, drunken sorry excuse for a man, and I wish never to see you again. I thank God you refused to marry me. It's the only good thing to come out of all this heartache." She laughed hollowly. "I'm not your wife! Oh, God, I'm not, and I'm so glad!"

"You're upset," he persisted. "I don't blame you, but I'll make it up. I love you, I must have you." He moved closer to her, a hungry, determined look on his handsome face.

Alarm jolted through Sylvain. She was alone in the chandlery. John Spencer wouldn't be back for at least another hour. The sisters were across town. She was in danger and she knew it.

Backing away, she said cautiously, "Randolph, you're not yourself."

"But I am. Come to me, darling," he begged huskily, reaching out for her.

"No, Randolph, no — "

"Yes, Sylvain," he growled and bore down on her.

"Touch her and I'll kill you," came a deep deadly voice.

Randolph felt a firm hand on his shoulder. He whirled, blinked, and found himself looking up into the dark and very angry face of Hilton Courteen.

"See here," Randolph said indignantly, "you're out of line, aren't you, stranger?" He wrenched himself from Hilton's grasp.

"No, Baxter," Hilton said coldly, "you're the one who's out of line. The lady wants you to leave. So do I."

Randolph looked from Hilton to Sylvain. "He's right, Randolph. I want you out of here. Don't ever return."

Randolph grew surly. He leaned toward Sylvain and said nastily, "You prefer this common riverman's bed to mine?"

"That's it!" Hilton Courteen seized Randolph by the scruff of the neck and hauled him toward the door. "Unless you wish to be called out, you'll stay away from Miss Fairmont." Hilton followed Randolph outside and added, "A word of advice: You'll find, Mr. Baxter of the Mississippi Baxters, that I'll be more of a challenge than Edwin Fairmont was."

"He won't bother you again, Sylvain," Hilton said, stepping back inside.

She was glaring at him, her gray eyes smoky. The color seemed to move like restless mist. "I want you here about as much as I wanted him."

"What kind of thanks is that for saving you?" he teased gently.

"No one asked you to save me, Courteen. I'm a big girl and I've been looking out for myself for a long time."

"I know you have and I — "

She raised both hands, palms forward. "I don't care if you've ventured down here to gloat or to console: either is equally offensive to me. I'm Jean Lafitte's daughter, Mr. Courteen. I know it, you know it, the world knows it. Well, that's just fine with me. I know my place and I stay in it, and I'll appreciate it if you'll stay in yours." She whirled and walked away from him.

"To hell with our places. I've something for you, Sylvain, something you want."

"No, Courteen." She fixed him with that gray glare. "I want nothing from you. You're no different from Randolph Baxter. The two of you are brothers under the skin, Courteen. Bluebloods. Arrogant aristocrats. Spineless upper-crust fops. Pampered, pitiful panty-waists."

"Jesus, do I deserve all that?"

"Yes," she said explosively, "you do. What do you want from me? What? Are you upset because you weren't around to collect your pound of flesh when my world blew up in my face? Do you feel cheated because you missed out on all the fun? Is that it, Courteen?" Fury had turned her golden skin to a bright red.

"Sweetheart," he said grimly, "what have they done to you? God in heaven, what have they done?"

"They?" she said harshly. "You're they, damn you! Now get out. Get out of here, Courteen. Get back to silk stocking row where you belong. I don't want you here. I've my friends, my life, my world. You don't belong in it. Get out!"

"I'm going, Sylvain," he said flatly, "but if you ever need me, I'll come."

"I need no one. Get out!"

When he'd left, Sylvain found she was trembling. She made it to the long counter and held on to it for support, breathing heavily, her head throbbing.

When she'd finally calmed down a bit, she went behind the counter and sat down on the tall stool, fighting the pain in her stomach.

She was not sure which man's unexpected visit had upset her more.

She was still sorting out her feelings when John Spencer walked through the front door. One look and Sylvain knew he was ill.

She leaped up and ran to him. "What is it, John?" She quickly caught his arm when he staggered.

"I have a raging headache, child, and I'm a bit dizzy."

Chapter Twenty-One

Yellow fever!

The words truck terror in the heart of Sylvain Fairmont. She thought immediately of her dear friend Rosalie. The dreaded plague was a death sentence, and Sylvain knew she had to get her servants and the Spencers out of the city at once.

She told the Spencer sisters to pack only a few pieces of clothing and to be prepared to leave within the hour. Then she hurried from the chandlery and sought out Big Napoleon.

Breathlessly, she told him that Dr. Cornell had diagnosed John Spencer's illness as the fever. "Napoleon, get a cart somewhere," she said, "and find us a good strong horse or mule. We must get out of Mobile at once!"

Big Napoleon asked no questions, but went at once to do her bidding. He returned less than an hour later with a rattling cart pulled by a pair of flop-eared mules.

"I hope we're not too late," Sylvain said uneasily as they bumped along the crowded road to the chandlery. "It's been but two days . . . "

John Spencer was wheezing, his jaundiced body shaking violently, when Napoleon placed him in the cart. The Spencer sisters scrambled up beside him, silent in their terror.

The ride to the wharf was like a bad dream, the epidemic had spread rapidly, and everyone in Mobile was headed either for the waterfront or inland, away from the Gulf. The narrow streets were jammed with every kind of conveyance. The port looked like a city under siege. All the shops were closed and shuttered.

Thick black smoke curled toward the cloudless blue sky from hundreds of burning tar barrels. Cannons boomed and echoed in attempts to clear the air. People were shouting and screaming, some dropping in their tracks, victims of the fever.

The dock was pandemonium. Two huge steamers were sliding out of their berths, their decks overcrowded with passengers. Only one vessel remained in port.

Sylvain jumped on to the wooden wharf, calling over her shoulder, "Hurry, we must hurry!" Up the gangplank she flew, only to be stopped by a burly master-at-arms.

"I have money," she shouted, and shoved a wad of bills at him.

He looked at the money, at her, and then over her head. "Tell that big nigger he can't bring that sick man on this boat."

"But we must take him with us! He's alive, he'll get better."

"He ain't comin' on the *Jay Jernigin*, miss. Neither are them niggers. You and the two old ladies can board, but the others stay here!"

"Dear God, are you inhuman?" she shouted. "You've got to take us out of here! We'll pay and — "

"They ain't goin'," he boomed as a blast of the loud whistle announced the vessel's departure.

Sylvain ran to the sisters. "You two must get aboard. Hurry!"

"No," said Hester, "we heard the sailor. We will not leave John."

"You go on, Miss Sylvain," Big Napoleon urged. "I'll watch after them."

Sylvain looked from Big Napoleon to Delilah. Her faithful friend was nodding, "He be right, honey. You go. We'll be okay."

Sylvain looked again at the paddle-wheeler. In minutes it would back out of the harbor and cut through the calm waters of the Gulf. She could be on it. She could leave this horror behind, forget them all, start a new life.

"We'll all remain here," she said firmly and walked back to the cart. Behind her the *Jay Jernigin*'s bells clanged as the craft slid out of the berth and headed for the open waters of the Gulf.

The normally bustling port was now quiet. Tons of cargo sat on the deserted wharf. Rodents scurried out to feed on overturned baskets of perishables.

Like the ride to the wharf, the trip home was a nightmare. Dogs and cats prowled the silent streets in search of food. The scared citizens who remained stayed behind locked doors, sweltering in the heat, but terrified to venture out lest they catch the deadly plague. Sylvain could feel frightened eyes following them.

A mosquito landed on her perspiring neck, and she slapped it violently, biting back the gasp of panic rising in her tight throat.

"John's gone," Hester said calmly, then clutched her temples with both hands, her eyes registering intense pain. Marie Spencer moaned softly, then grew silent.

The death wagon rattled down the street, its old, tired driver calling hoarsely, "Bring out your dead! Any dead here today?"

Doors swung open and men came out to toss their dead on top of the mound of human refuse.

When the death wagon creaked past them, they saw the body of a once-beautiful young woman, her long golden hair shimmering in the sun, pale eyes wide open, a look of pain still in them. An infant slipped out of the death wagon and fell into the dust.

Delilah screamed.

Big Napolean stopped the cart, leaped down, and hurried to pick up the dead child. Sylvain watched as the gentle giant lifted the little body and walked to the wagon. Placing the baby beside the beautiful young woman, he drew her lifeless arm around the child and spread his shirt over them. The touch of dignity he offered them brought tears to Sylvain's eyes.

When he returned to the cart, Marie Spencer leaned forward and said, "Big Napoleon, don't let them take John like that."

"I won't, Miss Marie," he said softly. "I won't."

Captain Hilton Courteen was a frustrated man. No sooner had he arrived in New Orleans than word of the Mobile epidemic reached him. Cursing himself for not having stayed longer with his grandmother, he sought a steamer for Mobile, but none could be found. No captain would take his vessel to the beleaguered little city and Hilton had no choice but to remain at the Richardson Hotel and await word.

He was worried. Belle Courteen was past eighty and not a strong woman; should she contract the fever, she would not survive. And he was worried about someone else.

Sylvain Fairmont.

After agonizingly long weeks, a letter was delivered to his hotel. It was from Belle:

> Dearest Hilton:
> I'm so relieved you got out ot Mobile ahead of this tragic plague. More than one night I've offered grateful thanks for your safety. There's no doubt in my mind had you remained here with me, as I begged you to do, you'd have contracted the killing disease. It preys on those who have been weakened by other illnesses, such as your malaria.

I have escaped the fever, but I grieve for those
less fortunate. Hilton, they tell me nearly seven
hundred people have lost their lives in this
epidemic. Seven hundred! Isn't that hard to grasp!
Take care, grandson — or should I say, Captain?
Oh, yes, I checked for you. She survived. She
did not contract the fever. Sylvain Fairmont is
alive and well.

Hilton exhaled slowly. And then he smiled. Folding the
letter carefully, he dropped it on the table, pulled the
stopper from the whiskey decanter and poured himself a
drink. He tossed it down and took pleasure from the
warmth that spread down into his chest.

"She's alive," he said to the silent, sun-filled room. He
laughed and poured another drink. It would take more
than a yellow fever plague to kill the brave, beautiful
daughter of Jean Lafitte. "Here's to you, Lafitte!" He
raised his glass, drained it, picked up his frock coat, and
went in search of a poker game.

After a couple of months in New Orleans, Hilton grew
restless. So, with Jasper, he drifted north to Natchez,
Mississippi, settled into the stately Parker Hotel, and
hired a carriage to transport him to Briarfield plantation
to call on Jefferson Davis.

The morose man he'd left three years before had shed
his gloom. Jeff came down the steps smiling, his pale
gold hair gleaming in the sun, blue-gray eyes displaying
some of their old twinkle.

"Captain Courteen." Jeff's handshake was firm.

"Jeff." Hilton grinned down at his friend. "You're looking well. I'm delighted."

"Come in, come in, and tell me all about the war." Jeff
drew him into the house. "They say you're a hero."

"Hardly, Jeff." Hilton was anxious to change the subject. "And you? I hear you've been spending time up in

273

Washington City meeting prominent politicians, hearing the debates in Congress." He raised his eyebrows. "Could it be you're ambitious to become something other than a gentleman cotton planter?"

Jeff grinned and scratched his long, lean face. "My good friend George Jones knows everybody, and he's introduced me to a lot of important men. I had breakfast at the White House with President Van Buren."

"Are you entertaining the idea of running for office?"

"No, no." Jeff waved a hand in the air, then shook his head. "Of course, if Daniel Webster and the other extremists don't stop going about up north making abolitionist speeches, I may find it necessary to take our cause to the people." He indicated a worn leather sofa, and Hilton took a seat. Jeff poured two glasses of bourbon and said, smiling, "You couldn't have picked a more opportune day to arrive. I'm to attend a dinner party at the Le Noble plantation, and you'll go with me."

Hilton nodded. "I like Brian and Alexa."

"I'm sorry, Hill. I thought you knew . . . Brian Le Noble passed away a couple of years ago. Had a heart attack while out riding over his property. Never made it back to the main house."

"I'm sorry to hear that," Hilton said. "And Mrs. Le Noble? Is she managing all right without her husband?"

Jeff smiled again. "Alexa Le Noble is one rare woman, Hill. She's calm and cool and takes everything in her stride. She cared for Brian, but she didn't crawl into the grave with him. She's remained very social. Some of the richest, most powerful men in the South are regular guests at Beau Monde."

Hilton misread the light in his friend's eyes. "Two years is a long time." He smiled lazily. "Are you courting the lovely widow?"

Davis's smile fled. "Don't be absurd, Hill. There was only one woman for me. Sarah. No one will ever replace her." He brightened immediately. "I like Alexa, though, and as I said, she has some very influential friends. If a man ever did consider politics, she could be most helpful."

"Cap'n, what an unexpected joy to see you again. Welcome to Beau Monde." The stunningly beautiful Alexa Le Noble, wearing an immaculate white silk gown, diamonds glittering at her throat and ears, stood looking up at him.

"My dear, may I offer my belated condolences." Hilton kissed the hand she raised to him. "It's a pleasure to see you again, Mrs. Le Noble."

"You're kind, Cap'n Courteen." Alexa smiled beguilingly, her wide green eyes looking unwaveringly into his. "You'll be my table companion this evening?"

"I'd be honored, Mrs. Le Noble."

"Call me Alexa, Cap'n," she said and took his arm. Then she led him around the big drawing room, introducing him to her friends, leaning close to whisper something pertinent about each guest that would help him to remember them, and pleasantly stirring him with her sophistication and charm.

"I think, my friend," said Jeff Davis on their return to Briarfield, "that the glamorous Mrs. Le Noble is taken with you."

Hilton didn't deny it. "Alexa is an engaging woman." He turned to look at Jeff. "I was invited for dinner at Beau Monde tomorrow evening."

Jeff Davis chuckled. "I sure wasn't."

It was the first of many romantic evenings Hilton was to spend at the opulent mansion with Alexa Le Noble. The lady was intelligent, beautiful, and sensitive. She enjoyed opera, good food, fine wines, and staying up late. A good sport and a witty conversationalist, she laughed at his risqué stories. She despised injustice, loathed gossips, and refused to associate with anyone she considered a hypocrite.

Alexa never burdened others with her troubles, and she fixed meddlers with a cold green-eyed stare when they pried into her personal life. She was cool in touchy situations and ever the regal lady in public. And at home alone with Hilton Courteen she was open, relaxed, and very, very passionate.

He made love to her for the first time on a cold night in December. Hilton had come for dinner, and the pair had lounged on the patterned-velvet sofa sipping cognac from eggshell-thin crystal snifters. A blazing fire roared in the huge fireplace, and they'd talked little, content to enjoy the warmth of the fire, the fine brandy, and their seclusion.

It was past midnight when Hilton said drowsily, "It's getting late." He looked at Alexa. Her wide green eyes were fixed on him, inviting him to stay. "Either I leave now, or I'll not go at all. The choice is yours, my dear."

"I've never asked a man to stay with me in my life." She tilted her chin. "I won't ask you, Hilton Courteen."

Hilton smiled, then took her brandy snifter and set it aside. His fingers went to the jeweled pins in her upswept golden hair. He deftly pulled them from her elegantly dressed tresses and watched, fascinated, as her hair spilled down over her creamy shoulders.

Within moments the cool, sophisticated Alexa Le Noble's fashionable blue satin ballgown lay in a heap on the Aubusson carpet. Her eyes were closed, her breathing was rapid, and her lips were already bruised from the heated kisses being pressed on them.

Caring not at all that they were in the downstairs drawing room, Alexa Le Noble gloried in the touch of the hands divesting her of her lace-trimmed chemise and pantalettes and lifted not one finger to help.

She scattered kisses over his dark, handsome face and sighed and murmured encouragement while he leisurely disrobed her. She breathed in the clean male scent of him when he picked her up and carried her closer to the white marble fireplace. He stood with her in his arms, kissing her deeply while the flames warmed her bare back and she clung to him. Hands twining in the thick, dark hair, she kissed him wildly, passionately, and Hilton knew she was ready for his loving.

Gently he laid her on the rug, and she purred and watched, transfixed, while he stood above her, shedding his evening clothes.

When he was as naked as she, he remained standing looking down at her, his feet apart, his black eyes languidly sliding over her body. When he heard the tiny gasp of eagerness escape her lips, Hilton fell to his knees beside her. And when he bent and feathered kisses over her flushed face, Alexa Le Noble moaned.

He lifted his head to look at her and read the need in her expressive eyes. He took her at once and had hardly begun the practiced movements of his body in hers before she cried out in ecstasy.

An experienced and understanding man, Hilton tenderly kissed her flushed face and held her close. He knew what had happened. This beautiful, cool, cultured woman had been too long without a man. Hilton's own desire had not yet been slaked, but he slipped from her and gathered her into his arms. They had all night.

He began kissing her softly, gently, taking his time. In minutes Alexa Le Noble was pulling him to her, kissing him excitedly, pressing her warm body to his.

Alexa was again ready for him.

Chapter Twenty-Two

It was Mardi Gras once again.

Shrove Tuesday 1843 was cold and raw. Winds sighed and moaned and sought entrance to the small clapboard dwelling on Water Street. A few stars had already appeared in the clear sky. It would be another long, frigid night in Mobile, Alabama.

Sylvain felt a happy glow of anticipation as she dressed for the carnival. The three women in her small bedroom shared her excitement, fussing over her as if she were a queen preparing for her coronation. Marie Spencer smoothed the gathers in the long, full scarlet skirt while Delilah tied a flaming red silk scarf around Sylvain's shiny brown hair, carefully arranging the knot so that the ends of the bandanna would fall over her left ear.

Hester and Marie closely scrutinized Sylvain, their eyes slowly sweeping over the beautiful young woman who in the past few years had become very dear to them.

Sylvain's hair fell in thick locks about her oval face and the red silk bandanna accentuated the high color in her cheeks. The long-sleeved white blouse was feminine and lovely, its décolletage revealing her golden shoulders. A wide black taffeta sash hugged Sylvain's narrow waist, its streamers almost touching the hem of her red skirt. New slippers, purchased at an exclusive ladies' shop, peeked from underneath the swirls of red.

"You look lovely, dear," Hester said thoughtfully, "but I'm worried about those shoes. You know, it's been ages since you've worn anything like that. The heels are so high; they could be quite dangerous."

Sylvain smiled as she lifted her full skirts and looked at her feet. "I'll be very careful, Hester," she assured her friend. Then she exclaimed delightedly, "I don't feel like myself. I feel like . . . like — "

"A beautiful, free Gypsy girl, Miss Sylvain?" Delilah asked, grinning.

"Yes!" Sylvain turned and hugged her old friend, still impressed by Delilah's proper English. Gone was the Negro dialect. Delilah, in the past year, had begun to talk like Big Napoleon. She'd also begun grooming herself more carefully and was certainly more pleasant to everyone, especially Napoleon. She no longer complained about him, and when he entered or left a room, Delilah's dark eyes followed him, a little smile on her face.

"Such a pretty Gypsy," said Marie, her hands clasped in front of her. "Sister's worried about the slippers, it's the blouse that worries me, Sylvain. It's so revealing, I'm afraid you'll incite the young men to misbehave."

Sylvain laughed and reminded her, "Marie, you made the blouse yourself."

"I know, I know, but still . . . Well, I suppose as long as Big Napoleon is in the crowd somewhere, no harm will befall you."

"I can take care of myself," Sylvain reminded them. "I don't see why you all insist on making him go along."

"He is going!" Delilah tugged at the wide black sash, "and that is that! He won't bother you, but he'll be there should you need him."

"Very well. Is he ready?" Sylvain took the shiny golden earrings Hester handed her.

"Yes, Miss Sylvain. He's wearing a white suit with purple shoulder plates, a purple sash, and a purple turban." Delilah's eyes lit with pride. "He looks real grand

and you'll be able to see that bright turban over the heads of the crowd."

"Good." Sylvain looked at the servant, and Delilah read her mistress's thoughts in her expressive gray eyes.

"Come." Delilah motioned to the sisters. "Let's give our beautiful Gypsy a minute alone." To Sylvain, she said, "Honey, we'll be in the parlor."

Sylvain sighed with relief when they left the room. She looked at herself in the mirror and smiled. *Mardi Gras!* she thought excitedly. She was going to celebrate Mardi Gras again after all these years.

Sylvain whirled around giddily and told herself it would be wonderful. She was going to enjoy herself tonight. She looked again at the high-heeled slippers and lifted the skirt to gaze at her long legs gleaming in the sheer silk stockings. She bent one knee and turned a little, feeling daring and wanton and happy.

Dropping the skirts, she laughed at her foolishness, blew out the lamp, and went to the stairs. The Spencer sisters were talking softly in the parlor. What they were saying caused Sylvain to stop and listen.

"It says so right here in the *Mobile Examiner*: Mrs. Belle Courteen passed away." It was Hester speaking.

"Oh, dear," said Marie. "Wasn't she that tiny silver-haired lady we met at the last bazaar we attended six or seven years ago?"

"The very one," Hester confirmed. "You recall, sister, she was so talkative and friendly, and she had that handsome grandson who came to fetch her when the festivities ended. Hilton Courteen, his name was. This article says he's in town to settle her affairs."

Sylvain's hand tightened on the smooth banister. Hilton Courteen was in Mobile! Her pulse quickened at the thought. Would he be celebrating? Would he join the revelers parading down the crowded streets? Would he attend the masked ball?

Sylvain shook her head, and proceeded on down the stairs. What did she care if the rakish Mr. Hilton Courteen was in town? She didn't care. Not at all.

The winds lifted Sylvain's colorful skirts and blew her long, dark hair into her eyes, but she laughed and tossed her head. The city was aglitter with fireworks and twinkling holiday lights. Eyes shining behind her scarlet domino mask, Sylvain watched the shiny costumes and painted pennants. She was delighted by the papier-mâché masks and hats and outrageous fantasy creatures. Costumed celebrants swirled about her as she made her way joyfully down the avenue. Fireworks lit the clear, starry sky and echoed in her ears. Revelers wearing oversized masks and sparkling costumes embraced her, swung her about, offered her drinks from their goblets.

She saw Roman gladiators and medieval lords and kings, Cleopatras, Marie Antoinettes, and Madame Du Barrys. She clapped her hands and joined in their songs and merriment, feeling young and gay and carefree. And expectant. Could one of the tall celebrants be Hilton Courteen?

It was nearing midnight when she was swept dizzily up the stone steps of the Hotel Condé. The ballroom was crowded to overflowing for the masked ball. Sylvain, telling herself she was looking for no one in particular, let her eyes sweep about the room.

And there he stood.

At thirty-five, Hilton Courteen was at the peak of his virility. His shoulders, broad and powerful, strained the fine dark fabric of his well-cut evening coat. His jet-black hair gleamed in the light from the crystal chandeliers. His dark eyes flashed behind a black satin mask, and beneath a neatly trimmed mustache, his full, sensuous lips widened into a slow smile.

Suppressing a nervous giggle, Sylvain responded in a purely feminine way to the overwhelming sexual vitality of the tall, handsome man who seemed to be looking directly at her. He lifted a hand and spread his long brown fingers over his crackling white shirtfront and Sylvain's mouth grew dry.

Forgotten was the anger she'd felt toward him that long-ago day at the chandlery. Forgotten was the fact that this dangerously desirable man was the aristocratic enemy. Everything was forgotten in the face of his powerful magnetic attraction. He was a lusty, compelling, virile male. She was a tremulous, attracted, fascinated female. Her pulse pounding, Sylvain tore her gaze from him and spun around, struggling valiantly against a formidable foe.

Suddenly feeling very thirsty, Sylvain started through the crowd. Nervous and still unaccustomed to the high-heeled slippers, she tripped and her left ankle gave way. Horrified, she felt herself going down. *Dear Lord, no!* she thought. *I'm going to fall flat on my face in front of —*

A strong pair of hands encircled her slim waist, catching her, and an unmistakable deep voice said softly, "Miss Fairmont, may I have this dance."

Too stunned to reply, Sylvain felt his long arms close around her, pressing her to him, and heard him murmur close to her ear, "I've got you, sweetheart. I won't let you go."

Breathless from her close proximity to this strongly masculine man, Sylvain watched his black eyes gleam behind his mask, felt his breath on her cheek, melted against the warmth and strength of him.

Tonight she wanted that warmth, that strength. She pressed her face close to his throat and inhaled deeply of his clean, unique scent. His words thrilled her, and the touch of his strong, graceful hands rapidly enkindled her flesh.

Sylvain felt her knees trembling. He'd evoked in her a fiery stirring of desire, a feeling she thought had died completely long ago. But she assumed he felt nothing for her. He would have saved any lady in danger of falling on her face.

Sighing, she told herself this dark, mysterious man probably still considered her a bothersome child, someone he should look after, watch out for, defend.

Reluctantly lifting her head from his chest, Sylvain said, "It seems, Mr. Courteen, you are always coming to my aid."

"My dear, it's a supreme pleasure," he replied with a kind of lazy ease, "and one of which I shall never tire."

"You're very kind," she said, smiling.

Hilton squeezed her hand and laughed. "There are those who would disagree. Some might even say I have a selfish motive." He grinned devilishly.

"Oh?" she responded. "And what could you hope to gain by saving me from a fall?"

Hilton's reply caught her off guard. "I have always wanted to kiss that delicate hollow at the base of your throat."

She laughed softly and tilted her chin back in playful invitation. She gasped in surprise when he bent his dark head and kissed her throat, letting her feel his hot, open mouth briefly on tingling flesh.

"Hilton!" She dropped the formality of calling him Mr. Courteen. "We're in a roomful of people."

"So we are," he said coolly and casually glanced about, smiling at the masks that had suddenly turned their way.

Sylvain laughed gaily, charmed by his cavalier disregard for propriety. "Ladies don't usually laugh when I kiss them, Sylvain," Hilton told her.

"Haven't you heard, I'm not a lady," she said pleasantly.

"Thank the Eternal for that," he murmured and danced her toward a long table where pyramids of champagne glasses awaited thirsty revelers.

He told her he thought her bright Gypsy costume most becoming. She teased him for having worn evening clothes instead of a costume. He explained that he was dressed as the mysterious Stranger in Black. She expressed sympathy at his grandmother's passing. He assured her Belle Courteen had lived a long and full life, then smoothly changed the subject, smiling mischievously beneath his black mustache. He didn't mention the last time they'd met. She didn't either.

They sipped champagne and danced. They watched the other dancers, Hilton delighting Sylvain with his easy conversation and his casually possessive air. He stood close to her, his free hand at her waist, his dark head bending to her each time she spoke.

It was fun!

Sylvain had not had such a good time in years. She was growing relaxed, less afraid her handsome companion might turn on his heel and leave her at any moment. He seemed content to stay by her side and not the least concerned about the stares they drew from the costumed gentry at this fancy masked ball. The other celebrants' disapproval bothered Hilton Courteen none at all, and Sylvain derived a giddy kind of pleasure from that.

She'd been cast from their ranks while Hilton Courteen was still a favorite among them, sought after by the cream of the aristocracy. To see such a dashing gentleman of their league unabashedly paying court to Jean Lafitte's bastard — a waterfront waif, a young woman they believed had moral standards as low as those of the man who'd sired her — was too much.

Beautiful belles tossed their curls and wondered why the darkly handsome man insisted on wasting his time with one so obviously beneath him. Sylvain read their looks through their masks and felt a strange power — unlike any she'd ever experienced before.

That feeling increased when Hilton set their champagne glasses aside and, grinning down at her, said pointedly, "Gypsy lady, I'm much too warm."

He walked away from her, and Sylvan watched the tall, broad-shouldered form disappear among the potted palms surrounding the marble dance floor. She knew exactly where he was going. And she knew he intended that she follow.

Sylvain reached for another glass of champagne and sipped thirstily, struggling with her emotions. Good judgment told her it would be wise to remain indoors. If she stepped outside onto the cold balcony tonight, Hilton Courteen might take more from her than a few moonlight kisses.

Her pulse speeded at the thought. The man's raw masculinity had worked its magic on her. The gauntlet had been tossed at her feet. The Gypsy took the challenge.

Draining the glass of bubbly wine, she put it down and made her way through the crowd. At the tall French doors, she paused, then drew a deep breath and went out to Hilton.

He stood with his back to her, his long, lean fingers gripping the railing. He did not turn around. Sylvain smiled, remembering a night long ago when she'd done the same to him. Obviously he, too, remembered.

She stepped up behind him, slipped her arms underneath his, and clasped the railing, enclosing him. She stood on tiptoe and said close to his ear, "A little chilly to be outdoors without a wrap, isn't it?" His laughter filled her heart with joy and she ordered, "Turn around, Courteen."

Hilton turned, smiling, and cupped her upturned face in both his hands. "Ah, my little Gypsy," he teased, "it's you." He slowly lowered his mouth to hers. It was a very gentle, undemanding kiss. His lips softly tasted, teased, asked, in a tender caress that was delightful and pleasing to Sylvain. The bristles of his mustache tickled her mouth, strangely adding to her pleasure.

When his warm lips left hers and went to her temple, she sighed and put her hands on his broad chest. "You did want me to come out, didn't you, Hilton?"

He laughed and kissed her nose. "Sweetheart, there's never been anything I wanted more." He lowered his head once again, capturing her parted lips with his own. He let his hands slowly slide from her velvety cheeks to her throat, his fingers gently massaging her long, graceful neck, his thumbs skimming her sharp jawline.

Hilton felt her slim body molding itself to his, her sweet mouth opening to his deepening kiss. He lifted his head to look at her. His hands slipped to the bare, slender shoulders which shimmered like silver in the moonlight.

Sylvain was looking up into his masked face, loving the feel of his hands on her. Those hands were warm and strong and gentle, and they moved with deliberate slowness out from the curve of her neck to her shoulders. They lingered for an instant, caressing, stroking, then moved downward. She gasped when they slipped under her arms, the strong fingers gripping her rib cage, the thumbs making tiny, teasing circles atop the swell of her breasts.

Hilton groaned and gathered her to him, his arms going around her to press her close. His lips took hers in a kiss so fierce she sighed with surprised pleasure. His tongue moved inside her mouth, his lips burning with a heat that made her whole body grow warm.

She swayed against him, drowning in his kiss, feeling her will being molded to his, her innate sensuality bursting into flame, the sense of right and wrong wavering as Hilton's plundering mouth sought hers again and again. Her straining, sensitive body jumped to life and the clothes she wore felt binding, cumbersome, a nuisance.

She was suddenly vitally aware of her body, and of his, so gloriously different from her own. He was so tall and solid and strong. Her hands explored his back and waist, enjoyed immensely the feel of taut muscle beneath the finely tailored coat. She found herself wishing his long, lean back was not covered at all, that it was bare to her searching hands, her questing fingertips.

Hilton's mouth left hers and went to her ear. Hoarsely he murmured, "Ah, sweet Gypsy, come to my room." He lowered his head, and his lips played over the satiny skin of her shoulder.

"Hilton," she breathed, her eyes half-closed, "we can't — "

"Sylvain Fairmont can't," he agreed, his teeth nibbling on her flesh, "but the Gypsy girl can. Come. We won't remove our masks. We'll be two masked strangers through the long, lovely night." He pressed a kiss to the curve of her neck.

Sylvain shuddered. The sensual picture he'd painted heated the already warm blood racing through her veins. She could see the two of them, alone in his hotel room, their bodies bare, their eyes covered by masks.

"Yes," she whispered into the jet-black hair over his ear. "This Gypsy girl is as free as her ancestors. She will go with you." Her eyes closed.

Hilton kissed her again. Against her lips he whispered, "Gypsy, my gypsy."

Sylvain's heart pounded against her ribs, and, holding tightly to Hilton's hand, she leaned over the balcony and waved to Big Napoleon. He nodded and departed. Hilton Courteen, his dark gaze intent on the beautiful girl at his side, never saw the exchange.

Hilton led Sylvain up the stairs and into a spacious room done tastefully in subdued browns and tans. She quickly assessed the room and its expensive furnishings while Hilton shrugged out of his evening jacket.

The huge mahogany bed, hung with beige taffeta, brought a flush to her cheeks. French wallpaper patterned in white and brown flowers, complemented the deep brown rug. A marble-top pedestal table, a pair of walnut chairs, and a massive walnut chest of drawers completed the furnishings.

Candles flickered in crystal-globed wall sconces on either side of the bed. The heavy draperies of brown velvet were open, allowing silvery moonlight to filter through the sheer white curtains at the tall front windows.

Sylvain's gaze came back to Hilton, who stood in the middle of the room, gazing at her. She shivered when he held his arms out to her.

"Sweet Gypsy," he said, his voice low, persuasive, "come here."

With a bravado she did not feel, Sylvain crossed the room. Hilton untied the scarlet bandanna and let it flutter to the floor. He gently removed her gold earrings and slipped them into his pocket. And then she was in his arms again, his mouth devouring hers in a kiss of unrestrained passion, hers opening wide to his mounting ardor. His tongue played upon her lips, teasing, licking, then slid deep inside her mouth to greedily taste her sweetness.

Sylvain gloried at the invasion. His tongue filling her mouth sent the blood scalding through her veins, and her whole body went limp against him, unable to resist, not wanting to, longing to know the full power and pleasure of this extraordinary man's fiery lovemaking.

Her lips never left hers, as Hilton's hands clasped her small waist. Gently he lifted her off the floor and carried her across the room.

She wrapped her arms securely about his neck and continued to kiss him, moaning gently when he drew her tongue inside his mouth. Just when she'd grown accustomed to her new role and had begun to search out his tongue, stroking, tasting, pleasuring, he took his mouth from hers.

Surprised to see they were standing before a high chest of drawers, Sylvain gave him a questioning look as he lifted her higher and deposited her atop the walnut chest.

"Courteen, what are you doing?" She began to giggle nervously.

"Gypsy, I'm going to undress you." Sylvain felt a sudden stab of panic. Hilton removed one kid slipper, then the other, and bent to set the shoes on the floor. Her breath caught in her throat when his hands went to her ankle. "You weren't intending to come to my bed wearing your shoes and stockings, were you, sweetheart?" Before she could answer, those strong hands were moving up her calf to her knee.

Sylvain wondered fleetingly if Edwin Fairmont had ever set her mother atop a chest and removed her shoes and stockings. Did husbands do things like this to their wives? The thought left her head as rapidly as it had come. She ceased caring what other couples did as Hilton's fiery fingers began to perform an erotic ritual of lovemaking unlike anything she'd ever imagined.

His fingers had traveled up past her knee and were slowly lowering the red satin garter on her left thigh, pulling it down over her foot and dropping it on the chest. Sylvain tensed, waiting for his hands to come back to her tingling leg. He lifted her other foot and gently caressed it, rubbing, stroking until she squirmed and bit her lip, eager for his warm hands to make that journey back up her leg.

He sensed her impatience and smiled, the thick mustache twitching above his full, sensuous lips.

"Soon, my beautiful Gypsy," he murmured and his hands began their ascent up the slick silk of her left leg. The colorful skirt rose before his hands as Hilton followed the wispy silk midway up her thigh. His breath grew as short as Sylvain's. The seductive silk stocking and the warm female flesh were pleasing to his touch. "Sweetheart," he breathed and slowly peeled the stocking down her leg and over her foot.

The colorful skirt remained up, exposing her thigh. Hilton drank in the sight and he felt the rapid onset of desire. Still keeping to his languid pace, he lifted her bare foot in one hand and bent over it. His warm lips came to rest on the high instep, and he felt Sylvain begin to tremble.

"Hilton," she said through dry lips, "you're not going to — "

"Yes, darling, I am," he said, his lips toying with her foot, his tongue tracing the delicate blue veins, "I'm going to kiss all of you."

His lips moved as slowly as his hands had, kissing and licking a molten path up her leg until finally his mouth was pressed to her soft, sensitive thigh, feathering kisses over her smooth, warm skin.

Sylvain, eyes closed, lips open, head thrown back, held tightly to the chest and felt suddenly dizzy and faint and frightened. Her body seemed no longer to belong to her, it belonged to this masked man whose lips were searing her flesh with exquisite, intimate kisses. When he started on the right leg Sylvain felt she might burst into flames, and it was all she could do to keep from crying out to him to hurry, hurry, to move faster, to kiss her again and again.

Sylvain knew her face was as scarlet as her skirt and she was grateful he couldn't see her masked eyes, nor she his. She sat there holding on for dear life, her eyes squeezed tightly shut.

While his tongue and lips aroused her acutely sensitive sense of touch, his deep voice excited her as he murmured endearments and made promises of how he would love her through the cold winter night.

"Hilton, Hilton." She hardly realized she was calling his name.

"Yes, my sweet?" He lifted his head, his hands stroking her bare thighs. "What is it?"

Her eyes opened and she looked down at him. "Nothing," she breathed, "just Hilton, Hilton."

He smiled, lifted her from the chest, and kissed her. She met his kiss with a fire equal to the one claiming his body. Hilton was sure what he'd thought all along was true. She was as passionate as he. He knew she had lived on the river for several years, among sailors and whores and rivermen. He had little doubt she'd shared more than one seaman's bed.

Hilton didn't care. He was glad; it would make the night all the more enjoyable. And come morning, there'd be no tears and threats, no regrets, no accusations, no entanglements. There would be only pleasure. For her. For him. For them both.

Hilton led Sylvain to the big bed, sat on its edge and pulled her down onto his knee. While he took sweet, plucking little kisses from her soft, dewy lips, he opened the buttons of his white shirt and drew Sylvain's hand inside it, silently urging her to touch him. She let out a breath and spread her hand upon him. She squirmed on his knee and raked eager fingers through the thick black hair. She liked the feel of him, the pleasing textures of crisp hair and smooth skin. She thrilled to the heavy thudding of his heart under her fingers.

Growing bolder, she stroked his chest, pausing to examine hard flat nipples and corded ribs. And as she caressed him, she dipped to his mouth for more kisses. He let her take charge, offering himself for her exploration.

She licked at his lips and slid her tongue along their curves. She nipped harmlessly at his full bottom lip while her hands found and followed the heavy black line of hair going down his belly. She was so caught up in this new pleasure, she didn't realize that Hilton was casually lowering her blouse until she felt the cool air on her bare skin.

Her head shot up at once. Her breasts were now freed from blouse and chemise, and her first inclination was to cover herself. She threw her arms across her chest in a defensive gesture that baffled Hilton, though he said only, "Sweet, let me touch you the way you touched me." His hands gently moved hers away and he eased the sleeves of the blouse down over her arms and off.

Fear and doubt returning, Sylvain sat with her blouse resting in a white pool around her waist and heard him saying softly, "Beautiful, so very beautiful." Her back went rigid when his brown hand gently cupped a breast and he slowly bent to her.

Air exploded from her aching lungs when she felt his warm mouth press a kiss to her left breast. He moaned and opened his mouth to lick lovingly at the nipple until it became a diamond-hard bud beneath his tongue. He moved to the other breast and kissed its already erect, aching rosette.

Sylvain had never known such ecstasy. She arched her back and moaned, and when Hilton drew her sweetness deep into his mouth and gently sucked, she whimpered softly and grabbed hold of his hair.

"Hilton," she rasped, "darling. It's good, that feels so good."

For an instant his lips released their treasure and he murmured against her burning flesh, "Gypsy, you're sweet; God, you're sweet," and again his mouth hungrily took hers.

He kissed her and caressed her breasts until her breathing was labored and she began to writhe and call his name. Then it was no longer enough for him, or for her. He stood, bringing her up with him. While she looked trustingly at him through the tiny eye slits of her scarlet domino mask, Hilton finished undressing her, deftly removing the wide sash, scarlet skirt, petticoats, and linen pantalettes.

When she stood naked before him, Hilton felt the blood roaring in his ears and the painful swelling in his groin. He longed to drop to his knees and worship all of her beautiful body with his hands and mouth, but he could sense the tension claiming her, and he gallantly turned back the sheets, picked her up, and placed her in the middle of the bed.

Sylvain hurriedly snatched the covers up over her. Heart pounding furiously, she lay back and let her curious gaze go to the tall man undressing in the candle-light. White shirt discarded, he unbuttoned his dark trousers while Sylvain admired the manly beauty of his wide shoulders, his hair-covered chest, his smooth, long back.

He sat down on a chair and removed his shoes and stockings, stood up and gripped the waistband of his trousers and linen, sending both to the floor. Sylvain gasped. Face flaming, she stared at his awesome erection and fleetingly thought such a mating was not possible. She had seen only one man naked in her life — Big Napoleon, on the night she saved him from the beating. She'd had only a glance at his groin; he was flaccid at that time and she'd never dreamed a man could expand to such large proportions. The pulsing, powerful rod she saw before her could not possibly go inside her. She was sure of it.

Hilton stretched out on the bed beside her and Sylvain instinctively cringed. A long arm came over her waist, and he kissed her trembling lips. Weight supported on an elbow, he whispered softly, "Sweetheart, I won't hurt you. I'll pleasure you, trust me."

She couldn't speak. She nodded and gave thanks for the mask she wore. And then his masterful mouth went to work once again, kissing her cheeks, her ears, her throat, her mouth. His hand gently tugged the sheet from hers, pushing it down steadily while his lips brought her to the threshold of rapture.

She was aware that her body was no longer concealed from his gaze. Unashamedly he studied the lovely length of her, eyes leisurely traveling from face to small, round breasts, to slim midriff, to narrow waist, to rounded hips, to long, slender legs.

"You have skin the color of honey," he said thickly, "and it tastes even sweeter. Kiss me, Gypsy."

Their lips met and held, and while she surrendered completely to his kiss, Hilton's strong, lean hands moved provocatively over her body. He stroked her breasts, her belly, her thighs. His lips slipped from her mouth down over her chin and came to rest in the sensitive hollow he'd kissed on the dance floor.

Sylvain's hands clutched at the silky sheets, she turned her head to one side. A knuckle went into her mouth when Hilton again caressed her swelling breasts, circling the nipples with his tongue, raking his teeth across the taut tips. His hand played upon her belly, and her thighs seemed to part of their own volition.

His fingers raked through the curly triangle of dark hair between her legs and moved lower. She felt his fingers gently probing and there was fire in them. Her groin was ablaze and a fiery wetness sprang from it. He dipped his fingers into that wetness and began to caress her, stroking, touching, tracing tiny circles upon the slick, sensitive flesh.

Sylvain's head tossed from side to side upon the pillow. She breathed heavily and arched her back, her body afire, every muscle and nerve of her being now centered there between her legs where he was touching her. Her need increased by the second. She felt she might scream from the unfamiliar pressure rapidly building, and she became achingly aware that only that rigid male rod, hard and insistent, pressing against her thigh could bring her the blessed release she craved.

It was what she wanted, what she needed, what she had to have or die. She rolled a shoulder up off the bed and reached out for him. Tentative fingers coming to him, she winced when, as she reached out to touch him, that throbbing shaft of male power rose to meet her hand. A gasp of wonder escaped her lips and she enclosed him with her fingers, thrilling to his reaction.

"God, Gypsy, darling — "

"Please, Hilton, now!"

"Sweetheart!" Hilton murmured against her fevered cheek and immediately shifted his weight.

Masked eyes on her face, he thrust into her sharply. And stopped at once. "My God," he groaned, shocked. He tore the mask from his eyes and discarded it. "Sylvain, sweetheart," he whispered in awe. "Angel girl, I'm no stranger. I'm your lover."

Lying completely still within her, he gently removed her mask. He saw the unshed tears shining in her frightened eyes and felt his chest constrict. He kissed her tenderly and soothed, "I didn't know, love, I didn't know. Have I hurt you? Are you all right?"

Sylvain, her body screaming its outrage at that first hard jab of white-hot pain, nodded her head violently, willing herself not to cry, determined not to behave like some sheltered young bride.

"Don't stop," she managed. "I'm fine, just fine." But her eyes slid closed and tears gathered in them.

Hilton couldn't have stopped had she begged him. He wanted her more now than before. To know this beautiful, sensuous young woman had never lain with a man, had chosen to give her virginity to him, added an unexpected depth to the coupling, and Hilton silently vowed to guide her patiently, lovingly, putting his own pleasure after hers.

"Sweetheart," he whispered, kissing her eyelids, "the worst is over, I promise."

Slowly her eyes opened and she looked straight into his. "Hilton, I don't . . . what am I supposed to do? I — "

"Shhh, love." He pressed warm kisses to her tremulous lips. "You needn't do a thing. Just lie here and let me love you, sweet. Just rest here in my arms, all right?"

"Y-yes," she stammered, "I . . . I will."

He smiled down at her and said, "You're so beautiful, so sweet." He kissed her again and said into her mouth, "So warm and loving."

Weight perfectly balanced so that he would not crush her, he lay on top of her and tenderly kissed her mouth, her eyes, her ears, her shoulders, and felt her tight, tense body begin to relax.

When his lips returned to hers, she kissed him wildly and her arms went around his neck, her fingers into his thick hair. They kissed and kissed, and during those heated, flaming kisses, Hilton began to slowly move his lean hips. Almost without realizing it, Sylvain began to move with him.

"Yes, baby," he encouraged and continued to spread searing kisses over her face and shoulders and breasts. He began to thrust, gently at first, pushing farther into her. She clung to him and bit her lip, and soon much of the discomfort was magically gone. She could feel him sinking into her and pleasure began to claim her.

He smiled and smoothed the tumble of dark brown hair back from her face. His lips hovered just above her own and she lifted her head from the pillow, seeking his mouth. She clutched at the wide, brown shoulders and kissed him deeply, lifting her hips to his as he drove into her with thrusts slow and insistent.

Hilton, his brain and body fevered with his all-consuming need for release, fought valiantly against such selfishness, determined to give this golden-skinned girl the pleasure she had sought in coming to his bed. It was not easy. She kept lifting her sweet, burning lips to his. Her eager hands caressed his back, fingertips trailing fire along the cleft. Her sweet voice kept calling his name in a way that touched his heart. And her pliant woman's body kept clasping him, holding him, driving him dangerously close to the edge of ecstasy.

Sylvain lay beneath Hilton and gloried in his lovemaking. His body in hers now brought rapture. The pain had disappeared, and she could hardly recall it. She moved with him, for him, became a part of him, and it was exquisitely sweet. Sure the pleasure he was bringing was all there was, could ever be, she liked the slow, languid way his body moved. She wanted it never to end, to go on and on, to last.

Hilton read the look of elation on her beautiful face and knew she was ready to be led on into paradise, she moved in rhythm with him and was overjoyed to experience even greater pleasure. Her nails dug into his flesh and she bucked against him, her heart beating faster, body heating rapidly, the need for fulfillment growing to match his.

And then it began.

A wild, strange force was claiming her body, building, rushing, tearing, until . . . Sylvain never knew it was her own cries she was hearing. Eyes wide with shock, she shuddered and trembled and clung to her lover with all her strength, experiencing the full wonder of her first climax.

Hilton held her spasming body, his hands clutching her rounded bottom, giving her all she wanted, riding out the storm, until finally, knowing she'd reached the pinnacle of passion, he let himself go. He groaned and shuddered and finally collapsed, his long body deadweight upon her.

She didn't mind. She turned her face to his and kissed his hair, his perspiring cheek, his shoulder. She was happy in a way she had never dreamed possible, so peaceful and contented she wanted to lie here under Hilton Courteen for as long as she lived.

Slowly Hilton eased off of her, gathering her to him, his lips feathering kisses on her brow. His eyes half closed, he murmured, "Rest, sweet love, rest." And to Sylvain's surprise, he fell asleep.

She did not. She lay awake in the candlelight and studied the dark, handsome face. Never had she seen a face so strong yet so beautiful. She let her fingertips trace the white scar that slashed through his heavy black eyebrow and smiled recalling how brave he'd been that day. She loved the girlishly long black eyelashes resting on his high brown cheekbones, the straight, prominent nose, that wide, sensuous mouth that knew so well how to kiss.

She moved her head a little and let her appreciative eyes slip down over the broad brown chest with its thick mat of black hair. She shivered, recalling how it felt to have that hair pressing against her naked breasts. Her gaze went on down his abdomen and lower to that part of his which had just given her such pleasure.

All of him was beautiful, so beautiful.

She let her eyes move back up to the lean brown hand resting on her belly. It, too, was beautiful. His fingers were long and tapered, and strong, oh, so strong. His nails were short and clean. He wore no jewelry, and she was glad. She'd heard that most gamblers wore flashy stickpins and diamond rings, and she was grateful he eschewed that mark of his trade.

To her he was not a gambler; he was Hilton Courteen, a gentleman, an aristocrat, a wealthy planter's son. He was far too fine and beautiful to be a gambler. He was much too gallant and respected. He was . . . he was . . . far, far above her.

Sylvain felt a twinge of pain stab her heart. She was lying here in bed with a man whose social class would never allow him to . . . to care for her. He'd taken her to bed for the night, but it meant nothing to him. Nothing. He'd sought amusement for an evening, a playmate for carnival night, a warm body to share his bed.

Sylvain lifted her head from the pillow and looked again at the handsome face, so calm and serene in sleep. "What have I done?" she agonized, absently noting how the black hair grew in appealing swirls about his perfectly shaped ears. "This is Hilton Courteen I'm in bed with! A man renowned for his conquests. I must go, get up and flee at once."

Sylvain eased Hilton's hand from her stomach and slid away from him. The movement awakened him and his black eyes opened. He reached out and pulled her back to him, nuzzling her neck. "Don't get up, darling." He kissed her throat, then lifted his head and looked down at her with such tenderness she wanted to weep. "My sweet girl, why didn't you tell me?" He brushed a kiss on her lips. "I didn't know you were a virgin, Sylvain. God, honey, I wouldn't have . . . " He shook his head.

Terrified by his tenderness and the confusion she was engulfed in, Sylvain fought the only way she knew how. "Don't feel bad, Courteen. You see, I purposely chose you to take my virginity."

Touched, he said, "I'm so grateful and happy, sweetheart, but I don't see why — "

"Because," she said, purposely seeking to hurt him, "I knew it wouldn't bother you, as it would a decent gentleman."

His eyes went cold, then blazed. "You're absolutely right, Gypsy. You chose well. I think only of myself at all times, and right now, I desire you again." He grinned wolfishly, and his eyes narrowed with anger.

"No!" she cried and struggled to get up.

"Oh, yes, my calculating little charmer, I've been inside you and it pleases me to be there again." He pulled her back to him. "And what pleases me is all I care about, isn't that true?"

"Don't," she begged. "Let me go! I'm sorry I ever — "

"As am I," he muttered and kissed her. She squirmed and fought and tried to resist him, but Hilton was having none of it. She'd pricked him and she'd pay. He would show her unrestrained passion, unleashed desire, an animal-like mating. He had patiently introduced her to making love; now he would acquaint her with raw lust.

His hands clasped the sides of her head and his mouth ground into hers, hungry and demanding. Sylvain shocked him, and herself, with her fiery response. His probing tongue invaded her mouth, and she met it with her own. They moaned and held each other tightly, their mouths melded, their naked bodies pressing, their hearts racing together.

They tumbled about on the bed, kissing, caressing, pawing each other like animals. Hands were everywhere, exploring, seeking, taking and giving wild pleasure. Burning lips branded kisses into faces, throats, shoulders, chest, and bellies, each almost fighting the other for the privilege of covering bare flesh with eager, hungry lips.

And then Sylvain was lying on her back, pulling her lover to her. Hilton thrust fiercely into her, and both gasped with pleasure. They mated violently, clinging to each other, whispering unintelligible words of endearment.

Rapidly, rhythmically Hilton moved in her, plunging deeply, one hand gripping her long dark hair, the other underneath her, lifting her to him. And all the while his smoldering black eyes were looking straight into her huge pewter ones.

Sylvain blinked when he released her hair and abruptly rose to his knees, taking her with him. He sat back on his heels, his knees wide apart, then pulled her legs across his thighs, and gripped her buttocks.

Her arms around his neck, she threw her head back and gloried in this strange new way of loving. Hilton guided her hips to accept his deep thrusts and leaned to her to lick her throat. Her eyes slid closed. She was aware of so many things: of her long, loose hair spilling down her back, tickling her, of Hilton's hot mouth and tongue pressing kisses to her sensitive skin, of the silky bristles of his mustache brushing her, of his hard chest pressing her naked breasts, of his strong hands gripping her hips, her bottom, of his sinewy thighs supporting her legs, of his huge shaft thrusting into her wet warmth.

It was pure heaven, all of it. Everything about it.

She felt herself losing control. Her eyes flew open, and she gripped Hilton's shoulders and looked into his eyes. He read the message in that heated gaze, felt her sweet body gripping him tighter, felt his own body meeting her demands.

"Yes!" he rasped and loved the expressions crossing the beautiful face before him. And when at last Sylvain screamed out, he gathered her close to his chest and followed her into heaven.

They clung to each other, their bodies covered with a sheen of perspiration, their hearts thudding wildly, their breathing labored. They kissed each other in sweet gratitude, sitting there in the middle of that big bed with the candlelight flickering on their glistening bodies.

It was an interlude neither would ever forget, a time of absolute bliss, a few moments of beautiful tenderness, a period of serenity beyond compare. Both felt it, shared it, savored it, reluctant to release it.

So for several sweet moments they remained as they were, Hilton still inside her, she clinging to him, her face resting on his shoulder, each softly calling the other's name. When at last Hilton felt her slender body go completely limp against his, he gently lowered them both to the bed and slid out of her.

He held her close in his arms, saying nothing, sure she was almost asleep. Soon he did sleep, and so he never heard her confession.

"Hilton," she whispered softly, her swollen lips pressing kisses on his chest, "I love you. I love you, darling."

Hilton awoke with the first pink haze of dawn and looked at the lovely girl asleep beside him. She'd turned in her sleep. She lay on her back, her long dark hair flowing about her on the pillow. A slender leg was turned out, the sole of her foot resting on the inside of her other knee.

Hilton swallowed hard and rose from the bed. Gently he pulled the sheet up over her. Then he dressed.

He knew he had to leave, had to go now before she woke. She'd told him what she wanted from him. He had given it to her. She'd made it clear he meant nothing to her and that she thought him no part of a gentleman, had little use for him.

Hilton walked to the walnut chest, drew her gold earrings from his pocket, and placed them by her stockings and the bright red garter. Then he took the emerald ring from his valise and laid it beside the earrings.

He leaned down to look at her one last time. His hand automatically reached out to touch her cheek, stopped short, and fell to his side. Dark eyes tortured, he grabbed up his coat and valise and left the room.

Sylvain awoke when the strong winter sun flooded the opulent room. Her eyes opened to the unfamiliar beige silk canopy. Then it all came back. She purred happily and turned to look at her lover.

She sat up, foolishly looking about for Hilton. The harsh truth dawned, and Sylvain drew her knees to her chest and softly cried. Shamed, hurt, tired, she sat in the middle of the rumpled bed and wept.

But not for long.

After a moment, she wiped her eyes on the beige sheet and rose. Anger was rapidly driving away all other emotions. She hated Hilton Courteen almost as much as she hated herself. But not quite. What had happened between them was her fault, no one else's. She knew the kind of man he was, and yet she'd eagerly gone to his bed. Had she really expected him to be lying there beside her with words of love to go with the morning coffee?

Sylvain shivered, recalling the intimate night they'd shared, the things he'd done to her, her confession of love for him. Obviously that confession had meant nothing at all to the heartless Hilton Courteen. And why should have it? Dozens of women had fallen in love with him — high-born, beautiful, rich women.

Sylvain, dressed now, went to the tall chest for her stockings. She put her hand on the wispy silk and gasped. There on the walnut chest lay her dear mother's emerald ring. She grabbed it up and smiled despite her agony. She had no idea where Hilton had gotten it, and she didn't care. It was precious to her, and she was glad to have it back.

She slipped the emerald onto her finger and admired it. And she wondered: Was it all she was ever to have of Hilton Courteen?

Chapter Twenty-Three

In the darkened dining room, only a single candle had been lighted. The great old chandelier was dust-covered, never used. A small, dim circle of light fell on the white tablecloth and on the seated man.

The gold gargoyle-head of an ebony cane gleamed in the flickering candlelight and made a heavy thudding sound as the man tapped it absently against his open palm. Eerie shadows danced on the crumbling wall coverings. A mouse meandered brazenly along the baseboard near the man's feet. The air was hot, and fetid with the stench of unwashed flesh.

Hyde Rankin, shirtless, the thick black hair covering his chest and skinny arms drenched with sweat, laid down the ebony cane. He picked up a table knife and dislodged a sliver of meat caught between his molars. He swilled whiskey from a waterglass. Before him a china plate held the scraps of the dinner he'd finished over two hours earlier. His cold eyes, gleaming in the half light, held a look of rage.

Scratching his armpit, Rankin, whiskey dribbling down his stubbled chin, called out in the stillness.

"Yancey!" The veins stood out on his narrow forehead. "Yancey, get your black ass in here this minute!"

Yancey Jones, the slim, mannerly black who acted as butler at the crumbling Riverbend plantation, appeared immediately in the arched doorway, his eyes round with fear.

"Yessuh, Mast' Rankin?"

"Come closer, Yancey." Hyde Rankin took another long pull from the whiskey glass and picked up the evil-looking cane. "Step up here close so I can see you." Unquestioning, the black obeyed. "Yancey, you're aware Mrs. Rankin left me two days ago."

Yancey ducked his head and mumbled, "I's powerful sorry, Mast' Rankin, 'bout that."

"I see," Rankin said coolly. "And Betty Lou? She sorry, too?"

Yancey blanched at the mention of his wife. "Ah, yessuh, yessuh, she be sorry, too, suh."

Eyes narrowed, Hyde Rankin lifted a long arm and swept all the china from the table. The loud crash caused the nervous black man to jump. Hyde Rankin laughed softly.

"Startle you, Yancey?" Rankin said in a low voice. "It seems that's the only way to get you people's attention."

Yancey kept his head bowed, afraid to look at the evil man who was his master. He wished again, as he had so many times in the past, that he'd taken his wife, Betty, and their two children and fled into the swamps, as many other slaves had done since Hyde Rankin had come to Riverbend.

Rankin rose to his feet. "Yes, Yancey, I lost my dear wife. Know why?" He waited for the black to speak. Yancey said nothing. Rankin struck the table with his cane. "Know why?" he shouted.

"No, suh."

"Mrs. Rankin heard some terrible lies about me, Yancey. And she believed them." His voice was threatening. "Ever hear anything bad about me, Yancey?"

"No, suh." Yancey began to tremble.

Rankin grinned sadistically. "Bring Betty Lou in here, Yancey."

"But, Mast', she be cleanin' the kitchen. She be — "

Rankin's cold, hard eyes fixed the trembling black man. "When I get through with her, she won't be able to clean anything." He eased back down into his chair and scratched his hairy chest. "Mrs. Rankin overheard your Betty Lou whispering about me, Yancey. Betty Lou said some terrible things, and now my wife's left me."

"Oh, Mast' Rankin, no, that — "

"I'm most unhappy about this turn of events," Hyde Rankin interrupted. He chuckled suddenly. "I went to all the trouble to marry that dour, ugly old bitch so I would be considered a respectable family man. I even bedded her a few times, distasteful as it was, so she'd believe ours was a real marriage." Rankin shook his head. "Get Betty Lou in here and strip her down."

"No, suh, Mast' Rankin. Whip me 'stead of Betty." The terrified black automatically began unbuttoning his shirt. "I be the one that told," Yancey said hopefully. "Whup me, suh, not Betty Lou."

Betty Lou silently appeared and stepped into the dimly lit room. Young and intelligent, she moved up to the dining table and smiled down at Hyde Rankin. "Mast' Rankin," she spoke in a calm, determined voice. "You not want to whip my Yancey. Yancey, he know somethin' what's goin' to make you rich."

Hyde Rankin eyed the young woman. "He does?" His voice was derisive. "That right, Yancey? You're going to make me rich?"

Shooting an alarmed, silencing look at his pretty wife, Yancey shook his head, "Naw, Mast' Rankin, I don't know nothin' 'bout — "

"There's gold at Riverbend." Betty Lou ignored her husband. "Pirates buried it years ago right here on the plantation."

Hyde Rankin's mouth gaped open. "Gold on my land?" His eyes took on a glow. It didn't sound outlandish to him. The pirate Lafitte had slept with Serena Fairmont,

had fathered her child. It was entirely possible this remote plantation had once been a hideaway of Lafitte's.
"Where is it, Yancey?"

"Mast', I don't know. I jes' hear 'bout — "

Again Betty Lou broke in. "He don't know, Mast', but
there's slaves out in the quarters what do know."

Eyes gleaming with excitement, Rankin rose from his
chair. Picking up the vulgar cane, he circled the table
and came to Betty Lou, stepping up very close to her.
She stood her ground, her eyes holding his. His long
bony fingers entwined in her hair and he gave the curly
locks a hard yank, then cupped the crown of her head,
tilting her face up to his. "You better be telling the truth,
Betty," he murmured menacingly. "I've lost my wife because of your loose tongue. This better not be just another one of your lies." He gave an evil smile, then
guided her around the long table and forcefully shoved
her to the floor amid the broken china and bits of food.
"Clean it up," he ordered, unmoved by her shriek of
pain.

He turned to Yancey. "We'll speak to the field hands."

"Yessuh." Yancey eyes were on his wife. "Firs' thing in
the mornin'." He started toward Betty Lou.

"No, Yancey." Hyde Rankin twirled the ebony cane
underneath his arm. "Tonight."

"But it be past midnight, Mast'."

"Good for you," Rankin said hatefully, "you've learned
to tell time. Come!"

Groggy, blinking slaves stumbled from their quarters,
some half dressed, others still in their nightclothes. Hyde
Rankin, slapping the gold tip of his cane against his open
palm, looked at the baffled throng before him.

"Where's the gold hidden?" said Rankin in a cold, flat
voice. "Take me to it."

The slaves mumbled and looked at one another.
None answered. Rankin stalked along in front of them,

pointedly looking at each one, his light, angry eyes sending terror through them all. He rubbed his chin and grinned. With the speed of a striking serpent, Hyde Rankin's hand shot out and he grabbed a tall black youth by the arm and jerked him close to his face.

"Shall I start the whipping with you, son? Want to be beaten here in front of the others?"

"No, suh." The terrified boy shook his head.

Hyde Rankin released him. Again he paced back and forth before them, making certain his threatening, evil presence was felt by every person there. "Hear me, all of you: This is my land you live on, my beds you sleep in, and my gold you're keeping from me. I want it, and I want it tonight." He paused and studied the cane; then smiled. "I believe I'll start with the youngest and work my way up to the oldest." He stopped before a young father holding his five-year-old girl in his arms. With the tip of his cane, Rankin tickled the sleeping child's back. "How about it, Rufus, shall I start the beatings with your daughter?"

"Please, Mast'," the father pleaded, clutching the child closer.

"It's me you're huntin'." Saul, an old gray-haired man, stepped through the crowd. "Let the others go. They don't know 'bout the gold." A buzz went through the cluster of frightened slaves as they listened to old Saul say, "There's treasure buried here at Riverbend. But not even I know where."

Too old and tired of living to be afraid, Saul told Hyde Rankin what he knew of the gold. "Jean Lafitte's messenger give to old Kashka, a slave what's dead, gold and diamonds to hide at Riverbend. Kashka, he did it and tol' no one where he hid it."

"My God, man!" Hyde Rankin glared at the tired old slave. "Kashka told you of the gold but refused to tell you where it was buried?"

"I didn't want to know," Saul said evenly.

"Damn you for a fool, old man!" Hyde Rankin spat out the curse. Clutching the old slave by the collar of his frayed nightshirt, he ordered, "You'll show me Kashka's grave." He called four of the strongest men out of the group. "Get shovels and follow us. We're going to dig up Kashka's body. I mean to have that gold!"

The frigid February weather changed rapidly. The day following the masked ball was balmy, springlike, beautiful. Sylvain walked home along the sun-splashed avenues and felt a hundred times colder than she'd been parading down the same streets the evening before.

The lovely day and the colorful gypsy costume she wore mocked her. She stepped cautiously along in her dainty high-heeled slippers and wished she could turn back the clock, change the tide of events, alter the course she had so willingly taken.

She could not.

What was done was done and there was no going back. The pain in her temples, the ache in her heart, the unfamiliar tenderness between her legs were punishing reminders of what had happened in Hilton Courteen's hotel room.

To her despair, waves of desire surged through her at the thought of the dark, handsome man who'd taught her what it was to be a woman. Masterfully he'd stirred her to raging, blazing desire, then had given her exquisitely glorious release, a culmination so earth-shattering she could still feel the tiny tremors race through her at the recollection.

Sylvain neared the Water Street house and sighed wearily. Would they question her? Would they scold and berate her and add to her shame? Would the sisters look at her with that barely veiled disgust of the old days? Would Delilah get her alone and tell her she'd behaved no better than a waterfront tart?

Mercifully, the Spencer sisters were not at home. Big Napoleon was at the chandlery, so only Delilah awaited her. The tall black took one look at the sad young woman and held out her arms.

"Delilah," Sylvain said, clinging to her old friend, "he left me alone. Hilton Courteen went away without a word after I . . . after we. . . . "

Delilah hushed her. "Come upstairs. We'll give you a nice hot bath and wash your hair, and you'll feel much better."

Sylvain followed her servant up to the second floor, then sat in the wooden tub while Delilah soaped the long dark tresses gently, speaking softly as she worked. "The Lord looks at our hearts, Sylvain. He knows you're good. He knows you've suffered." She laid the soap aside and kneaded Sylvain's tight scalp. "You have to take each day as it comes, honey. Here's the question you must ask yourself: Did you have a grand time last night?" Her busy fingers paused, and she gently turned Sylvain's head.

Sylvain looked Delilah in the eye. "Delilah, I never knew such joy existed. I never dreamed that a man and a woman could give to each other such pleasure. It was wonderful. Unlike any bliss I've ever known."

Delilah smiled, and her hands again grew busy. "Maybe it's not that wonderful for all couples, honey. Maybe what was between you two was very special."

Sylvain shut her eyes tightly. "No. If it had been, he would not have left me. Would he?"

"Honey, I can't answer that. But I know this: till you're an old, old woman, you will always remember the Mardi Gras of 1843 and the wonderful time you had. No one can take that away from you. People have lived on less." She looked at the emerald ring on Sylvain's finger. "You have that sweet memory, and you got your emerald back as well."

Hilton's handsome, passion-hardened face flickered before Sylvain's closed eyes. "Delilah," she said softly, "have I ever told you you're a very intelligent woman?"

Delilah laughed softly.

The censure Sylvain was afraid she'd see in the eyes of the Spencer sisters was not there. When they returned home that afternoon, they were as kind and sweet as always. They said nothing of the Mardi Gras, nor did she. Sylvain never knew if Delilah — or perhaps Big Napoleon — had covered for her, and she didn't care. She was simply grateful she hadn't lost the respect it had taken her so long to gain.

After dinner that evening, the sisters relaxed in the parlor, Hester reading aloud to Marie, who was embroidering a scarf for Sylvain's bureau. Delilah was busy in the kitchen.

Restless, Sylvain wandered into the small back courtyard as dusk was falling. She sat down on the wooden settee Big Napoleon had built the summer before and looked up at the quarter-moon rising in a sky full of twinkling stars.

A wave of loneliness swept over her, and a feeling of deep melancholy tore at her heart. Thoughts tumbled over one another. Had her mother felt in Jean Lafitte's arms the way she'd felt in Hilton Courteen's? Always before, she'd wondered how her dear, regal mother could have given herself to a man she hardly knew, a man she was never to see again. She looked at the beautiful emerald on her finger and sighed.

"The Colombian emerald belonged to Jean Lafitte." Big Napoleon's voice was soft.

Sylvain looked up at the gigantic black man standing before her. She motioned for him to sit beside her. "Big Napoleon, I'm Jean Lafitte's daughter." The two had never before discussed it. "Did Delilah tell you the ring came from Lafitte?"

Big Napoleon eased down on the long wooden settee. His dark eyes were kind. "No, Miss Sylvain. Once I lived on Grand Terre with Lafitte."

Speechless, Sylvain stared at the big man who'd been with her for the past five years. "You knew my father? You knew Jean Lafitte?"

Napoleon nodded. "Knew and respected him."

Awed, Sylvain said, "Please. You must tell me all you know about my father."

The big, gentle man talked for the better part of an hour while Sylvain listened, engrossed, to stories about her real father.

"Tell me how you came to know Lafitte," Sylvain gently urged. "I've always wondered about your precise English. You weren't born a slave."

"No, Miss Sylvain, I was not." He smiled, his white teeth flashing. "I'm the son of an African queen and a white man. My father was an admiral in His Majesty's Royal Navy. He was ordered to Africa to quell a small summertime disturbance. There he met my mother." Big Napoleon's massive shoulders lifted in a shrug. "My father loved my mother, but he was married to a proper lady back in England. Each year he came to visit us. He brought gifts and books, and he tutored me." He paused. "When I turned twenty, I was restless for adventure, so I sailed, against my mother's wishes, to the West Indies. The ship I was on was attacked by pirates. I was captured and taken to New Orleans to be sold at the slave auction. I escaped and fled into the swamps. Near death, thirsty, lost, I wandered through the maze of marshes until I could go no farther. I lay down to die and was found the next day by Lafitte himself. He asked no questions; he took me in and cared for me."

"Why did you leave him, Napoleon?"

Big Napoleon looked pensive. "When Lafitte went to Galvez, he asked me to stay in Barataria, said he'd return one day." He looked at her. "He never made it back. I wandered too close to civilization, and the slave catchers got me. I was brought here to Mobile and sold at auction to Hyde Rankin." He smiled then and added, "And you saved me from death, just as your father saved me all those years ago."

"Napoleon, do you believe there's treasure buried at Riverbend?"

"I know it," he stated emphatically. "Lafitte chose me to transport a cache of gold and diamonds to Riverbend to be hidden there."

Sylvain sat up straighter. "Do you know where the booty is?"

He shook his big head. "No, Miss Sylvain. Your father sent me through the swamps with the gold. I delivered it to a man called Kashka. He was to hide it and tell no one, save Jean Lafitte, where it was concealed. I carried a sealed letter back to Lafitte, telling where Kashka hid the gold. Lafitte read it and put it into the candle flame. They were the only two who ever knew where the treasure was placed. And now they are both dead."

Sylvain nodded. "Was Kashka an African prince, too?"

"No, Miss Sylvain. Kashka was a Christian like you. He even had the same profession as Jesus."

"He was a carpenter?"

"Yes, ma'am."

"Ummm," Sylvain mused and fell silent. The two of them sat there in the warm February night, their thoughts identical.

"Big Napoleon?" Sylvain finally broke the silence.

"Yes, Miss Sylvain?"

"Is there any chance we could find that treasure?"

"You're forgetting that Riverbend belongs to Hyde Rankin. He'd kill us if he caught us on his property."

"Riverbend is mine! Jean Lafitte gave it to my mother. Rankin stole it as surely as if he'd taken a gun and held us up." Her eyes were fierce and hate welled up in her anew.

"That's true. Nonetheless, the man now has legal possession — "

"We could slip through the swamps at night. He'd never know we were there." She gave him a hopeful look.

"Miss Sylvain, we're too far away. It would take time and patience."

"We'll move to New Orleans!" she exclaimed. "I'll save all the money I possibly can. Then in a year, perhaps less, we'll sell the chandlery and purchase another when we get to New Orleans. At night you and I can search for the gold!" Her eyes danced.

"You're the boss," he said, not wanting to shatter her hopes. "You want to move back to New Orleans, I'll go along with it. But on one thing I must put my foot down."

"What's that, Big Napoleon?"

"I'm not taking a young white woman into those swamps at night. I'll go in alone or not at all."

"We'll see."

Alexa Le Noble relaxed on the long blue velvet chaise, her closed eyes covered with pads saturated in witch hazel. She had only an hour to rest before the Sunday evening buffet. She had to be relaxed and at her best; it was to be a special evening.

James Polk, who'd been speaker of the House for four years before he became the governor of Tennessee, was to be the honored guest. Jeff Davis was already planning to travel throughout Mississippi making speeches on behalf of Polk's election to the presidency. Hilton had returned only this afternoon from Baton Rouge. He'd been gone for days making swings throughout Mississippi and Louisiana, advocating the annexation of Texas to the Union.

Alexa smiled. Finally Hilton was showing the keen interest in politics she and Davis had long hoped to see. Alexa was sure Jeff would soon be a representative in

Congress. And that would be only the beginning for the ambitious Davis. Wouldn't it be satisfying if Hilton, with her help, entered into the political arena and gave up his gambling once and for all? It would be very thrilling to one day find herself the envied wife of the respected, handsome Senator Hilton Courteen of the great state of Mississippi.

Alexa's smile broadened at the thought, then quickly fled. Hilton had not been the same since his grandmother's death. Since he'd returned from Mobile more than a year before, he'd been withdrawn, distracted, moody. It was not like him, and it worried her, though when she questioned him, she'd gotten no answers.

She was baffled by his strange behavior. In many ways he was more attentive to her than ever, yet he seemed to be going through the motions, trying too hard, as though his heart was not in it. She couldn't imagine what had happened in Mobile to bring about the change, but something definitely had.

Alexa removed the cotton pads from her green eyes and sat up. She rose and crossed the plush carpet to her dressing room. Thumbing through her many elegant gowns, she told herself she was being foolish. Her lover would be in her arms before the warm spring night was over, and she'd drive everything else right out of his handsome head.

She would. She had to. She loved Hilton Courteen. More, much more, than she'd ever loved her husband.

Hilton Courteen stepped off the gangplank of the steamer *Glenda Ruth* and strolled eagerly toward Natchez Under the Hill. He ducked out of the bright sunshine into a smoke-filled card room on bustling Silver Street. He blinked in the dim light and cautiously made his way between the green baize-covered tables where nattily dressed gentlemen played poker on this warm Sunday afternoon.

He saw an acquaintance seated at a table. One chair stood vacant. Smiling he made his way there. Three of the men remained seated while the fourth, a tall, darkly handsome youth, rose.

The young man thrust out his hand to Hilton and smiled engagingly. "I'm Dawson Harpe Blakely, Cap'n Courteen. I understand you made some rousing speeches in Vicksburg, Jackson, and Baton Rouge. Betting men say you'll be a state senator within five years. Like cards as much as speechmaking, Cap'n?"

"Dawson," drawled Hilton, "poker's my passion." Both men laughed and took their seats at the table.

Within two hours, young Dawson Blakely had accumulated all the cash on the table.

Hilton rose, grinned, and clasped the boy's hand. "Dawson, you're one fine poker player."

"Thanks, Cap'n Courteen, I'll give you a chance at me any time you want it."

Hilton pulled a gold watch from his trousers pocket and said, "I'll hold you to that. For now, I must hurry. I have a dinner engagement with a beautiful lady."

Hilton Courteen stepped out of the tub in his Parker Hotel suite. He toweled himself dry and walked naked to the mahogany bureau. He drew out a starched white shirt and slipped into it, then stepped into his white linens and pulled on a pair of dark trousers. Black shoes and stockings on, he stood before a mirror and brushed his thick black hair, tied his cravat, and reached for his jacket.

He returned to the bureau, pulled out the middle drawer, and was lifting a snowy white handkerchief from a neat stack when his eyes fell on a small beige glove nestled among the handkerchiefs. Swallowing hard, Hilton lifted the glove from the drawer and looked at it. He smiled and raised it to his lips for a moment before returning it to the drawer.

He laughed at himself for his romantic foolishness, but the laughter rang hollow in his ears.

An old and insistent longing filled him once again. He couldn't forget the one glorious night he'd spent in the arms of the glove's owner. Carnival night with Sylvain Fairmont had left him permanently scarred. He'd never be the same man again.

Wearily, Hilton sank down onto the soft bed and sighed. As he had so many nights in the last year, he saw her beautiful oval face, the smoky eyes, the succulent lips. He groaned and recalled her body, its color rich as pale honey, stretched out beside him in the candlelight. And he heard again the soft, sweet voice calling his name in ecstasy.

And Hilton knew.

He would never forget Sylvain Fairmont.

By the time he stepped into the Davis coach for the ride out to Beau Monde, Hilton had made up his mind, and he wasted no time in telling his friend of his decision.

Jeff Davis's eyes widened, then narrowed. "Hill, while I'm sure Sylvain Fairmont is a sweet child, you know very well such a marriage would end your promising political career. Good Lord, look how they treated powerful old Andy Jackson over Rachel."

"I'm more than willing to give up my political future for Sylvain."

Jeff Davis shook his head. "I believe you, my friend, and although I can't pretend I'm pleased with your decision, I do admire you." He touched Hilton's sleeve. "One thing more: Is this girl in love with you?"

Hilton laughed, his full lips lifting beneath his black mustache. "Nope."

No one in the room could tell by Hilton's behavior that he was planning to leave Natchez. He stood at Alexa's side and shook hands with the illustrious guests, easily charming the ones he hadn't met, finding definite favor in the twinkling eyes of Governor Polk. The older man drew him aside and told Hilton he'd heard glowing reports coming the cities where he'd been delivering speeches.

"I tell you, son," the governor confided, "it's men like you and Jeff Davis who will keep the Democrats strong and in power. You've both got bright futures before you."

It was not until the last couple had finally departed that Hilton closed the heavy front door, strode into the drawing room, and poured two glasses of brandy. Alexa smiled adoringly at him from the long sofa and patted the cushion beside her.

Hilton drew a breath and came to her. "My dear," he said in clear, decisive tones "you know I'm very fond of you."

Alexa straightened, took the brandy snifter from him and said, "I've said those very words to gentlemen I no longer wanted to call on me."

Hilton looked steadily into her green eyes. "I can't deny it, Alexa. You see, for too long I've been unfair to you. And to myself."

"I'm listening." She steeled herself, and continued sipping her brandy.

"I buried my grandmother over a year ago, Alexa. While I was in Mobile, I attended the Mardi Gras ball."

"You told me, darling." She smiled knowingly. "You probably met some frivolous young lady and spent the night with her. It doesn't matter, Hilton. Those things happen. I'm not shocked or displeased. I don't expect you to be a saint, my love." She looked hopefully at him.

"It was more than carnival night frivolity. I love the girl. I'm going to marry her if she'll have me." He drained his brandy glass in one long draft.

"No," breathed a stunned Alexa Le Noble. "I thought you and I . . . We get along so well and . . . there's more. Much more. You have your political career to consider.

You're on your way. Imagine how far you can go if you . . . if we — "

"My mind's made up," he said quickly. "For what I've done to you, I'm sorry. I never meant to hurt you, my dear. I'm very — "

" . . . fond of me," she finished bitterly.

"Yes."

"Who is she, Hilton? Tell me her name."

"Miss Sylvain Fairmont," Hilton said, smiling.

"Sylvain Fairmont," Alexa repeated the name, her brow creased in thought. "Sylvain Fairmont. Where have I heard . . . ?" Her eyes grew wide. "Hilton, good Lord, don't you know who Sylvain Fairmont is?"

He nodded his dark head. "Jean Lafitte's beautiful daughter."

"Exactly!" Alexa stared at the smiling man. "You can't be serious, darling. Why, the entire South knows about her. You'll be throwing away any chance you have of becoming a senator."

Hilton touched Alexa's ivory cheek. "My dear, for Sylvain I'd give up the presidency."

"You love her that much?"

"More than my own life." He rose and helped Alexa to her feet. "Walk me to the door."

"I think not," she said, looking into his eyes. "I abhor females who cry, and I might do just that if I see you walk out that door for the last time."

"As you wish," said Hilton and leaned down to kiss her cheek. "Sorry," he murmured, and strode away.

"Hilton," she called after him. He paused, turned, and looked at her.

"Do you realize just what you're giving up? Wealth, power, a life of splendid ease?"

Hilton Courteen smiled. "My dear, it won't be the first time."

Chapter Twenty-Four

A pale, weakened Hilton Courteen descended the gangplank of the *Judith Ann* as soon as the big steamer slid gracefully into a berth at the New Orleans landing in the hot June sunlight.

The malaria had flared again on the trip down the river, and Hilton had spent the journey fevered and shivering in his bunk. Eager to get to a clean hotel room where he might regain his health before proceeding to Mobile, Hilton lifted his arm and hailed a cab.

Jasper, close on his heels, said solicitously, "You need a full week in bed, yessuh. We get you to the hotel, I go for a doctor."

"I've no need of a doctor, Jas." Hilton stepped tiredly into the coach and laid his dark head against the worn leather cushion. "The Richardson," he said to the driver and closed his eyes.

"Yessuh." The driver flicked the reins and turned the carriage around. They clopped down Magazine Street, a broad thoroughfare crowded with saloons, barrelhouses, bagnios, dance halls. And a brand-new ship chandlery.

Hilton never saw the sign that had gone up only two days before: Spencer's Chandlery.

At a small white cottage near the swamps and on the Ramparts, Sylvain directed the unpacking. She smiled when Napoleon carried the champagne brocade sofa into the parlor. The gold chairs followed, and the gilt mirror. The square piano had been sold in Mobile. Sylvain knew it was foolish to transport the sofa and chairs, but she couldn't bear the thought of parting with the fine furniture her mother had so prized.

Delilah came in from the kitchen, a dish towel around her middle, a crisp white tignon covering her hair. In her hand was a fragile crystal dish. "Miss Sylvain," she said, dark eyes serious, "what will folks think about us living in one of these houses where gentlemen keep their octoroon *placées*?"

Sylvain looked at Big Napoleon and saw the twinkle in his brown eyes. Her gaze swung back to Delilah. She clasped her hands before her and said, "My stars above, I do hope it won't ruin my reputation." Then she burst into peals of laughter. Napoleon's throaty chuckle mingled with hers.

Delilah looked from one to the other, eyes snapping, lips pursed. Then she saw the humor of it. Her full lips curved first into a slight grin, finally into a full-blown smile, and she began to laugh. The three old friends laughed so uproariously that the Spencer sisters came downstairs to investigate. When Sylvain could speak, she explained that the three of them had found it amusing that Delilah was still concerned with propriety.

"Do you two mind so very much that we're living here where young quadroon women are kept in houses by gentlemen who will never be allowed to marry them?"

"My dear," Hester spoke resolutely, "This house is so much more pleasant than the one in Mobile, we are delighted with it. Aren't we, sister?"

"We are, Sylvain," Marie said, nodding. "Why the house is freshly painted and we have that nice cool gallery and the flowers and trees. It's a lovely place." She paused and smiled guiltily. "I met a young lady while I was out back beating a rug. She lives in the house next door. She told me her name was LouAnne and she invited me to come for tea some afternoon." She glanced at her older sister. "Do you suppose it would be all right if I went."

Sylvain hugged her. "I think it would be a very neighborly thing to do."

A week had passed. Sylvain, alone in the new chandlery on Magazine Street, stood on a high rung of a tall stepladder, arranging newly arrived merchandise on a top shelf at the back of the store. She hummed as she worked, a sweet, mellow love song that so often ran through her head she hardly realized she was humming it.

It was warm on this still June day. Sylvain's heavy, dark hair had been pinned haphazardly atop her head. She wore a cool calico dress of yellow and white checks, the first few buttons of the tight bodice undone for comfort. She stood on the ladder in her stocking feet, stretching a slender arm upward.

The newly hung bell tinkled loudly.

"Be with you in a minute," she called in a warm, friendly voice and continued with her chore.

The customer made no reply. He stepped in out of the sun, and the pupils of his dark eyes dilated. He lounged against the door frame, arms crossed, lips lifting into a satisfied smile beneath his black mustache.

Hilton's appreciative gaze went to the slender girl on the stepladder. Heart speeding pleasantly at the sight of her, he carefully appraised the slim woman who'd haunted him for far too long.

Her small feet, showing beneath her full skirts as she stretched up on tiptoe, made him long to kiss them, just as he had that night they spent together. The slender waist, the long, graceful neck, the glossy dark hair — all presented such a pleasing picture that Hilton was tempted to storm across the room, pull her from the ladder, and devour her with hungry kisses until she was panting and breathless in his arms.

"All finished," she announced and moved one foot down a rung. Catlike, Hilton sprang to her aid, his hands encircling the narrow waist. "What the devil . . . ?" Sylvain sputtered and twisted her head around.

"May I give you a hand, Sylvain?"

It was all a blur to Sylvain, so hurriedly did she look at him, then away. She saw black hair, a deeply tanned complexion, a straight, proud nose, a strong, sculptured jaw. Eyes as black as midnight burning with a hot light, and a mouth, full and sensuous, smiling from beneath a thick blue-black mustache.

Her hands plucked at the strong, brown ones holding her waist. Sylvain was at once plagued . . . and pleased . . . to see him. Both were shocked at the electricity that crackled between them.

"Will you let me go?" Sylvain's voice was not as forceful as she would have liked.

"Certainly," said Hilton, setting her on the floor and reluctantly releasing his hold on her small waist.

She whirled around to look up at him. Weakened by the leashed sensuality of the broad-shouldered man before her, she hastily reminded herself that this indecently handsome man was a scoundrel, a rogue, a heartless blue-blooded cad who'd taken her virginity and left her without so much as a by-your-leave.

Her gray eyes turned to moving smoke and her hands went to her hips. "What in blazes are you doing here, Courteen?"

"I've come for you," he announced calmly, and watched the fire flash in her beautiful eyes as her skin turned a deep crimson with anger.

"Of all the pigheaded, conceited, insensitive fools I've ever known, you take the prize!"

Unruffled, he nodded. "I try always to be first at anything I attempt." He thought for a moment she was going to strike him.

She took a step closer, chin lifted, eyes snapping. "Listen to me, so I won't have to repeat myself, Courteen: I don't know what you're doing here, but unless you wish to purchase something, you will leave!"

Hilton smiled lazily, looked around, and picked up a small compass from the counter. "I'll take this."

"Fine!" said Sylvain. She grabbed the compass from his hand and added bitingly, "The needle points toward the door. Why don't you follow it?"

"Not yet. I've not told you why I've come."

Sylvain shoved the compass at him, folded her arms, and said, "What have you come for?"

"You, sweetheart."

Her pulse jumped at the endearment. "Me?" She tossed her dark head.

"You, darling." He shoved his hands into his trousers pockets to keep them from reaching out for her. "Sylvain, I've not spent one day when you were not in my thoughts." His dark eyes were almost hidden beneath the lowered lids, and the smile had left his lips. "I should never have left you. I've come back for you."

Her arms fell to her sides. She balled her hands into tight fists and fought the dizziness his confession had caused. "I care nothing for you, nothing," she snapped. "You're an arrogant fool, Courteen."

"That may well be," admitted readily, "but let me warn you, sweetheart, I'm not easily dissuaded. A fool? Perhaps, but a most determined one, my love." His hands came slowly out of his pockets, and he moved dangerously close to her.

Feeling an involuntary tremor rush through her body, Sylvain lowered her head, eyes on the V of his open white shirt. Hilton lifted his hand to her face. A long, lean finger skimmed over a soft, golden cheek. Languidly, he stroked her dark, upswept hair, then raised her face toward him. He let his black hypnotic eyes command hers to look into them. She trembled, but her gaze held his.

Hilton placed his hands on either side of her face and would not let her look away.

In that deep, unforgettable voice he said, "Sylvain I should never have left you. I'm back because I love you, and I intend to make you love me." Her eyes widened and she caught her breath. "I love you, sweetheart," he drawled softly. "And I mean to have you."

He gently released her face, took one of her cold hands in his own and lifted it, He turned it over and bowed to press a soft kiss into her palm.

Sylvain regained her equilibrium. She jerked her hand free and pointed to the door.

"Get out!"

From that day forward, Sylvain lived in constant fear — and hope — that she'd look up to see him coming through the door of the chandlery. Or that she'd walk into a room and he'd be there. The knowledge that he was in New Orleans added a measure of dread — and anticipation — to her every waking hour.

She didn't believe his confession of love. He was, she assumed, back in New Orleans for a visit and in search of amusement. She was woman enough to realize he'd gladly take her to bed again, and wise enough not to let him do so. There was little doubt in her mind that once he'd had her again, he'd behave just as he had before. Sated, he'd stroll right out of her life, tossing her aside as though she were one of his soiled white shirts.

That was not going to happen.

It had been eighteen months since that night of passion at the Condé and still she awoke murmuring his name. Those first weeks had been filled with agonies of a kind and dimension she'd never expected to experience over a man. She would not suffer that way ever again.

Hilton Courteen would not remain in New Orleans for very long, she told herself. Soon, he'd go back to Natchez and the beautiful widow she'd read of in the newspapers. It was said Alexa Le Noble was a member of the Old Guard, a fabulously wealthy widow, and madly in love with Hilton Courteen.

"Mrs. Le Noble," Sylvain addressed the absent woman that night when she climbed into her bed, "for you I feel most sorry. You're in love with a man who loves no one but himself. While you're breathlessly awaiting his return, he's down here brandishing that fatal charm on every unsuspecting female whose path he crosses." She laughed in the darkness and raised her arms up over her head.

The laughter died rapidly, and Sylvain bit the inside of her cheek. Once again she resolved not to let Hilton Courteen into her heart.

Ever.

"What you think you goin' to do?" Jasper scratched his gray head and watched his master dress. "It be only two o'clock in the afternoon. You ain't never gone out this early before."

Hilton took a drink of coffee from a china cup on the side table. He shoved the gold studs through the French cuffs of his starched white shirt and said, "I'm going out to make us some money." His lips twitched.

Jasper glared at him. "You actin' like a fool. Only two things you know how to do is soldierin' and gamblin'."

Hilton laughed and stepped into his impeccable dove-gray trousers. "True enough, Jas." He looked at the old man. "I resigned from the army, so what does that leave?"

Jasper shook his head. "You ain't got a lick of sense. You coulda been some big 'portant congressman or senator and be married with that rich highborn lady, Alexa." The old man sighed wearily. "Had the chance to behave like a Courteen's s'posed to, but no, you jes' leaves it all behin' and comes down here and starts that infernal gamblin' again."

"Correction, Jas. I never quit gambling." He slid his long arms into the perfectly tailored gray frock coat. "Nor do I intend to. However, there is one small problem." Hilton absently stroked his mustache.

"What dat be?"

"I have no money. Got any cash hidden away?"

Jasper gave a loud harrumph and shuffled into the adjoining servant's bedchamber, closing the door loudly behind him. He lifted the mattress and pulled out a worn leather purse stuffed full of bills. Hilton had always insisted on paying his faithful valet. In flush times he'd forced money on the old man, assuring him he had earned it. Jasper had little opportunity to spend cash, so the purse always bulged.

"Thanks, Jas." Hilton took the folded bills and stuffed them into his pocket. "I'll pay you back."

It was another unlucky session at the poker table. Early in the evening Hilton rose from his green silk-padded chair in the plush gambling hall, Toussaint's, nodded to the gentlemen at the table, and strode away.

A man of medium height, snow-white hair, swarthy complexion, light blue eyes, and thin pink lips stepped from behind an ornately carved interior door. His alert eyes fell on the tall, dark gentleman crossing the carpeted room, and he smiled.

Hurrying to catch up to the longer-legged man, Jacques Gayarre intercepted Hilton before he reached the Chartres Street door. "Let me buy you a drink, Cap'n Courteen." Jacques clasped Hilton's shoulder. The richly attired Frenchman guided Hilton up the marble steps and into his lushly decorated private office.

Splashing burgundy into a couple of wine glasses, the owner of Toussaint's said conversationally, "Lose much this evening, Cap'n?"

Hilton lounged comfortably in a fine armchair of soft green velvet. "No, Jacques." He grinned and added, "You see, I had very little to lose." He sipped the wine.

The Frenchman half sat, half leaned on his huge rosewood desk. "Cap'n Courteen, come in with me." He lifted a hand in a sweeping gesture. "I need you here at Toussaint's."

Hilton's dark brows lifted. "Jacques, you heard me. I have no money left . . . and no prospects."

"There are better times ahead," Jacques Gayerre said confidently. "Take my offer."

"I can't pay my share."

"You've always played straight with me and my casino. The high stakes gamblers love to play with you . . . and against you."

Hilton set his wineglass aside, steepled his long fingers and said, "I'll work for you, Jacques. I'll deal faro or blackjack or vingt-et-un, even poker, but there'll be no partnership."

"I'm offering you a share in — "

"And I'm turning it down, Jacques." Hilton reached for his wine. "If you want me to be a croupier, drum up some business for you, I'm your man."

Knowing Hilton was far too stubborn and proud to accept the offer of a partnership because in his mind it smacked of charity, Jacques Gayerre sighed and said, "The moneyed men play late at night. You'll work from eight in the evening to four in the morning."

Hilton drained his wineglass, rose, and shook hands with his old friend and new employer. He looked at the ornate gold clock behind the Frenchman and said, "It's seven-fifteen. I'll go back to the Richardson, clean up, change into evening clothes, and be back in time to deal tonight."

"Fine, Cap'n," said Jacques Gayerre. "Take the back poker table. The heavy spenders prefer it."

Hilton Courteen had studied tactics at West Point. He'd applied those tactics successfully in the Seminole War. He'd gambled from the time he was a boy of fourteen, and he'd learned early on how to make the odds work in his favor.

A wise, worldly man, he knew full well a mixture of tactics and gambling skill was called for in his quest to win the spirited Sylvain Fairmont. Hilton guessed, and rightly so, that Sylvain would be expecting him to show up at the chandlery in the next day or two. So, much as he longed to see her, he stayed away. With a will of iron, Hilton steered clear of the Spencer Chandlery for over a month, silently suffering, cleverly planning, coolly stalking with his very absence.

On the day following his unexpected appearance at the chandlery, Sylvain jumped each time the bell jangled. Eyes going swiftly to the front door, she'd heave a sigh of surprised relief to see it was not the tall man whose presence so unnerved her.

Never admitting it to herself, she looked all day for Hilton to stride commandingly through the door. When the sun had slipped low on the western horizon and it was time to lock up and leave, Sylvain sighed dispiritedly and walked home.

It was the same the next day. She was tense, edgy, distracted. By week's end she was beginning to relax. He had not returned. He hadn't meant one word he'd said to her, just as she'd known he had not. Obviously, he'd quickly lost interest when he realized it would take at least a small amount of effort to get her into his bed. He'd dismissed her from his mind and gone on to other pursuits.

Good.

Relieved that the scarily sexy man would not be bothering her, Sylvain quickly brushed aside the mild disappointment she was feeling and turned her thoughts to acquiring a sturdy, reasonably priced bateau for the planned search into the swamps behind Riverbend. She'd cajoled and demanded, and finally Big Napoleon, against his better judgment, had given in to her wishes. She'd be allowed to go with him to hunt Lafitte's hidden treasure. Her treasure.

When more than a month had passed with no sign of the elusive Hilton Courteen, Sylvain was certain the dashing scoundrel had returned to Natchez and his rich widow. She no longer had butterflies when the bell tinkled. She didn't look up expectantly. She hardly ever thought about him.

It was past quitting time. Sylvain had stayed late at the chandlery to close out the ledger books at month's end. Her eyes were strained from looking too long at neat, tiny rows of numbers when she finally slammed the big book shut, pinched the high bridge of her nose, and rose from the uncomfortable stool.

It was hot — sticky, muggy, stiflingly hot. Sylvain's hair was limp and heavy on her neck. Perspiration beaded her upper lip and forehead. Her chemise clung damply to her skin and she could feel tiny trickles of moisture pooling between her breasts and behind her knees. Her faded purple dress was soiled and dusty from unpacking crates. She felt wilted and unclean and was glad she'd had no customers for the past couple of hours, that no one had seen her looking so frightfully unkempt.

Twisting her long hair into a careless knot, she shoved it on top of her head and speared it with a couple of pins, then picked up her reticule and left the chandlery. She stood outside the door in the fading sun, silently cursing the stubborn lock she'd put off having repaired. Temper short, she fumbled and poked with the large metal key, muttering and twisting so vigorously that her hastily pinned hair came tumbling down.

"May I be of assistance?" came that deep, self-assured voice, and Sylvain whirled around to see an impeccably attired Hilton Courteen leaning lazily against the building, arms folded over his broad chest, one foot crossed over the other. He looked as cool and clean as if he'd just stepped from his tub.

While she stared, open-mouthed, he pushed away from the wall and came to her. Expecting him to take the worrisome key from her shaking hand, she winced when, ignoring the door, he lifted her thick hair and gently repinned it atop her head.

Sylvain let go of the key, snatched at the pins he'd so painstakingly arranged, and tossed them to the ground. She shook her head, letting the heavy hair cascade about her shoulders.

Hilton chuckled.

"I do not need your help!" she snapped as he turned his attention to the door.

"Very well," he said and stepped back. "It's all yours."

She pushed past him and again tried to lock the door. She jiggled the key. She turned it. She twisted it. She stamped her foot. She muttered under her breath. Finally, she gave a great sigh of defeat.

"Give up?"

Seething, she whirled on him and said, "Lock the blasted door!"

He smiled, put his long fingers on the key, and skillfully turned it until he heard the click. He withdrew the key, presented it to her, and said, "A good oiling will solve the problem. I'll come around tomorrow and take care of it."

"You'll do no such thing," she warned and walked away from him.

Easily he caught up to her. "I don't like you walking the streets alone at this hour. I'll see you home."

She halted. "You will not."

Hilton shrugged and looked down at her. Thinking surely she had to be the most appealing female he'd ever seen, he fought the fever in his blood that blazed when he looked into those huge smoky eyes flashing angrily up at him. Calmly he said, as though surprised, "You don't want me to escort you home?"

"Good Lord, are you dim-witted, Courteen? No! I do not want you to walk me home, nor will I allow it. You're to stay away from me. I have no use for you and your kind!"

"I hope, my dear, you'll give me the chance to soften your opinion of me."

"Never!" She turned on her heel and stormed away from him.

Hilton, smiling, watched her march angrily down the banquette. He remained where he was until she was no more than a tiny moving dot of purple against the sunset. He sighed, turned, and strode away, taking with him the vision of the adorably angry young woman whose heart he was determined to win.

Hilton's nightly presence at Toussaint's gambling hall produced the results Jacques Gayarre had hoped for. The sharp-witted and nimble-fingered gentry of New Orleans hastened to the club to have a go at Cap'n Courteen.

Dazzling, well-dressed gamblers in their black broadcloth coats and trousers, white shirts with frills and ruffles, black ties and black high-heeled boots sauntered confidently into the hall, diamonds flashing on their well-groomed hands, showy brocade vests fastened with gold or pearl buttons. All gravitated to that prized back table where Cap'n Courteen held court nightly, his long brown fingers dealing cards with skill and precision, his dark, hooded eyes unreadable, his manners impeccable.

Men of great wealth and prominence won and lost thousands. On more than one occasion, Hilton obligingly moved his game upstairs to a private salon to accommodate the wishes of the high stakes gamblers. Without so much as a flicker of his dark eyelashes, the cool, controlled Hilton watched gentlemen stake their vast plantations, their city real estate, their slaves, and anything and everything of value that they possessed.

Captains of steamers lost their generous salaries, ship owners their cargoes, planters the money made from the sale of their yearly crops. The sporting men took it all in stride, as did Hilton Courteen. A gambling man himself, he felt no pity for the losers, no envy of the winners.

These were games of skill and chance, and not for the weakhearted. Hilton was an honest, respected dealer and player, and if he dealt a hand that caused a gentleman to lose all that he had, he made no apologies and none were expected.

Soon it was not only the gentlemen of New Orleans who were frequenting Toussaint's. The ladies of the Crescent City, too, had heard that the charming rogue was back in town. Many a Creole belle persuaded her father or her beau to escort her to the glittering gambling palace. Married women cajoled and begged and got their way, showing up after dark in lavish gowns.

Since poker was not a ladies' game, Jacques Gayarre casually asked Hilton to take over the roulette wheel until midnight. Asking no questions, Hilton stepped behind the green velvet rope, nodded to the players, and lifted the shiny white ball between thumb and forefinger while eager bettors rushed to push brightly colored chips onto their favorite numbers.

Within minutes there was not an empty velvet chair at the roulette table and customers stood three deep behind the players, many leaning over to place a bet while the white ball whirled around the varnished wheel.

Several flirtatious ladies, married and single, found an excuse to touch the lean brown hand pushing chips their way. Sparkling, full-lashed eyes lifted longingly to the strong masculine face across from them.

They were wasting their time. Hilton was a changed man, a man so deeply in love he was barely tempted by the constant parade of pampered, pretty females bent on catching his eye. His black eyes never dropped to the exposed bosoms around his roulette table. His gaze never met and held the bold, provocative eyes constantly upon him.

There was one woman for him. A tall dark-haired goddess with smoky eyes and golden skin and a demeanor at once so cool yet fiery that she presented an exciting challenge to his male ego. The very thought of her caused his blood to heat and filled his tall, powerful body with longing.

Sylvain in her faded purple dress with her unruly hair a tangled mess about her head was more beautiful by far to Hilton than the bejeweled, richly gowned women who would willingly come into his arms if he snapped his long fingers.

His arms, and his heart, belonged only to the woman who wanted neither.

Chapter Twenty-Five

Devon Vaughn lifted deep blue eyes to the peeling wall-paper in the drawing room. Nose wrinkling with distaste, he strode across the spacious room to draw back the curtains to the sun. He coughed when he pulled on the dusty, tattered drapes, and grimaced.

"I know Riverbend needs a bit of sprucing up, Devon," said Hyde Rankin apologetically.

"Hyde, the place is falling down around your ears. You led me to belive that Riverbend was a luxurious mansion with fine furniture and priceless art and sculpture."

"It will be all those things again, and more." Rankin smiled. "Come. I have something to show you."

The two men ascended the stairs to the master suite. Inside, Devon's eyes moved about the musty room with mounting displeasure while Hyde, recalling the loss of Philip in Mobile, anxiously rushed to pull from a bureau drawer a worn leather map.

He spread the map on his rumpled bed and explained, "This is a map of my property." He tapped a fore-finger on the leather. "Here we are now, here's the house." Devon nodded, looking down at the map. "All the outlying areas of Riverbend are clearly marked." Rankin rubbed his chin. "On this land — my land — is enough gold to buy everything you've ever dreamed of having."

Devon's blue eyes widened. "Gold here at Riverbend?"

"I'm not speaking of gold ore. I'm saying there's a fortune in gold coin hidden here. Pirates concealed it years ago, and it's mine. Ours."

"Where is this gold?"

"I'm not certain, but it's only a matter of locating it. In no time the gold can be in our hands and we'll refurbish Riverbend. We'll have fine clothes and gleaming coaches, satin sheets and imported wines, trips abroad. Anything we want."

Devon looked at the map, then looked again at the room with its worn carpet and faded furnishings. There was an aura of decay about the dwelling that made him shiver. Even his stomach felt queasy. He shuddered and hurried across the room, throwing open the tall French doors with such determined force that a soiled pane of glass fell out and shattered on the gallery. Devon rushed to the balcony's sagging railing and drew a deep, welcome breath of fresh air.

Hyde Rankin followed, stepping up beside him. "I've never lied to you. There's gold here, Devon."

Devon looked at the tall man standing beside him, then turned to let his gaze take in the sprawling plantation with its unkempt lawns, weed-choked orchards and gardens, idle sugarcane fields, crumbling slave quarters, and the dark, thick-foliaged swamps beyond. Somewhere there was gold. Bright, shiny gold. Valuable, spendable gold.

"Hyde, how soon can we start looking for our gold?"

"At once," said a happy Hyde Rankin.

Sylvain felt the wispy hair on the nape of her neck rise. The night was starless and overcast. Heavy clouds hung over the delta land. It was the blackest sky she'd ever seen, the air so thick and humid it required an effort just to breathe. A night bird shrieked in the stillness. Crickets scraped their hind legs together in a never-ending chorus. A steamer's whistle sounded faintly from the river.

Sylvain, one hand clutching the gunwale of the flat-bottomed bateau, the other holding the bull's-eye lantern, ducked to avoid low-hanging moss.

Behind her, Big Napoleon rhythmically poled the long bateau through the cobwebby gloom of the cypress swamp bordering Riverbend. Alert to any danger, the gigantic man worried less about the creatures inhabiting the lowland than about the armed slaves guarding the entrance to the old plantation.

Sylvain was the opposite. In the lamplight she caught sight of enormous water moccasins resting in the knees of cypress stumps, and felt her flesh crawl. Through the murky waters, slick black snakes swam uncomfortably close to the bateau, and on the slimy clay banks of the bayou, alligators, awakened by their presence, slithered into the water or rode lazily on rotting logs.

Immense cottonwoods and sycamores, thickly dotting the shallows, were the resting place of more night creatures. From the fog-shrouded gloom came the high, keening screams of a panther and Sylvain winced. Terribly frightened, she turned wide, disbelieving eyes on Big Napoleon when the boat stopped in the mire and he wordlessly stepped over the side.

The water lapped at his knees. Sylvain held the long pole as he lifted the bateau, freeing it from the snag, while curious alligators swam toward the intruder and a cottonmouth slid past Napoleon's legs. Too terrified to scream a warning Sylvain jerked her head toward the deadly reptile. The boat freed, Big Napoleon stepped back into it a split second before the poisonous snake struck, its dripping fangs meeting wood instead of flesh.

Wondering if all the gold on earth was worth this dangerous foray, Sylvain, the bull's eye lantern raised, spotted the steeple-cross of Seachurch in the distance and sighed with relief. In minutes Big Napoleon was pulling the long bateau, with her in it, onto dry land.

Big Napoleon said close to her ear, "Snuff out the lantern, Miss Sylvain. We'll go the rest of way in darkness." She obeyed, took his big square hand, and followed him through the dense undergrowth.

As they neared the old slave church, Sylvain gasped. There in the cemetery beside the old chapel, a mound of fresh dirt was piled high beside an open grave. As curious as she, Big Napoleon moved closer, taking her with him.

Sylvain clasped a hand over her mouth to keep from screaming. There on the ground lay a bleached white skeleton. The skull had been ground to powder.

Pulling away from Big Napoleon, Sylvain went to the headstone and leaned close.

"Kashka," she breathed.

Napoleon nodded and whispered. "Rankin knows about the gold. He dug up Kashka."

"He's searching?"

"Yes, Miss Sylvain. Come, let's go to work."

Sylvain was preoccupied, her thoughts on the elusive treasure, when next she encountered Hilton Courteen. It was early on a Sunday morning. She had come to the French Market to choose fresh fruits for breakfast. Bottom lip sucked behind her teeth, she was absently choosing large purple plums and depositing them in the wicker basket that hung from her arm. She felt someone's gaze on her; her eyes slowly lifted.

Hilton Courteen was standing across the wooden stalls from her, eating a ripe golden peach, his dark eyes watching her every move. He smiled disarmingly and came around the fruit-laden tables to her.

Momentarily wondering why he was up at such an early hour, she glanced again at the tall figure attired in evening wear. He had not yet been to bed. Or at least, he'd not been to sleep. It was apparent he'd been out all night.

" 'Morning, sweetheart," Hilton caught up to her, slipping the basket from her arm and holding out the peach. "Care for a bite?" His lips were gleaming with the fruit's sweet juice.

"Certainly not," she said scathingly and tried to reclaim her basket. Hilton changed hands, placing it out of her reach.

"You don't know you're missing." He grinned and deposited the half-eaten peach in a refuse barrel. "I don't suppose you'd reach into my pocket and get my handkerchief, would you?"

"Don't hold your breath."

He laughed, drew the snowy white handkerchief from his coat pocket, and wiped his mouth while she watched, frowning. "You missed a spot," she said when he lowered the handkerchief.

"I did? Where? I can't see my face."

"Here," she said and yanked the linen from his hand. She lifted it to his face and blotted the left corner of his mouth, choosing to ignore the warm black eyes boldly caressing her and the restless power emanating from him. She handed the handkerchief back and again reached for her fruit basket.

"Not yet," he told her, then took her arm and chuckled when she pulled free.

Sylvain had no choice but to walk along beside him. Together they strolled away from the markets, past the Cabildo, the arsenal and calaboose, and toward the Esplanade. To her chagrin, she found her old curiosity was still quite strong; she was more than a little tempted to ask him where he had been all night. But she'd have cut her tongue out before she'd have done so.

"I'm sure you must wonder why I'm up and in evening clothes, Sylvain."

"Me?" she said quickly, feeling as though she'd been caught. "It never entered my mind, Courteen."

"Yes, it did, sweetheart, so I'll set your mind at ease. I'm a croupier at Toussaint's gambling parlor on Chartres. I get off work at four in the morning."

Sylvain gave him a withering look. "Isn't dealing cards a bit beneath you, Courteen?"

"Not at all. However, if it displeases you, I'll quit. I can understand if you'd rather I — "

"For heaven's sake, I don't care what you do." She stopped walking and glared at him. "That's not completely true," she added. "There *is* one thing: I want you to leave me alone!" She hurried away while Hilton, smiling, called to her.

"Sweetheart," his deep voice carried, attracting the attention of shoppers and strollers in the rapidly filling square. "You forgot something."

Sylvain whirled around to see the full wicker basket of purple plums and golden peaches dangling from his raised hand. She sighed and said, "Bring it here, will you please?"

Hilton made no reply. He merely lowered the basket to his side and slouched into a relaxed, feet-apart masculine stance that wordlessly told her he had no intention of moving. Sylvain stormed back to the tall, annoying man, jerked the basket from his hand, and whirled away while his deep, mocking laughter made her mutter all the way to the peaceful little cottage on the ramparts.

While Sylvain continued her fruitless pursuit of Lafitte's hidden treasure, Captain Hilton Courteen continued his fruitless pursuit of Sylvain. Both undertakings were monumental, and more than once they were both tempted to give up, to concede defeat, to leave the prize unclaimed.

Neither would do so.

Sylvain regularly — at least once a week — made the dangerous journey with Big Napoleon through the steamy swamps bordering Riverbend, intent on finding her father's lost gold.

And Hilton regularly — once, sometimes twice, a week — made it a point to be where Sylvain was. He'd drop by the chandlery, killing time until she ran him out. Or he'd be waiting in the late evening to ask if he might walk her home; her answer was always the same.

Newly married Jeff Davis and his eighteeen-year-old bride, Varina, showed up in New Orleans on their honeymoon in early March of 1845. They checked into the swanky St. Charles Hotel and promptly invited Hilton to dine with them.

Kissing the dark-haired bride and shaking hands with a beaming Jeff Davis, Hilton took a seat in the elegant dining room and congratulated his old friend. "You're a lucky man, Jeff." He smiled warmly at the young dark-eyed bride. "My dear, a pleasure to meet you."

The trio enjoyed a long, leisurely lunch, and Hilton learned the new Mrs. Davis was not only attractive but bright and charming as well.

Over coffee, Jeff said, "I suppose you're pleased Texas is finally a part of the Union, Hill."

Hilton smiled. "Delighted. I understand Mexico is furious and has broken off relations with the U.S."

Jeff Davis confirmed it. "There's going to be trouble, Hill. Mexico is declaring the Nueces River the boundary between Texas and Mexico. Texas claims it's the Rio Grande."

"If Texas says it's the Rio Grande, then it is."

"I concur," Davis said. "But enough of that. Where's the lovely Sylvain? I thought surely you'd have won the lady by now."

"No," Hilton said truthfully. "She refuses to have anything to do with me, Jeff."

Varina smiled at Hilton and said graciously, "Cap'n Courteen, give her time. My, my, you're so handsome, she's bound to give in soon."

A jealous Jeff frowned at his wife, but she swiftly wrapped her arms around one of his and said coquettishly, "Now, Jeffy, don't be foolish. You know I think you're just the cutest, cuddliest man alive." She gave his jaw a peck, and the thirty-six-year-old Davis's eyes sparkled with happiness.

More than a year had passed since Hilton's return to New Orleans, and neither Hilton nor Sylvain was closer to the longed-for goals. Hilton had not won Sylvain. Sylvain had not found the gold.

The country was still in the grip of a long, devastating depression. Business at the chandlery had been disappointingly slow all winter. To make matters worse, an extraordinary number of storms in the Gulf had delayed dockings, postponed voyages, and left the Spencer Chandlery in deep trouble.

Sylvain had barely enough cash to feed the family. Rent on the Ramparts cottage was due. The coffers were empty. What would she do?

An image of Hilton Courteen flashed through her mind as she walked wearily home from the chandlery. She couldn't ask him; she wouldn't. There had to be some other answer.

Deep in thought, she walked past the grogshops and gaming halls. She paused before a gambling den called Lucky's, and an idea struck her. Pulse quickening, Sylvain took a shiny silver quarter out of her reticule. She looked at the coin then looked at the closed door of Lucky's.

Squaring her slender shoulders, she clutched the coin firmly in her hand and swept through the door. Her nerve almost deserted her. All about her were men. She was the only woman, and that fact had gone unnoticed by no one.

Hilton Courteen sat playing poker at a table less than thirty feet from Sylvain. His black eyes widened when he saw her, and his first inclination was to rise immediately, go to her side, and escort her out into the street. Instead, he remained in his chair, cigar smoke curling up about his dark head.

A short, swarthy man wove among the crowded tables, stopping when he reached Sylvain. Eagerly he eyed her curves, his mouth watering, then possessively took her arm and said, "I'm Pierre Jousset, owner of Lucky's. Let me show you around."

Sylvain jerked her arm free. "I've been around."

Hilton, witnessing the exchange, laughed quietly and found he'd lost interest in poker. "Deal me out," he said and rose. He went to stand at the bar, eyes following the only woman he'd ever loved. She sauntered over to the lotto parlor, ignoring the looks and whispers from astonished males.

Sylvain purchased a lotto card with her quarter. She studied her card as she sat amid amused men who were furiously marking cards, certain their numbers would win.

Sylvain bit the inside of her cheek and put a large X across the number twenty-six. Her age. And number thirty-four. Delilah's age. Forty-two, for Big Napoleon. She shook her head. She wasn't sure of the sisters' ages. She marked the number six because her birthday came in the sixth month. She looked at the card. Only four numbers. She had to mark one more. She wrinkled her brow.

She marked a big X across number thirty-seven.

Hilton Courteen was thirty-seven years old.

Sylvain hardly had time to hand in her card before the game began. Her wide eyes were fastened on the man taking his position on a raised platform behind a big globe containing ninety-nine consecutively numbered balls. The tiny white balls were all mixed. The "roller" pressed a spring at the bottom of the globe and one ball fell out.

"Number thirty-four." His voice was loud, deep.

Smiling excitedly, Sylvain eagerly awaited the next number and laughed aloud when she heard him say forty-two. The man continued to release one ball at a time, calling out its number. Excitement was building in Sylvain's breast.

He'd called out four of her marked numbers. All she needed was one more!

The roller kept releasing the tiny balls. He kept announcing the number written on the fallen ball. Any second someone would win. Someone would have all five numbers in a row. Someone would take the entire amount of money put up by all the players. Someone would walk away with —

"Number thirty-seven."

"Lotto!" Sylvain shot from her chair, shouting so loudly every eye in the room fell upon her. She didn't care — she'd won! She hurried to one of the collectors to have her card tallied. She stood at his elbow while he checked the card, and when he nodded his head, she clapped her hands with excitement.

After the house had taken its fifteen percent cut, Sylvain was handed a whopping fifty-three dollars. She was rich. Glowing, she made her way back through a throng of unhappy men. They hadn't minded when she laid out her quarter to purchase one card, but they were not pleased that she'd taken the biggest pot of the day, and they were letting her know it.

"Damned petticoats ought to stay out of man's domain," sniped an anemic-looking man.

"No lady'd come in a place like this." A huge drunken drifter rose to his feet, and Sylvain, stuffing her money into her reticule, felt uneasy when she saw a couple of sore losers blocking her path to the front door.

Hilton Courteen stepped between the pair, came to her, tucked her hand around his arm, and said loudly, "If I've told you once, I've told you a dozen times, I will not put up with my woman coming here. Your place is at home with our children, and that's where you're going right now!"

Sylvain opened her mouth, but his eyes silenced her. Seething, she let him lead her out of the smoke-filled room while men chuckled and hooted. "That's tellin' the wench, Cap'n," shouted a toothless, burly seaman. "Let her have it when you get her home."

"If you need money so badly, why didn't you come to me?" Hilton asked when they were outside.

Sylvain pulled away from him, "Courteen, get this through your head: I want neither your pity nor your protection."

He smiled and leaned close. "How about my passion?"

"Oh!"

It was less than a week later that Hilton had a bit of good fortune. He strolled into the Spencer Chandlery at the noon hour, shortly after Hester and Marie had arrived with a linen-draped tray containing a large hot lunch for Sylvain and Big Napoleon.

Sylvain was munching on a piece of pan-fried chicken when Hilton came through the front door. Used to his intrusions, she continued with her meal while Hester and Marie looked with interest at the tall, dark man approaching them.

His handsome face broke into a smile of recollection. "The Spencer sisters," he said in that drawling, smoothed-tongued voice. "Hester and Marie, isn't it?"

The two middle-aged ladies looked at each other, then back at the imposing man smiling at them. Hester spoke. "Cap'n Courteen," she said, amazed, "you remember us?"

"I most certainly do." His dark eyes twinkled. "It was eight . . . no, nine years ago, I believe. The Mobile bazaar. I came to see my grandmother home, and one of you gave me a piece of the most delicious pecan pie I've ever tasted."

"It was I, Cap'n Courteen," Marie excitedly informed him.

"I made it, Marie," scolded Hester. "You made the peach." Her gaze went back to Hilton. "Your grandmother was such a pleasant lady, Cap'n."

Sylvain, seated behind the counter, continued to eat her lunch as if Hilton were not there, but she almost choked on her lemonade when, after the three had carried on a lengthy and spirited conversation, Hester said to Hilton, "Cap'n, we'd be so honored if you'd come to our home for dinner some evening soon."

Sylvain set down her glass and held her breath, knowing only too well what his answer would be.

"Why, Miss Spencer," he promptly accepted, "I'd be delighted to join you all for dinner." He cast a quick, triumphant glance in Sylvain's direction. "Just name the day."

The smiling Spencer sisters looked at each other. "Would tomorrow be too soon, Cap'n?" Marie's hopeful eyes were on his face.

"Perfect," replied Hilton Courteen.

Sylvain patted her mouth with a white linen napkin and had no choice but to smile sweetly when Hester said to her, "Dear, I had no idea you knew Cap'n Courteen." Her eyes returned to Hilton.

"I suppose I failed to mention it." Sylvain shot him a forbidding look over the sisters' heads.

"I've known Sylvain since she was a little girl," Hilton said easily. "We've been friends ever since."

"It's too good to be true," exclaimed Marie while Hester said. "Now, Cap'n, we live in a nice little cottage on the Ramparts. Shall I draw you a map of how — "

"I'm sure Cap'n Courteen has visited the Ramparts houses many times," Sylvain broke in.

If either sister caught her meaning, they carefully concealed it. Hilton ignored the remark. "I can find my way," he said lightly. "I must go. So nice to see you ladies again. I look forward to tomorrow." He came to Sylvain. His hand went to her elbow, slid slowly down to her wrist and encircled it. She longed to snatch it free, but didn't wish to fuss with him before the observing sisters.

He took advantage of the situation. He laced his long brown fingers through hers and said, "I wish I could stay longer, dear, but I really must be going."

"That's quite all right," she told him coldly and tried unsuccessfully to free her hand.

Pretending not to notice, he drew her with him toward the door, saying his good-byes to the sisters. At the portal he urged her out, but she refused to go.

"Until tomorrow, then," he said softly, then released her hand and was gone.

"Such a fine, handsome boy," said Marie Spencer, her light green eyes sparkling.

Sylvain stared at the pair. "That fine boy," she informed them, "is a thirty-seven-year-old man. A croupier over at Toussaint's."

"Pardon, dear?" Hester said.

"A croupier. The man deals poker at a fancy gambling hall." Sylvain smiled and eagerly awaited the sisters' reaction.

The pair considered the information. Then Hester said earnestly, "Young men must begin somewhere. I'm sure the handsome captain will soon find something more suited to his talents."

Sylvain rolled her eyes.

Chapter Twenty-Six

Sylvain was half amused, half annoyed when she stepped into the Ramparts cottage the next evening shortly after six. The small parlor fairly shone. The woodwork and floors had been polished to a high gleam and the furniture rearranged so that the two gold chairs faced the long champagne sofa across the square marble-topped table.

A bouquet of freshly cut flowers, carefully arranged in a tall crystal vase, graced the table, concealing a bad crack. The tall mirror had been moved from behind the sofa to the wall across from it — a wall whose covering had faded from years of bright Louisiana sun falling upon it each morning.

Sylvain smiled and followed the pleasing aromas wafting from the small kitchen. She walked through the door just as Hester took a huge smoked Virginia ham from the oven. In the window sill, not one, but two freshly baked pies were cooling.

"Dear," Marie looked up from the snap beans she was seasoning, "you'd better hurry. Cap'n Courteen will be here at seven sharp."

Hester nodded her agreement, sticking a long fork into the tender, juicy ham. "Delilah's waiting upstairs, Sylvain. Scoot on up and get in your bath."

"Are you sure we'll have enough to eat?" Sylvain kidded. Besides the giant ham and the snap beans, there were

Irish potatoes boiling, hot bread baking, sugared yams swimming in honeyed juice, fruit salad of oranges and apples and walnuts, beets, buttered carrots, and stewed squash.

Hands going to her powdered cheeks, Marie said nervously, "I hope so. Can you think of anything else the captain might want?"

Sylvain couldn't keep from laughing. She'd never seen the sisters so excited and she silently vowed she'd not spoil the evening for them. She'd behave. She'd be civil to him if it killed her. After all, he'd be here only for an hour. She could sit on a straight-edged razor that long.

"I'm sure, Marie, the captain will find everything he wants on the table tonight. You two must have been cooking all day."

"We didn't mind," Hester raised a hand to her shiny forehead. "The captain's so big and tall I'm sure he has a hearty appetite."

"I wouldn't know," Sylvain said and let Marie shoo her up the stairs. Delilah waited in her bedchamber, a tall black sentry beside the door, snowy white towel across her shoulder, long-handled brush in her hand.

"We've got to hurry," she said, eyes flashing, not bothering to greet Sylvain. "He'll be here by seven."

"You, too?" Sylvain shook her head. Across the room a steaming tub was waiting. Upon her feathered bed, a freshly pressed frock of blue striped taffeta lay.

"I don't know what you mean." Delilah's hands went to the hooks at the back of Sylvain's faded calico work dress.

Sylvain shrugged away. "You know exactly what I mean, Delilah Fairmont. My best dress laid out. Jasmine-scented bathwater." Her gray eyes narrowed. "Are you forgetting who our dinner guest is?"

"Why, he's Cap'n Hilton Courteen and — "

"He's the heartless scoundrel who left me naked and alone in a Mobile hotel room!"

"Shhh." Delilah's dark eyes grew fierce, and she flew to the door to swiftly shut it. "Do you want the sisters to hear you?"

"I don't much care," Sylvain told her. "Maybe if they knew what the man's really like, they wouldn't be so eager for him to sit at their table."

"I think you're too hard on the captain, honey." Delilah turned Sylvain and again fussed with the hooks. "Maybe if you'd just give him a chance, he'd show you that — "

"He'll get no chance. None." Sylvain stepped out of her soiled dress and spun around. "I won't spoil the evening for the sisters, but neither will I be a party to this . . . this . . . farce. Civility is all that man can expect from me. Now get out of here and let me bathe." She snatched at the straps of her chemise. "And hang that taffeta gown right back in the armoire. I'm not wearing my best for the likes of Courteen."

Delilah looked disappointed, but obeyed. "I'll fix your hair for you when you get out of the tub."

"You'll do no such thing, Delilah. I'll take care of it." She waved her hand dismissively.

Alone, she shoved her hair on top of her head and snatched a blue hair ribbon from the bureau. She hastily tied the ribbon around the heavy mass of dark hair and stepped into her bath. Sighing with the pleasure of it, she sank into the welcome heat, resting her head against the tub's wooden rim.

Wishing she could remain seated in the sweet-smelling water until Hilton Courteen had come and gone, she soaped her long legs and arms and wondered why most of life consisted of doing things she did not wish to do.

She was drying herself when she heard the commotion downstairs. Her heart skipped a beat, but she was determined Hilton would not think she'd attempted to make herself pretty for him.

Stalking to the armoire, Sylvain stood looking at the few frocks she owned. She purposely chose her oldest, plainest one. She'd always hated the dress. It was a sickly blue with a tight bodice and tiny cap sleeves. The skirt was too skimpy to be fashionable, the wide ruffle around its hem adding little fullness.

Certain she looked her worst, Sylvain descended the stairs to greet their guest.

Hilton rose politely when she entered the small parlor and beheld a woman so beautiful he almost lost the cool demeanor that was second nature to him. She looked all scrubbed and clean, her dark, beautiful hair attractively arranged atop her well-shaped head. A blue satin ribbon secured the glossy locks, but a few rebellious strands curled appealingly around her high cheekbones, her small ears, the lovely nape of her neck. She wore a sky-blue dress with a bodice that strained across her high, small breasts, and when she crossed the room he noticed how the soft fabric of the skirt clung to her rounded hips. He swallowed hard when he was rewarded with a fleeting glimpse of firm female bottom enchantingly outlined in the narrow-skirted frock.

Never had she looked so desirable.

"Courteen," she said, refusing to offer her hand.

"Sylvain, how are you this evening?" His voice held that deep resonance that was almost a caress.

"Tired," she informed him and frowned when she realized the sisters had chosen the gold chairs, leaving her only the champagne sofa on which to sit. She sank down onto its softness and cleared her throat loudly when Hilton sat down much too close to her.

"If you don't mind . . . " She looked daggers at him and felt like shoving an elbow into his ribs when he ignored her request and remained where he was, turning his attention back to the sisters.

Feeling as though she might suffocate, she wiggled and squirmed and found the small parlor so filled with his presence that the whole cottage seemed to vibrate with a dangerous, powerful excitement. He was out of place in this feminine atmosphere. His twinkling dark eyes, the blackness of his thick hair and mustache, the swarthiness of his skin, the coiled strength in his long, lean body, the indolent grace, the deep drawl, the teasing, sensual smile — all combined to cause an involuntary flutter of her heart.

Sylvain could tell by the Spencer sisters' expressions that they, too were wholly susceptible to the magnetism this man so effortlessly exuded. They couldn't take their eyes off him, and their usually pallid faces held tinges of high color. They were not the stuffy, pristine preacher's daughters on this night. They twittered and laughed and fidgeted, responding to the highly virile male in their midst.

While they'd easily fallen under his spell, Sylvain was determined she would not be guilty of the same.

Later, at the dining table, the sisters eagerly passed their guest platters and tureens of food. They were delighted when he took generous portions, piling his plate high.

"I do hope, Cap'n Courteen," Marie trilled, smiling at him, "you aren't uncomfortable being with so many females." She giggled.

"Miss Spencer," Hilton said, looking directly at her, "I can think of nothing more pleasant than being in a room filled with ladies. As a fellow cadet, Ed Poe, once said of women, 'No nobler theme ever engaged the pen of a poet.'"

Both sisters sighed, enthralled, and Hester turned to Sylvain. "Dear, that's Edgar Allan Poe the captain is speaking of."

"Really?" Sylvain cut into a slice of ham. "Tell me, Courteen, was that before or after you and your fellow cadet were cashiered out of West Point?"

"Sylvain!" Hester reprimanded while Marie gasped.

Hilton turned amused eyes on her. "I believe it was after," he drawled and went right on charming the two middle-aged ladies who were gazing adoringly at him.

His empty plate was removed by the hovering Delilah, and he was asked which kind of pie he wanted, pecan or peach. Sylvain, watching him covertly, knew what his answer would be.

"I'll have a slice of each," he announced, making both sisters equally happy.

"You're going to be late to the card parlor," Sylvain taunted, and took a sip of black coffee. "It's nearly eight."

"Kind of you to worry, my dear, but I told my employer I wouldn't be there until nine. I have a full hour before I must leave."

"Good," said the sisters in unison while Sylvain fumed.

That hour finally passed and Hilton bid the sisters good night, promising to return again and soon. In the smoothest of maneuvers, he captured Sylvain's elbow and guided her to the front door. She found herself outside under the rapidly rising moon with the disturbingly attractive, exasperatingly determined man.

At the front gate he turned to look down at her. "Sylvain, it's February."

She smirked up at him. "How astute you are, Courteen. Why, you'll be learning to count any day now. Won't that be handy?"

Ignoring the sarcasm, he said simply, "Mardi Gras time." Sylvain drew a sharp breath. "Celebrate with me." His black eyes held hers and he whispered, "Gypsy."

The blood in her veins stirred and she felt breathless. She gazed up into his black eyes and recalled vividly how he'd looked lying naked above her on that other occasion when he'd called her Gypsy. She could feel the heat and power emanating from him, and she felt herself swaying him.

"No!" she caught herself and stepped back. "Don't ever call me that again, Mr. Hilton Courteen!" Her gray eyes shone with unshed tears of anger and frustration, and Hilton knew he'd gone too far.

"Honey, forgive me," he said softly and reached out to touch her cheek.

She spun away so rapidly his fingers touched air, and Hilton had a feeling it was all he'd ever be allowed to touch, that this proud, beautiful woman he so wanted could never be captured.

Fortunately, Hilton had two strong allies in the Spencer sisters. Either they did not notice the animosity Sylvain felt for the dark man, or they chose to ignore it. They liked the captain and continued inviting him to the little cottage on the Ramparts.

He never turned down an invitation. Sylvain was cool to him, polite but distant. Often she refused to come downstairs, pleading fatigue, if he was in the parlor. It was on one of those occasions when she'd remained upstairs that Hilton asked the sisters if he might look in on her.

Not quite certain it would be proper for the handsome man to go inside a young lady's bedchamber, even with the sun still up, they put their heads together, whispered, and finally issued a verdict.

Speaking for them both, Hester said resolutely, "Sister and I have decided you may look in on Sylvain as long as you promise to leave the door wide open."

Hilton smiled. "I wouldn't dream of closing it."

Sylvain heard the heavy footsteps on the stairs and panicked. He knocked softly on the door and opened it before she could answer. He stood there in the doorway, his eyes leisurely moving over her, and she realized, too late, that she was wearing only her white batiste nightgown, the thin fabric barely concealing her nakedness.

She saw the fire leap into his eyes before he discreetly lowered them. To the floor he said, "I've leased a gig, Sylvain. I thought you might like to go for a ride."

"You thought wrong," she said and frantically grabbed at the sheet.

"I'll show you the places where Jean Lafitte conducted his business." His eyes lifted once again and he smiled. He saw the open-mouthed look of interest and knew she was considering his offer. He took swift command.

Leaving the door wide open, Hilton crossed to the armoire, took out a frilly cotton frock, and brought it to the bed. "Shall I help you dress?" His full lips stretched wide beneath his mustache.

Sylvain snatched the dress from his hand and pointed to the door. He nodded and said, "Meet you downstairs in ten minutes."

Sylvain almost forgot she was with the enemy when Hilton helped her into the light two-wheeled carriage. The gig was small. She was seated close to him, but she didn't mind, because no sooner had he clicked to the fine-looking roan stallion than he began to speak of Jean Lafitte.

She longed for knowledge of her father, and Hilton Courteen seemed not in the least reluctant to talk about the famous privateer. She leaned close to hear him over the clattering of horse's hooves on the cobblestones. He turned and smiled at her. "Your father was a very intelligent man, Sylvain. He spoke several languages, lived like royalty, and was very handsome."

Her eyes alive with interest, Sylvain wet her lips and said, "Tell me all that you know of him, Courteen."

He nodded. "He was received in the finest drawing rooms in New Orleans, conducted business with this city's most respected citizens." Hilton laughed suddenly and told her, "Lafitte had a droll sense of humor. He led Louisiana Governor Claiborne a merry chase, and the governor became so frustrated he posted a proclamation offering a five-hundred-dollar reward for the capture of Jean Lafitte. Your father took the opportunity to once again show the boldness that endeared him to the people of New Orleans. The very next day, Lafitte strolled right into the city and read a copy of the proclamation nailed to a lamppost."

"He wasn't arrested?"

"No one touched him, sweetheart. All the posted proclamations disappeared that night, and in their place Lafitte posted his own, offering fifteen hundred dollars for the capture and delivery of Claiborne to Grand Terre. It was signed 'Jean Lafitte.' "

Sylvain laughed. "Is that true, Courteen?"

"It is, and that's only one of the many tales about him." He continued talking, his audience of one so enthralled she'd entirely forgotten any animosity she felt toward him.

Hilton showed Sylvain the blacksmith shop on St. Philip and Bourbon streets, stopping the gig to let her look at the low one-story building with its gently sloping roof where the Lafitte brothers had held secret meetings. He pointed across the street to a small cottage and courtyard where Pierre Lafitte had lived.

"Is Pierre alive, Hilton?"

"No, darling, he's gone, too." He patted her hands, which were folded in her lap. "Lafitte had a shop over on Royal. Want to see that?"

"Yes, please." She let her eyes drift back to the small blacksmith shop, trying to envision inside its walls the handsome Frenchman who'd fathered her.

It was a wonderful outing and Sylvain enjoyed every moment of it. As they started back to the cottage, Hilton was telling her of Lafitte's part in the Battle of New Orleans. " . . . And when the victors returned to New Orleans, the whole city awaited them. General Jackson rode at the head of the parade, and the brothers Lafitte were right behind him, heroes all. Your father, Jean Lafitte, was the toast of New Orleans."

Sylvain was glowing. "Hilton, did you know Lafitte owned Riverbend?"

"No, sweetheart, I didn't." He smiled suddenly and said, "Maybe there really is treasure hidden there. Remember showing me that gold doubloon when you were a little girl?"

Sylvain nodded and considered telling him that she and Big Napoleon were searching for the booty. She promptly decided against it. He'd scold and warn and forbid her to continue, and she didn't want to hear it. "I remember," she answered.

The sun had disappeared when the pair pulled up before the small white cottage. Hilton lifted Sylvain down from the tiny gig and couldn't believe his ears when she said warmly, "Courteen, why don't you come in for coffee?"

From that afternoon, Sylvain treated Hilton less like an intruder, more like a friend. There were frequent rides together through the old city, Hilton pointing out cabarets and coffee houses where Jean Lafitte had sipped absinthe and held court in his glory days.

Sylvain never tired of the excursions and soon persuaded Hilton to show her all he knew of New Orleans, the bad along with the good. Ever curious, her gray eyes sparkled with excitement when he drove her into the section of the city called "the Swamp."

"Better slide close to me," he coaxed as the coach rolled through the half-dozen blocks crowded with seamy flesh-pots.

"I'm not frightened, Courteen," she said flippantly as they rolled down Girod Street where even the police were afraid to set foot.

Hilton took her wherever she wished to go. They roamed the old city together on summer Sunday afternoons, taking pleasant, leisurely rides through the Vieux Carré with its quaint charm — the iron-lace balconies, the tree-shaded courtyards, the marble fountains.

They visited Congo Square at Rampart Street and Orleans Avenue, Sylvain delighted at the sight of so many happy, laughing black people gathered to enjoy their free time dancing and singing, all dressed in their most colorful clothes. She laughed happily when she spotted Big Napoleon and Delilah and waved frantically to the dancing pair.

Down St. Charles Avenue she and Hilton rode, past the magnificent St. Charles Hotel with its immense dome and Corinthian portico, and Hilton told her that grand as it was, he still preferred the St. Louis Hotel in the French Quarter. She nodded and absently wondered how many nights he'd spent in both grand hotels. And with whom.

Hilton showed Sylvain all the gambling houses, Elkin's and Charton's, and Pradat's on Canal Street, St. Cyr's, Hewlett's, and Toussaint's on Chartres.

Sylvain gazed thoughtfully at Toussaint's and asked, "Is it opulent, Courteen?"

"Why don't you visit me some evening and find out for yourself?"

She was tempted, but she declined. "It's getting late. Let's go to the river."

The levee was always their last stop before he took her back to the cottage. She never tired of watching the big paddle-wheelers steam in and out of the port. Smiling, Hilton would watch, not the big boats, but her beautiful face as she excitedly pointed out each vessel, speaking the names aloud, thrilled when one she hadn't seen before moved slowly into its berth.

"You know, Hilton," she said wistfully one Sunday, "someday I'm going to get on one of the biggest side-wheelers and ride all the way up the Mississippi, clear to St. Louis." She turned and smiled at him. "Wouldn't that be fun?"

"It would," he replied and wished he could rush her aboard this very day, whisk her into a grand stateroom, and make love to her all the way upriver.

On those beautiful summer evenings when the light was fading and soft warm breezes lifted tendrils of Sylvain's dark hair, Hilton Courteen was in exquisite agony.

He loved her to distraction and desired her so completely he could hardly bear to be with her and not possess her. But he dared not do anything to endanger losing the ground he'd gained. If she thought of him as a man, if she ever recalled their blazing night of passion, she didn't let on.

In some ways those weeks and months were the worst of his life. Never before had he wanted something he couldn't casually reach out and take. Never before had he desired a beautiful woman who did not willingly come into his arms.

Never before had Hilton Courteen been in love.

Sylvain, truly her father's daughter, had become expert at hiding her feelings. She could spend hour upon hour with Hilton and never give any indication she thought of him as anything more than a friend.

In fact, she never looked into those flashing black eyes that she did not feel she'd surely drown in their fiery depths. She never watched the sensuous lips move beneath the thick black mustache that she did not wish they were pressed against hers. She never heard that deep, caressing voice speak her name without experiencing a girlish thrill. And never did she watch those strong brown hands move so gracefully that she did not long to feel them moving upon her.

Sylvain told herself what she felt for Hilton was nothing more than meaningless physical desire. The man was a sexual animal and she simply responded to his lusty magnetism like any healthy female. As long as she held him at arm's length, where was the danger? After all, he was witty and entertaining. An amusing companion, nothing more.

Summer faded and a cold, dismal winter spread over the Southland. Hilton spent bleak Sunday afternoons at the cozy little cottage on the Ramparts, basking in the glow of Sylvain's warmth and beauty, his heart leaping each time she casually laid a hand on his sleeve, or smiled fetchingly at him, or drowsily leaned her dark head on his shoulder and dozed before the fire.

Once she sat beside him on the champagne sofa, feet curled under her, reading to him from a book of Shelley's

poetry, a book he'd given to her. Her voice sweet and
clear, she read with great feeling and inflection, and Hilton
listened and watched her soft, sweet lips move. She paused,
lowered the book, and looked at him with gray eyes that
were unfathomable. She lifted a hand to his left eyebrow
and tenderly traced the white scar.

"Did it hurt, Hilton?" she said dreamily. "When they cut
you that day, did it hurt?"

Afraid to move, afraid to speak, Hilton lolled back
against the cushions and let her soft fingertips toy with his
scarred eyebrow. She puckered her lovely lips and he
thought for one heart-stopping instant she was going to
kiss the scar. Abruptly her hand fell away. She raised the
book of poetry and once again read as though the intimate
interlude had never happened.

Winter fled and a balmy, flower-scented spring saw Captain Hilton Courteen still calling on the young beauty in
the Ramparts cottage. Sylvain's family fully approved.
The Spencer sisters were extremely fond of the dark,
handsome man. Big Napoleon had become friendly with
Hilton. Delilah, herself a woman in love, knew Sylvain
cared deeply for Hilton but stubbornly refused to admit it.

Hilton, on an evening off from Toussaint's, visited Sylvain
and the family, relaxing on the wide gallery of the cottage.

The sisters said their good-nights and went up to bed,
Big Napoleon and Delilah had disappeared to the back
courtyard, and Hilton and Sylvain were alone. To his
delight, Sylvain made no move to go inside. They sat
together, enjoying the warm weather, the sounds of the
city, the silvery Louisiana moonlight.

It was late when finally she turned to him and said softly,
"Hilton, you must leave. I'm very sleepy."

He put up no argument. He rose and helped her to her
feet. They stood facing each other. For a long moment
Hilton stared at her. Then he reached out, his hand
shaking a little, and pulled her against him. His lips

brushed her cheek and moved to her mouth. Sylvain responded.

Hilton carefully kept a tight rein on his passions. He kissed her softly, his lips warm and tender on hers. The caress was brief, fleeting, gentle. Sylvain's mouth left his and she turned her head away, but his arms continued to hold her and against her temple he said raggedly, "Sweetheart, I want to take you out for an evening. Say you'll go with me."

Head spinning, heart hammering, Sylvain battled with her warring emotions. His arms were warm about her, his hard body pressed against hers. Tempted to yield, to turn her face back up to his, to kiss him hungrily, she sighed and pushed gently on his chest. Hilton released her.

As though they'd never touched, he said hurriedly, "Sylvain, have you ever been to the Theatre d'Orleans?"

"You know very well I've never been there."

He shoved his hands into his tight trousers pockets and smiled at her. "Let's go to the opera."

"I can't." Sylvain felt a small shiver of excitement at the idea. Since the time her mother had told her of going to the ornate theater, she'd longed to see it. "You know I can't go, Courteen."

"Why not?"

"That's a foolish question. Only the upper crust attends the opera and — "

"Afraid, Sylvain?"

"Afraid?" She laughed at him. "I'm afraid of nothing, Courteen."

"Then say you'll come." His eyes flashed in the moonlight. Terrified at the prospect of being in a room filled with the cream of New Orleans society, Sylvain tossed her head back, looked up into those challenging dark eyes, and smiled at him.

"I'll come."

Chapter Twenty-Seven

On the warm May night when Sylvain stood in the moonlight and said to Hilton Courteen, "I'll come," neither knew that the Congress of the United States had that day declared war on Mexico.

Hilton had suspected it was coming. He had decided to go to Mexico, for Cot Campbell, when it came, but he hadn't revealed his plans to Sylvain. She had agreed to go to the opera with him only if he'd allow her the opportunity to save the money for a new gown. And that would take some time.

He'd laughed happily and assured her he'd buy her a gown.

He was immediately sorry he'd suggested it when she turned angry eyes on him and loftily informed him that she did not take charity from him or anyone. She'd supported herself from the age of eighteen and hadn't starved yet, thank you very much! She would be properly gowned for their evening among his fancy friends, so he could just stop worrying!

Hilton had wisely remained silent throughout her tirade and carefully concealed his amusement. Lips twitching in an effort to keep from grinning, he'd watched her storm up and down the aisles of the chandlery, arranging merchandise that didn't need arranging, before finally sweeping back to stand before him.

Hands on her hips, she'd said brusquely, "I have gone over my ledger books, Hilton Courteen, and I'll have enough money for a new frock in July. I consulted the calender and will go to the Theatre d'Orleans with you on Friday night, July twenty-fourth. In a new gown. Is that satisfactory?" Her eyes dared him to disagree.

Hilton smiled at last. "My dear, that will be perfect." He clicked his heels together and gave her an exaggerated bow. "Would I be out of line if I brought the lady flowers on that grand occasion?"

Sylvain looked into the devilish black eyes and smiled. "A white gardenia would be appropriate, I believe."

"You'll wear it in your hair?" His eyes went to the tousled mass of curls atop her head.

"I'll wear it where I please," she told him pertly.

"As my lady wishes," he said, bemused, and backed away thinking he'd never known a more stubborn — or a more enchanting — woman in his life.

Colonel Jefferson Davis, having resigned his safe seat in Congress to serve his country, arrived in New Orleans on July 21, a sweltering Tuesday afternoon. His eager regiment, over nine hundred enthusiastic volunteers representing the cream of the Delta youth, awaited their leader. Many of the young men had with them their personal servants, their prized horses, baskets of wines and delicacies. All were from families of wealth and prominence.

One volunteer in the regiment was no longer young, no longer rich.

One month older than the blond, slim thirty-eight-year-old Colonel Jeff Davis, Hilton Courteen strode through the troops to shake hands with his old friend.

Over dinner that evening, Jeff Davis, eyes sparkling, asked Hilton, "Any luck yet?"

Hilton took a drink of burgundy and smiled. "As a matter of fact, Sylvain has agreed to accompany me to the opera this Friday night."

Jeff Davis pushed his plate away. "Care for company?"

"Not a chance, my friend." He offered the colonel a cigar. "This could well be the only evening I'll ever have with her." His dark eyes grew somber.

Jeff Davis lit his cigar, shook out the match, and said, "Hill, I know what she means to you. I'd not think less of you if you didn't go to Mexico with me." He smiled devilishly and added, "There's a chance we can beat them even without you."

"I have to go, Jeff. For Cot."

Davis nodded. "Have you told Sylvain you're going?"

Hilton looked sheepish. "Not yet. How did Varina take the news?"

Davis sighed. "She's angry with me, Hill, for leaving her alone. She's so strong-willed." The smile crept back to his lips. "But then, she's a woman, and such an adorable one."

Hilton nodded. He knew a great deal about strong-willed, adorable women.

The white cottage on the Ramparts hummed with excitement all that Friday. While Sylvain sat in the sunny back courtyard with Delilah towel-drying her freshly washed hair, Hester Spencer was in the small kitchen pressing a new gown of rose silk. Marie polished the worn furniture, readying the small parlor for the important evening.

It was midafternoon. The captain would arrive at eight o'clock. Every female at the cottage was looking forward to this night. The sisters had heard of the famous Theatre d'Orleans, and they were like proud parents whose only child had been invited to spend a glittering evening at the opulent landmark. They'd made the new ball gown and felt certain their darling Sylvain would be the loveliest lady there. They were doubly certain her escort would be the most handsome gentleman.

Delilah was pleased her stubborn charge had finally agreed to go out with the captain. She knew Sylvain as

364

no one else did. Knew the young beauty was in love with
Hilton Courteen, though she refused to admit it. She also
knew the handsome captain was the only man capable of
taming the wild spirit of Jean Lafitte's headstrong daughter and that Hilton Courteen's protective arms was where
the fiery Sylvain belonged.

Across town on that hot, muggy afternoon, Captain
Courteen walked through the front door of the Spencer
Chandlery. Big Napoleon, alone in the shop, looked up
and smiled.

"Cap'n Courteen," he greeted him, "I'm afraid you've
missed Sylvain. She left at noon."

Hilton shook the big black's hand. "It's you I've come
to see, Napoleon."

"Me, Cap'n? What can I do for you?"

Hilton shoved his hands deep into his pockets. "Napoleon, I'm leaving on Sunday."

"The Mexican War?"

"Yes."

"You haven't told her."

"No, I haven't. I'll tell her this evening. I want you to
do me a service."

"Glad to, Cap'n."

"Say you'll watch after her while I'm gone." He smiled
then. "I know she's an obstinate handful and awfully
hard to handle, but" — he sighed — "I love her,
Napoleon."

"I know you do, Cap'n." He shook his head. "She's a
remarkable woman. From the night she saved me from
Hyde Rankin, she's never failed to amaze me."

"Hyde Rankin?" Hilton was puzzled, and Big Napoleon realized immediately that Sylvain had told Hilton
nothing of Hyde Rankin, or of their nighttime excursions
into the swamps. Like her father, the young woman kept
her own counsel, solved her own problems, asked for no
quarter.

"Not important, Cap'n." Big Napoleon waved a hand in the air.

"I'm going to marry her if I come back from the war," Hilton stated. "Tell me you won't let anything happen to her." His black eyes were pleading.

At that moment, Big Napoleon decided he'd never again escort Sylvain into the dangerous swamps. This man trusted him to take care of her and he was going to do it, whether she liked it or not. He put out a hand to Hilton.

"Cap'n, I swear to you I'll not let anyone harm one hair on her head."

Hilton again shook Napoleon's hand. "I knew I could depend on you."

"Thank you, Cap'n."

Hilton turned to leave, paused, and said, "Sylvain tells me you and Delilah are getting married."

Big Napoleon beamed. "In August, Cap'n. Took me a long time to win that woman, but I finally did it."

Hilton grinned. "I hope I'll have the same good fortune."

The blistering Louisiana sun was slipping low when the gleaming black brougham rolled up before the cottage.

When Hilton Courteen stepped down from the carriage, Hester, Marie, and Delilah stared, open-mouthed, as he walked purposefully toward the house.

His dark, well-tailored evening clothes fitted him perfectly. The trousers were wide, in keeping with the new fashion. A stiff white bow tie topped a white pleated shirt exposed by a low-cut white vest. His shoes were black, narrow, and square-toed. He wore a silk London top hat and snowy white gloves. Under his arm was a box containing one fragrant white gardenia.

He came into the small foyer and stood, dark and imposingly handsome, while Sylvain gracefully descended the wooden stairs. His flashing eyes never leaving her,

Hilton felt his broad chest expand with possessive pride at the pleasing sight of her.

She was radiant in a gown of deep rose silk, its bodice drawn down into a long point, the waist shortened, the neckline a wide band of pleats, mitered at center-front. The skirt was very full with two wide flounces around its bottom. On her small feet were dainty rose slippers. Her hair was elaborately dressed, the long curls starting high on the temples, the hair at the back of her head set in a braided coronet that turned into a bun at the nape of her neck. An oyster-shell comb held the gleaming tresses in place.

"Miss Fairmont," said an adoring Hilton, "you are magnificent."

Her eyes shining, Sylvain descended the stairs, took his hand, and said, "You're very elegant yourself, Cap'n Courteen."

Hilton took the gardenia from its box and held the blossom out to her. He smiled when she lifted it toward her hair, stopped, and tucked it into the décolletage of her gown. His eyes went to the delicate flower's resting place and he felt the blood surge through his veins.

The handsome pair climbed into the shiny black carriage and departed while Sylvain's family waved and smiled and felt they might burst with pride.

Inside the closed coach, Sylvain was strangely reserved and polite. She made inconsequential small talk, pretended nonchalance, and began to tremble when they neared the old theater.

Hilton, on the other hand, was totally at ease, smiling and relaxed. When he saw the strained expression on her lovely face, he drew one of her small cold hands into both of his.

"Sylvain," he murmured, "if you'd rather not go, we needn't."

Thickly lashed gray eyes turned swiftly on him. "I wouldn't miss it for the world."

Hilton Courteen chuckled.

Her bravado wavered a bit when the fine brougham clattered down Orleans Avenue and came to a stop before the theater. As regally as she could manage, Sylvain, one hand in Hilton's, the other clutching the voluminous skirts of rose silk, stepped down onto the banquette and into the midst of the city's social set.

Fighting the desire to jump right back inside the carriage and flee, Sylvain took Hilton's arm and was swept into the ornate old theater. He stopped often to speak to old acquaintances, to introduce Sylvain, to kiss outstretched hands, to exchange pleasantries.

All about them grand ladies in colored silks, shimmering taffetas, and expensive laces chattered and smiled and clung to the arms of richly attired gentlemen. Gay bonnets and turbans, satin fans, beaded reticules, and cut flowers abounded.

Inside the theater Hilton led Sylvain to the dress circle. There it was possible to see — and to be seen. The dress circle was divided into boxes; each box had two rows of single seats, flanked by loges. Alone in their box, Sylvain and Hilton sat in the front row. Sylvain, eyes aglow, looked out upon the dazzling crowd and felt she'd never seen a grander display of good taste and good looks in her life.

She stared at the striking Creoles with their jet-black hair, milky skin, daring gowns, and flashing eyes. Soon she realized they were staring at her, too. The old unease filled her and she automatically reached for Hilton's hand.

"They're looking at us, Hilton," she whispered.

"Yes," he answered quietly, "they are."

She turned to him. "They're whispering about me. They're saying I'm — "

" — the most beautiful creature they've ever seen."

Unconvinced, she gave a little sigh of relief when the velvet curtain rose and all eyes went to the stage. Hers went there eagerly and she sat silently, listening to the famous diva, Madame Simone Rouvilliere, sing in romantic French.

She became aware of Hilton's eyes on her and she turned in the dim privacy to give him a questioning look. The expression she saw in his black eyes baffled her. It was a pensive, longing look that disappeared as soon as she turned. He smiled immediately, leaned toward her, and said, "Madame Rouvilliere looks like a plump, powdered infant. Come to think of it, her singing sounds a great deal like a baby squalling, doesn't it?"

"Hilton Courteen!" she whispered, shocked, and glanced nervously about to see if anyone had heard him. But when she turned her attention back to the performance, she had to agree. The diva was a rotund little woman with a round face, round belly, and great naked arms. Her small features were distorted as she lifted her voice to hit a hard-to-reach high note. Sylvain began to smile, finally to laugh softly. And she didn't turn away when Hilton's warm lips brushed her cheek.

Madame's performance mercifully ended, most of the patrons, including Sylvain and Hilton, drifted into the adjoining Orleans ballroom. Sparkling crystal chandeliers cast a gleam on walls paneled in fine woods. The vast structure was elaborately decorated with expensive marble statuary and costly oil paintings.

The ballroom itself was a long, high-ceilinged room with balconies overlooking the gardens in back of the St. Louis Cathedral. The dance floor was of hard cypress topped with oak. Hilton told Sylvain, as he took her in his arms, that the floor on which they stood was said to be the finest dance floor in the country.

She smiled and thought to herself that she was in the arms of the finest dancer in the country as well. Her opinion seemed to be shared by the beautiful ladies, and she knew they were wondering why the most glamorous bachelor in all New Orleans was at this glittering affair with someone so far beneath him. She wondered, too, but refused to spend this precious time pondering it. She was here. She was in his arms. She was in heaven.

It was warm in the great hall. Hilton escorted her to the rear of the ballroom and down a wide stairway to a flagstone courtyard. A smiling waiter passed with wines and cordials. Hilton chose two small glasses of Sazerac, and they sipped it as they strolled about the blossom-filled grounds. It was a lovely, hot, romantic night and Sylvain found herself wishing it never had to end.

Hilton had promised a midnight supper, and it was nearing the witching hour when he helped her up into the waiting brougham and told the driver to take them to Maspero's.

"Hungry, Sylvain?" he asked solicitously, as she settled back against the fine leather of the seat.

"Famished," she admitted, smiling.

They rode in silence and Sylvain was again aware of a somber look in Hilton's dark eyes. She turned to him, laid a hand upon his sleeve, and said, "What is it, Courteen? There's something on your mind. Tell me."

Hilton's gloved hand closed over hers and he said quietly, "I'm going away."

Her gray eyes widened. "The Mexican War?"

"Yes, dear."

Her hand tightened on his sleeve. "But, why? You're out of the army. No one's ordered you to go." Her usually calm voice had turned shrill. "You're a gambler, not a soldier."

"I have to go. Santa Anna killed my best friend at the Alamo. For what they did to Cot Campbell, I want revenge."

"Yes . . . I remember," she murmured, "you told me about him." She swallowed with difficulty. "When . . . when will you leave?"

"Sunday."

For what seemed an interminable time, she simply stared at him while he clutched her hand and looked into her eyes. Her lip began to tremble and she bit it. Her throat felt tight. Her eyes stung. He was leaving. He was going away and he might never come back.

"Hilton," she breathed.

"Yes, Sylvain?"

"I . . . I wish . . . " She took her hand from his and lifted it to his face. Fingertips gently stroking the smoothly shaven cheek, she said raggedly, "No! Hilton, I can't let you go." Her arms went around his neck.

"Sweetheart!" he murmured. His hand went to the coronet of braids at the back of her head. Then his lips swiftly found hers and he kissed her. She melted against him. They kissed hungrily, devouringly, anxiously, clinging to each other in a desperate embrace.

Hilton groaned and pulled her across his lap. "Sylvain," he breathed when their lips finally parted, "I love you. I'll always love you."

"Then don't go," she begged, arms tightening around him. "I need you. Don't leave me." And her mouth went back to his. Urgently she kissed him, willing him to stay, to give in, to never leave her.

His burning lips fed on hers while the heart inside his broad chest hammered heavily. Never had she kissed him the way she was kissing him now, and Hilton's long submerged desire flared white-hot under the sweetly sensual assault.

A gloved hand moved to the swell of her breast, and his lips slipped to her bare shoulder. He nibbled on the soft skin and heard her breathless voice say the words he'd thought would never come.

"I love you, Hilton," she whispered softly. "Darling, I love you. Don't go. Don't leave me."

"Oh, God, sweetheart," he groaned and again took her lips with his.

Their kisses grew ever hotter, deeper, longer. Their hands searched, explored, caressed. Sylvain's rose silk gown had slipped off her right shoulder, a full breast almost spilled from the bodice, temptingly exposed to Hilton's heated gaze. His white-gloved hand moved beneath her full pink skirts, gently stroking a well-turned knee.

Sylvain, mouth open wide to his kiss, found and opened two buttons of Hilton's shirt. Her fingertips went inside, anxiously stroking crisp black hair and warm brown flesh.

Lost in each other, neither was aware the brougham had halted. Young and passionate and deeply in love, they were on the way to total, uninhibited lovemaking when a discreet tapping on the side of the carriage made them both blink in confusion.

The driver cleared his throat, stepped back from the open side window, and announced, "Maspero's, Cap'n Courteen."

Disheveled, breathing heavily, arms pressing her close, Hilton looked into Sylvain's eyes. He swallowed hard, and asked, "Are you hungry?"

"Only for you," she whispered. She smiled then, a promising feline smile as her eyes slid closed and she pressed her open lips to his throat.

"We've changed our minds, Edward," Hilton's deep voice cracked. "The St. Louis Hotel, please."

"Yessuh."

The room was quiet and private. A single lamp was lighted. Rich velvet bed-hangings reached from high ceiling to lushly carpeted floor. Frothy, gauzy mosquito netting enclosed the huge four-poster. Fine Irish linen sheets, as white as snow, were spotless and pleasingly cool.

Atop those fine hand-embroidered white sheets, a slender, long-limbed young woman lay naked on her stomach, the pale gold of her bare flesh shimmering in the lamplight. Heavy sable-brown tresses had been unbound and now spilled over the silky pillow. Beside her, a man stretched upon his side, as naked as she, his lean body very dark against the whiteness of the bed. The first frantic, frenzied coupling was over.

The pair had hurried anxiously into the grand hotel suite, barely closing the door before they were at each other. In a state of passion, they'd clawed at their clothes discarding them where they fell. They'd mated immediately, panting and eager, unable to wait.

Now, much later, there was time for languid loving, time for Hilton to show Sylvain the full wonder of lovemaking, time to introduce her to all the glorious secrets of her slim, golden body, time to acquaint her with the male strangeness of his, time to assure her he was deeply, completely, everlastingly in love with her.

Hilton's strong brown hands caressed Sylvain's bare bottom while his lips pressed tender kisses over her shoulders and he softly spoke to her of love.

She lay supine, a slender arm folded beneath her cheek. And she purred and squirmed and arched her body and trustingly let her experienced, tender, worshiping lover instruct her, arouse her, delight her.

Lips and mustache brushing gentle kisses along the sensitive cleft of her back, Hilton said all the things a woman in love wants to hear.

"You're the only woman I've ever loved, sweetheart." His strong fingers lightly kneaded her pale buttocks. "You have no idea how many tortured, sleepless nights I've dreamed of having you in my arms like this."

"Why did you leave me on carnival night, Hilton?" She sighed softly. "I told you I loved you and yet you — "

"My love, I never heard you. I thought you didn't want me, didn't love me."

"I did. I've loved you ever since, Hilton."

The soft kisses continued. "And I've loved you since first I kissed you on the cold balcony of the Condé Hotel.

he night of the Victory Ball." His warm lips moved down
ier back. He kissed the two deep dimples at the base of
ier spine.

Sylvain sighed. "Hilton, you know it won't work for
is."

His tongue teased. "It will. Soon as I get back from
Mexico, we'll marry."

Sylvain's eyes closed. "I'm afraid, Hilton."

"You're mine, sweetheart. There's nothing to be afraid
of."

Her hand clutched the cool sheets, and a bare foot
kicked the air. "You're an aristocrat, Hilton. If you marry
me, people will talk about you, about me."

Hilton's mouth moved provocatively over her bottom
and slid down her thigh. Nibbling playfully at the backs
of her knees, he said, "Sweetheart, I don't give a damn
what anyone says about me." He lifted his dark head.
"And should anyone be foolish enough to say one unkind
word about you, it'll be their last." He continued to kiss
even as he reassured. "Sylvain, I took you to the opera
tonight. You saw how it will be when you're Mrs. Hilton
Courteen. You'll be able to go anywhere you choose, do
anything you please."

"Hilton, if you marry me, we . . . there might be . . .
children."

Hilton rose up and gently turned Sylvain over onto her
back. His black eyes were on her face, and he touched
her cheekbone and laughed. "Sweetheart, I guarantee
you there will be babies, and I'll be delighted to father
the descendants of Jean Lafitte. Now kiss me and tell me
you'll be my wife."

Her hands went into the thick hair at the sides of
his head and she pulled his mouth to hers. Against his
lips, she murmured, "I will. I love you, Courteen. So
much."

When their lips parted, his mouth went to ear. "Have I
mentioned that I'm a very jealous man, Sylvain?"

She giggled. "I've not even so much as kissed a man since you made love to me." She turned her head and looked at him. "Can you say the same?"

"No" — he was ever truthful — "but I promise you this: I'll never make love to another woman now that have you. You're all I want, all I'll ever want. You're my beautiful baby, my precious love."

And then his mouth and hands were moving over her once again, his lips sliding down a shoulder to her breasts. His mouth captured a rosy nipple, his hand stroked her flat stomach. While she lay looking at his dark, handsome head, Hilton paid homage to her beautiful body, sending shivers of sensation throughout her until she writhed and breathed his name and became dazed and unaware of her surroundings.

When his warm open lips spread moist fire to the trembling flesh of her thighs, and his teeth gently sank into their warm inner sides, Sylvain gasped and pulled frantically at his hair. Only then did he move up over her and take her with slow, insistent thrusts of his hard male body, making her his grateful prisoner. There in the lamplight in their sheltered, enclosed world, he lovingly guided her from tenderness to arousal to passion to wild abandon to glorious release.

And back again.

Bright sunlight streamed into the spacious room Sylvain awakened and stretched. She put out a hand and felt only the cool linen sheet. Panic caused her heart to pound. Hilton was not in the bed. She was alone.

He'd left her, just as he had that other time. He'd made love to her, lied to her, and left her. He was cruel, cold, a scoundrel. How could she have been such a fool?

Sylvain bolted upright. And she saw him. Through the filmy mosquito net, she saw him. He was across the room, seated, wearing only his dark trousers, feet and chest bare. His head was pressed back against the tall brocade chair. He was asleep.

Puzzled, alarmed, Sylvain looked for something to throw on. There was nothing. She slid her long, golden legs over the edge of the bed and lifted the gauzy netting. Naked, she padded to him.

Eyes on his sleeping face, she knelt between his bent knees. "Hilton?" she said cautiously, "What is it?"

His black eyes fluttered open and he looked at her. "Morning, darling." He cupped her chin in his hand.

"What's wrong?" she asked, her heart beating erratically.

"Sweetheart" — he smiled at her — "nothing's wrong. I have night sweats occasionally and I didn't want to disturb you."

Her hand went to his cheek. "Hilton, you're feverish. You're sick, darling."

"No." He captured her hand and kissed it. "Sylvain, I have malaria. It flares at the damnedest times." He looked embarrassed.

"My darling," she murmured and wrapped her arms around his trim waist. She leaned her head against his bare chest and told him, "I love you, Hilton Courteen, and I'm going to make you feel better." She kissed his hard abdomen and lifted her head. "Now you'll do as I tell you. You're my patient and I'm going to nurse you back to health."

Hilton pushed her long hair back off her face and nodded. "I belong to you. Do with me as you will."

Sylvain lithely rose and put out her hand. He took it and let her drape his long arm around her shoulders. She guided him to the bed, then unbuttoned his tight trousers and pulled them down over his slim hips. She lifted the mosquito netting, tied it up, and bade him lie down.

"I'll be right back," she said, touched his burning cheek, and rushed away. Moments later, wearing his long-tailed white shirt, she returned carrying a basin of

cool water. She lovingly bathed his long, lean body
tirelessly moving the dampened cloth over broad chest
flat belly, and long legs. And as she worked, she crooned
to him as though he were a small boy.

Within an hour the fever had departed and Hilton
dozed. Relieved, Sylvain leaned over to him, pressed a
soft kiss on his scarred eyebrow, and whispered, "Sleep
my love. I'll be right here. I'll never leave you, never."

Hilton awoke two hours later. He felt the bed. She was
not there. Panic causing his heart to hammer, he sat up
and shouted, "Sylvain!" She appeared immediately in the
doorway, a vision in his white dress shirt. She smiled a
him and approached the bed.

"Better, darling?"

"My God, I thought you'd gone. Thought I'd lost you."

She lunged into his arms. "You'll never lose me, Hilton
I love you, darling. Now and forever." She sprinkled
happy kisses over his face.

"You mean it?"

"I do."

"Then take off that damned shirt and show me."

It was five in the afternoon before they ate their firs
meal. A linen-draped table was rolled into the sitting
room of their suite. They dined half dressed, he in hi
trousers, she in his shirt. They ate ravenously, she o
roast duckling and wine sauce, he of oysters garnished
with lemon slices. Both sipped champagne. Dessert was
thick wedges of dark chocolate washed down with snif
ters of fine Armagnac and *café au lait* in china cups.

Sylvain took a bite of chocolate, chewed, and said
"Good Lord, Hilton!"

"What, love?"

"My family!" She jumped up from the table. "They'l
be worried sick."

"Sit down, darling." He waved her back into the chair
"I took care of it."

Skeptical, she remained standing. "How? And when?"

"Last night when I paid the driver, I sent him to the ottage to speak with Big Napoleon."

Her face reddened. "What will they think? The sisters nd — "

"Come here."

Sylvain dropped the block of chocolate onto her plate nd circled the table. Hilton pulled her down onto his lap nd wrapped his arms around her. "You are mine, you elong to me. You're in my care and you're not to worry bout what anyone thinks or says. Understand?"

She snuggled against his bare chest. "I know, Hilton, ut the sisters will — "

"Tomorrow we'll go to the cottage and tell them we lan to marry when I get back from Mexico."

"Hilton."

"Ummm?"

"Marry me now. Marry me tonight." She lifted her ead.

"No, sweetheart."

"Why not?"

His hands framed her face. "I don't want you to be a vidow should I not come back."

Her hands lifted to clasp his wrists. "Promise me you'll ome back." Her eyes were frightened now.

"Kiss me, sweetheart," said Hilton Courteen and pulled er down to him.

At sunset the lovers bathed together in a marble tub. At dusk they made love on the sitting room sofa. At nidnight they clung to each other in the four-poster bed. At sunrise they stroked each other awake. At noon they lined on caviar and kisses. At two they took one last ook at their love nest, dressed, and departed.

"I have to go by the Richardson to tell Jas to be packed nd ready to leave by five," Hilton told Sylvain when he landed her into a carriage.

"Jas? Your servant?"

Hilton nodded.

"You're taking him to Mexico?"

"Yes," Hilton nodded. "I hope he's up to the journey. He's so old he's — "

"Would he stay with me?"

"Sylvain, you can't take care of him. Jas is — "

"Your friend." She smiled. "He'll live with us while you're gone. Big Napoleon and Delilah are getting married. There'll be an extra bedroom."

"You sure?"

"Let's go get him."

Jasper showed Sylvain none of the contrariness he so often turned on Hilton. His old eyes shone with relief when Hilton told him he would not be going to Mexico.

"I be lots of help to you, Miz Sylvain." He bobbed his gray head. "I can drive the carriage or serve the meals or protect you. Anythin' you needs, old Jasper do it for you."

Hilton winked at her. She smiled at the old slave and said, "You'll be a great comfort to me while Cap'n Courteen is away."

"My baby," Delilah cried and hugged Sylvain when she and Hilton announced to the family that they were in love and would be married on his return. Big Napoleon smiled at Hilton over the heads of the women and gently pulled Delilah away.

Then it was the sisters' turn. Teary-eyed, they embraced Sylvain and shyly put on their hands to Hilton. He swept them both into his arms and hugged them soundly, saying, "Help Sylvain clean up, I want her to see me off."

"Yes, yes, Cap'n," said Hester and rushed Sylvain up the stairs.

Hilton told them all good-bye at the cottage, hugging his fragile old manservant whose tired eyes were brimming with tears. Into the old man's ear, he whispered, "Don't know what I'll do without you down there, Jas ut I need you to look after Sylvain. You understand, on't you?"

"I does," the old servant whispered, and his back got a ittle straighter. He was needed here. For Hilton Courteen, e'd stay.

Sweetheart, meet Colonel Jefferson Davis." Hilton pre-ented her to the tall blond officer standing in the sun on he New Orleans levee.

Colonel Davis kissed her hand and said, "My dear, vhat a pleasure to meet you. Hill has spoken of you ften. I hope you'll not hold me responsible for taking im away from you."

"Colonel Davis, I hold you responsible for nothing, ut I'd be forever in your debt if you'd see to it he returns afely." She smiled up at Hilton. "I love the captain, you now."

Charmed by her straighttorward manner, Jefferson Davis grinned. "I'll bring him back. And when this is all ver, make Hill bring you up to Briarfield. My Varina is oing to like you."

"Thank you, Colonel."

Davis smiled. "*Adieu*, my dear," he said quickly and trode to the gangplank of the waiting *Alabama.* The iant steamer's whistles gave two sharp blasts, and ylvain's breath caught in her throat.

Hilton's hand was on her arm. "Kiss me good-bye, weetheart."

Sylvain threw her arms around his neck and embraced im. Mindless of the crowd swarming about them, of the atcalls and whistles from young volunteers leaning over he railing of the *Alabama,* she clung to her lover, drink-ng from his mouth, drawing strength from his tall, solid ody, memorizing the sound and scent and feel of him.

Her slim fingers spread upon his broad shoulders as he pressed him close. On her right hand, the Colombian merald glittered in the bright July sun.

Eyes closed, Sylvain never saw the nondescript young man peering enviously at the emerald ring. Nor did she see him stroll across the wooden landing to a dark, ferret-face man leaning against a load of cargo. She didn't hear the youth whine to his companion, "I want that emerald ring, Hyde."

She saw and heard none of it. For her there was only Hilton Courteen. Hilton reluctantly removing her arms from around his neck. Hilton hurrying up the gangplank of the *Alabama*. Hilton leaning over the varnished rail to blow her kisses. Hilton's dark, handsome head silhouetted against the blue Louisiana sky. Hilton.

Only Hilton.

Chapter Twenty-Eight

The *Alabama* became but a tiny speck on the horizon. A terrible sense of emptiness overtook Sylvain, a despair so intense it became an acute physical pain. She'd felt so safe in his arms. Now he was gone and she was once again alone. Telling herself, as she had so many times in the past, that she'd wait until night to weep, Sylvain sighed heavily, turned and walked back to the carriage.

"He'll come back," Big Napoleon said with quiet authority. "The captain will come back."

Sylvain smiled at the black man of noble ancestry and let him lift her into the carriage. "He will," she said. "He has to come back."

"The captain asked me to look after you." His gaze swung to her face. "We will not be going into the Riverbend swamps again. It's far too dangerous." His voice was determined.

Sylvain's first impulse was to protest. She opened her mouth to object, then closed it. She said simply, "Perhaps you're right. I now have something else to live for, something more valuable than Riverbend and Lafitte's gold."

Big Napoleon, relieved, grinned and said nothing.

Sylvain missed Hilton desperately, and anxiously looked forward to his letters. He was good about writing, but modest and closemouthed about his soldier's life in nothern Mexico. The letters consisted mainly of expressions of love and loneliness, often so intimate and personal she blushed at the words.

Each time a letter arrived, she saw the eager look in old Jasper's eyes and realized he was dying to read every word his charge had written. Sylvain read to him from the impersonal parts and explained that the rest was private. He'd nod his head and wander away, muttering to himself.

On an oppressively hot Saturday, the day of Napoleon and Delilah's wedding, two letters arrived from Captain Hilton Courteen: one for Sylvain, one for Jasper.

Sylvain called the old man from his room and watched, delighted, when his eyes lit and his shaking hand reached out to take the letter. Painstakingly, he loosened the seal and took out the short missive. By the time he'd unfolded the letter, Sylvain was lowering her own, a smile on her face.

She looked at the old servant. He was squinting and holding the letter at arm's length. She stepped forward, reaching out for the message.

"Jasper, I'll be happy to read the Captain's letter to you."

The old man drew the piece of paper close to his narrow chest. Loftily, he announced, "Thanks jes'de same, but it be personal. You understan', Miz Sylvain."

Sylvain patted his shoulder. "I certainly do, Jas. Take the chair by the window; the morning light is perfect for reading."

"I'll do dat," he bobbed his head and shuffled away.

Jasper was still seated in the chair with his letter when the wedding party was ready to depart for Congo Square.

"Jasper," Sylvain said, "you're not ready. It's time to leave. Don't you remember? Today is Delilah and Big Napoleon's wedding day."

He blinked at her and she could tell by the expression in his eyes he'd completely forgotten about the wedding. "It be so hot, Miz Sylvain, I bes' jes' stay here at home."

Sylvain smiled and said, "Sounds like a wise idea. Stay in out of the sun. Take a nap after a while."

"I will." He grinned and raised the prized message from Mexico, "I'll read my letter again from de cap'n, see if I missed anythin'."

Sylvain nodded, glad the old man was comfortable. It was terribly hot, and he'd surely tire long before the wedding festivities came to an end.

Sylvain and the Spencer sisters stood in the black crowd assembled at Congo Square and watched a shy, beaming Delilah become the wife of a proud, noble Big Napoleon. Delilah was striking in a soft, full dress of white cotton and lace. Her bare shoulders gleaming in the sun, she stood beside the splendid Napoleon, her eyes aglow, knees trembling.

The tiny black preacher, attired in a long tailcoat and a bright scarlet shirt, pronounced the pair man and wife, and the approving crowd shouted and clapped when Big Napoleon took Delilah in his arms and kissed her.

The dancing began immediately.

Slaves from the outlying plantations and freemen of color chose their partners and hurried to the center of the square while an ancient man rattled two huge bones on the head of a cask, the rhythmic drumming stirring their blood.

Big Napoleon and Delilah led the others in the bamboula, a feverish dance from Africa. Sylvain and the sisters watched, fascinated, as the usually sedate Napoleon, brightly colored ribbons with bits of metal tied about his ankles, pranced back and forth and leaped into the air shouting in a deep voice, "Dansez bamboula! Badoum! Badoum!" until the other men took up the chant and the women swayed from side to side chanting strange words.

Sylvain enjoyed the changing expressions on the faces of the sisters almost as much as the spectacle itself. The two ladies held hands and gasped and pointed and blushed and enjoyed every moment of the celebration.

The three stood on the fringes of the crowd beneath cotton awnings, and ate little ginger cakes and drank lemonade and had themselves a time. It was nearing sundown when Delilah and Big Napoleon said their good-byes and slipped away, Napoleon telling Sylvain they'd be home in a couple of days. She nodded, hugged Delilah, and wished them both every happiness.

It had been a happy day. Sylvain was eager to tell old Jasper all about it.

She never got the chance.

Clutching the prized letter in his right hand, the old servant lay dead in the doorway of her bedroom. Behind him the room was in disarray. An empty silk jewelry box lay at his feet.

The Colombian emerald was gone.

Hilton's letters were less frequent. Sylvain worried, but kept up with the war through the *Picayune* and the *Bee*. On September 30, 1846, the *Picayune* printed a dispatch from Monterey, Mexico: "Under a galling fire of copper grape, Colonel Jefferson Davis and his regiment took the fort. Three days of intense fighting followed and the city which the Mexicans had thought impregnable fell."

All over the United States, word of Monterey's fall spread, and victory bonfires flamed in public squares. Sylvain hurried to the Place d'Armes to hear the speeches praising General Zachary Taylor's brave army. Colonel Jefferson Davis and Major Hilton Courteen were given a modest share of praise and Sylvain's heart swelled with pride. Hilton hadn't bothered to tell her he'd been breveted to major.

"In two days, I'll be forty years old," said a pensive Captain Robert E. Lee to his old friend Major Hilton Courteen.

Hilton lifted dark eyes from the well-thumbed tactical map spread out before him. He leaned back in his chair and drew a cigar from his breast pocket and smiled. "Robert, I'd say January nineteenth, 1847, is as good a day as any to turn forty."

"I'd agree, were I staying here," mused Lee. He rose and paced about the tent, hands clasped behind his back. "Can you believe it, Hill? I've been taken from General Taylor's command and put under General Scott, far from the sound of cannon, on the very eve of battle. Will I never be allowed near the front? Will I be a captain on my fiftieth birthday?"

Hilton, a cigar planted firmly between even white teeth, cheered his friend. "Robert, while I hate to see you leave, I fully believe you're the fortunate one. You know damned well President Polk is trying to squeeze old Taylor right out of this war. He's named Scott commander in chief, and he's taken nearly all of Taylor's troops away and handed them over to Scott at Vera Cruz." Hilton paused, drew on his cigar, and added, " 'Old Rough and Ready' has had his wings clipped, Robert. It will be you and Winfield Scott who'll capture Mexico City."

Robert Lee was unconvinced. "I'll never hear a shot fired if I don't — "

"Robert, Hilton." Colonel Jefferson Davis threw back the tent flap and marched in. To Hilton; "You're out of the hospital, good, good." Then to Robert Lee; "I understand you're going with Scott."

"Those are my orders, sir. Glad to have you back." Lee shook Davis's hand and inquired of Mrs. Davis. Colonel Jefferson Davis's face went pink. He'd ridden home to Mississippi at the request of his young wife. He was embarrassed that Varina had put up such a fuss as to make a field officer leave his post during a war. He'd reminded Varina that no Davis woman would ever have done such a thing. His temper, however, had swiftly

386

evaporated when she tickled him and murmured, "I missed my Jeffy so much I just had to see you for a few days."

"Mrs. Davis is doing well," the colonel assured Captain Lee, and turned his attention to Hilton. "The fever all gone? Feeling fit again? When did you get out of the field hospital?"

"It was nothing, Jeff. A flare-up of malaria. I got back yesterday. I'm good as new now."

"Just as well you are. We'll surely be in battle within weeks."

Hilton exchanged glances with Robert Lee.

"You see, Hill?" Robert shook his head. "I'm being sent right out of the theater just as the curtain rises."

"Listen, Robert, I — "

"Write what letters you'd like me to see delivered," Captain Lee told the men and quietly left the tent.

Hilton sat down at once and wrote to Sylvain:

> My dearest love,
> I'm here on the tablelands of Mexico at the foot of the Sierra Madre. General Santa Anna's army is proceeding closer.
> My health is fine, darling; do not worry. And do not believe all that you read in the newspapers. I'm no hero, my love, though for your sake I'd like to be one.
> You're with me each minute of the day. My lonely arms ache for you, sweetheart, and when I lie down to sleep, I close my eyes and see your beautiful face before me.
> I've a lucky charm that goes into battle with me. It's a small beige glove that once belonged to the most enchanting fourteen-year-old-girl in Louisiana.
> Keep all your sweet kisses for me. Goodnight, darling.
> Your Hilton.

Hilton folded the short letter and went to find Robert Lee.

Two days later, Captain Robert Lee rode away from Taylor's command to join General Winfield Scott.

On February 21, a lone rider on a lathered horse brought word to General Zachary Taylor's tent that the mighty Mexican cavalcade was less than a day's march away.

"We're outnumbered by at least four to one, General," the excited messenger declared. "We haven't a chance against Santa Anna."

Major Hilton Courteen and Colonel Jeff Davis watched the old general's face turn a bright shade of crimson as he bellowed, "By God, we'll show Santa Anna that twenty thousand Mexicans don't scare us!" The general whirled and shouted orders, "Colonel Davis, you're to move all troops north immediately. Don't stop until you get them to some high ground we can hold and protect!"

Far away and far below, Major Hilton Courteen could see the campfires of Santa Anna's mighty Mexican army. He stood in the cold February moonlight on the lonely mesa and watched his enemy.

Tomorrow they'd be here. Hilton yawned, walked back to camp and went to bed. He folded his long arms beneath his head. A sense of anticipation filled him. He was going up against Santa Anna at last.

He was ready.

The morning of George Washington's birthday dawned warm and clear. Major Hilton Courteen awoke refreshed and rested. With a spring in his step he walked to breakfast while the Third Indiana regimental band played "Hail, Columbia."

By midmorning, high clouds were forming in the clear Mexican sky. A smell of rain filled the air. The wind changed directions. Now it came from the south, blowing directly into the tense faces of the American soldiers.

At straight-up noon Zachary Taylor mounted Old Whitey as Santa Anna's advance guard of 2,500 horsemen charged down the valley. The resplendent Mexican dictator had sent his surgeon general with an arrogant demand for surrender. The American forces were surrounded by 20,000 armed men and could not possibly avoid total destruction.

Fuming, General Taylor politely declined the request, and the Americans braced themselves for an onslaught. The waiting was the worst part of it.

Major Hilton Courteen, Whitney rifle in his hands, a brace of 1845 Van Dreyse six-shot revolvers stuffed into his waistband, sat astride a big bay stallion. Eyes on the approaching Mexican army, nerves calm, Hilton sat as still as a statue in the warm Mexican sun, surrounded by the First Mississippi Rifles.

The guidon fluttered in the wind.

A young private galloped along the line. "The watchword is 'Honor to Washington.'"

"Soldier, hold there," said Major Courteen.

"Sir?" the boy reined in his horse.

"Name and age?"

"Private Walters, David R., Second Illinois, age fourteen, sir."

"Fall in behind me, Private Walters." Hilton's black eyes never left the enemy.

"Yes, sir," said the fuzz-faced youth and wheeled his snorting gelding in close to Hilton.

Santa Anna's richly caparisoned lancers galloped forward, their ranks tight and precise, as the Americans watched the garrison close.

Steadily they came, thousands of hoofbeats thundering across the valley, sabers gleaming in the sunlight.

"Look to your front," ordered Major Courteen as he moved his stallion out to prance behind his troops. "Mark your targets," he said in a steady, even voice. "Mark your target when it comes."

On he moved. Private Walters on his heels.

Along the right flank Major Courteen cantered, eyes on the enemy. "Fire!" he shouted at last, and a barrage of bullets hailed through the air.

The Mexicans moved in three heavy columns on the Americans. The American left flank broke and turned. Hilton's right flank stood their ground. General Zachary Taylor, at the center, every inch the brave leader, calmly rode Old Whitey out onto the field in plain view of both armies, exposing himself to cannon and shot, cool and calm in the face of death. The appearance of the old war-horse had a magical effect; the soldiers took heart and rallied. The left formed and held.

General Taylor ordered Colonel Davis and the Mississippi Rifles to the attack. Hilton charged alongside Jeff Davis into the heaviest fire of the battle. Jeff Davis took a bullet in the heel. Colonel Davis continued advancing. Hilton heard the whizzing of bullets and felt a small sting to his jaw.

Side by side the old West Point comrades, wounded, uncaring, led the valiant Mississippians against Santa Anna's swarm as, suddenly, thunder boomed and the clouds opened up and rain came in a torrential downpour.

Never had Hilton Courteen felt younger, stronger, more alive. While rain pelted his face and washed away the blood streaming from his jaw, Hilton, knee-reining his well-trained mount, thundered across the plain. The American volley was so destructive the frightened Mexicans finally fled.

His rifle out of ammunition, Hilton swiftly scabbarded it and drew the Van Dreyse six-shooters. Aiming carefully, he continued to fire and laughed aloud when he saw old Zach Taylor again ride his mount into the thick of the battle. Bullets had torn through Taylor's clothing,

390

slit his shirt, ripped out the lining of his coat, and still the steely general never slowed his horse.

Hilton spurred his bay, six-shooters blazing. The horse shot forward, then reared. Snorting and neighing, the big stallion went to his knees, then fell dead, shot through the eye. Hilton rolled over his head and landed on his feet, pistols still raised.

"Here, Major," called the young voice of Private David Walters and Hilton turned to see the boy looking down at him. The lad was leaning from the saddle, a long arm extended. Hilton took the youth's hand and swung up behind him.

The wounded major and the fourteen-year-old private rode on to meet the enemy.

In New Orleans, Sylvain had read chilling reports of the war. Santa Anna's 20,000 soldiers confronting General Taylor's depleted force could mean only disaster.

News of the amazing victory reached the port city, and Sylvain, eyes wide, read the dispatch in the *Picayune*: "The whole head of the column fell . . . a more deadly crossfire was never delivered. It was just past noon. Thunder cracked and rain fell in a sudden torrent. Part of the Mexican Army retreated to the protection of caves." The report went on to praise the heroic fighting of Colonel Jefferson Davis and the men of his command. One other soldier was mentioned: " 'For gallant and meritorious service,' the wounded Major Hilton Courteen was breveted colonel."

Sylvain lowered the *Picayune* and breathed easily for the first time in days. He was alive. That was all that mattered. He'd be coming home.

Sylvain had lived for this day and finally it had come. June 9, 1847. She and every other citizen of New Orleans stood in the Place d'Armes awaiting the returning heroes of Buena Vista.

Her pulse quickened when she heard the martial music growing closer. Cannons fired. Drums rolled. Women wept. Men shouted and cheered. Sylvain, hands clasped before her, stood on tiptoe, her eyes on the foot soldiers parading grandly into sight.

Behind the hundreds of marching men, Colonel Jefferson Davis rode in an open carriage, gaunt and in pain, but smiling warmly at the crowd. Flowers were tossed into the slow-moving carriage from balconies along the way. Creole women in summer dresses dropped wreaths and garlands to the soldiers from the galleries of the Pontalba buildings.

And then she saw him.

Mounted on a splendid beast whose shiny coat was as jet black as the rider's gleaming hair, Colonel Hilton Courteen, sitting his horse with natural grace, was magnificent in full dress uniform. A blouse of sky blue stretched tautly over his broad chest, the proud golden eagles of colonel on his epaulets. His trousers a dark blue, bright yellow sash about his trim waist, and shiny saber riding his thigh, campaign hat jauntily upon the pommel of his saddle, he was all masculine grace and beauty.

Hilton smiled at the cheering crowd, saluted fellow soldiers lining Government Street, nodded to beautiful women, and looked so devastatingly handsome Sylvain felt she couldn't get a breath.

She tried very hard to retain her composure. She lifted a hand high in the air to wave and softly called his name.

As though Sylvain had reached out and laid a soft hand upon his arm, Hilton could feel her eyes on him. He looked directly at her, and her heart began to pound. She wasn't sure when she started through the crowd. She didn't know she'd anxiously elbowed people out of her way so that she could reach him.

She was in the square at his side, her hand on his hard, blue-trousered leg. He pulled up on his gleaming black mount, leaned down and wrapped a long arm about her narrow waist. Hilton lifted her from the cobblestones, kissed her deeply, lingeringly, while people whistled and clapped and laughed.

Against her cheek, he murmured, "I love you. I want you. Meet me at the Ramparts cottage in one hour," while Sylvain's lips brushed the fresh scar on his left jaw. He didn't give her the opportunity to answer. His lips took hers once again in a brief kiss before he gently lowered her to the ground and moved on.

Hands on her flushed cheeks, Sylvain stood there in the June sun smiling foolishly while butterflies took wing inside. "Hilton," she breathed, then turned and ran happily through the crowd.

At parade's end, Hilton was surrounded by adoring throngs. Eager voices called, "Colonel Courteen, a drink, let us buy you a drink."

Longing to hurry at once to Sylvain, Hilton graciously let himself be swept into Turpin's Cabaret. He stepped up to the long polished mahogany bar, lifted a booted foot to the brass railing, and said to the barkeep, "Tafia, please, Sam."

"A toast, a toast to the colonel," shouted a cherub-faced man with snow-white hair and sideburns.

"A toast to the colonel," the others chimed in. Hilton, feeling foolish, lifted his glass of sugarcane rum. Smiling at the admirers, glass in hand, his dark eyes fell on a hand not raised in toast.

On the little finger of that hand was a unique emerald surrounded by tiny pearls. Hilton set his glass of tafia on the bar. Eyes narrowed, he made his way through the puzzled crowd, his jaw hard, his mind racing.

He stopped beside a pock-faced man staring warily into the mirror behind the bar. A long ebony cane lay upon the bar, its shiny gold head gleaming. The man lifted his glass, swilled down straight whiskey, and wiped his mouth on the back of his hand.

The hand wearing Sylvain's emerald.

Hilton said nothing. He stood at the man's elbow, tall, imposing, threatening. Slowly the man turned to look at him.

"Anything I can do for you, Colonel?"

"Yes," said Hilton Courteen. "You can tell me what you're doing with Sylvain Fairmont's emerald." His eyes were deadly.

The ferret-faced man snorted with laughter and conceded, "Colonel, that high-and-mighty girl you speak of is not a Fairmont at all." He looked about at the now silent crowd. Leaning closer to Hilton, he said laughingly, "That haughty little bitch is nothing but a pirate's unwanted bastard."

His laughter and his breath were knocked from him by the swift right fist of an enraged Hilton Courteen. Hilton crouched down and lifted the man's bony hand. He took the emerald and quickly slipped it onto his little finger. "Come near her ever again, speak her name without respect, you're a dead man."

He rose and turned away.

Should he finish off the vermin? Hilton decided against it. He was home; he'd take care of Sylvain for the rest of her life. No further harm would come to her.

He strode away, unhurriedly walking among the excited men, who parted to let him pass.

"Colonel! Look out!" someone shouted, but it was too late.

Hilton felt the deadly blow one split second before his long legs folded and he crumpled to the wooden floor.

Hyde Rankin, eyes wild, ebony cane with its bloodied gold head raised, ran past the startled patrons, out the door of Turpin's and down Marigny Street.

Chapter Twenty-Nine

He looked deathly pallid beneath his deep tan, otherwise strangely unharmed. A small square bandage on the left side of his head was barely visible. His brown shoulders and chest were dark against the white sheets, long arms resting outside the covers.

His dark eyes were closed, and his breathing was slow and even, so Sylvain could almost pretend he was asleep. He looked much as he had when he'd peacefully napped in their St. Louis Hotel suite on that glorious weekend before he'd gone off to war.

She smiled, recalling how she'd sat cross-legged in their bed and watched him sleep. There'd been no sheet draping his body then. He'd lain gloriously naked before her and she'd let her curious eyes caress every inch of his beloved body. When she'd tired of only looking at him, when she'd wanted his arms around her, she'd needed do no more than lean over him and tickle him with her long hair or slide her tongue along the sculpted contours of his lips.

Would that it were so simple now. If only she could softly speak his name and see those black eyes open to look at her. If she could place a light hand on his smooth shoulder and gently shake him until he awoke and pulled her down to him. If it were possible to —

A door quietly opened and a silent nurse preceded the physician into the room. Sylvain rose from her chair and looked hopefully at the doctor.

Dr. James Dunn leaned over the bed and lifted Hilton's left eyelid. He peered for a long moment into the depths of the dark pupil, released the lid, and repeated the action on the right. He then peeled away the tiny bandage and looked at the minute wound that had done such damage.

"Doctor?" Sylvain questioned. "Is he better? Will he be — "

"Young lady," Dr. Dunn took Sylvain's elbow and guided her out into the corridor of Mercy Clinic. "I wish I could give you good news. I cannot. Colonel Courteen is still in a coma. He is not improving, nor will he with the care I can offer."

"But, Dr. Dunn, he must — "

"The only hope I can see for the colonel is a Memphis brain surgeon who has brilliantly pioneered in this field. He's recently introduced a new procedure whereby he drills a tiny hole in the cranium and drains off fluid. It's dangerous and there's no assurance of success." He folded his arms across his chest and shook his head.

"What's the alternative, Dr. Dunn?"

"There is none. I've seen these kinds of cases all my life, and the condition usually leads to death in a matter of days, two weeks at the longest. On rare occasions a patient comes out of the coma and survives. More often than not, they simply lie there and starve to death, never regaining consciousness."

"This Memphis doctor? Who is he? How soon can he be here?"

"Dr. Theodore Kilborne is at the Kilborne Clinic. He might come, but" — Dr. Dunn paused — "he's a busy, noted specialist. He's very expensive. *Very.*"

Sylvain's face fell.

She had no money. Hilton had no money. He'd sent his army pay directly to her each month and it had gone to take care of the family. She didn't have the money to pay a noted surgeon. She had nowhere to get the money.

"I'm sorry." The doctor patted her shoulder. The nurse stepped out of Hilton's room and followed the physician down the quiet corridor.

Sylvain drew a deep breath and went back to Hilton. Dusk had fallen, and the lamp had been lighted on the white metal table by his head. Thunder rumbled in the distance. A gentle breeze stirred the thin white curtains at the room's one window.

Sylvain stood looking down at the man she so adored. Leaning over him, she tenderly kissed the scar in his left eyebrow, the small war scar on his jaw, and finally his cool, still lips.

"My darling," she breathed, "you can't leave me; I will not let you." She sat down on the bed and laid her cheek on his chest. Beneath her ear, his slow, steady heartbeat drummed and his chest was warm to the touch. "I'll think of something, Hilton," she murmured and let her hand slide down the length of his arm to his hand.

She sat up immediately and lifted his brown hand to her lap. Tears stinging her eyes, she slipped the Colombian emerald from his little finger and twisted it, heart filled to overflowing with love for this fearless man who lay unconscious and near death.

She absently felt the ring's inscription with thumb and forefinger.

La croix.

That was the inscription inside the emerald ring.

La croix.

It was a message! It was Lafitte's revelation.

The gold was hidden in the cross!

Sylvain put the ring back on Hilton's finger, kissed his cool lips, and told him, "Hang on, my love. I'm going to save you. You'll have that operation. You'll live, my darling. Please, please hold on."

She flew out of the room and down the hall. Grabbing a startled nurse, she said breathlessly, "Please go at once to Colonel Courteen's room and watch over im. I must leave, but I'll send Miss Spencer to stay ith him."

She didn't wait for a reply but swept down the steps of e clinic and into the night, her heels clicking sharply n the cobblestones. She caught a definite scent of rain the muggy New Orleans air and grimaced. Big Napo- on stepped forward from his post on the deserted street.

"The colonel, is he — "

"No, no, he's the same." Sylvain's eyes flashed. She rabbed his arm, "Napoleon, you told me old Kashka as a carpenter."

Puzzled, Napoleon nodded. "What has that to do with e colonel?"

"The cross!" she ignored his question. "Lafitte's gold is the cross atop Seachurch. Come!"

"How do you know?" He lifted her into the gig.

"The inscription in the ring . . . *La croix*. I didn't see it ears ago. How could I have been so blind?"

At the Ramparts cottage an uncomfortably pregnant Delilah held her swollen belly and tried to keep the fear om her voice.

"If you don't find the gold tonight," she said to Sylvain nd her husband, "promise me you'll give up for good."

"We promise." Sylvain spoke for them both while Big Iapoleon gently pulled his worried wife into his arms nd Sylvain said to the Spencers, "Marie, you will stay ere and look after Delilah." She turned to Hester. Hester, you must go to Mercy Clinic and sit with the colonel." She caught Hester's arm. "As soon as you get here, tell Dr. Dunn to wire Dr. Theodore Kilborne in Memphis. Dr. Kilborne must depart for New Orleans at nce. He's going to save Hilton."

t was past midnight when Big Napoleon and Sylvain oled through the fog-shrouded swamps of Riverbend. he summer storm was closing in on them, and already usts of winds blew through the lacy Spanish moss

hanging from the cypresses. Lightning lit the night sk
and thunder split the silence.

Giant drops of rain peppered the murky waters aroun
the bateau. Alligators, roused by the mounting storm
slithered from their napping places on the banks an
splashed easily into the bayou.

The cottonmouths and water moccasins seemed rest
less, swimming rapidly, crazily through the mudd
marshes. Other snakes, their slippery black bodies illu
minated by the lightning flashes, slithered down vine
and dead tree stumps.

Sylvain bit the inside of her cheek and told herself th
treasure would be worth the risk. All the times she an
Big Napoleon had made their treacherous way throug
this eerie, uninhabitable marsh had been dangerous, bu
tonight was the last time. No more frightening midnigh
excursions through this quagmire. No more braving quick
sand and snakes and alligators and panthers.

Tonight would be the last time.

Sylvain felt a rush of hope when she saw the slim
banks and recognized the outline of the big cypress cros
against the stormy sky. Mindless of the rain pelting he
face, she let Napoleon lift her out of the boat. He turned
back for his ax, swung it over his right shoulder, and
silently followed Sylvain through the undergrowth to
Seachurch.

The rain now came in sheets, quickly saturating
the soft earth and stinging the adventurers plunging
doggedly through the wet jungle. Sylvain's cotton skirts
were drenched and sticking to her, and she silently be-
rated herself for not having changed into something less
cumbersome. Her shoes stuck in the mud, the earth
sucking at her feet until she felt she could hardly lift
them.

Dashing her wet, heavy hair back out of her eyes, she
trudged on, destination in sight, goal firmly set, gold
within reach.

Finally they stood before Seachurch. The storm was violent now. Lightning skittered across the sky in great streamers that lit up the old slave church. The thunder boomed deafeningly close. To be heard above the din, Big Napoleon leaned down to Sylvain, cupped his big hand around his mouth, and said into her ear, "I'll climb to the roof. After I'm up, Miss Sylvain, you hand the ax to me."

"All right," she shouted, then screamed in terror when a bolt of lightning struck the church. Beams split, timber groaned, wood shattered. Big Napoleon grabbed the terrified Sylvain and pulled her to safety as the tall cypress cross took a direct hit, teetered, and crashed to the wet ground at their feet.

At Mercy Clinic the lightning and the subsequent loud clap of thunder made Hester Spencer, who was dozing in her chair, jump in alarm. She rose and hurried to Hilton's bedside.

Again lightning lit the small room and Hester's hands flew to her face. A trickle of bright red blood was flowing from Hilton's nose, saturating the pillow beneath his head.

"Dear God," murmured Hester as Hilton's eyes opened.

"Sylvain?" he called softly.

Hester Spencer, pressing a clean white bandage to the lifesaving crimson flow, whispered, "Colonel Courteen?"

"Sylvain?" he said again and lifted his hand.

Hester took it and murmured soothingly, "Colonel Courteen, she's not here right now, but she'll be back in the morning."

"Not here?" He lifted his head.

"Please, Colonel, lie back," Hester urged, pushing gently on his chest.

"Where is she? Where's Sylvain?"

Hester debated. Never in her life had she told a lie. Wishing she did not know the answer, she smiled weakly and said, "Colonel, she and Big Napoleon went down to the old Riverbend plantation."

"What in God's name for?" Hilton pushed himself up onto an elbow, his black eyes questioning, his hand pressing the gauze to his nose.

Hester sighed. "You must lie down, Colonel Courteen. I'll go for the doctor and — "

Hilton caught her arm. "Miss Hester, why did they go to Riverbend?"

Hester looked at the strong fingers grasping her wrist. "Sylvain believes there's gold down there at an old slave church. Dr. Dunn said you need a specialist, so she and Big — "

"Get me my trousers."

"No," Hester scolded, "I'll do no such thing. You can't get out of bed!"

Hilton, his head throbbing, sat up. "I'll get them myself." He began to push the sheet down to his waist.

"Please!" Hester was incensed. She hurried across the room for his trousers, her face flushed. She draped the pants across his lap and rushed out of the room, calling over her shoulder, "I'm telling the doctor! He won't let you leave this clinic!"

Sylvain clung in terror to Big Napoleon, her eyes riveted on the ruptured wooden cross. Even in the darkness, they could see gold coins, thousands of them, and sparkling diamonds as large as walnuts glinting inside the cross. Another bolt of lightning illuminated the open cross, and the gold and diamonds glittered so brightly she and Big Napoleon blinked in shocked wonder.

They looked from the booty to each other. Wordlessly, they scrambled to the treasure, eagerly dipping into the cold, wet metal and stone. Laughing like two small children, they crouched and swiftly began scooping up the gold and the sparkling gems.

Mindless of the storm with its driving rain, Sylvain and Big Napoleon laughed and shouted and congratulated each other.

"May I say I share your delight?"

Sylvain, hands filled with gold doubloons, looked up to see Hyde Rankin, an evil smile on his wet face, standing not ten feet away. Beneath his left arm was the vulgar ebony cane with its gargoyle head. In his right hand was a long-barreled pistol, and it was pointed directly at her.

"You've saved me a great deal of trouble, Miss Lafitte." He grinned wickedly. "I've grown weary hunting my gold and now you've found it for me. So convenient. Now I have the treasure, and I've no choice but to kill you for trespassing." He laughed harshly.

The gold coins slipped through her fingers and she rose slowly. She started to speak, but Napoleon took her arm and pulled her behind him. Then he picked up his ax and said, "You'll have to get through me first, Rankin."

Hyde Rankin snorted. "All six chambers of this revolver are filled, nigger. Surely there's enough to finish you both."

"Come near this girl and I'll split your head wide open," Big Napoleon promised calmly.

Sylvain never saw Rankin fire, but she heard the shot and saw Big Napoleon's huge body jerk. She screamed. Big Napoleon remained on his feet.

"Run, Miss Sylvain," Big Napoleon commanded, but Sylvain clung to his back, unable to move. Big Napoleon swiftly shook her off, and shoved her out of the way. Again he shouted, "Run!" Ax in hand, he raised his powerful arm and moved toward Hyde Rankin. Another shot was fired, and another. The huge black grunted in pain, but did not fall.

"Damn you, you black bastard!" shouted Rankin and watched the big man, blood streaming down his chest, remain standing. Rankin's hands were shaking now, and his eyes were filled with fear, but he raised the pistol and pumped the three remaining shots straight into the brave giant bearing down on him.

Then he let out a cry of fear and threw the gun at Napoleon. Big Napoleon rocked unsteadily on his feet. His big hand went to his bullet-riddled chest. He opened his mouth to speak.

No words came.

Blood gushed from his mouth and his knees buckled. Sylvain, screaming, was at his side instantly. His dark eyes lifted to her face and in them she saw the message.

Run.

Foolishly she pressed a hand to the dying man's chest, trying to stop the flow of blood. And then a great sob escaped her lips when she realized that there was no heartbeat.

Big Napoleon was dead.

"The nigger can't help you now." Rankin's voice was very near.

She grabbed for the ax in Big Napoleon's right hand, but Rankin's foot crashed down on the handle before she could snatch it up. She whimpered, but was up at once and running, her wet skirts lifted high, her feet bare. Sylvain stumbled across the soggy ground. The rain continued to come in heavy sheets and great puddles of water formed everywhere. Sylvain looked back to see Hyde Rankin, the ax slung over his shoulder, coming after her.

Her blood froze. She wished fleetingly that his gun was loaded. She'd prefer being shot to being butchered with and ax.

"I'm coming for you, Miss Lafitte," Hyde Rankin taunted as he crashed through the dripping forest after her. "I'll get you just like I got that old bitch they named you after." He laughed evilly and continued to call to her through the rain. "It's all her fault you know. Sister Sylvain, ugly dried-up old hag! She told my secret, so I killed her. Did you know that, Miss Lafitte?"

Sylvain, breath burning in her throat, blood pounding in her ears, heart hammering with fear and exertion, ran through the jungle, picking her way along a remembered path from childhood, skirting the nearby swamps, angling steadily toward the river.

Rankin's voice was growing fainter and Sylvain grew hopeful. "Miss Lafitte," he hollered, "where are you? I'm growing irritated. You're annoying me just like that old darkie that caught me stealing your ring. I had to kill him. Now I have to kill you."

Sylvain tried desperately to keep her head. She had to make it to the river. If she could only make it to the river, perhaps she could hide beneath the wooden levee or in the old gate house.

The rain continued, and the bayou waters were rapidly rising. Sylvain, out of breath, felt if she didn't stop for a second, she'd collapse. Hand at her throat, she slowed, looked back, and saw something moving through the shadows.

Swallowing hard, she gulped for air and plunged on, her bare feet now bruised and bloodied. Her side ached, her knees were jelly, but still Sylvain ran headlong through the dense underbrush. Rain and tears filling her eyes, thick, foggy mist rolling before her, she never saw the cypress log in her path.

She crashed to the ground and released a cry of hopelessness and despair. She landed on her stomach, hands and face in the mud. She tasted blood and dirt as she pushed herself up. She felt a heavy boot on her back. She looked up to see the vile Rankin standing over her, a sadistic grin on his pockmarked face. In his right hand was the heavy ax.

"Beg me for your life, you little tramp," he said cruelly, then laughed.

Jean Lafitte's blood was surging through Sylvain's veins and she replied calmly, "Never." She closed her eyes and waited for the ax to fall.

Enraged by her unexpected bravery, Hyde Rankin thre[w]
his cane down and lifted the heavy ax high in the air.

A shot rang out.

Sylvain screamed while Hyde Rankin, the ax slidin[g]
from his hand, blood spurting from his shoulder, looke[d]
around in shocked surprise. She quickly rolled over an[d]
sat up.

Hilton, pale and sick, stood there in the steamy mis[t,]
the gun still smoking in his hand. "Beg *me* for your lif[e,]
Rankin." His deep voice was deadly.

Hyde Rankin staggered toward Hilton. "Please," h[e]
whined, "don't kill me, Colonel Don't kill — "

Hilton pulled the trigger. Hyde Rankin fell dead at h[is]
feet.

Sylvain slowly stood up, then stooped and picked u[p]
the ebony cane from the mud. She stood over Hyd[e]
Rankin. His eyes were wide open, filling with rain. Look[k]
ing down at the evil, ugly face, she lifted her knee an[d]
broke the ebony cane in two. She threw the splintere[d]
cane onto the man's still form. The gold gargoyle-hea[d]
fell into the bloody pool that was his chest.

Sobbing hysterically, she ran to Hilton's sheltering arm[s.]

The rains continued throughout the night. Riverbend[']
levee broke. Through the devastating crevasse in th[e]
embankment, the water gushed toward the sugar plant[a]
tion, flooding the lower floor of the crumbling mansio[n,]
sending the few remaining slaves fleeing for their live[s,]
and washing the body of the evil Hyde Rankin into th[e]
mighty Mississippi to be carried downriver into the Gu[lf]
and finally to the vast Atlantic ocean.

Chapter Thirty

In the glaring sunlight of a perfect September day, Colonel and Mrs. Hilton Courteen happily boarded the *Pride of the Mississippi* for a long honeymoon trip up the Mississippi. Mrs. Courteen did not travel light. Valises, bags, steamer trunks, and hat boxes were filled with ball gowns of rich satins and silks, frothy underthings, daring nightgowns, shoes, bonnets, parasols, and toiletries.

Hilton had patiently waited throughout the summer to marry his love. Sylvain insisted that although she wanted only a quiet wedding at the cottage, she was going to have all the finery she ever dreamed of for the steamboat honeymoon.

He'd agreed, only to find that postponing the wedding meant he would not be allowed to make love to her until after the ceremony.

"Darling, humor me," she'd said, toying with the buttons of his shirt. "Think how much you'll want me if we wait."

"Sweetheart," he'd reminded her, "we've been waiting. I've been in Mexico for almost — "

"I know, Hilton, but it will be exciting this way." She laughed and kissed his mouth. "It will make our honeymoon very special."

Hilton had groaned, reluctantly acquiesced, and spent the rest of the summer in sweet agony. Now that the day had finally arrived, Hilton had to agree that perhaps

406

Sylvain had been right. Expectation making his heart accelerate, he swept his bride up the long gangplank of the *Pride*, wearing a happy smile.

The mighty vessel was already building steam, it whistles blowing, crew shouting. Soon they'd be backing away from the landing and he could whisk his beautiful wife into their stateroom and make love to her at long last.

Sylvain, clinging to Hilton's arm, glowed with happiness. Radiantly beautiful in an expensive traveling suit of beige linen, her heavy dark hair swept up under a small brimmed bonnet, brown silk parasol lifted in the sun, she urged her husband toward the polished railing.

Lifting a gloved hand in farewell, she felt the big steamer begin to move and she laughed with delight. "Good-bye," she called to the family far below. The Spencer sisters madly waved handkerchiefs while Delilah, her three-month-old son Napoleon gurgling in her arms, smiled and nodded her head.

Sylvain blew a kiss and turned to see Hilton tipping his hat to them. Another sharp blast of the whistle and the huge *Pride of the Mississippi* moved away from the wharf. The journey to St. Louis had begun.

"Shall we, darling?" asked an eager Hilton Courteen.

"Shall we what?"

Hilton swallowed. "Retire to our cabin?"

Sylvain laughed gaily. "Why, Hilton Courteen, I've not seen any of this magnificent steamer. Surely you intend to show me about." She lowered her parasol and let her fingers slide up the lapels of his fine jacket. She wet her lips and added, "I can't imagine why you're so eager to go to our quarters." She swayed closer, teasing him, adding to the anticipation, building the sweet tension.

On to her, Hilton decided to play along. Smoldering black eyes on her tempting mouth, he said casually, "There's no hurry, far as I can see." He grinned at the look of surprise that came into her expressive gray eyes.

"You've never seen a side-wheeler as grand as the *Pride*. Come, I'll take you on a tour."

"Wonderful," she said and hoped he wouldn't make her pay too long for her game-playing. In truth, she could hardly wait to be alone with her dark, handsome husband. The touch of his hand on her arm was enough to fan the fire burning inside her, and the sight of his tall, powerful frame in the well-tailored suit of dove gray, with those revealing trousers stretching tightly over his slim hips and long well-shaped legs, made her breathe faster.

"Come," he said, smiling rakishly. "Let's go above deck."

He handed her up a wide, ornate companionway with fine fluted banisters. As they walked along the starboard side of the craft, Hilton pointed out the fine Gothic detail of the pillars and guardrails. Sylvain nodded, smiling, and admired the intricately carved flowers and acorns and curlicues.

Hilton drew her past rows of staterooms with doors of dark walnut and windows of colorful stained glass and on to the grand saloon. Insisting they go inside, he led her past a long impressive bar of fine heavy marble. Behind the bar, a mirror stretched the length of the long room. A Brussels carpet muffled their footsteps and in the corner a gleaming grand piano stood beside a gold harp. Snowy white linen tablecloths graced the tables, and velvet chairs caught the sunlight streaming through the stained-glass skylights.

Hilton pulled out a chair and offered her a seat. He raised his arm, and a smiling steward hurried forward. Hilton ordered a bottle of wine. It was served in shiny silver goblets, the finest Sylvain had ever seen.

Hilton lounged languorously back and drank his wine slowly, poured another, and looked to be in no hurry to leave. Sylvain lifted her empty goblet. Black eyes holding hers, wide lips curved in a smile, he refilled it. They sat there in the grand saloon and leisurely drank the wine, spoke unhurriedly of inconsequential things, pretending they were not dying to go to their cabin.

After an hour, Hilton rose, helped Sylvain to her feet, and they left the regal room just as dusk was falling and lights were flickering on in the long row of crystal chandeliers, the dark wood taking on a silken sheen.

Outside, the night was filled with stars. Sylvain smiled, certain her husband would now escort her to their stateroom. He did not. He guided her up a narrow companionway to the hurricane deck, emerging forward of the huge black smokestacks. Puzzled, she looked up at him. He put a hand on her waist and urged her on up to the high texas deck.

"The pilothouse." He pointed to the gleaming glass-enclosed structure where a man with iron-gray hair, pipe between his teeth, and alert eyes guided the big steamer through the muddy waters.

"The texas is where I like to ride. Up here you can see the whole river, all the smaller boats, the plantations lining the banks."

"It's breathtaking, isn't it, Hilton?" Sylvain looked at the lights twinkling on along the river as darkness engulfed the giant waterway.

"Yes, darling, it is." Hilton stepped up behind her where she stood clinging to the railing.

"I love the paddle-wheelers. I have since I was a child."

"I recall." His breath ruffled her hair.

Sylvain inhaled deeply and leaned her head back on her husband's shoulder. All pretense and playfulness fell away. "Till the rest of my days are done, Hilton Daniel Courteen, I shall remember this moment. I love you, darling." Slowly she turned and looked up into his black eyes. "Please, husband," she whispered, "take me to our cabin. Make love to me, Hilton."

His eyes were hot and dark on her face. He trembled. "Whatever you want, love."

nside the plush stateroom, Hilton Courteen, his heart hudding against his ribs, took his satin-nightgowned bride n his arms and pressed her to him, enjoying the sight of ner scantily clad backside reflected in the silver-framed nirror behind her.

Hilton, wearing only his gray trousers, let his wanton vife sprinkle kisses over his bare chest while his eyes 'emained fixed on the slender golden body in the mirror. He deftly exposed that beloved body by slowly lifting the gown up her long legs and hips to her waist.

While Sylvain's parted lips played over his warm chest, she was vaguely, delightfully aware of the sensuous slither of satin as it moved up over her body. She shivered and ner kisses grew hotter. With undulating body and lambent tongue, the shameless Mrs. Courteen went about driving her husband mad with desire.

Hilton, eyes glazed with passion, breathing labored, admired the symmetry of her figure, the well-shaped slender legs, the firm rounded buttocks, the narrow waist. His hands gently stroked the bottom he'd bared while Sylvain's hot mouth and tongue fanned the flames of passion burning within him.

For a time they stood there, playing, teasing, waiting. Then all at once, Hilton groaned, took Sylvain's arm, and set her away from him. He slid the satin gown up over her head and dropped it. She stood there in the lamplight, naked, desirable, proud. She threw her head back and looked brazenly into his eyes, but her slender body trembled involuntarily beneath his searing, sweeping gaze.

Hilton found her utterly irresistible, an intoxicating mix of brazen sensuality and sweet vulnerability.

"Sweetheart," he murmured and in seconds he was naked and pulling her into his arms. He kissed her hungrily, moaning into her mouth while she wrapped her arms around his neck and clung to him. When their lips parted, Sylvain's husband wordlessly turned her until she

was facing away from him. He pulled her back against hi
tall, hard frame, and their heated eyes met in the silver
framed mirror.

To Sylvain Courteen's shock — and delight — he
hot-blooded husband, his parted lips on her hair, stood i
the middle of the room and made love to her while bot
watched in the mirror. Sylvain daringly looked at thei
reflected images while Hilton's strong hands cupped he
aching breasts, his warm palms covering the sensitiv
crests. In slow, circular movements, Hilton urged th
blossoming centers into peaks of passion. Then his lea
fingers plucked gently at the taut nipples until Sylvai
sighed and trembled and spoke his name.

Those magic, graceful hands moved slowly down ove
her body, caressing, stroking, spreading fiery pleasur
while his black, blazing eyes held hers in the mirro
Over her ribs his hands swept upon her belly, then cuppe
her hips and slid down her golden thighs.

"Look at me, darling," he said when her eyes slippe
closed in elation.

Rising to his softly spoken challenge, Sylvain opene
her smoky eyes opened as her husband's masterful han
moved between her slightly parted legs. A soft soun
escaped her lips. Unashamedly, she stood writhing agains
him, enjoying to the fullest the feel and the sight of hi
dark fingers so intimately loving her.

It was just as joyous for her husband. His breath wa
shallow and that most male part of him swelled to rigi
hardness. She could feel the powerful throbbing agains
her buttocks and dizzily recalled how it felt to have i
inside her.

"Hilton," she breathed and it was close to a sob.

"Sylvain," he answered huskily.

And then they were on the bed, loving each othe
fiercely, passionately, completely. Two sleek, eager bod
ies entwined in the act of loving, one soft, slender, golden

he other hard, lean, dark. Two becoming one. For the moment, for the night, for a lifetime.

Years of waking early caused Sylvain's eyes to open when the first dim light of morning filtered through the stained-glass window of the stateroom. Her husband, used to gamblers' hours, slumbered on. Sylvain, smiling contentedly, raised herself on an elbow and watched him sleep. Her eyes ran adoringly over the rugged body beside her.

He lay with one long arm up over his head. His face was turned to one side, dark hair falling onto his forehead. Sunlight glinted on the thick crisp hair of his chest. He was all muscled power and swarthy beauty, and Sylvain felt very fragile and feminine against his awesome masculinity.

She shivered with pleasure against his warmth and Hilton slowly awoke by degrees. His black eyes came open and he turned his head. She laid a gentle hand on his shoulder and the touch of her fingers on his skin stirred him.

He looked up to see her leaning over him, her long tousled hair falling about her face. A lean brown hand reached up and took a handful of that shiny hair. He smiled drowsily, and said in a sleep-heavy voice, "I had a dream, a wonderful dream."

"What?" she asked, her voice breathless.

"I dreamed we were married and on a long, idle honeymoon up the Mississippi."

"Hilton," she murmured as he pulled her down to him, his hot mouth closing over hers. His warmth and power rapidly ignited her desire, and Sylvain gloried in her husband's exquisite lovemaking.

Chapter Thirty-One

It was sundown. The bell was calling the hands in from
the fields. Sylvain stood on the broad back gallery o
Riverbend plantation waiting for her husband. The scen
of magnolia and jasmine sweetened the warm air and
brought a pleased smiled to the lips of Riverbend's happy
mistress.

Her eyes swept over the vast lawns, neatly manicured
and tended, and her heart swelled with contentment
The orchards were blooming, the slave quarters had
been repaired and newly whitewashed. The flood
damaged sugarcane fields were now planted with row
upon row of cotton.

The empty sugar factory, the unused gate-house, and
the ruined Seachurch had been torn down. A new slave
church had gone up in a better location. High on the
bluffs of the Mississippi, the gleaming white Seachurch
was filled to capacity each Sunday morning. Beside the
chapel, the graveyard lay high and dry, far from the
encroaching swamps.

Big Napoleon was there. And old Jasper. Edwin and
Serena Fairmont rested there. Sylvain had asked Hilton
to have them brought home to Riverbend. His answer
had been a gentle kiss and a promise. A week later she
was kneeling at their graves, cut flowers in her hands.

It was a place of peace and beauty, the sounds of the
river tumbling by far below, steamboat whistles softly

calling to those who would never again travel down the ancient stream. It was here that she would rest one day, beside Hilton, here on the banks of a river that rolled on forever into the sea.

The main house had been restored to its former splendor. Priceless furniture had been ordered from Europe and floated downriver from New Orleans. Serena Fairmont's beloved champagne brocade sofa and gold chairs had been reupholstered and moved into the place of honor in the drawing room. They graced the elegant room just had they had when the regal golden-haired lady had reigned over the mansion and just as they would when Sylvain joined those in the high graveyard and her sons and daughters dwelled in the great house.

Sylvain strolled along the gallery and sighed with satisfaction. Her life was one long, lazy dream of happiness. She was back at Riverbend. She slept each humid, flower-scented night in the huge master bedroom with Hilton's long arms about her, his hard, bare body pressed to hers, his warmth a constant, silent reminder of protection and safety. And love. Through the tall French doors thrown open to the spring nights, the sound of the slaves softly singing in the distance added to her peace. And sometimes in the deep still of the night, a steamer's whistle sounded from the river, half waking her, making her smile in the darkness and snuggle closer to her sleeping husband.

Home.

She was home. Riverbend. Her Riverbend. She had it back, just as she had always known she would.

FREE!!
BOOKS BY MAIL
CATALOGUE

BOOKS BY MAIL will share with you our current bestselling books as well as hard to find specialty titles in areas that will match your interests. You will be updated on what's new in books at no cost to you. Just fill in the coupon below and discover the convenience of having books delivered to your home.

PLEASE ADD $1.00 TO COVER THE COST OF POSTAGE & HANDLING.

- -

BOOKS BY MAIL

320 Steelcase Road E.,
Markham, Ontario L3R 2M1

210 5th Ave., 7th Floor
New York, N.Y., 10010

Please send Books By Mail catalogue to:

Name _____
(please print)

Address _____

City _____

Prov./State _____ P.C./Zip _____

(BBM1)